Thomas Longueville

The Life of a Conspirator

Being a biography of Sir Everard Digby by one of his descendants

Thomas Longueville

The Life of a Conspirator
Being a biography of Sir Everard Digby by one of his descendants

ISBN/EAN: 9783337013240

Printed in Europe, USA, Canada, Australia, Japan

Cover: Foto ©Raphael Reischuk / pixelio.de

More available books at **www.hansebooks.com**

THE LIFE OF A CONSPIRATOR

SIR EVERARD DIGBY KNIGHT, OE 1605.

THE LIFE OF
A CONSPIRATOR

BEING A BIOGRAPHY OF SIR EVERARD DIGBY

BY

ONE OF HIS DESCENDANTS

BY THE AUTHOR OF
"A LIFE OF ARCHBISHOP LAUD," BY A ROMISH RECUSANT, "THE
LIFE OF A PRIG, BY ONE," ETC.

WITH ILLUSTRATIONS

LONDON
KEGAN PAUL, TRENCH, TRÜBNER & CO., Ltd.
PATERNOSTER HOUSE, CHARING CROSS ROAD
1895

PREFACE

THE chief difficulty in writing a life of Sir Everard
Digby is to steer clear of the alternate dangers of
perverting it into a mere history of the Gunpowder
Plot, on the one hand, and of failing to say enough
of that great conspiracy to illustrate his conduct, on
the other. Again, in dealing with that plot, to condemn all concerned in it may seem like kicking a
dead dog to Protestants, and to Catholics like joining
in one of the bitterest and most irritating taunts to
which they have been exposed in this country
throughout the last three centuries. Nevertheless,
I am not discouraged. The Gunpowder Plot is an
historical event about which the last word has not
yet been said, nor is likely to be said for some time
to come ; and monographs of men who were, either
directly or indirectly, concerned in it, may not be
altogether useless to those who desire to make a
study of it. However faulty the following pages
may be in fact or in inference, they will not have
been written in vain if they have the effect of
eliciting from others that which all students of
historical subjects ought most to desire—the Truth.

I wish to acknowledge most valuable assistance

received from the Right Rev. Edmund Knight, formerly Bishop of Shrewsbury, as well as from the Rev. John Hungerford Pollen, S.J., who was untiring in his replies to my questions on some very difficult points; but it is only fair to both of them to say that the inferences they draw from the facts, which I have brought forward, occasionally vary from my own. My thanks are also due to that most able, most courteous, and most patient of editors, Mr Kegan Paul, to say nothing of his services in the very different capacity of a publisher, to Mr Wynne of Peniarth, for permission to photograph his portrait of Sir Everard Digby, and to Mr Walter Carlile for information concerning Gayhurst.

The names of the authorities of which I have made most use are given in my footnotes; but I am perhaps most indebted to one whose name does not appear the oftenest. The backbone of every work dealing with the times of the Stuarts must necessarily be the magnificent history of Mr Samuel Rawson Gardiner.

CONTENTS

CONTENTS

CHAPTER V.

CHAPTER VI.

CHAPTER VII.

CHAPTER VIII.

CHAPTER IX.

CHAPTER X.

CHAPTER XI.

CHAPTER XII.

CHAPTER XIII.

CHAPTER XIV.

CHAPTER XV.

CHAPTER XVI.

CHAPTER I.

Nothing is so fatal to the telling of an anecdote as the prelude :—" I once heard an amusing story," &c., and it would be almost as unwise to begin a biography by stating that its subject was a very interesting character. On the other hand, perhaps I may frighten away readers by telling them at starting, this simple truth, that I am about to write the history of a young man of great promise, whose short life proved a miserable failure, who terribly injured the cause he had most at heart, for which he gave his life, a man of whom even his enemies said, when he had met his sad fate :—" Poor fellow. He deserved it. But what a pity !"

If the steady and unflinching gaze of one human being upon another can produce the hypnotic state, it may be that, in a much lesser degree, there is some subtle influence in the eternal stare of the portrait of an ancestor. There is no getting away from it unless you leave the room. If you look at your food, talk to a friend, or read a book, you know and feel that his eyes are still rivetted upon you ; and if you raise your own, again, towards his, there he is, gravely and deliberately gazing at you, or, you are half inclined to think, *through* you at something beyond and behind you, until you almost wish that you could be thrown into some sort of cataleptic condition, in which a series of scenes could be brought before your vision from the history of the long-dead man, whose representation seems only to exist for the purpose of staring you out of countenance.

In a large country house, near the west coast of Wales, and celebrated for its fine library, hangs a full-length portrait which might well impel such a desire. It represents a tall man, with long hair and a pointed beard, in a richly-chased doublet, a lace ruff and cuffs, very short and fringed trunk hose, and a sword by his side. He has a high forehead, rather raised and arched eyebrows, a long nose, hollow cheeks, and a narrow, pointed chin. His legs are thin; his left hand is placed upon his hip; and with his right he holds a cane, which is resting on the ground. At the bottom of the picture is painted, in Roman characters, "Sir Everard Digby, Knight, OB. 1606."

Few people care for genealogies unless their own names are recorded in them. The keenest amateur herald in matters relating to his own family, will exhibit an amazing apathy when the pedigree of another person is offered for his inspection; the shorter, therefore, my notice of Sir Everard Digby's descent, the better. He was descended from a distinguished family. It had come over from Normandy with William the Conqueror, who had granted it lands at Tilton, which certainly were in its possession in the sixteenth century, though whether the subject of my biography inherited them, I am not quite sure. The first Sir Everard Digby lived in the reigns of Henry I. and Stephen.[1] This powerful family sided with Henry VII. against Richard III.; and on one occasion, King Henry VII.[2] "did make Knights in the field seven brothers of his. house at one time, from whom descended divers houses of that name, which live all in good reputation in their several countries. But this Sir Everard Digby was the heir of the eldest and chiefest house, and one of the chiefest men in Rutlandshire, where he dwelt, as his ancestors had done before him, though he had also much living in Leicestershire and other shires adjoining." He was the fourteenth in direct eldest male descent from Almar, the founder of the family in the eleventh century. Five of his forefathers had borne the name of Everard Digby, one of whom was killed at the battle of Towton in 1641. Sir Everard's father had also

---

[1] *Harleian MSS.*, 1364.

[2] *Narrative of the Gunpowder Plot*, Father Gerard, p. 87.

N.B.—"The Narrative of the Gunpowder Plot," and "The Life of Father John Gerard," are both published in one volume, entitled *The Condition of Catholics under James I.*, edited by Father John Morris, S.J.: Longmans, Green & Co., 1871. It will be to this edition that I shall refer, when I quote from either of these two works.

been an Everard, and done honour to the name; but literature and not war had been the field in which he had succeeded. He published four books.[1] The only one of these in my possession is his *Dissuasive from taking the Goods and Livings of the Church*. It is dedicated "To the Right Honourable Sir Christopher Hatton, Lord High Chancellor of England, &c."

The author's style may be inferred from the opening of his preface :—"If my pen (gentle reader) had erst bin dipped in the silver streames flowing from Parnassus Hill, or that Apollo with his sweet-sounding harp would vouchsafe to direct the passage thereof unto the top of the high Olympus; after so general a view of great varietie far and neere, I might bouldly begin with that most excellent Poet Cicelides Musę paulo maiora canamus." I leave my readers to judge how many modern publishers would read any further, if such a book were offered to them in these days! Still, it is interesting as showing the style of the times.

Father Gerard, an intimate friend of the Sir Everard D'gby whose life I am writing, mentions [2] "the piety of his parents," and that "they were ever the

---

[1] See *Bibliographia Britannica*, Vol. iii. p. 1697. The books were :— I. *Theoria Analytica ad Monarchiam Scientiarum demonstrans.* II. *De Duplici Methodo, libri duo, Rami Methodum refutantes.* III. *De Arte Natandi ; libri duo.* IV. *A Dissuasive from taking the Goods and Livings of the Church, &c.*

[2] *Narrative of the G. P.*, p. 88.

most noted and known Catholics in that country "
(Rutlandshire); and Mr Gillow, in his *Bibliographical
Dictionary of English Catholics,*[1] states that they
" had ever been the most staunch and noted Catholics
in the county of Rutland." But here I am met with
a difficulty. Would a Catholic have written such a
passage as the following, which I take from the
Dissuasive ? It refers to that great champion of
Protestantism and Anglicanism, Queen Elizabeth.

" I cannot but write truely," he says, " that which
the Clergie with the whole realme confesse plainely :
That we render immortell thankes unto Almightie
God, for preserving her most Roiall Majestie so
miraculouslie unto this daie, giving her a most religious
heart (the mirror of all Christian princes) once and
ever wholly consecrated to the maintaining of his
divine worship in his holy Temple. From this cleare
Christall fountaine of heavenlie vertue, manie silver
streames derive their sundrie passages so happelie into
the vineyarde of the Lorde, that neither the flaming
fury of outward enimies, nor the scorching sacrilegious
zeale of domesticall dissimulation, can drie up anie one
roote planted in the same, since the peaceable reigne
of her most Roial Majestie."

The writer of the notice of Sir Everard Digby in
the *Biographia Britannica*[2] appears to have believed his father to have been a Protestant; but on
what grounds he does not state. So familiar a friend

---

[1] P. 62.   [2] Vol. iii. p. 1697.

as Father Gerard is unlikely to have been mistaken on this point. Possibly, however, in speaking of his "parents," he may have meant his forefathers rather than his own father and mother. This seems the more likely because, after his father's death, when he was eleven years old, Sir Everard was brought up a Protestant. In those times wards were often, if not usually, educated as Protestants, even if their fathers had been Catholics ; but if Sir Everard's mother had been remarkable for her "piety" as a Catholic, and one of the "noted and known Catholics" in her county, we might expect to find some record of her having endeavoured to induce her son to return to the faith of his father, as she lived until after his death. The article in the *Biographia* states that Sir Everard was "educated with great care, but under the tuition of some Popish priests": Father Gerard, on the contrary, says that he "was not brought up Catholicly in his youth, but at the University by his guardians, as other young gentlemen used to be"; and in his own *Life*,[1] he speaks of him as a Protestant after his marriage. Lingard also says[2] that "at an early age he was left by his father a ward of the crown, and had in consequence been educated in the Protestant faith." I can see no reason for doubting that this was the case.

---

[1] *Life of Father John Gerard*, p. clii.
[2] *History of England*, Vol. vii. chap. i.

At a very early age, Everard Digby was taken to the Court of Queen Elizabeth, where he became "a pensioner,"[1] or some sort of equivalent to what is now termed a Queen's page. He must have arrived at the Court about the time that Essex was in the zenith of his career; he may have witnessed his disgrace and Elizabeth's misery and vacillation with regard to his trial and punishment. He would be in the midst of the troubles at the Court, produced by the rivalry between Sir Walter Raleigh and Sir Charles Blount; he would see his relative, Cecil, rapidly coming into power; he could scarcely fail to hear the many speculations as to the successor of his royal mistress.

He may have accompanied her[2] "hunting and disporting" "every other day," and seen her "set upon jollity"; he may have enjoyed the[3] "frolyke" in "courte, much dauncing in the privi chamber of countrey daunces befor the Q. M."; very likely he may have been in attendance upon the Queen when she walked on[4] "Richmond Greene," "with greater shewes of ability, than" could "well stand with her years." During the six years that he was at Court,

---

[1] S. P. James I., Gun. P. Book, Part II. No. 135, Exam. of Sir E. Digby —"He confesseth that he was a pencon to Quene Elizabeth about six yeres, and tooke the othe belonging to the place of a pencioner and no other."

[2] Lord Henry Howard to Worcester.

[3] Letter of Lord Worcester, Lodge III. p. 148.

[4] MS. Letter. See Lingard, Vol. vi. chap. ix.

he probably came in for a period of brilliancy and
a period of depression, although there is nothing to
show for certain whether he had retired before the
time thus described in an old letter [1] :—" Thother
of the counsayle or nobilitye estrainge themselves
from court by all occasions, so as, besides the master
of the horse, vice-chamberlain, and comptroller, few
of account appeare there." If Lingard is right,
however,[2] he gave up his appointment at Court the
year before Elizabeth's death, and thus luckily
escaped the time when, as he describes her, she
was [3] " reduced to a skeleton. Her food was nothing
but manchet bread and succory pottage. Her taste
for dress was gone. She had not changed her clothes
for many days. Nothing could please her; she was
the torment of the ladies who waited on her person.
She stamped with her feet, and swore violently at
the objects of her anger."

One thing that may have had a subsequent influence
upon Digby, while he was at the Court of Elizabeth,
was the violence shown towards Catholics. In the
course of the fourteen years that followed the defeat
of the Spanish Armada before the death of the Queen,[4]
" the Catholics groaned under the presence of incessant
persecution. Sixty-one clergymen, forty-seven laymen, and two gentlemen, suffered capital punishment
for some or other of the spiritual felonies and treasons

---

[1] MS. Letter. See Lingard, Vol. vi. chap. ix.   [2] History, Vol. vii. chap. i.
[3] *Ib.*, Vol. vi. chap. ix.   [4] Lingard, Vol. vi. chap. iii.

which had been lately created." Although he had been brought up a Protestant, " this gentleman," says Gerard,[1] " was always Catholicly affected," and the severe measures dealt out to Catholics whilst he was at Court may have disgusted him and induced him to leave it.

I have shown how Father Gerard states [2] that Sir Everard Digby was educated "at the University by his guardians, as other young gentlemen used to be." It is to be wished that he had informed us at what University and at what College ; when he went there and when he left ; as his attendance at Court, together with a·very important event, to be noticed presently, which took place, or is said to have taken place, when he was fifteen, make it difficult to allot a vacant time for his University career.

The young man,—he did not live to be twenty-five, —whose portrait we have been looking at, is described in the *Biographia Britannica*[3] as having been " remarkably handsome," " extremely modest and affable," and "justly reputed one of the finest gentlemen in England." His great personal friend, the already-quoted Father Gerard,[4] says that he was " as complete a man in all things that deserved estimation, or might win him affection, as one should see in a kingdom. He was of stature about two yards high," " of countenance" "comely and manlike." " He was skilful in all

<hr>

[1] *Narrative of the G. P.*, p. 88.   [2] *Ib.*
[3] *Vol. iii.* p. 180.   [4] *Narrative of the G. P.*, p. 88.

things that belonged to a gentleman, very cunning at his weapon, much practised and expert in riding of great horses, of which he kept divers in his stable with a skilful rider for them. For other sports of hunting or hawking, which gentlemen in England so much use and delight in, he had the best of both kinds in the country round about." "For all manner of games which are also usual for gentlemen in foul weather, when they are forced to keep house, he was not only able therein to keep company with the best, but was so cunning in them all, that those who knew him well, had rather take his part than be against him." "He was a good musician, and kept divers good musicians in his house; and himself also could play well of divers instruments. But those who were well acquainted with him"—and no one knew him better than Father Gerard himself—"do affirm that in gifts of mind he excelled much more than in his natural parts; although in those also it were hard to find so many in one man in such a measure. But of wisdom he had an extraordinary talent, such a judicial wit and so well able to discern and discourse of any matter, as truly I have heard many say they have not seen the like of a young man, and that his carriage and manner of discourse were more like to a grave Councillor of State than to a gallant of the Court as he was, and a man of about twenty-six years old (which I think was his age, or thereabouts)." In this Father Gerard was mistaken. Sir Everard Digby did not live to be twenty-

six, or even twenty-five. Gerard continues :—" And though his behaviour were courteous to all, and offensive to none, yet was he a man of great courage and of noted valour."

We began by examining a portrait : let us now take a look at an old country-house. Turning our backs on Wales, a country which has little to do with my subject, we will imagine ourselves in Buckinghamshire, about half way between the towns of Buckingham and Bedford, and about three miles from Newport Pagnell, a little way from the high road leading in a north-westerly direction. There stands the now old, but at the time of which I am writing, the comparatively new house, known then as Gothurst.

Perhaps one of the chief attractions in Elizabethan architecture is that, by combining certain features of both classical and gothic architecture, it is a result, as well as an example, of that spirit of compromise so dear to the English nation. If somewhat less picturesque, and less rich and varied in colour, than the half-timbered houses of Elizabethan architecture, the stone buildings of the same style are more massive and stately in their appearance, and the newly-hewn stone of Gothurst [1] presented a remarkably fine front, with its pillared porch, its lengthy series of mullioned windows, and its solid wings at

---

[1] " Antiently Gaythurst," says Pennant in his *Journey*. It is now called Gayhurst.

either side. It was built upon rising ground, which declined gradually to the rich, if occasionally marshy, meadows bordering on the river Ouse.[1] It was a large house, although, like many others built in the same style, the rooms were rather low in proportion to their size.[2] The approach was through a massive gateway,[3] from which an avenue of yews—which had existed in the time of the older house that formerly stood on the same site—led up to the square space in front of the door. Near the gateway was the old church, which was then in a very indifferent state of repair,[4] and below this were three pieces of water. Beyond them ran the river Ouse, and on the opposite side stood the old tower and church of Tyringham. If the house was new, it was very far from being the pretentious erection of a newly-landed proprietor. Yet the estate on which it stood had more than once been connected with a new name, owing to failures in the male line of its owners and the marriages of its heiresses, since it had been held by a De Nouers, under the Earl of Kent, half-brother to William the Conqueror. It

[1] See Pennant's *Journey from Chester to London*, p. 437, *seq.* Also Lipscomb's *History and Antiquities of Bucks*, Vol. iv. 158, *seq.*

[2] The house is still standing, and is the residence of Mr Carlile. The further side was enlarged, either in the eighteenth or very early in the nineteenth century, in the style of Queen Anne ; but this in no way spoils the effect of the remarkably fine old Elizabethan front.

[3] This has disappeared.

[4] Poem on *Everard Digby*, written by the present owner of Gothurst, and privately printed.

had passed [1] by marriage to the De Nevylls in 1408 ; it had passed in the same way to the Mulshos in the reign of Henry VIII., and I am about to show that, at the end of the sixteenth century, it passed again into another family through the wedding of its heiress.

Mary Mulsho, the sole heiress of Gothurst, was a girl of considerable character, grace, and gravity of mind, and she was well suited to become the bride of the young courtier, musician, and sportsman excelling " in gifts of mind," described at the beginning of this chapter. It can have been no marriage for the sake of money or lands ; for Everard Digby was already a rich man, possessed of several estates, and he had had a long minority ; moreover, there is plenty of evidence to show that they were devotedly attached to one another.

The exact date of their marriage I am unable to give. Jardine says [2] that Sir Everard " was born in 1581," and that " in the year 1596 he married " ; and, if this was so, he can have been only fifteen on his marriage. Certainly he was very young at the time, and Jardine may be right ; for, at the age of twenty-four, he said that a certain event, which is known to have taken place some time after their marriage, had happened seven or eight years earlier than the time at which he was speaking.[3] I have made inquiries in local registers and at the Herald's College, without obtaining any further light upon the question of the

---

[1] See Pennant's *Journey*, p. 438.   [2] *Criminal Trials*, Vol. ii. p. 30.
[3] S. P. Dom. James I., Gunpowder Plot Book, Part II. No 135, B.

exact date of his wedding.   One thing is certain, that his eldest son, Kenelm, was born in the year 1603. In that same year Everard Digby was knighted by the new king, James I.   He may have been young to receive that dignity ; but, as a contemporary writer [1] puts it, " at this time the honour of knighthood, which antiquity preserved sacred, as the cheapest and readiest jewel to preserve virtue with, was promiscuously laid on any head belonging to the yeomandry (made addle through pride and contempt of their ancestors' pedigree), that had but a court-friend, or money to purchase the favour of the meanest able to bring him into an outward room, when the king, the fountain of honour, came down, and was uninterrupted by other business ; in which case it was then usual for the chamberlain or some other lord to do it."   It is said that, during the first three months of the reign of James I., the honour of knighthood was conferred upon seven hundred individuals.[2]

We find Sir Everard and Lady Digby, at this period of our story, possessed of everything likely to insure happiness — mutual affection, youth, intelligence, ability, popularity, high position, favour at Court, abundance of wealth, and a son and heir.   How far this brilliant promise of happiness was fulfilled will be seen by and bye.

[1] Osborne's *Traditional Memorials*, p. 468.   I quote from a footnote on page 147 of the *Somers Tracts*, Vol. ii.
[2] See Lingard, Vol. vii. chap i.

CHAPTER II.

YOUNG as he was, Sir Everard Digby's acquaintance was large and varied, and Gothurst was a very hospitable house. Its host's tastes enabled him thoroughly to enjoy the society of his ordinary country neighbours, whose thoughts chiefly lay in the direction of sports and agriculture; but he still more delighted in conversing with literary and contemplative men, and when his guests combined all these qualities, he was happiest. One such, who frequently stayed at Gothurst, is thus quaintly described by Father Gerard.[1] Roger Lee "was a gentleman of high family, and of so noble a character and such winning manners that he was a universal favourite, especially with the nobility, in whose company he constantly was, being greatly given to hunting, hawking, and all other noble sports. He was, indeed, excellent at everything, &c." In short, he appears to have been exactly the kind of man to make a congenial companion for Sir Everard.[2]

[1] *Life of Father John Gerard*, p. cxxxvi.

[2] I write of Sir Everard and Lady Digby; but it is improbable that he had received knighthood at the period treated of in this chapter.

So intimate was he at Gothurst, even during the life of Lady Digby's father, who had died at the time of which I am about to write, that, on his visits there, he frequently took with him a friend, who, like himself, was an intelligent, highly-educated, and agreeable man, of good family, fond of hawking, hunting, and other sports, and an excellent card-player.

Both Lee and his companion were Catholics, and, as I explained in the last chapter, Sir Everard Digby, although brought up a Protestant, was " Catholickly inclined, and entertained no prejudice whatever against those of the ancient faith " ; indeed, in one of his conversations with Lee he went so far as to ask him whether he thought his friend would be a good match for his own sister, observing that he would have no objection to her marrying a Catholic ; "for he looked on Catholics as good and honourable men." Considering the pains, penalties, and disabilities to which recusants, as they were called, were then exposed, this meant very much more than a similar remark would mean in our times. And not only was he unprejudiced, for he took a keen interest in the religion of Catholics, and the three men talked frequently on that subject, the speakers being usually Lee and Digby, the friend putting in a word occasionally, but for the most part preferring to stand by as a listener.

None of Lady Digby's family were Catholics ;[1] her

---

[1] *Life of Father John Gerard*, p. cl.

father had been an ardent Protestant, and possibly, as is not uncommonly the case, the long conversations about Catholicism would have more interest to one who had been brought up in an extreme Protestant atmosphere, than to those who had been accustomed to mix among people of both religions. At any rate, it is pretty evident that the young wife often sat by while her husband and his guests talked theology, and that she had gradually begun to form her own ideas upon the subject.

In considering life at a hospitable country house, nearly three hundred years ago, it is well to try to realise the difference between the conditions under which guests can now be obtained and those then existing. Visitors, and letters to invite them, are now conveyed by railway, and our postal arrangements are admirable; then, the public posts were very slow and irregular, many of the roads were what we should call mere cart-tracks, and it took weeks to perform journeys which can now be accomplished in twenty-four hours.

Our present system of filling our country houses just when we please, and then taking a quiet time alone, or visiting at other country houses, or betaking ourselves to some place for amusement, was impossible early in the seventeenth century; at that period, the only chance of seeing friends, except those living close at hand, was to receive them whenever they found it convenient to come, and to make country houses, as it were, hotels for such acquaintances who chanced to be passing near them on their journeys. People who were on visiting terms not uncommonly rode or drove up to each other's houses, without special invitation; and, even when invited, if the distance were great, owing to the condition of the roads and the frequent breakdowns in the lumbersome vehicles, it rarely could be foreseen when a destination would be reached. Yet a welcome was generally pretty certain, for, before the days of newspapers, to say nothing of circulating libraries, hosts and hostesses were not hypercritical of the guests who might come to relieve their dulness, and the vestiges still remaining of the feudal hospitality of the baron's great halls made them somewhat liberal and unfastidious as to the social standing of those whom they received; nor was it very rare for unknown travellers, who asked leave to take a short rest at a strange house, to meet with a cordial welcome and liberal entertainment.

There was nothing out of the common, therefore, in guests so well known at Gothurst as Roger Lee and his favourite companion riding up to that house unexpected, yet certain of being gladly received; but, on a certain occasion, they were both disappointed on reaching its arched and pillared doorway, at being told that their host had gone to London. The kind and graceful reception given by their hostess, however, did much to make up for his absence.

The long, if rather low rooms, with their wide,

mullioned windows, the good supply, for those times, of books, and the picturesque grounds, with the river flowing through them, made Gothurst a charming house to stay at, and Sir Everard's man-cook [1] no doubt made the creature comforts all that could be desired. For those who cared for sport, there was plenty of agreeable occupation, for there were hawks and hounds and well-filled stables. The young hostess, who had been brought up among men who spent their lives in country amusements, could converse about horses, dogs, and hunting if required; most probably, too, she often carried a hawk on her wrist; and, as she shared her husband's tastes for literature and serious reflection, she could suit herself to almost any company.

Her two guests were prepared to talk about any topic that might seem most pleasing to their hostess, and it was soon clear that she wished to renew the conversations about religion which she had listened to with so much attention when her friends had been last in her house in the company of her husband. They were no less ready to discuss the same subject with her, and the more she listened to them, the more she questioned them, and the more she thought over their replies to her difficulties, doubts, and objections, the more inclination did she feel towards the creed they professed. She was well aware that her husband, at

---

[1] Even his under-cook was a man. Cal. Sta. Pa. Dom., 1603-10, p. 266.

the very least, had a high respect for it; that he already admitted the truth of a great part of it, and that, in discussing it with Lee and his friend, he had propounded arguments against it rather as those of others than as his own; and when, after considerable solitary reflection while her visitors were out of doors, she felt very nearly assured that the Almighty could not approve of people professing a variety of creeds; that of several religions, all teaching different doctrines, only one could be right; that if God had revealed a right religion, he must have ordained some one body of men to teach it, and that there was only one body which seemed to have any claim to such tremendous authority, and that the Roman Catholic Church. These thoughts made her earnestly wish to talk the matter over with one of its priests, and consult him on the question of her own position in respect to so all-important a subject.

To meet with a priest was not easy in those times. Such priests as there were in England rarely, if ever, declared themselves, except to Catholics or would-be Catholics; for to make such a declaration, in this country, amounted to self-accusation of the crime of High Treason. Her two guests were Catholics, and would undoubtedly know several priests, and where they could be found; but to reveal their names or their whereabouts would be dangerous, both to those priests and to themselves, and Lady Digby felt some hesitation in interrogating them on such points. At last,

rather than place one of her husband's favourite companions in a position which might be unwelcome or
even compromising, she determined to consult, not
Roger Lee, but the friend he had brought with him.
When she had delicately and nervously told him of
her wish to see a priest, she was far from reassured by
observing that he was with difficulty repressing a
smile.[1]   Could it be that he thought her a silly woman,
hurriedly contemplating a change of religion on too
scanty consideration ?   Or was the finding of a priest
so difficult a thing just then as to make a wish to
attempt it absurd ?   His expression, however, soon
changed, and he told her, gravely enough, that he
thought her desire might very possibly be fulfilled ;
at any rate, he promised to speak to Roger Lee about
it.   " In the meantime," he added, " I can teach you
the way to examine your conscience, as I myself was
taught to do it by an experienced priest."   She was
inclined to smile, in her turn, at such an offer from a
mere sportsman ; so, thanking him, she allowed the
subject to drop.

He had not left her very long before Roger Lee
entered the room, and, as he immediately told her
that he had heard of her wish to have some conversation with a priest, it was clear that his friend
had lost no time in imforming him of it.   Her
surprise may be imagined when Lee proceeded to
tell her that his companion was himself a priest !

[1] Life of Gerard, p. cli.

At first she refused to believe it.[1] "How is it possible he can be a priest?" she asked, "has he not lived rather as a courtier? Has he not played cards with my husband, and played well too, which is impossible for those not accustomed to the game? Has he not gone out hunting, and frequently in my hearing spoken of the hunt, and of hawks in proper terms, without tripping, which no one could but one who has been trained to it?"

She gave many other reasons for disbelieving that he could be a cleric; and, finally, only accepted the fact on Roger Lee's reiterated and solemn assurances.

"I pray you," she then said, "not to be angry with me, if I ask further whether any other Catholic knows him to be a priest but you. Does . . . know him?"

"Yes," replied Lee, "and goes to confession to him."

Then she asked the same question concerning several other Catholics living in the county, or the adjoining counties—among others, a lady who lived about ten miles from Gothurst.

"Why," said Lee, "she not only knows him as a priest, but has given herself, and all her household, and all that she has, to be directed by him, and takes no other guide but him."

At this, she admitted that she was thoroughly satisfied. Whereupon Lee remarked of his friend—

[1] *Life of Father John Gerard*, p. cli.

"You will find him, however, quite a different man when he has put off his present character."

"This," wrote the priest himself, who was Father John Gerard, second son of[1] Sir Thomas Gerard,[2] a Lancashire Knight, and an ancestor of the present Lord Gerard. "This she acknowledged the next day, when she saw me in my soutane and other priestly garments, such as she had never before seen. She made a most careful confession, and came to have so great an opinion of my poor powers, that she gave herself entirely to my direction, meditated great things, which, indeed, she carried out, and carries out still."

I can fancy certain people, on reading all this, saying, "How very underhand!" I would ask them to bear in mind that for Father Gerard to have acted otherwise, and to have gone about in "priestly garments," under his own name, would have been the same thing as to have gone to the common hangman and to have asked him to be so obliging as to put the noose round his neck, and then to cut him down as quickly as possible in order that he might relish to the full the ghastly operation of disembowelling and quartering. To this it may be replied that to conceal his identity might be all very well, but that it was quite another thing to stay at the house of a

---

[1] This Sir T. Gerard was committed to the Tower on an accusation "of a design to deliver Mary Queen of Scots out of her confinement."—*Burke's Peerage*, 1886, p. 576.

[2] *Life of Gerard*, p. clii.

friend under that concealment, and, in the character of a layman and a guest, to decoy his host's wife from her husband's religion, in that host's and husband's absence, thus betraying his friendship and violating his hospitality.

My counter-reply would be, that his host had frequently discussed religious questions with both himself and Lee, and had shown, at least, a very friendly feeling towards Catholics in general and their religion ; that, as has already been proved, he had in so many words declared himself free from any objection to the marriage of his own sister with a Catholic ; nay, that he wished to see her [1] " married well, and to a Catholic, for he looked on Catholics as honourable men ; " and that Lady Digby had determined to become a Catholic after due consideration and without any unfair external influence. As to his revealing his priestly character to her and exercising his priestly functions on her behalf, it must be observed that she had expressed a particular wish to see and to converse with a priest, without any such action on her part having been suggested to her by either Gerard or Lee, and that, if Gerard had continued to conceal his own priesthood, she would have simply been put to the trouble, and possibly the dangers, of searching for some other priest. If it be further objected that he ought at least to have waited until her husband's return, I must so far repeat myself as

[1] *Life of Father John Gerard,* p. cli.

to point out that a man who had stated that he would have no objection whatever to his sister's being married to a Catholic, might be fairly assumed to have no objection to finding himself also married to a Catholic. Again, since Lady Digby was convinced that her soul would only be safe when in the fold of the Church, it would be natural that she should not like to admit of any delay in her reception into it. This being the case, the guests had their duties to their hostess, as well as to their host. It is unnecessary to enter here into the question whether wives should inform their husbands, and grown-up sons and daughters their parents, before joining the Roman Catholic Church; I may, however, be allowed to say that I believe it to be the usual opinion of priests, as well as laymen, as it certainly is of myself, that in most cases, although possibly not absolutely in every case, their doing so is not only desirable, but a duty, provided no hindrance to the following of the dictates of their consciences will result from so doing. Where it would have such an effect, our Lord's teaching is plain and unmistakeable—"He that loveth father or mother more than me, is not worthy of me."

Some Protestants are under the impression that a conversion like Lady Digby's, in which she consulted, and was received into the Church by, a "priest in disguise" is "just the sort of thing that Roman Catholics like." There could be no greater mistake !

It is just what they do not like. The secrecy of
priests in the reign of James I. was rendered necessary
by persecution : so was that of the laity in housing
and entertaining them : so also were the precautions
to conceal the fact that mass was said in private
houses, and that rooms were used as chapels.

Now I would not pretend for a moment that such
a condition of things was wholesome for either priests,
Jesuits, laymen, or laywomen. There are occasions
on which secrecy may be a dire necessity, but it is,
at best, a necessary evil, and its atmosphere is
unnatural, cramping, dangerous, and demoralising,
although the persecution producing it may lead to
virtue, heroism, and even martyrdom. The persecutions of the early Christians by the Romans gave
the Church hundreds of saints and martyrs ; yet
surely those persecutions did not directly tend to the
welfare of Christianity ; and I suppose that the
authorities of the established Church in this country
would scarcely consider that Anglicanism would be
in a more wholesome condition if every diocese and
cure were to be occupied by a bishop or priest of the
Church of Rome under the authority of the Pope,
although the privations of the dispossessed Anglican
clergy, and the inconveniences of the Anglican laity,
might be the means of bringing about many individual
instances of laudable self-denial, personal piety, and
religious zeal. On the same principle, I think that a
Catholic student, with an elementary knowledge of the

subject, when approaching the history of his co-religionists in England during the reign of James I., would have good grounds for expecting that, while many cases of valiant martyrdom and suffering for the faith would embellish the pages he was about to read, those pages would also reveal that the impossibility of priests and religious living a clerical life, and the necessity of their joining day by day in the pursuits and amusements of laymen—laymen, often, of gaiety and fashion, if nothing more—had led to serious irregularities in discipline; that the frequent intervals without mass, or any other religious service or priestly assistance, had had the effect of rendering the laity deficient in the virtues which religious exercises and sacraments are supposed to inculcate; that the constant and inevitable practice of secrecy and concealment had induced a habit of mind savouring of prevarication, if not of deception, and that in the embarrassing circumstances and among the harassing surroundings of their lives, clergy as well as laity had occasionally acted with neither tact nor discretion. No one is more alive to the sufferings or the injustices endured by English Catholics in the early part of the seventeenth century, or more admires the courage and patience shown by many, if not most, of those who bore them, than myself; and it is only in fairness to those sufferers, and with a desire to look at their actions honestly, and, as much as may be, impartially, that I approach the subject in this spirit. I have laid the more emphasis on the dangers of secrecy, be it ever so unavoidable or enforced, because of their bearing upon a matter which will necessarily figure largely in the forthcoming pages.

Lady Digby had no sooner been received into the Church than she became exceedingly anxious for the conversion of her husband, but news now arrived which made her anxious about him on another account. A messenger brought the tidings that Sir Everard was very seriously ill in London, and Lady Digby at once determined to start on the journey of some forty-five or fifty miles in order to nurse him. Her guests volunteered to go to him also, and they were able to accomplish the distance, over the bad roads of that period, much more rapidly than she was.

I will let Father Gerard give an account of his own proceedings with Digby for himself.[1] "I spoke to him of the uncertainty of life, and the certainty of misery, not only in this life, but especially in the next, unless we provided against it; and I showed him that we have here no abiding city, but must look for one to come. As affliction often brings sense, so it happened in this case, for we found little difficulty in gaining his goodwill.

"He prepared himself well for confession after being taught the way; and when he learnt that I was a priest, he felt no such difficulty in believing as his wife had done, because he had known similar

____
[1] *Life of Father John Gerard*, p. cliii.

cases, but he rather rejoiced at having found a confessor who had experience among persons of his rank of life, and with whom he could deal at all times without danger of its being known that he was dealing with a priest. After his reconciliation he began on his part to be anxious about his wife, and wished to consult with us how best to bring her to the Catholic religion. We both smiled at this, but said nothing at the time, determining to wait till his wife came up to town, that we might witness how each loving soul would strive to win the other."

When Digby had recovered and had returned to Gothurst with his wife, they both paid a visit to Father Gerard at the country house, some distance from their own home, at which he lived as chaplain. This was probably Mrs Vaux's house at Stoke Pogis, of which we shall have something to say a little later. While there, he was taken ill even more seriously than before. His life became in danger, and the best doctors in Oxford were sent for to his assistance. They despaired of curing him, and "he began to prepare himself earnestly for a good death." His poor young wife, being told that her husband could not recover, began "to think of a more perfect way of life," in case she should be left a widow. It may be thought that she might at least have waited to do this until after the death of her husband, but it is possible, and even probable, although not mentioned by Father Gerard, that Sir Everard himself desired her to consider what manner of life she would lead when he should be gone. She would be a very young widow with a large property, and Sir Everard would doubtless feel anxious as to what would become of her.[1] "For some days," says Father Gerard, "she gave herself to learn the method of meditation, and to find out God's will with regard to her future life, how she might best direct it to his glory. This was her resolution, but God had otherwise arranged, and for that time happily."

Gerard himself was, humanly speaking, the means of prolonging Digby's life, for, in spite of the verdict of the great physicians from Oxford, that nothing could save him, Father Gerard refused to give up all hope, and persuaded him to send for a certain doctor of his own acquaintance from Cambridge. "By this doctor, then, he was cured beyond all expectation, and so completely restored to health that there was not a more robust or stalwart man in a thousand."

Not very long after he had become a Catholic, Digby was roughly reminded of the illegality of his position, by a rumour that his friend, Father Gerard, who had gone to a house to visit, as a priest, a person who was dying, was either on the point of being, or was actually, in the hands of pursuivants. This news distressed him terribly. He immediately told his wife that, if Father Gerard

---

[1] *Life of Father John Gerard*, p. cliii.

were arrested, he intended to take a sufficient number of friends and servants to rescue him, and to watch the roads by which he would probably be taken to London ; and that "he would accomplish" his "release one way or another, even though he should spend his whole fortune in the venture." The danger of such an attempt at that period was obvious. Certainly his desire to set free Father Gerard was most praiseworthy, but whether, had he attempted it in the way he proposed, he would have benefitted or injured the Catholic cause in England, may be considered at least doubtful. A rescue by an armed force would have meant a free fight, probably accompanied by some bloodshed, with this result, that, if successful, the perpetrators would most likely have been discovered, and sooner or later very severely dealt with as aggressors against the officers of the law in the execution of their duty, and that, if unsuccessful, the greater proportion of the rescuing party would have met their deaths either on the field at the time, or on the gallows afterwards. To attempt force against the whole armed power of the Crown seemed a very Quixotic undertaking, and the idea of dispersing the whole of his wealth, whether in the shape of armed force or other channels, in a chimerical effort to set free his friend, however generous in intent, scarcely recommends itself as the best method of using it for the good of the cause he had so much at heart. This incident shows

Digby's hastiness and impetuosity. Fortunately, the report of Father Gerard's arrest turned out to be false; so, for the moment, any excited and unwise action on Sir Everard's part was avoided.

CHAPTER III.

A CHANGE of religion causes, to most of those who make it, a very forcible wrench. It may be, probably it usually is, accompanied by great happiness and a sensation of intense relief; no regrets whatever may be felt that the former faith, with its ministers, ceremonies, and churches have been renounced for ever; on the contrary, the convert may be delighted to be rid of them, and in turning his back upon the religion of his childhood, he may feel that he is dismissing a false teacher who has deceived him, rather than that he is bidding farewell to a guide who has conducted him, however unintentionally, unwittingly, or unwillingly, to the gate of safety. Yet granting, and most emphatically granting, all this, we should not forget that there is another view of his position. Let his rejoicing be ever so great at entering that portal and leaving the land of darkness for the regions of light, be the welcome he receives from his future co-religionists as warm as it may, and be his confidence as great as is conceivable, the convert is none the less forsaking a well-known country for one that is new to him, he is leaving old friends to enter among strangers, and he is exchanging long-formed habits for practices which it will take him some time to understand, to acquire, and to familiarize.

A convert, again, is not invariably free from dangers. Let us take the case of Sir Everard Digby. A man with his position, popularity, wealth, intellect, and influence, was a convert of considerable importance from a human point of view, and he must have known it. If he lost money and friends by his conversion, much and many remained to him, and among the comparatively small number of Catholics he might become a more leading man than as a unit in the vast crowd professing his former faith ; and although, on the whole, the step which he had taken was calculated to be much against his advancement in life, there are certain attractions in being the principal or one of the principal men of influence in a considerable minority. I am not for a moment questioning Digby's motives in becoming a Catholic ; I believe they were quite unexceptionable ; all that I am at the moment aiming at is to induce the reader to keep before his mind that the position of an influential English convert, at the beginning of the seventeenth century, like most other positions, had its own special temptations and dangers, and my reasons for this aim will soon become obvious.

In comparing the situation of a convert to Catholicism in the latter days of Elizabeth or the early days of James I., with one in the reign of Victoria, we are met on the threshold with the fact that terrible bodily pains, and even death itself, threatened the former, while the latter is exposed to no danger of either for his religion. In the matter of legal fines and forfeitures, again, the persecution of the first was enormous, whereas the second suffers none. But of these pains and penalties I shall treat presently. Just in passing I may remark that many a convert now living has reason for doubting whether any of his forerunners in the times of Elizabeth or James I. suffered more pecuniary loss than he. One parent or uncle, by altering a will, can cause a Romish recusant more loss than a whole army of pursuivants.

Looking at the positions of converts at the two periods from a social point of view, we find very different conditions. Instead of being regarded, as he is now, in the light of a fool who, in an age of light, reason, and emancipation from error, has wilfully retrograded into the grossest of all forms of superstition, the convert, in the reigns of Elizabeth and James, was known to be returning to the faith professed by his fathers, one, two, or, at most, three generations before him. It was not then considered a case of "turning Roman Catholic," but of returning to the old religion, and even by people who cared little, if at all, about such matters, he was rather respected than otherwise.

Now it is different. During the two last generations, so many conversions have apparently been the result of what is known as the Oxford Movement, or of Ritualism, that converts are much associated in men's minds with ex-clergymen, or with clerical families; and to tell the truth, at least a considerable minority of Anglicans of good position, while they tolerate, invite to dinner, and patronise their parsons, in their inmost hearts look down upon and rather dislike the clergy and the clergy-begotten.

At present, again, a prejudice is felt in England against an old Catholic, *prima facie*, on the ground that he is probably either an Irishman, of Irish extraction, or of an ancient Catholic English family rendered effete by idleness, owing to religious disabilities, or by a long succession of intermarriages. It would be easy to prove that these prejudices, if not altogether without foundation in fact, are immensely and unwarrantably exaggerated, but my object, at present, is merely to state that they exist. Three hundred years ago, whatever may have been the prejudices against Catholics, old or new, they cannot have arisen on such grounds as these, and if Protestants attributed the tenacity of the former and the determined return of the latter to their ancient faith rather to pride than to piety, there is no doubt which motive would be most respected in the fashionable world.

The conduct of the Digbys, immediately after their conversion, was most exemplary. They threw

themselves heart and soul into their religion, and
Father Gerard, who had received them into the
Church, writes [1] of Sir Everard in the highest terms,
saying :—" He was so studious a follower of virtue,
after he became a Catholic, that he gave great
comfort to those that had the guiding of his soul
(as I have heard them seriously affirm more than
once or twice), he used his prayers daily both
mental and vocal, and daily and diligent examination of his conscience : the sacraments he frequented
devoutly every week, &c." " Briefly I have heard it
reported of this knight, by those that knew him
well and that were often in his company, that they
did note in him a special care of avoiding all occasions of sin and of furthering acts of virtue in what
he could."

He read a good deal in order to be able to enter
into controversy with Protestants, and he was the
means of bringing several into the Church—"some
of great account and place." As to his conversation, " not only in this highest kind, wherein he
took very great joy and comfort, but also in ordinary
talk, when he had observed that the speech did tend
to any evil, as detraction or other kind of evil
words which sometimes will happen in company,
his custom was presently to take some occasion to
alter the talk, and cunningly to bring in some other
good matter or profitable subject to talk of. And

[1] *A Narrative of the Gunpowder Plot*, p. 69.

this, when the matter was not very grossly evil, or spoken to the dishonour of God or disgrace of his servants ; for then, his zeal and courage were such that he could not bear it, but would publicly and stoutly contradict it, whereof I could give divers instances worth relating, but am loth to hold the reader longer." Finally, in speaking of those "that knew him" and those "that loved him," Father Gerard says, "truly it was hard to do the one and not the other."

Like most Catholics living in the country, and inhabiting houses of any size, the Digbys made a chapel in their home, "a chapel with a sacristy," says Father Gerard,[1] "furnishing it with costly and beautiful vestments ;" and they "obtained a Priest of the Society" (of Jesus) "for their chaplain, who remained with them to Sir Everard's death." Of this priest, Gerard says[2] that he was a man "who for virtue and learning hath not many his betters in England." This was probably Father Strange,[3] who usually passed under the *alias* of Hungerford. He was the owner of a property, some of which, in Gloucestershire, he sold,[4] and " £2000 thereof is in the Jesuites' bank" said a witness against him. He was imprisoned, after Sir Everard Digby's death, for

---

[1] *Life of Father John Gerard,* p. clv.
[2] *A Narrative of the Gunpowder Plot,* p. 89.
[3] *Father H. Garnet and the Gunpowder Plot,* by Father Pollen, p. 15.
[4] *Records of the English Province.* S.J. Series, ix. x. xi., p. 3.

five or six years.[1] In an underground dungeon in
the Tower[2] "he was so severely tortured upon the
rack that he dragged on the rest of his life for thirty-
three years in the extremest debility, with severe
pains in the loins and head. Once when he was
in agony upon the rack, a Protestant minister began
to argue with him about religion; whereupon, turning to the rack-master, Father Strange[3] "asked him
to hoist the minister upon a similar rack, and in like
fetters and tortures, otherwise, said he, we shall be
fighting upon unequal terms; for the custom every-
where prevails amongst scholars that the condition
of the disputants be equal."

Another Jesuit Father, at one time private
chaplain to Sir Everard Digby, was Father John
Percy,[4] who afterwards, under the *alias* of Fisher,
held the famous controversy with Archbishop Laud
in the presence of the king and the Countess
of Buckingham, to whom he acted as chaplain for
ten years. He also had been fearfully tortured in
prison, in the reign of Elizabeth; and if he recounted
his experiences on the rack to Sir Everard Digby,
the hot blood of the latter would be stirred up
against the Protestant Governments that could per-
petrate or tolerate such iniquities.

In trying to picture to himself the "chapel with
a sacristy" made by the Digbys at Gothurst, a

<hr>

[1] *Ib.*, p. 5, and Stoneyhurst MSS.   [2] *Ib.*, p. 3.
[3] *Ib.*, p. 4   [4] *Records*, S.J. Series, i., p. 527.

romantic reader may imagine an ecclesiastical gem, in the form of a richly-decorated chamber filled with sacred pictures, figures of saints, crucifixes, candles, and miniature shrines. Before taking the trouble of raising any such representation before the mind, it would be well to remember that, in the times of which we are treating, that was the most perfect and the best arranged chapel in which the altar, cross, chalice, vestments, &c., could be concealed at the shortest possible notice, and the chamber itself most quickly made to look like an ordinary room. The altar was on such occasions a small slab of stone, a few inches in length and breadth, and considerably less than an inch in thickness. It was generally laid upon the projecting shelf of a piece of furniture, which, when closed, had the appearance of a cabinet. Some few remains of altars and other pieces of " massing stuff," as Protestants called it, of that date still remain, as also do many simple specimens used in France during the Revolution of last century, which have much in common with them. To demonstrate the small space in which the ecclesiastical contents of a private chapel could be hidden away in times of persecution, I may say that, even now, for priests who have the privilege of saying mass elsewhere than in churches or regular chapels—for instance, in private rooms, on board ship,[1] or in the ward of a hospital—altar, chalice,

---

[1] In his *Mores Catholici* (Cincinnati, 1841, Vol. II. p. 364), Kenelm H. Digby says that " Portable altars were in use long before the

paten, cruets, altar-cloths, lavabo, alb, amice, girdle, candlesticks, crucifix, wafer-boxes, wine-flask, Missal, Missal-stand, bell, holy-oil stocks, pyx, and a set of red and white vestments (reversible)—in fact, everything necessary for saying mass, as well as for administering extreme unction to the sick, can be carried in a case 18 inches in length, 12 inches in width, and 8 inches in depth. Occasionally, as we are told of the Digbys, rich people may have had some handsome vestments; but a private chapel early in the sixteenth century must have been a very different thing from what we associate with the term in our own times, and however well furnished it may have been as a room, it must have been almost devoid of " ecclesiastical luxury."

Here and there were exceptions, in which Catholics were very bold, but they always got into trouble. For instance, when Luisa de Carvajal came to England, she was received at a country house— possibly Scotney Castle, on the borders of Kent and Sussex—the chapel of which [1] " was adorned with pictures and images, and enriched with many relics. Several masses were said in it every day, and accompanied by beautiful vocal and instrumental music." It was " adorned not only with all the

eleventh century. St Wulfran, Bishop of Sens, passing the sea in a ship, is said to have celebrated the sacred mysteries upon a portable altar."

[1] *The Life of Luisa de Carvajal,* by Lady G. Fullerton, p. 154, *seq.*

requisites, but all the luxuries, so to speak, of Catholic worship;" and Luisa could walk "on a spring morning in a pleached alley, saying her beads, within hearing of the harmonious sounds of holy music floating in the balmy air." What was the consequence? "The beautiful dream was rudely dispelled. One night, after she had been at this place about a month, a secret warning was given to the master of this hospitable mansion, that he had been denounced as a harbourer of priests, and that the pursuivants would invade his house on the morrow. On the receipt of this information, measures were immediately taken to hide all traces of Catholic worship, and a general dispersion took place." I only give this as a typical case to show how necessary it then was to make chapels and Catholic worship as secret as possible.

Sir Everard Digby was anxious that others, as well as himself, should join the body which he believed to be the one, true, and only Church of God, and of this I have nothing to say except in praise. An anecdote of his efforts in this direction, however, is interesting as showing, not only the necessities of the times, but also something of the character and disposition of the man. In studying a man's life, there may be a danger of building too much upon his actions, as if they proved his inclinations, when they were in reality only the result of exceptional circumstances, and I have no wish to force the inferences, which I myself draw from the following facts, upon the opinions of other people; I merely submit them for what they are worth.

Father Gerard says[1] that Sir Everard "had a friend for whom he felt a peculiar affection," namely, Oliver Manners, the fourth son of John, fourth Earl of Rutland, and said by Father J. Morris[2] to have been knighted by King James I. "on his coming from Scotland," on April 22nd, 1603, but by Burke,[3] "at Belvoir Castle, 23rd April 1608." He was very anxious that this friend should be converted to the Catholic faith, and that, to this end, he should make the acquaintance of Father Gerard; "but because he held an office in the Court, requiring his daily attendance about the King's person, so that he could not be absent for long together," this "desire was long delayed." At last Sir Everard met Manners in London at a time when he knew that Father Gerard was there also, "and he took an opportunity of asking him to come at a certain time to play at cards, for these are the books gentlemen in London study both night and day." Instead of inviting a card-party, Digby invited no one except Father Gerard, and when Manners arrived, he found Gerard and Digby "sitting and conversing very seriously." The latter asked him "to sit down a little until the rest should arrive." After a short silence Sir Everard said:—

---

[1] *Life of Father John Gerard*, p. clxvi. *seq.*

[2] *Ib.*, footnote to p. cciii.

[3] *Peerage*, 1886, p.1173.

"We two were engaged in a very serious conversation, in fact, concerning religion. You know that I am friendly to Catholics and to the Catholic faith ; I was, nevertheless, disputing with this gentleman, who is a friend of mine, against the Catholic faith, in order to see what defence he could make, for he is an earnest Catholic, as I do not hesitate to tell you." At this he turned to Father Gerard and begged him not to be angry with him for betraying the fact of his being a Romish recusant to a stranger ; then he said to Manners, "And I must say he so well defended the Catholic faith that I could not answer him, and I am glad you have come to help me."

Manners " was young and confident, and trusting his own great abilities, expected to carry everything before him, so good was his cause and so lightly did he esteem " his opponent, " as he afterwards confessed." After an hour's sharp argument and retort on either side, Father Gerard began to explain the Catholic faith more fully, and to confirm it with texts of Scripture, and passages from the Fathers.

Manners listened in silence, and " before he left he was fully resolved to become a Catholic, and took with him a book to assist him in preparing for a good confession, which he made before a week had passed." He became an excellent and exemplary Christian, and his life would make an interesting and edifying volume.

All honour to Sir Everard Digby for having been the human medium of bringing about this most happy and blessed conversion ! It might have been difficult to accomplish it by any other method. In those days of persecution, stratagem was absolutely necessary to Catholics for their safety sake, even in everyday life, and still more so in evangelism. As to the particular stratagem used by Digby in this instance, I do not go so far as to say that it was blame-worthy ; I have often read of it without mentally criticising it ; I have even regarded it with some degree of admiration ; but, now that I am attempting a study of Sir Everard Digby's character, and seeking for symptoms of it in every detail that I can discover of his words and actions, I ask myself whether, in all its innocence, his conduct on this occasion did not exhibit traces of a natural inclination to plot and intrigue. Could he have induced Manners to come to his rooms by no other attraction than a game of cards, which he had no intention of playing? Was it necessary on his arrival there to ask him to await that of guests who were not coming, and had never been invited ? Was he obliged, in the presence of so intimate a friend, to pretend to be only well-disposed towards Catholics instead of owning himself to be one of them ? Need he have put himself to the trouble of apologising to Father Gerard for revealing that he was a Catholic ? In religious, as in all other matters, there are cases in which artifice may be harmless or desirable, or even a duty, but a thoroughly straight-forward man will shrink from the " pious dodge " as much as the kind-hearted surgeon will shrink from the use of the knife or the cautery.

Necessary as they may have been, nay, necessary as they undoubtedly were, the planning, and disguising, and hiding, and intriguing used as means for bringing about the conversions of Lady Digby, Sir Everard Digby, and Oliver Manners, though innocent in themselves, placed those concerned in them in that atmosphere of romance, adventure, excitement, and even sentiment, which I have before described, and it is obvious that such an atmosphere is not without its peculiar perils.

It is certainly very comfortable to be able to preach undisturbed, to convert heretics openly, and to worship in the churches of the King and the Government; yet even in religion, to some slight degree, the words of a certain very wise man may occasionally be true, that [1] " stolen waters are sweeter, and hidden bread is more pleasant." Nothing is more excellent than missionary work; but it is a fact that proselytism, when conducted under difficulties and dangers, whether it be under the standard of truth or under the standard of error, is not without some of the elements of sport; at any rate, if it be true, as enthusiasts have been heard to assert, that even the hunted fox is a partaker in the pleasures of the chase,

[1] Proverbs ix. 17.

the Jesuits had every opportunity of enjoying them during the reigns of Elizabeth and James I.

Besides a consideration of the personal characteristics of Sir Everard Digby, and the position of converts to Catholicism in his times, it will be necessary to take a wider view of the political, social, and religious events of his period. Otherwise we should be unable to form anything like a fair judgment either of his own conduct, or of the treatment which he received from others.

The oppression and persecution of Catholics by Queen Elizabeth and her ministers was extreme. It was made death to be a priest, death to receive absolution from a priest, death to harbour a priest, death even to give food or help of any sort to a priest, and death to persuade anyone to become a Catholic. Very many priests and many laymen were martyred, more were tortured, yet more suffered severe temporal losses. And, what was most cruel of all, while Statutes were passed with a view to making life unendurable for Catholics in England itself, English Catholics were forbidden to go, or to send their children, beyond the seas without special leave.

The actual date of the Digbys' reception into the Catholic Church is a matter of some doubt. It probably took place before the death of Elizabeth. That was a time when English Catholics were considering their future with the greatest anxiety. Politics entered largely into the question, and where politics include, as they did then, at any rate, in many men's minds, some doubts as to the succession to the crown, intrigue and conspiracy were pretty certain to be practised.

CHAPTER IV.

THE responsibility of the intrigues in respect to the claims to the English throne, at the beginning of the seventeenth century, rests to some extent upon Queen Elizabeth herself. As Mr Gardiner puts it :—[1] " She was determined that in her lifetime no one should be able to call himself her heir." It was generally understood that James would succeed to the throne; but, so long as there was the slightest uncertainty on the question, it was but natural that the Catholics should be anxious that a monarch should be crowned who would favour, or at least tolerate them, and that they should make inquiries, and converse eagerly, about every possible claimant to the throne. Fears of foreign invasion and domestic plotting were seriously entertained in England during the latter days of Elizabeth, as well as immediately after her death. " Wealthy men had brought in their plate and treasure from the country, and had put them in places of safety. Ships of war had been stationed in

[1] *History of England,* from the Accession of James I. to the outbreak of the Civil War, 1603-1642, Vol. i. p. 79.

the Straits of Dover to guard against a foreign invasion, and some of the principal recusants had, as a matter of precaution, been committed to safe custody.[1]

When James VI. of Scotland, the son of the Catholic Mary Queen of Scots, ascended the throne, rendered vacant by the death of Elizabeth, as James I. of England, no voice was raised in favour of any other claimant, and[2] "the Catholics, flattered by the reports of their agents, hailed with joy the succession of a prince who was said to have promised the toleration of their worship, in return for the attachment which they had so often displayed for the house of Stuart." King James owed toleration, says Lingard, " to their sufferings in the cause of his unfortunate mother ; " and " he had bound himself to it, by promises to their envoys, and to the princes of their communion."

The opinion that the new king would upset and even reverse the anti-Catholic legislation of Elizabeth was not confined to the Catholic body : many Protestants had taken alarm on this very score, as may be inferred from a contemporary tract, entitled [3] *Advertisements of a loyal subject to his gracious Sovereign, drawn from the Observation of the People's Speeches*, in which the following passage occurs :—" The plebes, I wotte not what they call them, but some there bee

---

[1] Gardiner's *History of England*, Vol i. p. 85.

[2] Lingard, Vol. vii. chap. i.

[3] Somers Tracts, Vol. ii. p. 147. From the Cotton Library, Faustina, c. 11, 12, fol. 61.

who most unnaturally and unreverentlie, by most egregious lies, wound the honour of our deceased soveraigne, not onlie touching her government and good fame, but her person with sundry untruthes," and after going on in this strain for some lines it adds :—" Suerlie these slanders be the doings of the papists, ayming thereby at the deformation of the gospell."

[1] On the other hand, there were both Catholics and Puritans who were distrustful of James. Sir Everard cannot have been long a Catholic, when a dangerous conspiracy was on foot. Sir Griffin Markham, a Catholic, and George Brooke, a Protestant, and a brother of Lord Cobham's, hatched the well-known plot which was denominated "the Bye," and, among many others who joined it, were two priests, Watson and Clarke, both of whom were eventually executed on that account. Its object appears to have been to seize the king's person, and wring from him guarantees of toleration for both Puritans and Catholics. Father Gerard acquired some knowledge

[1] " James was an alien." "Supposing that on such principles King James was rejected, who would come next? The Lady Arabella Stuart, descended from Margaret, daughter of Henry VII. in the same manner as King James, save that her father was a second son, and King James's father was the eldest. But she had the fact of her birth and domiciliation within the kingdom of England as a counterpoise to her father's want of primogeniture." "Without openly professing Roman Catholicism, she was thought to be inclined that way, and to be certainly willing to make favourable terms with the Roman Catholics." Introduction by J. Bruce to *Correspondence of King James VI. of Scotland with Cecil and others.*

of this conspiracy, as also did Father Garnet, the Provincial of the Jesuits, and Blackwell, the Arch-priest; and they insisted upon the information being laid instantly before the Government. Before they had time to carry out their intention, however, it had already been communicated, and the complete failure of the attempt is notorious. The result was to injure the causes of both the Catholics and the Puritans, and James never afterwards trusted the professions of either.

So far as the Catholics were concerned, the "Bye" conspiracy unfortunately revealed another; for Father Watson, in a written confession which he made in prison, brought accusations of disloyalty against the Jesuits. It was quite true that, two years earlier, Catesby, Tresham, and Winter—all friends of Sir Everard Digby's—had endeavoured to induce Philip of Spain to invade England, and had asked Father Garnet to give them his sanction in so doing; but Garnet had "misliked it," and had told them that it would be as much "disliked at Rome." [1]

Winter had arranged that if Queen Elizabeth should die before the invasion, the news should be at once sent to the Spanish court. For this purpose, a York-shire gentleman, named Christopher Wright, and one Guy, or Guido, Faukes, or Fawkes, "a soldier of fortune," of whom we shall have more to say by-and-bye, were sent to the Court of Spain in

[1] Dodds' *Church History of England*, Vol. iv. p. 8. Tierney's Notes.

1603. Although Father Garnet disapproved of the plan, he had given Wright a letter of introduction to a Jesuit at the Spanish Court. Neither Wright nor Fawkes were able to rouse King Philip, who said that he had no quarrel with his English brother, and that he had just appointed an ambassador to the Court of St James's to arrange the terms of a lasting peace with the English nation. Knowing something of this, Father Watson used it as an instrument of revenge against the Jesuits, who, he knew, had intended to warn King James against his own attempt to entrap him.[1] "It is well known to all the world," he wrote, "how the Jesuits and Spanish faction had continually, by word, writing, and action, sought his majesty's destruction, with the setting up of another prince and sovereign over us; yea, and although it should be revealed what practises they had, even in this interim betwixt the proclaiming and crowning of his majesty." And then he enumerated some of these "practises," among others, "levying 40,000 men to be in a readiness for the Spaniard or Archduke; by buying up all the great horses, as Gerard doth; by sending down powder and shot into Staffordshire and other places, with warning unto Catholics to be in a readiness; by collection of money under divers pretences, to the value of a million;" "by affirming that none might yield to live under an heretic (as they con-

[1] Dodds' *Church History of England*, Appendix i. p. xxxv.

tinually termed his majesty);" "and by open speech that the king and all his royal issue must be cut off and put to death." In making these bitter and, for the most part, untrue accusations against the Jesuits, he complained that he was "accounted for no better than an infidel, apostate, or atheist, by the jesuitical faction," and that he was never likely "to receive any favour" from his majesty "so long as any Jesuit or Spaniard" remained "alive within this land."

Undoubtedly, during the cruel persecutions of Elizabeth, Jesuits, as well as secular priests, and Catholic laymen too, for that matter, had hoped that her successor on the English throne might be of their own religion; they had good cause for doing so; the Pope himself had urged the enthronement of a Catholic monarch for their country, and in fairness, it must be admitted that not a few Englishmen, who considered themselves royalist above all others, had at one time refused to regard Elizabeth herself as the legitimate possessor of the British crown; but, when James had been established upon the throne, with the exception of a few discontents, such as the conspirators in the "Bye" plot and the diminutive Spanish party, the English Catholics, both lay and clerical, acknowledged him as their rightful king. Pope Clement VIII.[1] "commanded the missionaries" in England "to confine themselves

<hr>

[1] Lingard, Vol. vii. chap. i.

to their spiritual duties, and to discourage, by all means in their power, every attempt to disturb the tranquillity of the realm;" he also ordered "the nuncio at Paris to assure James of the abhorrence with which he viewed all acts of disloyalty," and he despatched "a secret messenger to the English Court with an offer to withdraw from the kingdom any missionary who might be an object of suspicion to the Council."

Unfortunately, the discovery of the two conspiracies above mentioned, in which Catholics were implicated, weighed more with James than any assurances of good-will from the Pope or his emissaries. Had not Watson given King's evidence? Had not foreign invasion been implored by Catholics? Had they not intended "the Lady Arabella" as a substitute for his own Royal Majesty upon the throne? And had they not treasonably united with their extreme opposites, the Puritans, in a design to capture his precious person, with a view to squeezing concessions out of him, if not to putting him to death? To some extent he did indeed endeavour to conciliate the higher classes among his Catholic subjects, by inviting them to court, by conferring upon them the honour—such as it was—of knighthood, as in the case of Sir Everard Digby, and by promising to protect them from the penalties of recusancy, so long as by their loyalty and peaceable behaviour they should show themselves worthy of his favour and his confidence, but he absolutely and abruptly refused all requests for toleration of their religious worship, and more than once, he even committed to the Tower Catholics who had the presumption to ask for it.

The times were most trying to a recent convert like Sir Everard Digby. I will again quote Lingard [1] to show how faithless was James to the promises he had made of relief to his Catholic subjects :—" The oppressive and sanguinary code framed in the reign of Elizabeth was re-enacted to its full extent; it was even improved with additional severities."

And then, after describing the severe penalties inflicted upon those who sent children " beyond the seas, to the intent that" they " should reside or be educated in a Catholic college or seminary," as well as upon " the owners or masters of ships who " conveyed them, and adding that " every individual who had already resided or studied, or should hereafter reside or study in any such college or seminary, was rendered incapable of inheriting or purchasing or enjoying lands, annuities, chattels, debts, or sums of money within the realm, unless at his return to England, he should conform to the Established Church, he says :—" Moreover, as missionaries sometimes eluded detection under the disguise of tutors in gentlemen's houses, it was provided that no man should teach even the rudiments of grammar without

[1] Vol. vii. chap. i.

a license of the diocesan, under the penalty of forty
shillings per day, to be levied on the tutor himself,
and the same sum on his employer."

And again, when James had been a year on the
throne, the execution of the penal laws enabled the
king . . . to derive considerable profit," says Lingard.[1]
" The legal fine of £20 per lunar month was again
demanded ; and not only for the time to come, but
for the whole period of the suspension ; a demand
which, by crowding thirteen separate payments into
one of £260, exhausted the whole annual income of
men in respectable but moderate circumstances. Nor
was this all. By law, the least default in these payments subjected the recusant to the forfeiture of all
his goods and chattels, and of two-thirds of his lands,
tenements, hereditaments, farms, and leases. The
execution of this severe punishment was intrusted
to the judges at the assizes, the magistrates at the
sessions, and the commissioners for causes ecclesiastical
at their meetings. By them warrants of distress were
issued to constables and pursuivants ; all the cattle
on the lands of the delinquent, his household furniture,
and his wearing apparel, were seized and sold ; and
if, on some pretext or other, he was not thrown into
prison, he found himself and family left without a
change of apparel or a bed to lie upon, unless he
had been enabled by the charity of his friends to
redeem them after the sale, or to purchase with

[1] VoL viL chap. L

bribes the forbearance of the officers. Within six months the payment was again demanded, and the same pauperizing process repeated."

It may be only fair to say, however, that Mr Gardiner thinks Lingard was guilty of exaggeration on one point; for he says[1] "the £20 men were never called upon for arrears, and, as far as I have been able to trace the names, the forfeitures of goods and chattels were only demanded from those from whom no lands had been seized."

A letter in Father Garnet's handwriting to Father Persons on these topics should have a special interest for us, as it was pretty certainly written at Gothurst, where he seems to have been staying at the time it is dated, October 4 and 21, 1605. It says[2]:—"The courses taken are more severe than in Bess's time. . . . If any recusant buy his goods again, they inquire diligently if the money be his own : otherwise they would have that too. In fine, if these courses hold, every man must be fain to redeem, once in six months, the very bed he lieth on : and hereof, of twice redeeming, besides other precedents, I find one here in Nicolas, his lodging," i.e., in the house of Sir Everard Digby. "The judges now openly protest that the king will have blood, and hath taken blood in Yorkshire ; and that the king hath hitherto stroked papists, but now will strike :—and this is without

---

[1] *History of England*, 1603-42, Vol. i. p. 329, footnote.
[2] I quote from *Dodd and Tierney*, Vol. iv., Appendix xvi., p. ciii.

any desert of Catholics. The execution of two in the north is certain : " — three persons, Welbourn and Fulthering at York, and Brown at Ripon, had in fact been executed in Yorkshire that year for recusancy.[1] Father Garnet continues :—" and whereas it was done upon cold blood, that is, with so great stay after their condemnation, it argueth a deliberate resolution of what we may expect : so that you may see there is no hope that Paul," *i.e.* Pope Paul V., "can do anything ; and whatsoever men give out there, of easy proceedings with Catholics, is mere fabulous. And yet, notwithstanding, I am assured that the best sort of Catholics will bear all their losses with patience : but how these tyrannical proceedings of such base officers may drive particular men to desperate attempts, that I cannot answer for ;—the king's wisdom will foresee."

Mr Gardiner, in noticing the fines levied on recusants, mentions[2] one point in connection with them which would be peculiarly vexatious to a man of Sir Everard Digby's temperament and position. "The Catholics must have been especially aggrieved by the knowledge that much of the money thus raised went into the pockets of courtiers. For instance, the profits of the lands of two recusants were granted to a footman, and this was by no means an isolated case."

Sir Everard Digby's great friend, Father Gerard,

---

[1] Challoner, ii. 12, 13.
[2] *History of England*, 1603-42, Vol i. p. 230.

also testifies at great length to the persecutions under Elizabeth and James.[1] Father Southwell was put " nine times most cruelly upon the torture," and the law against the Catholics " put to cruel death many and worthy persons," and " many persons of great families and estimation were at several times put to death under pretence of treason, which also was their cloak to cover their cruelties against such priests and religious as were sent into England by authority from His Holiness to teach and preach the faith of Christ, and to minister his sacraments."

Again, " their torturing of men when they were taken to make them confess their acquaintance and relievers, was more terrible than death by much, &c." " Besides the spoiling and robbing laymen of their livings and goods, with which they should maintain their families, is to many more grievous than death would be, when those that have lived in good estate and countenance in their country shall see before them their whole life to be led in misery, and not only themselves, but their wives and children to go a-begging." " And to these the continual and cruel searches, which I have found to be more terrible than taking itself. The insolencies and abuses offered in them, and in the seizures of goods, the continual awe and fear that men are kept in by the daily expectance of these things, while every malicious man (of which heresy can want no plenty) is made an officer in these

---

[1] *Narrative of the Gunpowder Plot*, p. 16. *seq.*

affairs, and every officer a king as it were, to command and insult upon Catholics at their pleasure." It may be readily imagined how the writer of all this would discuss this bad state of affairs with Sir Everard at Gothurst.

I have no wish to exaggerate the sufferings endured by Catholics during the reigns of Elizabeth and the early Stuarts. I willingly admit that in many cases the legal penalties were not enforced against them, nay, I would go further and frankly remind my Catholic readers—Protestants may possibly not require to have their memories thus stimulated—that half a century had not elapsed since Protestants were burned at the stake in Smithfield for their religion by Catholics. Besides all this, it is certain that toleration, as we understand it, is a comparatively modern invention, and that if Mary Queen of Scots had ascended the English throne, or if it had fallen into the hands of Spain, Protestants in this country might not have had a very comfortable time of it, especially in the process of disgorging property taken from the Church, and that, under certain circumstances, some of them might even have suffered death for their faith ; but, while readily making this admission, I doubt whether any Catholic government ever attempted to oblige a people to relinquish a religion, which it had professed for many centuries, with the persistency and cruelty which the governments of Elizabeth and James I. exercised in endeavouring to oblige every British subject to reject the religion of his forefathers. Instances are not wanting of Catholics dealing out stern measures towards those who introduced a new religion into a country ; this, on the contrary, was a case of punishing those who refused to adopt a new religion.

Nor was this the only ground on which the persecutions by James appeared unfair, tyrannical, and odious to Catholics. During the reign of Elizabeth they had endured their sufferings as the penalties of a religion contradicting that of their monarch. Perhaps they did not altogether blame her so much for her persecutions, as for persecuting the right religion in mistake for the wrong ; and, after all, they knew she had been persuaded by her Council that, for purposes of State, it was necessary to break off relations with the Apostolic See, and to maintain the newly-fangled Anglican faith ; they knew that the refusal of Rome to acknowledge her legitimacy, threatened the very foundations of her throne, and consequently made every Catholic seem a traitor in her eyes ; they knew, too, that the Holy See had favoured Mary Queen of Scots, whom she had regarded as her most dangerous rival. Under these circumstances, therefore, while they found their troubles and trials excessively bitter, they may not have been very profoundly astonished at them. But when James, after a brief respite, continued and even increased the persecutions of the previous reign, they looked at the matter in quite a different light. In the first place, they expected that the Protestant son of so Catholic a mother, who had suffered imprisonment and death because she was a Catholic, could scarcely become the friend and accomplice of those who had betrayed and martyred his mother. I am not trenching on the question of the martyrdom of Mary Queen of Scots ; I am merely writing of the feeling respecting her death, prevalent at that time among members of her own religion in this country. Secondly, unlike Elizabeth, James had no cause for fearing the Holy See ; it never questioned his legitimacy ; it had assisted him when King of Scotland ; its adherents in England had almost universally hailed his accession to the crown with loyalty and rejoicing ; and, as I have already shown, the Pope had sent messages to him, offering to assist in assuring the allegiance of the Catholics by removing any priests who might be obnoxious to him.

Even Goodman, the Protestant Bishop of Gloucester, wrote [1] :—" After Sixtus Quintus succeeded Clement Octavus, a man, according to his name, who was much given to mercy and compassion. Now to him King James did make suit to favour his title to the crown of England, which as King James doth relate in his book, *Triplici nodo triplex cuneus*, the Pope did promise to do." James said that he would show favour to Catholics [2] " were it not that the English would take it ill, and it would much hinder him in his succession ; and withall, that his own subjects

[1] *The Court of King James I.*, Vol. i. p. 82 *seq.*   [2] *Ib.*, p. 83.

in Scotland were so violent against Catholics, that he, being poor, durst not offend them. Whereupon the Pope replied, that if it were for want of means, he would exhaust all the treasures of the church and sell the plate to supply him." And again, says Goodman of the English Catholics and King James[1] :—
"And certainly they had very great promises from him." Nevertheless,[2] "he did resolve to run a course against the papists," and " at his discourses at table usually he did express much hatred to them."

Father Gerard writes that[3] there were "particular embassagies and letters from His Majesty unto other Princes, giving hope at least of toleration to Catholics in England, of which letters divers were translated this year into French and came so into England, as divers affirmed that had seen them." He was also "well assured that immediately upon Queen Elizabeth's sickness and death, divers Catholics of note and fame, Priests also, did ride post into Scotland, as well to carry the assurance of dutiful affection from all Catholics unto His Majesty as also to obtain his gracious favour for them. and his royal word for confirmation of the same. At that time, and to those persons, it is certain he did promise that Catholics should not only be quiet from any molestations, but should also enjoy such liberty in their houses privately as themselves would desire,

---

[1] *The Court of King James I.*, Vol. i. p. 86. [2] *Ib.* p. 87.
[3] *Narrative of the Gunpowder Plot*, p. 24.

and have both Priests and Sacraments with full toleration and desired quiet. Both the Priests that did kneel before him when he gave this promise (binding it with the word of a Prince, which he said was never yet broken), did protest so much unto divers from whom I have it. And divers others, persons of great worth, have assured me the same upon the like promise received from His Majesty, both for the common state of Catholics and their own particular."

It is dangerous to make too much of evidence against which there may be the shadow of a suspicion. Father Gerard's personal testimony can be accepted without the smallest hesitation ; but that of Father Watson, who was probably one of the priests he mentioned who "did kneel before" James when he made the solemn promise which Father Gerard heard of at second hand, should be received with more caution. Lord Northampton's statement in his speech at Sir Everard Digby's trial should certainly obtain very careful consideration. "No man," said he,[1] "can speak more soundly to the point than myself; for being sent into the prison by the King to charge him with this false alarm" (*i.e.*, the report that James had promised toleration to Catholics), "only two days before his death, and upon his soul to press him in the presence of God, and as he would answer it at another bar, to confess

<hr>

[1] *Criminal Trials*, Jardine, Vol. ii. p. 177.

directly whether at either or both these times he had access unto his Majesty at Edinburgh, his Majesty did give him any promise, hope, or comfort of encouragement to Catholics concerning toleration ; he did there protest upon his soul that he could never win one inch of ground or draw the smallest comfort from the King in those degrees, nor further than that he would have them apprehend, that as he was a stranger to this state, so, till he understood in all points how those matters stood, he would not promise favour any way; but did protest that all the crowns and kingdoms in this world should not induce him to change any jot of his profession, which was the pasture of his soul and earnest of his eternal inheritance. He did confess that in very deed, to keep up the hearts of Catholics in love and duty to the King, he had imparted the King's words to many, in a better tune and a higher kind of descant than his book of plainsong did direct, because he knew that others, like sly bargemen, looked that way when their stroke was bent another way. For this he craved pardon of the King in humble manner, and for his main treasons, of a higher nature than these figures of hypocrisy, and seemed penitent, as well for the horror of his crime as for the false-hood of his whisperings."

Probably Northampton may have exaggerated, possibly he may have lied, in making this statement ; but there is this to be remembered, that owing to his false testimony against the Jesuits, already recorded in this chapter, Father Watson must be regarded as a somewhat discredited witness, and it will not do for us Catholics to accept his verbal evidence against King James, and then to turn round and repudiate the evidence against the Jesuits in his own handwriting,[1] without some very strong reason for so doing. A reason of a certain strength does indeed exist; for Watson's evidence against James was given freely and uninterestedly; whereas his evidence against the Jesuits may very probably have been offered in the hope that it might be accepted as the price of pardon, or at least of some mitigation of the awful sufferings included in the form of death to which he had been sentenced.

Even if we altogether discard Watson's evidence of James's promises, enough remains to satisfy my own mind that the new king had given the Catholics more or less hope of toleration; and, if I am too easily satisfied on this point, there can be no sort of question that Sir Everard Digby, who was often with Father Gerard, and that many other English Catholics had been assured, rightly or wrongly, and believed, wrongly or rightly, that King James had solemnly promised to give them immunity from persecution, if not freedom of worship, and that he had basely and treacherously broken his faith with them and

[1] Quoted above. I copied from Dodd; but the original may be found in the S.P. Dom., James I., Vol. iii. n. 16.

sold them for the price of popularity among his far more numerous Protestant subjects : who, then, can blame them for considering themselves to have been most unjustly, perfidiously, and infamously treated by that monarch ?

It may be worth while to quote here again from Goodman, the Protestant Bishop of Gloucester, respecting the persecutions of the Catholics in the reign of James.[1] "Now that they saw the times settled, having no hope of better days, but expecting that the uttermost rigour of the law should be executed, they became desperate ; finding that by the laws of the kingdom their own lives were not secured, and for the coming over of a priest into England it was no less than high treason. A gentlewoman was hanged only for relieving and harbouring a priest ; a citizen was hanged only for being reconciled to the Church of Rome : besides, the penal laws were such and so executed that they should not subsist :— what was usually sold in shops and openly bought, this the pursuivant would take away from them as being popish and superstitious. One knight did affirm that in one term he gave twenty nobles in rewards to the doorkeeper of the attorney-general ; another did affirm, that his third part which remained to him of his estate did hardly serve for his expense in law to defend him from other oppressions, besides their children to be taken from home to be brought up

______
[1] *The Court of King James I.*, Vol. i. pp. 100-1.

in another religion. So they did every way conclude that their estate was desperate, etc." If objection should be taken to Goodman as a witness on the Protestant side, on the ground that he eventually became a Catholic, I would reply that, at the time he wrote what I have quoted, he was, as the editor of his *Court of James the First* says,[1] " an earnest and zealous supporter of the Church," of England, and of James I., Goodman himself writes[2] in that very book :—" Truly I did never know any man of so great an apprehension, of so great love and affection— a man so truly just, so free from all cruelty and pride, such a lover of the church, and one that had done so much good for the church." Such an admirer of King James might certainly be trusted not to say a word that he could honestly avoid about the ill-treatment endured by any class of his subjects during his reign.

[1] Introduction, p. viii.   [2] Vol. i. p. 91.

CHAPTER V.

Considering that the king had been led to distrust
the Catholics through the two lately discovered plots
in which some of their number had taken part, the
best policy for those who remained loyal, and these
were by far the majority, would have been to have
taken every opportunity of displaying their faithful-
ness to their sovereign, and, for those whose position
so entitled them, to present themselves as often as
they conveniently could at his Court, even if their
welcome was somewhat cold. Digby chose to follow
an exactly opposite course. He went to Court on
James's accession and received knighthood, and then
he returned to the country, only visiting London
occasionally, and then not going to Court. Like his
fellow-Catholics, he at first entertained hopes that the
new king was about to exhibit toleration, and as
much as any of them was he disappointed and em-
bittered as time speedily began to prove the contrary.
One cause of Sir Everard Digby's disgust at the aspect
of affairs, early in James the First's reign, may have
been that, as a courtier, he had expected much from

the Queen's being a Catholic,[1] and that not only
did no apparent good come of it, but her example
gave the greatest discouragement, as well as grave
scandal, to such of her subjects as professed her
own religion. Indeed, all that can safely be said
of her Catholicism, is that she was [2] "a Catholic,
so far, at least, as her pleasure-loving nature allowed
her to be of any religion at all." Nevertheless, "she
took great delight in consecrated,"—or, as Catholics
would say, blessed or sacred—"objects." She had
allowed herself to be crowned by [3] "a Protestant
Archbishop; but when the time arrived for the
reception of the Communion, she remained immov-
able on her seat, leaving the King to partake alone."
"Enthusiastic Catholics complained that she had no
heart for anything but festivities and amusements,
and during the rest of her life she attended the
services of the church sufficiently to enable the
Government to allege that she was merely an enemy
of Puritanical strictness." On one occasion, the

---

[1] In his *History of the Catholic Church in Scotland*, translated by Father
H. Blair, Canon Bellesheim says (Vol. iii. p. 347) that she was probably
received into the Church in 1600. But Father Forbes Leith, in his
Narrative (pp. 272 *seq.*) gives an authority stating it to have taken
place in 1598.

See also a very interesting article on "Anne of Denmark," by the
Rev. J. Stevenson, in *The Month*, Vol. 16 (xxxv.) pp. 256-265.

[2] *History of England*, from 1603-42. By S. R. Gardiner, Vol. i. p.
142. Also Degli Effetti to Del Bufalo, June ¹⁴⁄₂₄, ¹⁴⁄₂₄; Persons to
Aldobrandino, September ¹⁴⁄₂₄, *Roman Transcripts*, R.O.

[3] *History of England*, Gardiner, Vol. i, p. 116. Also Degli Effetti to
Del Bufalo, Aug. 11, ₁⁄₁, *Roman Transcripts*, R.O.

king, [1] "with some difficulty," had actually "induced her to receive the Communion with him at Salisbury, but she had been much vexed with herself since, and had refused to do it again. On Christmas Day she had accompanied him to Church, but since then he found it impossible to induce her to be present at a Protestant service. At one time Sir Anthony Standen, a Catholic, was employed by James on a mission to some of the Italian States, and he brought home with him some objects of devotion, as a present from the Pope to the Queen of England. These delighted her; yet, when the king heard of them, they were returned to the Pope through the Nuncio in Paris."

Now to any good Catholic, especially to an exceedingly zealous convert in his first fervour, like Sir Everard Digby, a Protestant king might be tolerable, provided he treated his Catholic subjects properly; but a court presided over by a queen, herself a convert, who was a most indifferent Catholic, if not an apostate,[2] would be odious in the extreme. It was difficult enough, in any case, to make many simple Catholics understand that there was anything very wrong in avoiding persecution by putting in an occasional appearance at the Protestant churches, without joining in the service, if they heard mass

---

[1] *History of England*, Gardiner, Vol. i. p. 142.

[2] In her *Queens of England*, Miss Strickland gives her authority for the statement that Queen Ann died "in edifying communion with the Church of England."

when they could, and went regularly to confession and communion; but the difficulty was immensely increased when they heard that the greatest lady in the land, who was herself a Catholic, did that very thing. Again, the country-gentlemen of high estate, Sir Everard Digby among them, suffered fines and penalties for their faith; yet here was the Catholic queen herself, contently living in the greatest luxury, and yielding on the most important points of her religion, in order to obtain it.[1] No wonder, therefore, that Sir Everard Digby absented himself from Court, however impolitic it may have been in him to do so.

In his country home, at Gothurst, he brooded, with much impatience, over the wrongs of his co-religionists, nor can it have been a pleasant reflection that at any moment his beautiful house might be broken into by pursuivants, who would hunt every recess and cupboard in it, in search of a priest, or of what Anglicans then denominated " massing-stuff." Should they suspect that the most richly carved pieces of oak-work concealed a hiding - place, the " officers of justice " would ruthlessly shatter them to pieces with axe or crowbar; his wife's private rooms

---

[1] Her practical concealment of her religion may have been chiefly on her husband's account. Father Abercromby, S.J., who received her into the Church, wrote that James I. said to her :—" Rogo te, mea uxor, si non potes sine hujusmodi (sacerdote) vivere, utaris quam poteris, secretissime, alias periclitabitur corona nostra." Bellesheim's Hist., p. 453.

would not be safe from the intrusion of the pursuivants, or the bevy of rough followers who might
accompany them ; and, if his house were filled with
guests, even were they Protestants, it would none the
less necessarily be given up to the intruders for so long
a time as they might choose to remain. The invasion
would be as likely to be made by night as by day ;
no notice would be given of its approach, and, as its
result, not only might the domestic chaplain be carried
off a prisoner, with his face to a horse's tail and his
legs tied together beneath its girths, but Sir Everard
himself would be liable to be taken away in the same
humiliating position, on a charge of High Treason.

The fine which Catholics had to pay must have
been sufficiently annoying even to a rich man like Sir
Everard Digby, and this annoyance would be greatly
increased by the knowledge that to poorer men it
meant ruin, as well as by the remarks of his less
wealthy Catholic friends that " after all, to him it was
a mere nothing."

The present was bad enough, and worse things were
expected in the future. Most of us know the fears
with which we hear that a Prime Minister of opposite
politics to our own is going to bring in a bill, in the
coming session, directed against our personal interests ;
even the coming budget of a Chancellor of the
Exchequer on our own side of the House, in a very
bad year, is anticipated with serious misgivings.
Imagine, therefore, the terrors of the Catholics whose

lives would already have been rendered unendurable, had the laws existing against them been put into full force, when they not only observed a rapidly increasing zeal among magistrates and judges in their proceedings against Romish recusants, but heard, on what appeared to be excellent authority, that additional, and most cruel, legislation against them was to be enacted in the Parliament shortly to be opened.

One of the most remarkable features in Sir Everard Digby's character was his extreme susceptibility to the influence of others ; and, for this reason, what may seem, at first sight, an undue proportion of a volume devoted to his biography, must necessarily be allotted to a description of the friends, and more especially one particular friend, under whose influence he fell ; and, if my readers should sometimes imagine that I have forgotten Sir Everard Digby altogether, or if they should feel inclined to accuse me of writing Catesby's life rather than Digby's, I can assure them that I am guiltless on both counts. For the moment, however, I must beg them to prepare themselves for an immediate and long digression, or rather an apparent digression, and warn them that it will be followed by many others.

To an impetuous man, zealous to the last degree, but not according to knowledge, few things are more dangerous than an intimate friend of similar views and temperament. Exactly such a friend had Sir Everard Digby. Here is a description of him by one who knew him well. [1] He "grew to such a composition of manners and carriage, to such a care of his speech (that it might never be hurtful to others, but taking all occasions of doing good), to such a zealous course of life, both for the cause in general, and for every particular person whom he could help in God's service, as that he grew to be very much respected by most of the better and graver sort of Catholics, and of Priests, and Religious also, whom he did much satisfy in the care of his conscience; so that it might plainly appear he had the fear of God joined with an earnest desire to serve Him. And so no marvel though many Priests did know him and were often in his company. He was, moreover, very wise and of great judgment, though his utterance was not so good. Besides, he was so liberal and apt to help all sorts, as it got him much love. He was of person above two yards high, and, though slender, yet as well proportioned to his height as any man one should see. His age (I take it) at his death was about thirty-five, or thereabouts. And to do him right, if he had not fallen into"—one particular and exceedingly "foul action and followed his own judgment in it (to the hurt and scandal of many), asking no advice but of his own reasons deceived and blinded under the shadow of zeal; if, I say, it had not been for this,

---

[1] Father Gerard's *Narrative of the Gunpowder Plot*, pp. 56, 57.

he had truly been a man worthy to be highly esteemed and prized in any commonwealth."

Be his attractions and virtues what they might, this man, Robert Catesby, had not anything like such an unblemished past as his friend, Sir Everard Digby. He was of an old Warwickshire and Northamptonshire family—he was the lineal descendant of William Catesby, who was attainted and executed for high treason after the battle of Bosworth Field.[1] Robert Catesby's father, who had been an ardent Catholic, had suffered considerable losses in his estate, and been imprisoned on account of his religion ; but Robert himself, on his father's death, apostatized, became exceedingly dissolute, and still further impoverished the family property by his extravagance. Goodman, Bishop of Gloucester, says of him :[2] "For Catesby, it is very well known that he was a very cunning, subtle man, exceedingly entangled in debts, and scarce able to subsist."

Some three or four years before Sir Everard Digby's conversion, Catesby had returned to the faith of his fathers. Whatever may have been the love of his God manifested by the reformed reprobate, his hatred of his queen, and afterwards of his king, was unmeasured. I have no desire to say anything in disparagement of Catesby's religious

---

[1] Dugdale's *Warwickshire*, p. 506. Jardine's *Criminal Trials*, Vol. ii. p. 26.   [2] *Court of King James I.*, Vol. i. p. 103.

fervour; but, considering that he had once abjured the Catholic faith, it may be no harm to remark that some people seem to like to profess the religion hated most by their enemies, and to exhibit zeal for it in proportion to that shown by their enemies against it. With several of his friends, Catesby joined the ill-fated conspiracy of the Earl of Essex, in the course of which he was wounded, taken prisoner, and finally ransomed for £3000 in all. When fighting for Essex, he greatly distinguished himself as a swordsman. Later, as I have already said, he was implicated in the intrigue that sent Christopher Wright and Guy Fawkes to Madrid in the hope of inducing Philip of Spain to depose James I. A modern Jesuit, Father J. Hungerford Pollen, has well said of him: [1] " The owner of large estates in the counties of Northampton, Warwick, and Oxford, honourably married, with issue to perpetuate the ancient family of which he was the only representative—such is not the sort of man we should have thought likely to engage in a desperate ad venture, and this presumption might be further strengthened by the consideration of his moral qualities. He was brave and accomplished, attractive to that degree which makes even sober men risk life and fortune to follow where he should lead, honest of purpose and truthful, and, above all, exceedingly zealous for religion. These qualities

---

[1] *Father H. Garnet and the Gunpowder Plot*, pp. 1 and 2.

should have, and would have, insured him from the frightful error into which he fell, had they not run to excess in more than one direction. Full of the chivalry that characterised the Elizabethan period, he was also infected with its worldliness, a failing which ill accorded with the patience every Catholic had to practice, and, moreover, his force of character carried him into obstinate adherence to his own views and plans. This it was that worked such ruin upon himself and all those who came in contact with him. Happy times may lead such men so to direct their energies, that the evil side of their character is never displayed, but times of great temptation often bring out the latent flaw in unexpected ways."

This is admirably put, except, perhaps, on one single point; and it is one of such importance that I will pause to consider it, especially as it applies to Sir Everard Digby, almost, if not quite, as much as to Catesby. In the reign of Elizabeth, it was not chivalry but the decay and abolition of chivalry and the chivalrous spirit which occasionally led to deeds which a knight-errant would have despised. As Sir Walter Scott says :—[1] "the habit of constant and honourable opposition, unembittered by rancour or personal hatred, gave the fairest opportunity for the exercise of the virtues required from him whom Chaucer terms a very perfect gentleman." Again he says :—" We have seen that the abstract principles

[1] *Essay on Chivalry.*

of chivalry were, in the highest degree, virtuous and noble, nay, that they failed by carrying to an absurd, exaggerated, and impracticable point, the honourable duties which they inculcated." Chivalry, therefore, acted as a wholesome check upon the barbarity, the licentiousness, and the semi-civilisation of the middle ages, and when it was abolished, the knights and nobles, in spite of all the glamour of refinement and education in the reigns of Henry VIII., Edward VI., Mary, and Elizabeth, still retained enough of the savage brutality of their forefathers to be occasionally very dangerous, when the discipline of chivalry had been withdrawn. " It is needless," says Sir Walter Scott, " by multiplying examples, to illustrate the bloodthirsty and treacherous maxims and practices, which, during the sixteenth century, succeeded to the punctilious generosity exacted by the rules of chivalry. It is enough to call to the reader's re-collection the bloody secret of the massacre of St Bartholomew, which was kept by such a number of the Catholic noblemen for two years,[1] at the expense of false treaties, promises, and perjuries, and the execution which followed on naked, unarmed, and unsuspecting men, in which so many gallants lent their willing swords." Now I am not going to enter here upon the question of Sir Walter Scott's historical accuracy, or its contrary, on this horrible massacre ;

---

[1] Where Sir Walter obtained his authority for this statement I do not know.

but might he not have extended his period " of treacherous maxims and practices," which "succeeded to the punctilious generosity exacted by the rules of chivalry," a few years later, and included, with the Massacre of St Bartholomew, the Gunpowder Plot? Catesby was quite a man of the type contemplated by Sir Walter Scott, gallant, charming, zealous, brave to a degree, and even pious, yet with something of the wild, lawless, and bloodthirsty spirit of the but partially-tamed savage, which every now and then asserted itself, until an even later period, unless it was kept under control by some such laws as those of chivalry. It was not, therefore, chivalry, but the *want* of chivalry, which led to the spirit, habits, and actions of Catesby and the other conspirators in the Gunpowder Plot.

I hope this digression—a digression from a digression—may be pardoned. It is high time that I returned to Robert Catesby in his relations to Sir Everard Digby.

· It was likely enough that Sir Everard Digby should become intimate with a zealous Catholic landowner in the neighbouring counties of Northamptonshire, and Warwickshire, especially as Catesby's mother's house, at Ashby St Legers, was little more than twenty miles from Gothurst; but probably the reason of his seeing so much of him was that Catesby's first cousin, Tyringham of Tyringham, lived only three-quarters of a mile from Gothurst, the two estates adjoining each other, either house lying within a short distance of the high road, on opposite sides of it.

Once on intimate terms, Sir Everard and Catesby were constantly together. In speaking of his master, Sir Everard's page, William Ellis, said in his examination [1] :—" both at London and in the countrie Mr Robert Catesby hath kept him companie."

In this not altogether desirable " companie," Sir Everard Digby spent much time " in cogitation deep " upon the treatment of his fellow-religionists and countrymen. Both men were exasperated by the persecution which was going on around them, by the fickleness of their king, and by the dangers to which they, their wives, their families—for Sir Everard, as well as Catesby, had a child now—and their estates were exposed. Perhaps most irritating of all, to country-gentlemen of high position, was the then prevalent custom of sub-letting, or farming, the fines and penalties levyable upon Catholics to men who squeezed every farthing out of them that was possible. To be persecuted and fined by an authorized public official was bad enough ; but to be pestered and tormented by a pettifogging private person who had purchased the right of doing so, as a speculation, must have been almost unendurable. The subject, however, which Digby and Catesby discussed most would probably be the severe anti-Catholic legislation which

[1] S. P. Gunpowder Plot Book, Part I. No. 108.

was apprehended from the new parliament. In this, said Catesby, the great danger lay. His surmises as to the form it might take would give him and his friend, Sir Everard, ample scope for contemplation, speculation, and conversation. The words of Scripture, " Sufficient to the day is the evil thereof," do not appear to have occurred to their memories.

In periods of trouble and danger, as indeed in all others, men of different dispositions and temperaments take different views and different lines of conduct ; there are optimists and pessimists, men who counsel endurance, men who advocate active resistance, men who advise waiting a little to see what may turn up, and men who urge that not a moment is to be lost. And so it was among the persecuted Catholics during the early years of the reign of James I. At the very time that men like Digby and Catesby were in the deepest depression of hopeless anxiety, the Spanish Ambassador was congratulating himself because he fancied he saw symptoms of the king's inclination to become [1] a convert to the Catholic Church. On the other hand, among those who took the most gloomy view of the prospect, there were very distinct phases of thought and action. "England will witness with us," says Father Gerard,[2] " that the greatest part by much did follow the

---

[1] *Roman Transcripts,* Sep. 24th, 1604, P.R.O., *Father H. Garnet an the Gunpowder Plot,* p. 4.

[2] *Narrative of the Gunpowder Plot,* p. 49.

example and exhortation of the Religious and Priests that were their guides, moving them and leading them by their own practice to make their refuge unto God in so great extremities. . . . This we found to be believed practically by most, and followed as faithfully, preparing themselves by more often frequentation of the Sacraments, by more fervent prayer, and by perfect resignation of their will to God, against the cloud that was like to cover them, and the shower that might be expected would pour down upon them after the Parliament, unto which all the chief Puritans of the land were called, and only they or their friends selected out of every shire to be the framers of the laws, which thereby we might easily know were chiefly intended and prepared against us."

But he says all were not quite so perfect, and of these imperfect there were two leading divisions. The first [1] " fainted in courage, and, as St Cyprian noteth of his times, did offer themselves unto the persecutors before they felt the chief force of the blow that was to be expected." Sir Everard Digby was not one of these. The second division were, as Father Gerard might most veraciously say, " much different from these, and ran headlong into a contrary error. For being resolved never to yield or forsake their faith, they had not patience and longanimity to expect the Providence of God, etc." It is to be feared that he may have noticed this want of patience and longa-

[1] *Narrative of the Gunpowder Plot*, p. 50.

nimity in Sir Everard Digby and his companions. "They would not endure to see their brethren so trodden upon by every Puritan," he goes on to say of this class, "so made a prey to every needy follower of the Court, or servant to a Councillor, so presented and pursued by every churchwarden and minister, so hauled to every sessions when the Justices list to meet, so wronged on every side by the process of excommunication or outlawry, and forced to seek for their own by law, and then also to be denied by law, because they were Papists; finally both themselves and all others to be denounced traitors and designed to the slaughter. These things they would not endure now to begin afresh after so long endurance, and therefore began amongst themselves to consult what remedy they might apply to all these evils," &c., " so that it seems they did not so much respect what the remedy were, or how it might be procured, as that it might be sure and speedy—to wit, to take effect before the end of the Parliament from whence they seemed to expect their greatest harm."

Those who followed the latter course may have included some who were in other respects good Christians; whether they showed the spirit of Martyrs and Confessors is another question.

Few things discouraged the English Catholics more than the goodwill and peaceful disposition shown to the new king by foreign Catholic kings and princes, notwithstanding that one final effort was made on their behalf by Spain, just as the treaty was being concluded with England for peace and the renewal of commercial intercourse. Velasco, the constable of Castile, who negotiated that treaty on behalf of Spain, was visited by Winter, at Catesby's suggestion, and urged to assist the English Catholics. Although he promised to speak on their behalf, he made it clear that his country would make no sacrifice to obtain toleration for them.[1] So far as he had promised, he kept his word. He told James that whatever indulgence he might show to them would be regarded by Philip as a personal act of friendship towards himself, and that they were prepared to make a voluntary offering annually in the place of the fines at that time imposed upon them by law; and he laid before him statistics of the distress to which very many respectable English families had been reduced by clinging to the faith of their forefathers.

James's reply was very decided. On any diplomatic question relating to the interests of England and Spain he would be ready and glad to confer with the Spanish representative, but the government of his own subjects was a domestic matter upon which he could not consent to enter with a foreigner. Besides this, he informed Velasco that, even were he himself inclined to better the condition of the Catholics, his doing so would offend his

[1] Lingard, Vol. vii. chap. i.

Protestant subjects to such an extent as to endanger his throne.

It would almost seem as if Velasco's endeavours on behalf of the Catholics had a contrary effect to that which had been intended; for, instead of granting them the smallest relief, James issued a proclamation, ordering the judges and magistrates to enforce the penal laws, and to adopt measures calculated to insure the detection of Catholic recusants. Before the judges started on their circuits, he called them together and charged them " to be diligent and severe against recusants."[1]   Accordingly, in the year 1604, about 1000 recusants were indicted in Yorkshire, 600 in Lancashire, and in the counties of Oxford, Berks, Gloucester, Monmouth, Hereford, Salop, Stafford, and in Wigorn, 1865.[2]   Of Buckinghamshire, Sir Everard Digby's county, I can find no return.   In all, the number of Catholic recusants convicted in the years 1604-5 amounted to 5500.   In July, a priest named Sugar was executed at Warwick, simply and only because he was a priest, and a layman, named Grissold, for " accompanying and assisting " him.[3]   In the Star Chamber, a man named Pound accused Sergeant Phillips of injustice in condemning a neighbour of his to death, for no other crime except that he had

---

[1] Tierney's Notes to Dodd, Vol. iv. p. 42.

[2] Dodd and Tierney, Vol. iv., Appendix xiv., pp. xciv., xcv.

[3] *Ib.*, Vol. iv. pp. 40, 41.

entertained a Jesuit. Not only did the lords of the Star Chamber confirm and approve of this sentence of Sergeant Phillips, but they condemned Pound himself to lose one ear in London and one " in the country where he dwelleth," and to be fined £1000, unless he would impeach those who advised him to make the suit. Fortunately this tremendous sentence was commuted, at the intercession of the French and Venetian Ambassadors, to standing for a whole day in the pillory.[1]

Bancroft had just ascended the archiepiscopal throne of Canterbury, full of zeal against the Papists. He urged his suffragan bishops to select the more wealthy and earnest among the Catholics, and, after first trying "sweet" and "kind means," to excommunicate them if they should refuse to conform. Forty days after their excommunication, the Bishops were to certify their names in Chancery, and then to sue out a writ *de excommunicato capiendo*, an instrument which subjected the delinquents to outlawry, forfeiture, and imprisonment, and deprived them of the right of recovering debts, of suing for damages, of effecting legal sales or purchases, and of conveying their properties either by will or otherwise.[2] Goodman, Bishop of Gloucester, writes[3] :—" The Spiritual Court did not cease to molest them, to

[1] Lingard, Vol. vii. chap. i.
[2] Tierney's Notes to Dodd, Vol. iv. pp. 41, 42.
[3] *Court of King James I.*, Vol. i. p. 101.

excommunicate them, then to imprison them; and thereby they were utterly unable to sue for their own." Nor were the rumours of an approaching increase of severities, to be enacted in the, ensuing parliament, mere exaggerated fancies. The denunciations of the Chancellor in the Star Chamber, and of Archbishop Bancroft at St Paul's Cross, confirmed the reports that sterner legislation against recusants was impending in the coming session. On the other hand, it is just possible that these official threats may have been uttered only to terrify the Catholics into submission, and with no very serious expectation of their fulfilment.

During those distressing times, Catesby's friends, among whom not the least was Sir Everard Digby, observed a change in his manner. He looked anxious and careworn; he was moody and abstracted at one moment, unusually loquacious and excitable at another. His mysterious absences from home were another source of uneasiness to those most intimate with him; so, too, were his large purchases of horses, arms, and gunpowder, which also attracted the attention of people who were not his friends; but he took great trouble to inform everybody that he was about to raise 300 horse, to join the English regiment which the Spanish Ambassador had prevailed upon King James to allow to be levied in England for the assistance of the Archduke in Flanders.[1]

[1] Jardine's *Gunpowder Plot*, pp. 60-1.

Nevertheless, his friends were not satisfied. If he were really going to join the army in the Low Countries, why these long delays?

Great as was their intimacy, Catesby was in the condition just described for many months without confiding the real reason of his activity to Sir Everard Digby; although it is probable that he warned him to be prepared for any emergency which might arise for the use of men, arms, and horses. Both Digby and Catesby were heartily tired of a state of passive endurance; the tyranny which was crushing the Catholics was daily increasing, and Sir Everard might very naturally suppose that while Catesby had no definite plan for resisting it, he wished to be ready in case foreign powers might come to their assistance, or the whole body of English Catholics, goaded to desperation, might rise in rebellion against their oppressors. Freely as he might appear to talk to Digby, and satisfied as the latter may have felt that he had the confidence of his friend, Catesby in reality feared to intrust a great secret, which was absorbing his attention, to the brave but straightforward master of Gothurst.

Another of Catesby's friends was less easy about him than Sir Everard Digby. Father Garnet, the Provincial of the Jesuits, suspected that some mischief was brewing, and seized an opportunity, when sitting at Catesby's own table, of inculcating the duty of patient submission to persecution. His host, who was his personal friend as well as a great respecter of his wisdom as a priest, showed considerable irritation. Instead of treating the Provincial of the Jesuits with his usual reverence and courtesy, he flushed up and angrily exclaimed[1]:—"It is to you, and such as you, that we owe our present calamities. This doctrine of non-resistance makes us slaves. No authority of priest or pontiff can deprive man of his right to repel injustice."

Another friend and frequent guest of young Sir Everard's, after he became a Catholic, should be noticed. A younger son of a Worcestershire family, Thomas Winter had attractions for Digby, in his profound zeal for the Catholic Church, his scholarship, his knowledge of foreign languages, his powers of conversation, and his military experiences, as he had served in Flanders, France, and, says Father Gerard, "I think, against the Turk." Unlike Catesby, he was "of mean stature, but strong and comely," and of "fine carriage." He was very popular in society, and "an inseparable friend to Mr Robert Catesby." In age he was about ten years older than Sir Everard. Whatever his zeal may have been for the Catholic Church, he did not always live in the odour of sanctity, and on one occasion he incurred the grave displeasure of Father Garnet by conveying a challenge to a duel from John Wright, one of the earliest conspirators in the Gunpowder Plot, to an

[1] Lingard, Vol. vii. chap. i.

adversary who had offended him. The combatants met, and Winter, as Wright's second, measured the swords of both duellists to ascertain whether they were of equal length; but the actual encounter was somehow prevented at the last moment.[1] Father Garnet says that he had a "hard conceit of him."

In dealing with the subject of Digby's friends, certainly his page, William Ellis, ought not to be forgotten. I have been unable to discover any details of his birth, except that he was heir to £80 a year—a much larger income, of course, in those days than in these—"if his father did him right." He entered Sir Everard's service at the age of seventeen, about May 1604.[2] How faithful he was to his master will appear by-and-bye.

Among Sir Everard's younger friends was Lord Vaux of Harrowden, a cousin of Catesby's. One reason of the intimacy is thus described by Father Gerard.[3] "Sir Everard had many serious occasions to come to my Lord Vaux's; and then in particular, as I have learned since, being come from his [Digby's] ancient house and chief living, which lay in Rutlandshire, from whence he could not go unto the house where his wife and family lay [Gothurst], but he must pass the door of Lord Vaux, his house, which also made him there an ordinary guest." To harbour

---

[1] S. P. Dom. James I., Vol. xix. n. 41. Garnet's statement.
[2] S. P. Dom. James I., G. P. Book, Part I., n. 108.
[3] *Narrative of the G. P.*, p. 138.

priests, and to defend the Catholic cause was no new
thing in the family of Vaux, for, some twenty or
thirty years earlier, Lord Vaux's grandfather had
been imprisoned and fined for sheltering Father
Campian in his house.[1] His grandmother had been
a daughter of John Tresham of Rushton, and of
his cousin, Francis Tresham, we shall hear something presently. His mother and his aunts, Anne
and Elizabeth, were most pious Catholics, but the
religious atmosphere in which he was brought up
does not seem to have led him to perfection; for,
although as a young man he suffered imprisonment
for his faith,[2] he afterwards had two sons, who bore
the name of Vaux, by Lady Banbury during her
husband's lifetime;[3] and, although he married her
after Lord Banbury's death, she never had another
child. Worse still, he left Harrowden and the other
family estates to his illegitimate children, instead of
to his brother, who succeeded him in the title, although his wife, on her side, claimed for her son that,
as he was born during her first husband's lifetime,
he had a legal right to the title of Banbury. Accordingly, this son changed his surname to Knollys,
and once actually sat, as Lord Banbury, in the House
of Lords. As is well known, his descendants went
on claiming and disputing the title until the year
1813, when their right to it was finally disallowed.

[1] *Records S.J.*, Series i. p. 329.   [2] *Life of Father Gerard*, p. clxxxv.
[3] *Burke's Peerage*, 1872.

But what specially concerns my story is that Sir Everard Digby was endeavouring to bring about a marriage for this (then) very young Lord Vaux, with the "Lord Chamberlain his daughter,"[1] as Father Gerard writes; and, in a footnote, is added "Earl of Suffolk.   Erased in Orig."   If this footnote is right, Sir Everard was probably trying to make a match for the youth with the very girl whom he eventually married, as Lady Banbury had been Elizabeth Howard, the eldest daughter of Lord Suffolk.   Suffolk was Lord Chamberlain,[2] and curiously enough (when we consider that he seems to have had negotiations with Sir Everard Digby with respect to a match between his daughter and Lord Vaux), in his capacity of Lord Chamberlain, he suspected and led to the discovery of the gunpowder laid in the cellar beneath the Houses of Parliament.[3]

Sir Everard visited a good deal at the house of Lord Vaux's mother, Mrs Elizabeth Vaux.   This was a house in Buckinghamshire at Stoke Poges, that had been built by Sir Christopher Hatton,[4] the Lord Chancellor, who had died childless.   It was let for a term of years to Mrs Vaux, and she not only estab-

---

[1] *Narrative of the G. P.*, p. 137.

[2] Gardiner.   *History of England*, Vol. x. p. 364.

[3] Gardiner's *History of England*, Vol. i. p. 249.

[4] It was to this Sir Christopher Hatton, that Sir Everard's father had dedicated his book *A Dissuasive from taking away the Livings of the Church*.

lished Father Gerard in it as her chaplain, but had
hiding-places and other arrangements made, so that
he could receive priests and Catholic laymen, as he
might think well, for the good of the cause of religion.
Here Sir Everard was probably thrown a good deal
with Catesby and Tresham, as they were both related
to his young host. Lord Vaux's two aunts, Miss
Anne Vaux and Eleanor, the wife of Edward Brooksby,
lived with him and his mother, and Miss Anne was
one of those who had serious misgivings as to the
mysterious conduct of her cousin, Robert Catesby.[1]
" Seeing at Winter's and Grant's "—Grant was a
popular Warwickshire squire, a Catholic, and celebrated
for his undaunted courage—" their fine horses in the
stable, she told Mr Garnet that she feared these wild
heads had something in hand, and prayed him to talk
to Mr Catesby and to hinder anything that possibly
he might, for if they should attempt any foolish
thing, it would redound to his discredit. Whereupon
he said he would talk to Mr Catesby."

Another account of what was probably the same
interview was given by Father Garnet himself, in his
examination of March 12th, 1605.

[2] " He sayth that Mrs Vaux came to him, eyther to
Harrowden or to Sir Everard Digby's at Gothurst,
and tould this exam[t.] that she feared that some

---

[1] *Father H. Garnet and the Gunpowder Plot*, Pollen, p. 20. P.R.O.,
March 11.

[2] S. P. Dom. James I., Vol. xix. n 40. See *Records S.J.*, Vol. iv. p. 157.

trouble or disorder was towards [them], that some of the gentlewomen had demanded of her where they should bestow themselves until the burst[1] was past in the beginning of the Parliament. And this exam[n] asking her who tould her so, she said that she durst not tell who tould her so: she was [choked] with sorrow."

An attempt was made, later, to represent the name of Vaux to be the same as that of Fawkes :—[2] "Mrs Anne Vaux, or Fawkes, probably a relative of the conspirator ;" for which there seems to be no foundation, and certainly there is none for the base imputation, in the same paragraph, of immorality between Anne Vaux and Father Garnet. Even the Protestant historian, Jardine, repudiates this calumny at considerable length.[3]

[1] This could not mean the projected "burst" of gunpowder, of which she could have known nothing, but an attempt of some sort, about that time, to obtain relief for the Catholics by force of arms, which she appears to have expected, or rather, to have feared.

[2] *Somers Tracts*, Vol. ii. p. 108, footnote.

[3] *Gunpowder Plot*, pp. 176-8.

CHAPTER VI.

In the summer of the year 1605, Sir Everard Digby spent a week in London, and stayed at the lodgings in the Savoy of his friend Roger Manners,[1] the eldest brother of Sir Oliver Manners, whose conversion to the Catholic faith has been already noticed. This Roger Manners married the daughter and heir of the famous Sir Philip Sydney, and eventually succeeded his father, as fifth Earl of Rutland. Although Sir Everard stayed with Roger Manners, he "commonlie dieted at the Mearmaid in Bred Streete."[2] He spent much of his time with the excellent Sir Oliver Manners, which was all very well; but, unfortunately, Robert Catesby also "kept him companie" a great deal; without, however, letting him know what was chiefly occupying him in London just at that time. Thomas Winter also came to see Sir Everard whilst he was in London, and his friendship with men who were conspiring to an evil end was endangering Digby without his knowing it. At that time he had no idea that any plot was in existence, although he was doubtless

---

[1] S. P. Gunpowder Plot Book, Part I, No. 108. [2] *Ib.*

aware that many Catholics were considering what steps could be taken to relieve their condition ; and the fact of his staying with Roger Manners proves that he had not come to London with any design of conferring with restless Catholics in a secret or underhand fashion.

After his visit to London, Sir Everard seems to have returned to Gothurst and to have continued his usual innocent country life, with its duties and pleasures. A letter among the Hatfield MS., written to him on the eleventh of June—his eldest boy's birthday by the way [1]— treats of otter-hunting, and it is likely enough that Sir Everard practised this sport in the Ouse as well as in the other rivers and brooks of Buckinghamshire.

About the end of August, or perhaps early in September, 1605, a large party met at Gothurst, as guests of Sir Everard and Lady Digby, but with an ulterior purpose. To pray for the much-oppressed cause of the Catholic religion in England, for their suffering fellow-religionists, and for themselves, they had agreed to make a pilgrimage together to the famous shrine of St Winefride at Holywell, in Flintshire,[2] which would entail a journey of a hundred and

---

[1] So it is usually believed, and so wrote Ben Jonson—"Upon his birthday, the eleventh of June"; —so, too, Richard Farrar—"Born on the day he died, the eleventh of June." But some authorities give a different date, and the question has been fiercely disputed.

[2] *Father H. Garnet and the Gunpowder Plot*, by J. H. Pollen, S. J., p. 15.

fifty miles.[1] Sir Everard does not appear to have accompanied it ; but, among those assembled at Gothurst who were to go on the pilgrimage were his young wife, Miss Anne Vaux, Brooksby and his wife, Thomas Digby, Sir Everard's brother, who had evidently followed his example and become a Catholic, Sir Francis Lacon and his daughter, Father Garnet, the Provincial of the Jesuits, a lay-brother named Nicholas Owen, who usually accompanied him, and Father Strange, Sir Everard's chaplain, making, with their servants and others, a party of pilgrims numbering little short of thirty. Later on, Father Darcy and Father Fisher also joined them. [2]

If, as it seems, Sir Everard did not go with the pilgrimage, the reason may have been that he was engaged in endeavouring to negotiate the proposed marriage between young Lord Vaux and a daughter of the Earl of Suffolk, although it seemed early to do so, as the boy was then only about fourteen.

" Riding westward,[3] the party of pilgrims would stop for the night at some Catholic friend's house, and in the morning the two priests would say Mass.

---

[1] A party, including ladies, would not be likely to travel faster than thirty miles a day over the bad roads, therefore it would take more than four times as long to go, then, from Gothurst to Holywell, as it would now take to go from Gothurst to the famous shrine at Lourdes, in the Pyrenees.

[2] Cal. Sta. Pa. Dom., 1603-10, p. 270.

[3] *Father Garnet and the Gunpowder Plot*, Pollen, p. 18.

Even at Shrewsbury, when they had to put up at an inn, and at 'a castle in a holt at Denbighshire,' the daily Masses were said without interruption, and even the servants were present. At St Winefride's Well, too, though the inn must have been small for so large a number, the Holy Sacrifice was again offered, and then the ladies went barefoot to the Well.[1] At Holywell they stopped but one night. Returning next day, they slept at a farmhouse seven miles from Shrewsbury, and after that they were again in the circle of their friends."[2]

About the end of September (1605) Sir Everard Digby went to stay at Harrowden with young Lord Vaux. While he was there, his host's mother, her sister-in-law, Anne Vaux, and Father Garnet came thither on their return from the pilgrimage. His friend Catesby also arrived from a visit to Lord Mordaunt[3] at Turville. Anne Vaux, who, as I have said, had been uneasy about Catesby's proceedings, was in a hurry for his departure to Flanders, where he was to command an English regiment. Father Garnet wrote a letter of introduction for him to a Jesuit priest in that country, and Catesby himself showed this letter to his nervous cousin,

[1] Jardine, in his *Narrative of the Gunpowder Plot* (p. 180), says that the ladies walked barefoot from Holt, that is to say, a distance of about twenty miles.

[2] *Father Garnet and the Gunpowder Plot*, pp. 18, 19.

[3] Henry, fourth Baron Mordaunt, was suspected of being concerned in the Gunpowder Plot. He was committed to the Tower, and fined by the Star Chamber. See Burke's *Dormant and Extinct Peerages*, p. 380.

assuring her that he was so anxious to start that he would spend £500 in obtaining a license[1] to go abroad with his men and horses, about which, he pretended, there was some difficulty.

After a few days' visit at Harrowden, the family seat of the Vaux's, which was then in a rather dilapidated condition,[2] Sir Everard Digby invited Catesby, Mrs Vaux, and Father Garnet to stay with him at Gothurst; and he started with Catesby to ride home, leaving his other guests to follow them. The distance between Harrowden and Gothurst was something like fifteen miles, and Digby and his friend became very confidential in the course of it.

Perhaps there are few occasions on which it is easier to converse freely than a long ride with a single companion; in most cases, no one can possibly be within earshot, therefore the voice need not be unnaturally lowered; the speakers are not confronting each other, and this prevents any nervous dread lest the mention of subjects on which either feels strongly should raise a tell-tale blush or a quiver of a lip or eyelid; and, if the topic should become embarrassing, the surroundings of those on horseback enable them to change it more easily, and with less apparent effort or intention, than under almost any other conditions. Lastly, the fresh country air, as

---

[1] *Father Garnet and the G. P.*, Pollen, p. 21.
[2] *Life of Father Gerard*, p. cxxxv.

it is inhaled in the easy exercise of riding, clears the brain and invigorates the energies, and when is it fresher or pleasanter than on a fine day at the end of September, such as we can imagine Sir Everard Digby and Robert Catesby to have enjoyed on their ride from Harrowden to Gothurst? Both of them, as we read, were fine men, fine horsemen on fine horses, and old friends; and they must have made a handsome and well-assorted pair, as they went their way along the roads, through the woods, and over the commons of Northamptonshire and Buckinghamshire.

Early in their ride, when they were well clear of the outskirts of the little market town of Wellingborough,[1] beside the famous Red Well of which, some twenty years later, Charles I. and his Queen were to dwell in tents, in order to drink its medicinal waters, Catesby told his companion that he had a communication of the greatest importance to make to him; that he was only at liberty to convey it upon an oath of secresy; and that from all others intrusted with the subject of this communication, the oath had not been accepted unless sealed and confirmed by Holy Communion—which alone would demonstrate its sacred and religious nature—but that, in the case of so honourable a man as Digby, a simple oath would suffice. This was paying a very flattering compliment, and, when Catesby drew a small poignard,

[1] S. P. Dom. James I., G. P. Bk., Part 2, No. 135.

handed it to him, and asked him to swear secresy upon it,[1] Sir Everard, thinking that the matter would concern some " stirres in Wales " on behalf of the persecuted Catholics, of which Catesby had talked at Gothurst during the summer, took the oath without much hesitation, and returned the little weapon.

Then Catesby began a long, earnest, and serious discourse. There can be little doubt that he would first dwell upon the desperate condition of their co-religionists in Great Britain, the hopelessness of redress or any improvement in their state, and the likelihood of their persecution becoming still more intolerable under the incoming parliament. At last, he told his patient and sympathetic listener that the time had come for action. They could expect no help from the king, no help from the parliament, no help from foreign Catholic princes or powers, no help from a general, an ordinary, and a legitimate rising among their Catholic fellow-countrymen ; there was nothing for it, therefore, but to help themselves. It was plain enough where, and from whom, their greatest danger lay. The few must be sacrificed to save the many. He had been reading his Bible[2]— the very Protestants who so cruelly oppressed them would commend that—and there he found instances in which the deliberate assassination of tyrants appeared to be not only tolerated but commended.

---

[1] S. P. Dom. James I., G. P. Bk., Part 2, No. 135.
[2] Lingard, Vol. vii. chap. i.

I cannot guarantee that Catesby said exactly all these things to Digby; I merely enumerate the arguments which he is stated, on good authority, to have used in persuading those who joined in his plot; and it is well known that he found no other of his adherents so difficult to convince as Sir Everard; therefore it is most unlikely that he omitted one of his pleas in this case.

Between the Catholics and the Protestants, Catesby considered that there was a regular warfare; no war could be conducted without bloodshed, and in war all was fair. It might even be maintained that the righteous Catholics were in the position of executioners, who should carry out the extreme sentence of death upon the iniquitous and murderous villains who, under the names of princes and rulers, were persecuting and slaying God's innocent people. Who were these princes and rulers? King James and his parliament. They richly deserved to die the death, and unless they were destroyed they would work even greater evils. Let the sword of justice fall upon them.

Were the Catholics to rise and invade the houses of parliament with drawn sabres? No. Such a thing would be impossible. Resort must be had to stratagem, a method to which holy men had often resorted in ancient times, as might be read in the sacred pages of the Old Testament. But, unlike the warriors of Israel, the modern Christian soldier fought less with the sword than with that much more powerful medium known as gunpowder. It had already been the principal agent of destruction in many great battles; let it be used in the strife between the oppressed English Catholics and the king with his parliament.

Before entering into details of the proposed attack, it would be well to consider that the end aimed at was not any private revenge or personal emolument.[1] The sole object was to suppress a most unjust and barbarous persecution by the only expedient which offered the least prospect of success. There could be no doubt as to its being lawful, since God had given to every man the right of repelling force by force. If Digby should consider the scheme cruel, let him contrast it with the cruelties exercised during so many years against the English Catholics; let him calculate the number of innocent martyrs who had been butchered by the public executioner, or had died from ill-treatment or torture in prisons; let him estimate the thousands who had been reduced by the penal laws against recusants, from wealth or competence, to poverty or beggary; and then let him judge whether the sudden destruction of the rulers who had been guilty of such fearful persecutions, and avowedly intended persecutions yet more atrocious, could be condemned on the charge of cruelty. Nay, more; unless a decisive blow were

[1] Lingard, Vol. vii. chap. i.

delivered very shortly, something like a massacre of Catholics might be expected, and,[1] " Mr Catesby tould him that the papistes throate should have been cutte."

Catesby would then tell his friend and companion, as they rode through the peaceful Midland scenery, with its horse-chestnuts and its beeches in their rich autumn colouring, on that September afternoon, how he must be a man, and nerve himself to hear the means which it was proposed to employ for carrying out the judgment of God upon their wicked oppressors.[2] Every Catholic peer was to be warned, or enticed from the House of Lords on a certain day, and then, by the sudden explosion of a large quantity of gunpowder, previously placed beneath the Houses of Parliament, the king and his councillors, his Lords and his Commons, were to be prevented from doing any further mischief in this world. As soon as the execution was over, the Catholics would[3] "seize upon the person of the young prince, if he were not in the Parliament House, which they much desired. But if he were," in which case, of course, he would be dead, "then upon the young Duke Charles, who then should be the next heir, and him they would erect, and with him and by his authority, the Catholic religion. If that did also fail them, then had they a resolution to take the Lady Elizabeth, who was in the keeping of the Lord Harrington in Warwickshire ;

[1] S. P. Dom. James I., Vol. xviii. n. 24.
[2] S. P. Dom. James I., Vol. xvi., No. 94, 20 Nov. 1605, B, C, and D.
[3] *Narrative of the Gunpowder Plot*, p. 85.

and so by one means or other, they would be certain to settle in the crown one of the true heirs of the same." How loyal they were!

On first hearing of this inhuman, detestable, and diabolical scheme, Sir Everard was overcome with horror, as well he might be, and it was with the greatest difficulty that Catesby induced him to consider it any further.[1] If Sir Everard had been a man of firm will and determination of character, he would have obeyed his conscience and resolutely followed his own good instincts; but instead of doing so, he was weak enough to listen with attention and interest to the arguments of Catesby. To a man of a religious mind like Sir Everard Digby, those of a Scriptural character would be some of the most persuasive, and his companion would hardly fail to point out the wholesale massacres and cruelties apparently sanctioned in the Old Testament.

If he so pleased, he could quote plenty of biblical precedents for slaying and maiming, on a far larger scale than was proposed in the Gunpowder Plot, which would be a mere trifle in comparison with some of the following butcheries :—" They warred against the Midianites," " and they slew all the males. And they slew the kings of Midian."[2] "They slew of them in Bezek ten thousand men." " And they slew

---

[1] Lingard, Vol. vii. chap. i.

[2] Numbers xxxi. 7, 8. For the benefit of my Protestant readers, I quote my Scripture from the Anglican version, to show them that there is nothing "apocryphal" in it.

of Moab at that time ten thousand men, all lusty, and all men of valour ; and there escaped not a man." [1] " David slew of the Syrians two and twenty thousand." [2] " The other Jews," " slew of their foes seventy and five thousand." [3] " Pekah the son of Remaliah slew in Juda an hundred and twenty thousand in one day, which were all valiant men, because they had forsaken the Lord God of their fathers," [4] just as King James and the English Government had forsaken Him, in Catesby's and Sir Everard's opinions.

If it were objected that all these fell in battle, and that it was quite a different thing to murder people by stealth in cold blood, could not Catesby have replied that " Jael Heber's wife took a nail of the tent, and took an hammer in her hand, and went softly unto him [Sisera], and smote the nail into his temple, and fastened it into the ground : for he was fast asleep and weary. So he died." [5] Jael Heber's wife was acting as hostess to a friend who had come into her tent for shelter and protection, and had fallen asleep. Yet Deborah and Barak sang in honour of this performance :— [6] " Blessed above women shall Jael the wife of Heber the Kenite be, blessed shall she be above women in the tent. He asked water, and she gave him milk ; she brought

---

[1] Judges iii. 29.
[2] 2 Samuel viii. 5.
[3] Esther viii. 16.
[4] 2 Chron. xxviii. 6.
[5] Judges iv. 21.
[6] Judges v. 24 *seq.*

forth butter in a lordly dish. She put her hand
to the nail, and her right hand to the workman's
hammer; and with the hammer she smote Sisera,
she smote off his head, when she had pierced and
stricken through his temples. At her feet he bowed,
he fell, he lay down: at her feet he bowed, he fell:
where he bowed, there he fell down dead." "So let
all thine enemies perish, O Lord."[1] Might not, and
ought not, the English Catholics to sing much such
a song in honour of Catesby, Digby, and their fellow-
conspirators, when the king and the Parliament should
be blown up, and fall, and lie down, at their feet,
where they should fall down dead? Was there not
something biblical and appropriate, again, in destroying the enemies of the Lord with fire? " Behold,
they shall be as stubble; the fire shall burn them."[2]
"Thou shalt be fuel for the fire; thy blood shall be
in the midst of the land."[3] And had not the very
gentlest of men, even the God-man, said, " I am come
to send fire on the earth?" Surely, too, if Holy
Writ did not specially mention gunpowder, it constantly threatened one of its ingredients, namely
brimstone, to the wicked !

Under the old dispensation, it was considered a
religious duty to fall upon the enemies of the Lord
and slay them; under the new, it would be as
religious a duty to get under them and slay them.
This was merely a detail, a simple reversal of the

<hr>

[1] Judges v. 31.   [2] Isaiah xlvii. 14.   [3] Ezekiel xxi. 32.

process, conducing to exactly the same results, and quite as Scriptural in its character.

A massacre by means of an explosion of gunpowder was neither a novel nor an exclusively Catholic notion. Persons observed, "There be recounted in histories many attempts of the same kynds, and some also by Protestants in our days: as that of them who at Antwerp placed a whole barke of powder in the great street of that citty, where the prince of Parma with his nobility was to passe: and that of him in the Hague that would have blown up the whole councel of Holland upon private revenge." [1]

Within the last half century, had not great earls and statesmen, in Scotland, conspired together to blow up with gunpowder the Queen's own husband, as he lay ill in bed, in his house; had not four men been destroyed by this means,[2] and had not the principal conspirator "declared," with how much truth or falsehood it is not necessary to pause here to inquire,[3] " that the Queen "—the very pious martyr-queen, Mary, herself,—" was a consenting party to the deed," [4] and had not that very pious queen married that very conspirator after he had brought about the murder of her first husband ?

It would be scarcely too much to say that, early in

---

[1] *Lingard*, Vol. vii. chap. i., footnote.

[2] *Ib.*, Vol. vi. chap. ii.

[3] Recent historical research tends to absolve Mary Queen of Scots from all imputation of complicity in this horrible crime.

[4] Bellesheim's Hist. Cath. Ch. of Scot., trans. H. Blair, Vol. iii. p. 112.

the seventeenth century, the ethics of explosives were
not properly understood. Catesby might argue that
gunpowder was a destructive agent, the primary and
natural use of which was to kill directly, and that its
indirect use, by exploding it in a tube, thereby pro-
pelling a missile, was a secondary, less natural, and
possibly less legitimate use. And, if it were objected
that to employ it in either way would be right in
war, but wrong in peace, he could bring forward the
exceedingly dangerous theory (which has been made
use of by Irish-American dynamitards in the nineteenth century), that oppressed people, who do not
acknowledge the authority of those who rule over
them, may consider themselves at war with those
authorities, a theory which Catesby's Jesuit friends
would have negatived instantly, if he had asked
their opinion about it.

Any attempt to prove the iniquity of Catesby's
conspiracy is so unnecessary that I will not waste
time in offering one. I have only to endeavour to
imagine the condition of mind in which he and his
friends were able to look upon it with approval,
and the arguments they may have used in its
favour.

Next to passages and precedents from Scripture in
support of his diabolical scheme, Catesby would be
well aware that its approval by authorities of the
Church, and especially by Fathers of the Society of
Jesus, would have most influence with his friend Sir

Everard. To the surprise of the latter, he informed him that he had laid the matter before the Provincial of the Society, and had obtained his consent to the scheme.

He admitted that the Jesuits were not fully aware of all the particulars; it was not intended to put them to the dangers of responsibility for the deed itself, or anything connected with it; already their very priesthood was high treason, and the last thing that Catesby and his friends desired was to add to their perils; but their approval of the design in general was of such importance that neither Catesby himself, nor any of those admitted into the secret, would have acted without it, and this Catesby declared he had obtained.

Upon a zealous convert, like Sir Everard Digby, such an assurance would exercise a great influence. Nor was it only of sacerdotal approval that Catesby boasted; he was able to add that he had obtained the consent, as well as the assistance, of John Wright, a Catholic layman and a Yorkshire squire; of Sir Everard's own friend, Thomas Winter; of his eldest brother, Robert Winter,[1] "an earnest Catholic," at whose house the pilgrims to St Winefride's Well had stayed for a night on their way thither; of Ambrose Rookwood, a Catholic,[2] "ever very devout," who had actually been one of the pilgrims; of John Grant,[3] a

---

[1] *Narrative*, G. P., Gerard, p. 71. [2] Ib., p. 85.
[3] Jardine's *Gunpowder Plot*, p. 52.

zealous Roman Catholic," who, like his brother-in-law, Robert Winter, had entertained the St Winifride's pilgrims for a night in his walled and moated house, and of Thomas Percy, a relative of the Earl of Northumberland's, and a very recent and earnest convert to the Church.

CHAPTER VII.

Believing that his principal friends, and the priests
for whom he felt the greatest veneration, had either
joined in or expressed their approval of the scheme,
Sir Everard began to be half inclined to consent to it.
Was there to be a great enterprise, entailing personal
activity and danger for the good of the Catholic cause,
and was he to shrink from taking part in it? Was
he alone, among the most zealous Catholic laymen of
England, to show the white feather in a time of peril?
Could he call himself a man if he trembled at the
very thought of bloodshed? Yet, in truth, the idea
of the cold-blooded massacre which was proposed
appalled him; fair fighting he would rather rejoice
in, but wholesale assassination was to the last degree
repulsive to his nature. Hesitating and miserable, he
reached Gothurst with his guest without giving any
definite answer to the question whether he would join
in the conspiracy.

When they were in the house, Catesby showed him
a book justifying proceedings which he claimed to be
similar to the proposed plot. "I saw," he wrote after-

wards to his wife,[1] "I saw the principal point of the case, judged by a Latin book of M. D., my brother's father-in-law." What book it may have been we have no means of knowing; but we do know that the perils of comparing parallel cases are notorious: and, unfortunately, the production of this book had the effect of turning the scale, and inducing Digby to join in the infamous plot.

Necessary as it is for a biographer of Sir Everard Digby carefully to consider all the arguments that are likely to have influenced him in consenting to the Gunpowder Plot, it is all-important to keep before the mind the cause which, on his own admission,[2] was the first and most potent of his assent to the conspiracy. This was[3] "the friendship and love he bare to Catesby, which prevailed so much, and was so powerful with him, as that for his sake he was ever contented and ready to hazard himself and his estate."

Sir Everard was a man of what may be termed violent friendship. We have already seen his almost immoderate attachment to Father Gerard. It was an excellent thing that he should have such a man for a firm friend; but his feeling towards him was something much more than that. Father Gerard was "his brother." The Jesuits make a rule of avoiding what

<hr>

[1] "Letters of Sir Everard Digby" in *Gunpowder Treason*, p. 177.
[2] Speech at his trial.
[3] *Gunpowder Treason*, by Thomas, Bishop of Lincoln, p. 55.

they term "particular friendships," and the great aggression of affection would certainly not come from Father Gerard's side. And now we find him loving Catesby to such an extent as to be "ready to hazard himself and his estate" "for his sake."

There is such a thing as an undue admiration for "the man who thinks as I do." It proceeds from a combination of pride and weakness. The man in question is the embodiment of "my" principles, and therefore to be worshipped, and, holding "my" principles, his decisions, which are presumably formed upon those principles, must be right, and "my" adoption of them will save me the trouble of forming any for myself. Such is the line of argument which men of Sir Everard Digby's type mentally follow. When, again, some difficulty presents itself, concerning which they have never thought at all, they argue to themselves after this fashion. "My friend agrees with me about A, B, and C, topics on which we are both well informed ; therefore I may safely follow his advice about D, a subject of which I at present know nothing, but about which, when I have studied it, I may logically assume that I shall agree with him."

Few men act on principle at first hand. To a vast majority, it is too invisible, intangible, difficult to define, and difficult to realise, to serve as either a guide or a support. Yet some of those who are least able, coolly, logically, and consistently to understand and adhere to a principle in the abstract, are the most enthusiastic in advocating, the most vigorous in defending, and the most extravagant in extending to the most extreme limits, its reflection, or supposed reflection, in the person and behaviour of a friend ; and they are apt, in their devotion to the friend, to forget the principle. It was thus in the case of Sir Everard Digby and Robert Catesby.   In his friendship with Catesby, Sir Everard was eager to be one of the most pronounced champions of the Catholic religion, yet when Catesby acted in direct opposition to the fundamental principles of that religion, Sir Everard clung to the visible friend to the neglect of the invisible principle, which, theoretically, he held to be more precious than life itself.

When one idea takes too forcible possession of the mind, although the objections to it may collectively be overpowering, if taken one by one, it is easy to dispose of them, and then to blind the eyes, to stifle the conscience, and to imagine a glamour of righteousness, unselfishness, and heroism, in iniquity, self-pleasing, and even cruelty.   Digby experienced this fatal facility.   He did not at once consent to Catesby's request without the least pretence of considering its merits ; but he combatted the objections to it one by one, and thus easily defeated them.   He endeavoured to regard the matter from Catesby's point of view, and he found the process simple, if not agreeable.

And here let me say that I wish I could honestly

represent Sir Everard as having consented hurriedly
to the plot in a hot-headed love of adventure. The
evidence, unfortunately, all points the other way.
He was persuaded with great difficulty by Catesby.
He disliked the look of the whole thing, and he finally
consented to it after cool and deliberate reflection. I
admit that he was impulsive ; I do not deny that, in
this instance, he may have acted on sudden impulse
at particular stages of his lengthened agony of doubt
and indecision, or that, after being too slow in
obeying his first impulse to refuse to hear another
word about the atrocious project, he may have
yielded too hurriedly to his later impulse to throw
in his lot with the friend whom he trusted ; but I
cannot excuse him on the ground that his adhesion to
the conspiracy was the result of a momentary con-
vulsion of enthusiastic folly.

He objected ; he feared the destruction of Catholic
peers ; he talked over the pretended opinions of the
Jesuit Fathers ; he read a so-called authority in a
book shown to him by Catesby ; he calculated the
chances of success and failure ; he thought over the
question of men, money, arms, and horses ; and then,
with false conclusions, on false premises, in a sort of
spasm of wrongheadedness, he, who had been depend-
ing excessively on clerical direction—even Jesuits
admit that there is such a thing as being over-directed
—suddenly acted, upon a question involving an
enormous issue, without any advice whatever except

that of the man who was tempting him to what, he must have seen, had, *prima facie*, the colour of a most odious crime. I am not forgetting that Catesby vaunted Jesuit approval; but what good Catholic would take clerical advice upon an intricate point at second hand from another layman? Or, to put it in another form, what prudent man would commit himself to a lawsuit simply because a friend told him that his lawyer recommended him to sue an adversary under very similar circumstances? Digby had good reason for knowing that the Jesuit Father, whose opinion he most valued—Father Gerard—would strongly object to what was proposed; but he fancied that he himself knew better what was for the good of the Church; so, after meekly wavering in a state of great uncertainty, like the weak man that he was, he suddenly yielded and agreed to partake in what he persuaded himself to be a pious act on behalf of his religion, but was in reality a piece of unprecedented pious folly; and few things are more certain than that, be his personal virtues ever so exalted, and his intentions ever so pure, the pious fool can do, and often does, more to injure the cause of religion than even the scientific fool to injure that of science, which is saying much.

It is now my duty to explain how grossly Sir Everard was deceived by Catesby, when he was assured that any Jesuit Fathers had approved of the conspiracy " in general, though they knew not the particulars." What I am about to write may appear a long digression ; but it should be remembered that it was chiefly upon Catesby's assurance of the approval of the Fathers of the Society of Jesus that Sir Everard consented to join in the conspiracy; therefore the amount of consent actually obtained from them, if any, is of the utmost importance to my story.

Here is Father Gerard's account of the so-called approval of the plot, which Catesby had extracted from Father Garnet, and on the strength of which he persuaded Sir Everard Digby and others to join in it.[1] "Having a great opinion both of the learning and virtue of the Fathers of the Society, Mr Catesby desired to get, by cunning means, the judgment of their Superior, so as he should never perceive to what end the question were asked." This makes Father Gerard's opinion of Catesby's shameful dishonesty in the affair unmistakably clear. "Therefore," he continues, "coming to Father Garnet, after much ordinary talk, and some time passed over after his arrival" (at a house in Essex, in June 1605, that is to say, about three months before he revealed the plot to Sir Everard) "one time he took occasion (upon some speech proposed about the wars in the Low Countries or such like)"—observe the fraud of this ! Catesby was to have command of a regiment in the "Low Countries," so he clearly intended to lead Father

---

1 *Narrative of the Gunpowder Plot*, p. 65 *seq.*

Garnet to suppose that he was contemplating a position in which he might very probably find himself when *there*—“to ask how far it might be lawful for the party that hath the just quarrel to proceed in sacking or destroying a town of the enemy’s, or fortress, when it is holden against them by strong hands. The Father answered that, in a just war, it was lawful for those that had right to wage battle against the enemies of the commonwealth, to authorise their captains or soldiers, as their officers, to annoy or destroy any town that is unjustly holden against them, and that such is the common doctrine of all Divines : in respect that every commonwealth must, by the Law of Nature, be sufficient for itself, and therefore as well able to repel injuries as to provide necessaries ; and that, as a private person may *vim vi repellere*, so may the commonwealth do the like with so much more right, as the whole is of more importance than a part ; which, if it were not true, it should follow that Nature had provided better for beasts than for men, furnishing them with natural weapons as well to offend as to defend themselves, which we see also they have a natural instinct to use, when the offence of the invader is necessary for their own defence.   And therefore that it is not fit to think that God, Who, by natural reason, doth provide in a more universal and more noble manner for men than by natural instinct for beasts, hath left any particular person, and much less a commonwealth, without

sufficient means to defend and conserve itself; and
therefore not without power to provide and use likely
means to repel present injuries, and to repress known
and hurtful enemies.   And that, in all these, the head
of the commonwealth may judge what is expedient and
needful for the body thereof."   Much of all this was
useless to Catesby's purpose ; but he waited patiently,
and when Father Garnet had finished speaking, he
answered, " that all this seemed to be plain in common
reason, and the same also practised by all well-
governed commonwealths that ever have been, were
they never so pious or devout.   But, said he, some put
the greatest difficulty in the sackage of towns and
overthrowing or drowning up (*sic*) of forts, which, in
the Low Countries"—the Low Countries again !
mark his deceitfulness—" and in all wars is endeavoured, when the fort cannot otherwise be surprised,
and the same of great importance to be taken.   How,
then, those who have right to make the war may justify
that destruction of the town or fort, wherein there be
many innocents and young children, and some perhaps
unchristened, which must needs perish withal ?   Unto
this the Father answered, that indeed therein was the
greatest difficulty ; and that it was a thing could never
be lawful in itself, to kill an innocent, for that the
reason ceaseth in them for which the pain of death
may be inflicted by authority, seeing the cause why a
malefactor and enemy to the commonwealth may be put
to death is in respect of the common good, which is to

be preferred before his private (for otherwise, considering the thing only in itself, it were not lawful to put
any man to death); and so because the malefactor doth
in re gravi hinder the common good, therefore by the
authority of the magistrate that impediment may be
removed.   But now, as for the innocent and good, their
life is a help and furtherance to the common good, and
therefore in no sort it can be lawful to kill or destroy
an innocent."

Determined as Catesby was to twist Father Garnet's
words into " a parallel case," he wanted something
more tangible than this to work upon.   Accordingly
he said:—" That is done ordinarily in the destruction
of the forts I spake of."   " It is true, said the Father,
it is there permitted, because it cannot be avoided ;
but is done as *per accidens*, and not as a thing intended by or for itself, and so it is not unlawful.   As
if we were shot into the arm with a poisoned bullet,
so that we could not escape with life unless we cut off
our arm ; then *per accidens* we cut off our hand and
 ngers also which were sound, and yet being, at that
time of danger, inseparably joined to the arm, lawful
to be cut off, which it were not lawful otherwise to do
without mortal sin.   And such was the case of the
town of Gabaa, and the other towns of the tribe of
Benjamin, wherein many were destroyed that had not
offended.   With which Mr Catesby, seeming fully
satisfied, brake presently into other talk, the Father
at that time little imagining at what he aimed, though

afterwards, when the matter was known, he told some friends what had passed between Mr Catesby and him about this matter, and that he little suspected then he would so have applied the general doctrine of Divines to the practice of a private and so perilous a case, without expressing all particulars, which course may give occasion of great errors, as we see it did in this."

If Sir Everard Digby had heard the conversation on which the vaunted "consent" of the Jesuits had been founded, there can be little doubt that he would have refused to have anything to do with the conspiracy on such grounds. Father Gerard probably heard the account of the interview, after the failure of the plot, from Father Garnet himself.

Father Garnet's own much shorter account of the conversation may be given here.[1] Mr Catesby "asked me whether, in case it were lawful to kill a person or persons, it were necessary to regard the innocents, which were present, lest they also should perish withal. I answered that in all just wars it is practised and held lawful to beat down houses and walls and castles, notwithstanding innocents were in danger, so that such battering were necessary for the obtaining of victory, and that the multitude of innocents, or the harm which might ensue by their death, were not such that it might countervail the gain and com-

---

[1] Hatfield MS., 110, 30. Father Garnet and the Gunpowder Plot, p. 7.

modity of the victory. And in truth I never imagined anything of the King's Majesty, nor of any particular, and thought it, as it were, an idle question, till I saw him, when we had done, make solemn protestation that he would never be known to have asked me any such question as long as he lived."

That Father Garnet believed Catesby to have deceived him and to have told untruths about him is evident from one of his letters written in orange juice in the Tower. He says[1] "Master Catesby did me much wrong, and hath confessed that he tould them that he said he asked me a question in Q. Eliz. time of the powder action, and that it was unlawfull. All which is most untrew. He did it to draw in others." Again he writes[2] "I doubt not Mr Catesby hath fained many such things for to induce others," Sir Everard Digby, of course, among the rest.

Some of the modern admirers of Father Garnet have maintained that the worse Catesby, the worse Garnet; the better Catesby, the better Garnet. Without suggesting the exact converse, I would venture to point out the danger to Garnet's memory in anything that might tend to show some sort of co-partnership in spirit and intention between himself and Catesby. All the facts lead me to a very different conclusion, and one which is much more to the

---

[1] *Records, S. J.*, Vol. iv., p. 108.

[2] *History of the Gunpowder Plot*, Jardine, Appendix, p. 329.

interest of Garnet's memory, namely, that Catesby deceived him from first to last, and that he was, in fact, the innocent dupe of Catesby. To begin with, Catesby, when, during the first half year of James's reign, Garnet desired him not to join in "some stirring, seeing the King kept not his promise," deceived Garnet by assuring him "he would not."[1] He deceived him in 1604, when, on Garnet's urging him not to take up arms, etc., against the king,[2] "he promised to surcease." He deceived him when he put a case before him on the question of slaying "innocents together with nocents," as if it concerned his projected campaign in Flanders, when it really concerned the Gunpowder Plot. He deceived him at the[3] "house in Essex," when he "assured" him "that all his plans were unexceptionable." He deceived him when he[4] "promised" "to do nothing before the Pope was informed by" "messenger." He deceived him at White Webbs, when he told him that what he had in hand was quite "lawfull." He deceived him at Harrowden when he said that he was going to start for the war in the Low Countries as soon as he possibly could.

In other places I either have shown, or will show, that he deceived all his fellow-conspirators, that he induced them to join in the plot on false pretences, and that he told the lie direct to Sir Everard Digby

[1] Examination, March 13. *Records, S. J.,* Vol. III., p. 157.   [2] *Ib.*
[3] *Father Garnet and the Gunpowder Plot,* Pollen, p. 8.   [4] *Ib.,* p. 10.

at Dunchurch. Undoubtedly he had a charming manner, he was an agreeable and well-informed companion; there is much in his history that is interesting, much that is romantic, much that excites pity, but let not any modern Catholics imagine that by attempting to minimise his misdoings they will do any credit to the cause of the Church; for the man began as a libertine, and, after a period of spasmodic piety, ended as a liar. Catesby was one of those people who are fond of asking for priestly advice, obey it only if it coincides with their own wishes, and have no scruple whatever in misquoting it to their friends. This race is not extinct, nor is it limited to the male sex. Sometimes the performance is varied: instead of misquoting the advice of the priest, these candid penitents misstate the case on which they ask the priest to form an opinion.

Such people are exceedingly dangerous, and do immense mischief to the cause of the Catholic Church. When we consider the evil that may be wrought by one inaccurate and not over-scrupulous woman of this sort, who says to her friends:—" Oh, you may be quite easy in your mind. I asked Father Dash, and he told me there was no harm whatever in it," of some action which that Father would have condemned in the most unqualified terms, what limit can be put to the disaster that a man like Catesby might bring upon a credulous friend such as Sir Everard Digby?

It is unfortunate that there should be men of the Digby class as well as the Catesby! A priestly judgment has to be given in a court in which the inquirer is witness for both plaintiff and defendant, as well as advocate for both plaintiff and defendant. The friend, therefore, of the inquirer, who is asked to accept the decision which he brings from that spiritual court, ought not to do so unless he feels assured either that he would lay his case with absolute impartiality before that tribunal, or that the judge would discredit his evidence if given with partiality. Now, knowing Catesby very intimately, had Sir Everard Digby good reasons for believing that he could be trusted as an absolutely impartial witness and an absolutely impartial advocate on both sides? or else that the priest consulted would certainly detect any flaw in the evidence of a man so notorious for his plausibility and his powers of persuasion? If not, and he was determined only to join in the enterprise on the condition that it had priestly consent, he was bound either to go and ask it for himself, or, if his oath of secrecy prevented this, to refuse to have anything further to do with the conspiracy. So far as I have been able to ascertain of the previous history of Robert Catesby, he was one of the very last men from whom I should have felt inclined to take spiritual advice or spiritual consent at second hand; and, on this point, I find it difficult to exculpate Sir Everard Digby, although the difficulty is somewhat qualified by an unhappy remark made to Sir Everard by Father Garnet, to be noticed presently.

But first let us notice an incident which, in the case of two men professing to be practical Catholics, is nothing short of astounding! As a modern Jesuit, the present editor of *The Month*, the chief Jesuit journal in this country, points out,[1] Catesby "peremptorily demanded of" his associates in the conspiracy, of whom Sir Everard Digby was one, "a promise that they would not mention the project even in confession, lest their ghostly fathers should discountenance and hinder it." Considering that that project, even when regarded in the most favourable light, was one likely to entail very intricate questions of conscience in the course of its preparation and its fulfilment, it is inconceivable how men called, or calling themselves, good Catholics could either make such a demand or consent to it.

[1] *The Month*, No. 369, p. 353-4.

CHAPTER VIII.

In the last chapter we saw how Catesby, by means of his infamous perversion of Father Garnet's words, induced several of his friends, among others, and last of all, Sir Everard Digby, to join in his conspiracy; but even with his extraordinary powers of personal influence and persuasion, his unscrupulousness, and his intimate friendship with Sir Everard, it is just possible that he might have failed in enlisting him as a conspirator, had it not been for a most unfortunate, and apparently unguarded, remark made by Father Garnet.

Garnet had been at his wits' end to put a stop to the dangerous inclination to civil rebellion which he had observed among certain of the English Catholics; and, in his despair, he had written to Father Claudius Aquaviva, the General of the Society of Jesus:[1]— "If the affair of the toleration go not well, Catholics[2] will no more be quiet. What shall we do? Jesuits cannot hinder it. Let the Pope forbid all Catholics to stir."

---

[1] *Narrative of the G. P.*, Gerard, pp. 72-3.

[2] "Wherein he meant belike Mr Catesby and some such whom he most feared," says Father Gerard; *ib.*

The date of this letter was August 29, 1604,[1] that is to say, more than a year before Sir Everard Digby had ever heard of the Plot. Now, will it be believed that when he was asked by Sir Everard Digby what the meaning of "the Pope's Brief was"[2] [which "Brief" it may have been matters little to my purpose; Lingard[3] thought it referred to that of July 19, 1603], Father Garnet was weak enough—can I use a milder term?—to reply "that they were not (meaning Priests) to undertake or procure stirrs: *but yet they would not hinder any, neither was it the Pope's mind they should, that should be undertaken for Catholick good.*" And this after all his anxiety that the Pope should be induced to "forbid all Catholics to stir!" I say "after," for if the conversation had taken place very much earlier, what reason would Sir Everard have had for saying :— "This answer, with Mr Catesbyes proceedings with him and me gave me absolute belief that the matter in general was approved, though every particular was not known." If the point be pressed that it *may* have been earlier, I would reply, be it so; for in the very initiatory stages of the Plot, Father Garnet learned that some scheme was in hand, although he knew nothing of its details, and even then he was most anxious to prevent any "stirr." Let me quote

[1] *Father Garnet and the G. P.*, p. 4.
[2] *Papers and Letters of Sir Everard Digby.* Paper 9.
[3] Hist. Eng., Vol. viii. Note H. H. H. 9.

Father Pollen.[1]   "About midsummer 1604, some steps in the Plot having been already taken, Catesby intimated that they had something in hand, but entered into no particulars.   Father Garnet dissuaded him.   Catesby answered, 'Why were we commanded before to keep out one that was not a Catholic, and now may not exclude him?'   And this he thought an 'invincible argument,' and 'was so resolved in conscience that it was lawful to take arms for religion, that no man could dissuade it, but by the Pope's prohibition.   Whereupon I [*i.e.*, Garnet] urged that the Pope himself had given other orders, &c.'"   Yet Garnet told Sir Everard Digby that priests "would not hinder any" "stirs" "that should be undertaken for the Catholick good," "neither was it the Pope's mind that they should."

A friend of my own, who is a great admirer of Father Garnet, as well as a deeply read student of his times, disagrees with me in my view of Father Garnet's speech to Sir Everard about the "stirrs."   He writes: —"It seems to me you make too much of *one word*, and not enough of the *known tenour* of his instructions." Well, in the first place, this one word is the chief thing that I have to deal with, in respect to Father Garnet.   I am not writing a life of Garnet, but of Sir Everard Digby; and as Sir Everard stated that on that one word, to a great extent, depended his belief that the plot was approved of by the Jesuits, and

[1] Father Garnet and the G. P., p. 4.

consequently his consent to join in that plot, it is scarcely possible for me to " make too much of it." Moreover, I expressly pointed out that it was contrary to " the known tenour of his instructions," and I emphasised the fact that it was a direct contradiction to those instructions, as well as to his wishes, and that it was given in a moment of good-natured weakness ; but I venture to suggest that that weakness, instead of being contrary to what we know of his character, was in remarkable accordance with it.

I will admit that I long hesitated to use the word " weakness " in connection with Father Garnet ; but he himself practically owned that he was not always free from it.

" I acknowledge," he wrote,[1] before his death, " that I was bound to reveal all knowledge that I had of this or any other treason out of the sacrament of confession.   And whereas, partly upon hope of prevention, partly for that I would not betray my friend, I did not reveal the general knowledge of Mr Catesby's intention, which I had by him, I do acknowledge myself highly guilty to have offended God, the King's Majesty and Estate, and humbly ask of all forgiveness, exhorting all Catholics that they no way follow my example." To Father Greenway, again, he wrote :—
[2] " Indeed, I might have revealed a general knowledge I had of Mr Catesby out of confession, but hoping of

[1] S. P. Dom. James I., Vol. xx. n. 12.
[2] Hatfield MS., 115 fol. 154.

the Pope's prevention, and being loth to hurt my friend, I acknowledge to have so far forth offended God and the king."

With all humility, I beg to submit that a feeble, unguarded, nervous and indulgent speech such as that about the " stirrs," attributed by Sir Everard Digby to Father Garnet, is not very inconsistent with that good Father's conduct, as described by himself in the above manuscripts.

The question whether Father Garnet did, or did not, die a martyr, however interesting, is altogether apart from my subject ; a life of Sir Everard Digby is in no way affected by that controversy ; nor am I taking upon myself the offices of Devil's Advocate in Garnet's case, when I endeavour to do justice to that of Sir Everard.

I fully admit that *if* Father Garnet was weak, his weakness was owing to an excess of kindheartedness and a loyalty to his friends that bordered on extravagance.   I am well aware that it is easy to be " wise after the event," and that that sort of wisdom is too cheap to justify confident or summary sentences on those whose surroundings in their own times were so complicated as to make it impossible to put ourselves exactly in their places.   Again, it may be that Sir Everard misheard or misunderstood Garnet, that his memory failed him, or even that he lied.   Yet, again, it is possible that Digby's letter may have been incorrectly transcribed, though I can see no reason for thinking this at all likely to be the case.

There is, however, another side to the question. The mischief which may be wrought by a holy, amiable, but weak man, especially one whose dread of giving pain to others, or putting them into bad faith, or making them give up all religion by saying more than they can bear, when it is his duty to speak plainly, fully, and decidedly, is almost unlimited ; and if we are to hesitate to form opinions of the actions and characters of those who have lived in the past, for the reasons given above, we must relinquish historical studies once and for ever. Lastly, we ought not to extol one character at the expense of another. Father Garnet's weak speech, if weak it was, to some extent excuses, or rather somewhat lessens, the guilt of Sir Everard Digby. We must try to put ourselves in Digby's place as well as in Garnet's ; nor do I see that Sir Everard's evidence need be discredited. It was not extorted under examination ; on the contrary, it was deliberately written to his wife, and whatever his faults may have been, deceit and dishonesty do not appear to have been among them.

But let me say one word now as to the difficulties in which Father Garnet was placed. Familiar as we are with the means through which he came to know of the plot, I will take the liberty of reminding my readers of them.[1] Suspecting that Catesby was scheming

[1] *Father H. Garnet and the Gunpowder Plot*, Pollen, pp. 10, 11.

some mischief, he had taxed him with it, and told him that, being against the Pope's will, it would not prosper. Catesby had replied that, if the Pope knew what he intended to do, he would not hinder it. Then Father Garnet urged him to let the Pope know all about the whole affair. Catesby said he would not do so for the world, lest it should be discovered; but he offered to impart his project to Father Garnet. This Father Garnet refused to hear. Catesby, with all his double-dealing, seems to have become filled with remorse and anxiety, for he revealed the plot to Father Greenway in confession, giving him leave to reveal it in his turn to Father Garnet, in the same manner and under the same seal.

It is difficult for Protestants to realise the secresy of the confessional. Not only can the confessor say nothing of what he has heard in it to anyone else, but he may not even speak of it to the penitent himself, unless the penitent specially requests him to do so, except in confession ; nor can he in any way act towards him, or concerning him, on the strength of it. On the other hand, the penitent, although sometimes bound in honour and honesty not to reveal what the priest may say to him confidentially, as man to man, is theologically free to repeat anything that the priest may have said to him in the confessional to the whole world if he so wills ; he can also, if he pleases, set the priest at liberty to speak either to himself about it, outside the confessional, or to any other particular person or persons whom he may choose to name, or to everybody, if he likes ; but, unless so liberated, if the confessor hears that his penitent is publicly or privately giving a wrong version of the advice given him in confession, he cannot set himself right by giving the true one.

Father Greenway, horrified at the disclosure, availed himself of Catesby's permission to confide it to Father Garnet in confession. The latter [1] " was amazed," and " said it was a most horrible thing, the like of which was never heard of, for many reasons unlawful, &c.," and he proceeded to reprimand Father Greenway very severely for even giving ear to the matter.[2] By this, Endæmon the Jesuit, who tells the story, probably means " for discussing" the matter, and not refusing to listen to any defence of it. A priest can hardly be blamed for " hearing " anything in confession ; yet this is what Endæmon says. Therefore it would appear that, whether Father Garnet acted imprudently or not, Father Greenway certainly did so—at any rate, in Father Garnet's opinion.[3]

The position in which Catesby was placed with regard to the sacraments of confession and communion is delicate ground for a layman to approach ; especially

---

[1] *Father Garnet and the Gunpowder Plot*, pp. 11, 12.

[2] See Endæmon Johannes, S.J., *Apologia pro Henrico Garneto*, p. 259.

[3] The following is the description of Father Greenway given in the Proclamation for his apprehension. " Of a reasonable stature, black hair, a brown beard cut close on the cheeks and left broad on the chin, somewhat long-visaged, lean in the face but of a good red complexion, his nose somewhat long and sharp at the end, his hands slender and long fingers, his legs of a good proportion, his feet somewhat long and slender."—S. P. James I., Vol. xviii. n. 21.

as nobody knows exactly what took place with regard to either.   I am told, however, by those who ought to know, that this much may be said from my own point of view, without danger of theological error.   Father Greenway, after telling Catesby in confession about the nature of the enormity he was meditating, must have refused him absolution and the sacraments if he persevered.[1]   After so striking a sentence, what possible room is there for thinking that Catesby could have gone on without even a *serious practical doubt* as to the lawfulness of his object?   Yet to have persevered with such a doubt would have put him at once into a state of *mala fides*.   And if he became in a state of *mala fides*, as he was in the habit of going to the sacraments every week, he must have done one or other of two things.   He must either have made sacrilegious communions, or he must have given up going to Holy Communion in order to commit the crime of proceeding with the Gunpowder Plot.

There is another point in connection with Catesby's confession which is worthy of notice.   When he first told the other conspirators that he had obtained the consent of a Jesuit to a case similar to the Gunpowder Plot, he could at least honestly say that no priest had at

---

[1] Although it may seem an insult to most of my readers, there are some who are so ignorant of Catholic matters, that it may be safer to explain that in saying Father Greenway must have refused absolution, I mean absolution for *past* sins.   Absolution cannot be given for future sins, as some Protestants have supposed, and a "dispensation to commit a sin" is an impossibility.   Certain Protestant writers have implied that both were given by the Jesuits to Catesby and his fellow-conspirators.

that time directly *condemned* the Gunpowder Plot itself as such ; but, when Father Greenway had distinctly done so, he still seems to have left them under the impression that the Jesuit Fathers approved of the conspiracy " in general, though they knew not the particulars." To do this was to *act* a lie ! But it seems to have been after he had heard Greenway condemn the Plot in confession that he said something of the same kind to Sir Everard Digby for the first time, and in that case he *told* a lie ! In short, if— mind, I say if—after hearing Greenway's denunciation of the Plot, which, according to Father Pollen,[1] was in July, he gave Sir Everard Digby to understand, on first telling him of the plot, in the following Septem- ber, that the scheme in general had the approval of the Jesuits, though they knew not the particulars, when he was well aware that he himself *had* told them the main particulars, and was certain that they did *not* approve of it, he obtained Sir Everard's adherence to the plot by a direct fraud, and acted the part of an unscrupulous scoundrel.

Some devout people have endeavoured to find excuses for Catesby—not for his action with regard to the plot, of course, but for the condition of mind into which he fell preparatory to it—on the ground that he was a good Catholic. What is a good Catholic ? I suppose a man who keeps God's commandments and obeys his Church. One commandment is, " Thou

[1] *Father Garnet and the Gunpowder Plot*, p. 13.

shalt do no murder " ; and one of the Pope's orders, in Catesby's time, was that the Catholics in England were not to rise against the Government. But then it is said that Catesby went to Holy Communion every week. Be it so ! Another historical character, one Judas Iscariot, committed a still worse crime immediately after receiving his First Communion.

Robert Catesby was one of those most dangerous men to his own cause, a Catholic on Protestant principles.   He acted in direct opposition to the commands of the Divine Founder of his Church, as well as to the precepts of the representative of that Divine Founder upon earth. He preferred his own private opinion to that of either. He considered his own Decalogue and Beatitudes juster and more sublime than the Almighty's, his own intentions for the welfare of the Church wiser than the Holy Father's, his own moral theology more orthodox than that of the Jesuits ; and then this Protestant in practice—for Protestantism is not exclusively restricted to protests against such matters as the supremacy of the Pope or transubstantiation—took it upon himself to pose as a prominent champion of the Catholic Church.

I am not denying that Catesby fancied he was doing right ; but whether that fancy was arrived at by right means or wrong is another question. He seems to have argued to himself that Pope, Priests, and Jesuits were not equal to the occasion ; that there were times, of which his own was one, at which papal, spiritual, and even biblical teaching must for the moment be set on one side whilst the secular arm struck a violent blow for the relief of God's suffering people; that, *ante factum*, the ecclesiastical powers could not consent to such a measure, but that, *post factum*, they would not only tolerate it, but approve of and rejoice at it. It came, therefore, to this, that on a most important point of morals—faith and morals, be it remembered, are the two chief provinces over which the Catholic Church claims power—a private individual, and not the Church, was to decide what was best; in short, Catesby was to protest against the teaching of the Church. Luther protested in matters of faith ; Catesby protested in matters of morals. Both men seem to have believed that the time would come when the Church would see that what they did was for its welfare.

It has been said that in Father Garnet we have one of the most remarkable instances in history of the secrecy of the confessional. On this point I venture no opinion ; but I am bold enough to say that in Robert Catesby we have one of the most remarkable instances in history of the abuse of the confessional. Perhaps no man ever did more to foster that superstitious horror of " auricular confession " which has so long prevailed, and still prevails in this country.

In passing, I may meet a possible inquiry as to how it came about that so much should be known concerning what Catesby had told Greenway in confession, and

what Greenway had told Garnet under the same sacred
seal. The explanation is simple. Catesby had not
only given Father Greenway permission to inform
Father Garnet of the plot, under seal of confession,
but had [1] "arranged that neither should be bound by
that seal when lawfully examined by their superiors."
Another question naturally presents itself, much more
connected with the man whose life I am writing, which
I confess I do not find it so easy to answer.   It is the
following :—When Father Garnet noticed the sudden
and suspicious confidences which had arisen between
Catesby and Sir Everard Digby,[2] after their ride from
Harrowden to Gothurst, did he, though tongue-tied as
to what he knew of Catesby's designs under seal of
confession, know enough *out* of the confessional to
warn Sir Everard against consenting to, or joining in,
any illicit schemes which Catesby might propose to him
and had he an extra-confessional *causa loquendi* ?

Let us suppose that he asked himself this question.
Even if he answered it in the affirmative, he might have
refrained from acting, through fear that, in his
vehemence in warning Sir Everard, there might be
a danger of his breaking the seal of the confessional ;
or that in vaguely putting Sir Everard on his guard,
he might raise the suspicion that knowledge obtained
in the confessional was the occasion, or the impelling
cause of that warning. Or he might reflect that, if

---

[1] *Father Garnet and the G. P.*, Pollen. p. 11.
[2] *Ib.*, pp. 21, 22.

cross-questioned by Sir Everard, it would be difficult
to remember, at a moment's notice, exactly how much
of his knowledge of Catesby's schemes was sealed by
confession, and how much unsealed.

Yet when he looked at his young host, and at his
charming and excellent wife, still a mere girl, but with
two little children beside her, in their beautiful and
happy home, the model of what a Christian home
ought to be, and a centre of Catholic society ; and
when he considered that hitherto Sir Everard Digby
had been as upright in character as in stature, and
as distinguished in virtue as in appearance, might he
not have told himself that any effort was worth making
to try to save him from a terrible crime and its terrible
consequences ?

He was the only man who could do so ! He alone
had "a general knowledge of Mr Catesby's intention,"[1] untrammelled by the secresy of either oath or
confessional, and he[2] "noticed the new intimacy that
had sprung up between Catesby and Digby," and sur-
mised truly enough that Digby had been "drawn in."
Yet it is evident from Sir Everard's letters from the
Tower, that Father Garnet never lifted a finger nor
uttered a word to hinder his host from joining, or
proceeding in, the conspiracy which was to work his
ruin. This is the more remarkable because Father
Garnet might have been expected not only to wish to

____

[1] His own admission. S.P. Dom. James I., Vol. xx. n. 12.
[2] Father Garnet and the G. P., Pollen, pp. 22, 23.

save Sir Everard from the guilt and the dangers of the Plot, but also to prevent a conspiracy which he so much dreaded from being strengthened by the support of a man of considerable wealth. The most probable origin of his inaction in this matter was the same weakness of character which had exhibited itself in his speech to Sir Everard about the Pope and the " stirrs," and in his failure to reveal his " general knowledge, had of Mr Catesby out of confession," whereby he said he offended God and the King.   His silence and inaction were certainly not owing to any temporary revival of confidence in his mind.   On the contrary, he wrote :— [1] " I remained in the greatest perplexity that ever I was in my life, and could not sleep a' nights."   He added, " I did offer up all my devotions and masses that God of his mercy and infinite Providence would dispose of all for the best, and find means which were pleasing unto Him, to prevent so great a mischief" [as the Gunpowder Plot].   " I knew that this would be infinitely displeasing to my Superiors in Rome, in so much as at my second conference with Mr Greenway, I said, ' Good Lord, if this matter go forward, the Pope will send me to the galleys, for he will assuredly think I was privy to it.' "

Far be it from me to presume to judge Father Garnet harshly ; his opportunities may have been much less, his difficulties may have been much

[1] *Ib.*, 23.

greater, than the evidence before us would seem to show ; but, as a biographer of Sir Everard Digby, I feel bound to express my regret that it should appear as if Father Garnet might have saved him from the terrible troubles that followed and failed to do so.

I began this chapter with a reference to those who plead extenuating circumstances for Catesby. Let me end it by referring to somewhat similar-minded critics, who, while they condemn the Gunpowder Plot as a most dastardly outrage, regard it as the hot-blooded attempt of a small party of Catholics driven to desperation by their sufferings. Of the sufferings of the English Catholics there can be no sort of doubt or question ; and none the less certain is it that, as a body, they bore them with patience and without any attempt at rebellion. Was, then, the small party of Catholics that conspired in the Gunpowder Plot composed of men so exceptionally exposed to sufferings for their faith as to be, more than any of their fellow-sufferers, " driven to desperation " ? It is well worth while to inquire. We will consult a Catholic contemporary, most unlikely to represent their lot as too easy, namely, the oft-quoted Father Gerard.[1]

Let us begin with Catesby, the originator and leader of the enterprise. The losses of his father on account of his religion do not concern the objects of the plot, as they were incurred long before and during a different

[1] *Narrative of the Gunpowder Plot.*

K

reign.   Catesby himself had certainly lost money, and a great deal of money ; but how ?[1]   "He spent much above his rate [income], and so wasted also good part of his living."   He was guilty of "excess of play and apparel."   He also had to pay "£3000 before he got out" of prison, where he had been put for joining in the ill-fated rising of Essex.   Even after all these losses, he was able to live among men of wealth, if not in his own country-house at Lapworth, in Warwickshire.

Ambrose Rokeby was [2] "a gentleman of good worth in the county of Suffolk, and of a very ancient family, and himself the heir of the eldest house."   At the time of the plot he had a great many horses, and was evidently a rich man.   John Grant was [3] "a man of sufficient estate."   Francis Tresham was [4] "a gentleman of Northamptonshire of great estate, esteemed then worth £3000 a year," a sum, of course, equivalent to a very large income in these days. Robert Winter was [5] "a gentleman of good estate in Worcestershire."   Thomas Percy,[6] although not a rich landowner, held the lucrative post of agent and administrator to his cousin, the Earl of Northumberland.   The "means were not great" of Robert Keyes, John and Christopher Wright, and Thomas Winter ; but most of them seem to have been able to live in good society, and their want of money

---

[1] *Narrative of the Gunpowder Plot,* p. 55.   [2] *Ib.,* p. 85.
[3] *Ib.,* p. 86.   [4] *Ib.,* p. 90.   [5] *Ib.,* p. 58.   [6] *Ib.,* p. 57.

was for the most part owing to their being younger sons, being "very wild,"[1] or living "in good sort and of the best,"[2] when their circumstances did not justify their doing so. As for Sir Everard Digby, it is scarcely necessary to repeat that he had been a rich man to begin with, and had increased his wealth by marrying an heiress. These, then, are the men who, we are told, were driven to desperation by their sufferings, and conspired together to commit a most horrible and murderous crime, while thousands of Catholics who were literally ruined, by fines for their religion which they were unable to pay, bore their troubles in silence, and with Christian fortitude and resignation.

In connection with this matter, there is one more point to be considered. The sudden and unpremeditated assault of a man in despair is sometimes to be excused, and often to be regarded with comparative lenience. What looks like murder at first sight, at second may prove to be only manslaughter, under such circumstances. Does any such excuse exist for the Gunpowder Plot? Was it a violent attempt made on the spur of the moment, or was it the result of lengthy, deliberate, and anxious forethought? Was it the work of an hour, a day, a week, or even a month. On the contrary, so far as can be ascertained, at least a year and a quarter, and more probably a year and a half,

---

[1] *Narrative of the Gunpowder Plot*, p. 59. [2] *Ib.*, p. 58.

of careful scheming and calculation were devoted to it.[1]

It has been said, in excuse for the conspirators, that there are reasons for suspecting the idea of the Gunpowder Plot to have been conceived in the first instance by Cecil, who had it suggested to Catesby, through a third person—possibly Mounteagle—with the deliberate intention of bringing discredit upon the English Catholics, and thereby giving cause for the enactment of severer measures for their repression. This may remind some of my readers that, at the height of the agrarian crime in Ireland, during the last quarter of the nineteenth century, many good Irish Catholics were persuaded, or persuaded themselves, that the outrages were invented, instigated, and encouraged, if not actually perpetrated, at the suggestion of the authorities at Dublin Castle, in order to throw discredit upon "the poor, oppressed Irish peasantry," and to give an excuse for "persecuting" them with renewed vigour.

As to the question whether Cecil originated the Gunpowder Plot as a bait with which to entrap Catholic priests, Jesuits, and laymen, if there be any grounds for it, it certainly has great historic interests ; but whether Cecil, or the Devil, or both, put the idea into the heads of the conspirators, little, if at all, affects their guilt.

[1] See Jardine's *G. P.*, p. 27 ; also *Father Garnet and the G. P.*, p. 4.

TOWARDS the end of the last chapter, I showed that the conspirators were for the most part in fairly comfortable circumstances, and that some of them were rich. It was not necessary to my purpose to enter into details concerning Guy Fawkes, who was an adventurer and a mere tool, or concerning Thomas Bates, who was Catesby's servant. Nor did I mention the Littletons—one a wealthy man, and the other a younger son, and a cousin of the former; for, although they joined in the rising after the discovery of the plot, and suffered death for it, they do not appear to have been among the sworn conspirators beforehand. But, before dismissing the subject of the riches or poverty of the plotters, I have something more to say.

Sir Everard Digby was chiefly enlisted by Catesby on account of his wealth. He promised to contribute £1500 towards the scheme, and to furnish, in addition, as much armour and as many arms, men, and horses as he might be able. Another large landowner was enlisted even later than Sir Everard, and for the same purpose. This was Catesby's cousin, Francis

Tresham, of Rushton, in Northamptonshire. He, like
Catesby and Percy, had been implicated in the rebellion of the Earl of Essex, so a plot was no novelty
to him, and he consented to help the new one with
money to the extent of £2000. Funds, again, were
to be found in another quarter. [1] "Mr Percy himself promised all he could get out of the Earl of
Northumberland's rents,"—in other language, he
promised to embezzle, and apparently with the pious
Catesby's full consent, every penny he was able of
his master's money—"which was about £4000."
Here, therefore, we have a fund of £7500, to say
nothing of what Catesby and the other conspirators
may have spent in the early stages of the plot.

In the reign of James I., a sovereign sterling was
worth very much more than it is at present; some
people say ten times as much;[2] so if they are right,
the Gunpowder Plot Fund amounted to £75,000 of
our money.

What became of it? All the work done was
voluntary and unpaid. The hiring of the cellar
under the houses of Parliament could not have been
a very heavy outlay; very many hundreds of pounds
cannot have been spent in gunpowder; and if a good
deal may have been invested in horses, that would
only exhaust a comparatively small portion of so
large a fund. Most likely the conspirators defrayed

---

[1] Thomas Winter's Confession. S.P., Gunpowder Plot Book, n. 114.
[2] See Dr Jessop, in *One Generation of a Norfolk House*, p. 285.

their own personal expenses while working for the plot, and even if they charged them to the fund, the men were so few in numbers that they cannot have amounted to much. Can it be that some immense bribe was given, or promised, to Guy Fawkes for the excessively dangerous part which he was to play in the drama? This is far from unlikely!

The fugitives, after the discovery of the plot, carried a good deal of cash with them as they rode about, trying to raise an insurrection. Sir Everard Digby alone took [1] "above £1000 in ready coin" with him. According to the authority quoted, this would be the equivalent of £10,000 nowadays, a large amount to carry about the country. Yet, as will be seen when the proper time comes, he apparently made no use of it. The financial aspects of the Gunpowder Plot are as curious as they are incomprehensible.

After giving his solemn promise not to divulge the conspiracy, Sir Everard evidently could say nothing about it to Lady Digby. It must have been a terrible trial to have the burden of that awful secret, with all its dangers to himself and those dear to him, on his mind when he looked upon his innocent, holy, and loving young wife, with her little boy, Kenelm, now two years old, toddling after her, and her baby, which had been born early in that year, in her arms, as she walked

[1] *Narrative of the G. P.*, Gerard, p. 92.

about the long, low rooms and corridors of Gothurst, or wandered about its sloping gardens and along the banks of the River Ouse. While the worst fear in her mind as she did so would be a visit from pursuivants, her husband knew of far more terrible dangers by which their hitherto happy home was threatened.

Already he was beginning to take precautions against possible failure and its fearful consequences. Of course, at Gothurst, as at every other house frequented by priests, there was a " priests' hole "; but Sir Everard now ordered preparations for concealment to be made upon a much more elaborate scale. It is nearly certain that the most celebrated of all artificers in priests' hiding-places was staying at Gothurst just at this very time.   His real name was Nicholas Owen, but he usually went by the name of " Little John." He was a Jesuit lay-brother, and he usually accompanied Father Garnet in his travels. It is recorded that he went to Gothurst with Father Garnet on his way to Holywell, and it may be assumed that he was with him when he returned. Nothing, therefore, would be simpler or easier for Sir Everard than, on the plea of a desire to increase his precautions for priests in case of a raid from pursuivants, to ask Little John to superintend the making of intricate places of concealment which should serve as refuges for himself and his fellow-conspirators in case of discovery, failure, or pursuit.

He could not have found a better workman for this purpose. Father Gerard writes of him :—[1] " He it was that made our hiding-places ; in fact he made the one to which I owed my safety." As he probably made the very curious hiding-places in Sir Everard Digby's house, I may claim to say something about him. Brother Foley calls him [2] " that useful, cunning joiner of those times," who " died a martyr for the faith, suspended from a Topcliff rack in the Tower of London, where he was divers times hung up for several hours together, to compel him to betray the hiding-places he had made, up and down the land ; but not a word could they force from his sealed and faithful lips." " The authorities, shocked at their own cruelty, gave out that he destroyed himself." [3] A Protestant writer accordingly calls him [4] " that Owen who ript out his own bowells in the Tower." Father Gerard denies this story at great length,[5] stating that the poor man suffered from hernia, and that although " the civil law doth forbid to torture any man that is broken," the executioners " girded " the afflicted part " with a plate of iron to keep in " the portion which threatened to protrude, but that " the extremity of pain (which is most in that kind of torment, about the breast " and the seat of the hernia, " did force out " the interior, " and so the iron did serve but to cut and wound his

<hr>

[1] *Life of Father J. Gerard*, p. lvii. [2] *Records, S. J.* Series I., p. 297.
[3] *Ib.*, p. 675, footnote.
[4] *The Foot out of the Snare.* By John Zee, London, 1624.
[5] *Gunpowder Plot*, p. 188-9.

body, which, perhaps, did afterwards put them in mind to give out that he had ripped his" part in question, "with a knife. Which, besides all the former reasons, is in itself improbable, if not impossible. For first, in that case, knives are not allowed but only in the time of meat, whilst one stands by, and those such as are broad at the point, and will only cut towards the midst."

As to his skill in making hiding-places, a Jesuit, Father Tanner, wrote of him that [1] "With incomparable skill he knew how to conduct priests to a place of safety along subterranean passages, to hide them between walls, to bury them in impenetrable recesses, and to entangle them in labyrinths and a thousand windings. But what was much more difficult of accomplishment, he so disguised the entrances to these as to make them most unlike what they really were." "When he was about to design" a hiding-place, he commenced the work by "receiving the Most Holy Eucharist, sought to aid its progress by continual prayer, and offered the completion of it to God alone, accepting of no other reward for his toil than the merit of charity and the consolation of labouring for the good of Catholics."

As I have shown, it may pretty safely be assumed that he was at Gothurst early in October 1605, just after Sir Everard Digby had been initiated into the

[1] *Collectanea S. J.* See *Records of the Eng. Prov. S. J.*, Vol. iv. pp. 247, 248.

plot; and, as the hiding-places at Gothurst about to be described are believed to have been made between his initiation and the discovery, with a view to concealment in connection with the gun-powder plot, the work must in that case have been done during October.

Lipscomb thus describes them :—[1] "In one of the apartments was formerly shewn a movable floor, which, to ordinary observers, offered nothing remark- . able in its appearance, but was made to revolve on a pivot, which, by a secret bolt, disclosed underneath it another room (receiving light from the lower part of a mullioned window, not discoverable exteriorily, unless at a very great distance)." From this secret room, he says "there were private passages of ingress and egress," "almost impossible of detection, even by the occupiers of the Mansion. Here were also some remarkably ingenious cabinets and drawers, for the deposit of papers, &c." Mr Walter Carlile, the son of the owner, and the occupier of Gothurst, or Gayhurst, as it is now called, informs me that Lipscomb's description of the secret room is perfectly correct; that, although it was demolished twenty years ago, greatly to his own regret, there are still all the traces of where it was and how it was managed; and that the "priest's hole" and some secret passages are yet in existence.

The secret room was not in the principal front,

---

[1] *Hist. and Antiquities of the Co. of Bucks*, Vol. iv. p. 159.

with its picturesque porch and gables; but at the end, at the right; that is to say, on the right as one stood facing the front. In the middle of this end of the house was a solid, square-headed projection, and it was the upper half of the room on the first floor of this projection which was converted into the secret room. The result was that, in this secret chamber the window came down to the floor, but did not rise to the top of the room, being in fact the upper half of the window which lighted the room beneath it. As the entire window was almost twice as high as it was broad, and divided into two equal parts, it was very well adapted for the purpose.

Lipscomb was probably right in calling this "a very artful contrivance for the concealment of the parties to the Gunpowder Plot"; there is certainly a tradition to the same effect, and, as will have been observed, I have adopted it; at the same time I will say candidly that I sometimes ask myself whether, after all, the "contrivance," with its pivotted floor, may not have been only intended as a hiding-place for priests, and not for conspirators, a theory which is somewhat supported by the knowledge that Sir Everard Digby was going to leave and shut up Gothurst a few days before the explosion was to take place, and even still earlier was going to send his wife and children to Mr Throgmorton's house at Coughton, which he had taken for them.

The energies of the conspirators, especially those of such an earnest Catholic as Sir Everard Digby, would be stimulated during October by the news that, that very month, two priests and a layman had been put to death for their religion. [1] "They were executed together with sixteen thieves and eight other malefactors ; and their heads were placed on London Bridge." A Spanish lady of high birth, who had come to England in the preceding May, wrote :— [2] "We can hardly go out to walk without seeing the heads and limbs of some of our dear and holy ones stuck up on the gates that divide the streets, and the birds of the air perching upon them ; which makes me think of the verse in the Psalms, 'They have given the dead bodies of thy servants to be meat for the fowls of the air," etc. Admitting that there may have been some exaggeration in this statement, it was by no means devoid of foundation in fact. The reports of such things would give the conspiracy the colour of a crusade, to men anxious to see it assume that hue.

We shall presently see that Sir Everard intended to turn his steps towards Wales, when the blow should have been struck, making sure of the support of Catholics so persecuted as the Welsh and the inhabitants of the border counties. Here is something about them. Less than five months before

[1] *Before and after the Gunpowder Plot.* By E. Healy Thompson, p. 4.
[2] *Life of Luisa de Carvajal.* By Lady Georgiana Fullerton, p. 226.

the attempt to blow up the houses of parliament, the Protestant Bishop of Hereford wrote to Salisbury :—[1] "On Wednesday last, at evening, Sir James Scudamore and other justices of the peace, with such aid as I could give them, went unto the Darren and other places adjoining to make search and apprehend Jesuits and priests . . . and did make diligent search all that night and day following, from village to village, from house to house, about thirty miles compass, near the confines of Monmouthshire, where they found altars, images, books of superstition, relics of idolatry, but left all desolate of men and women. Except here and there an aged woman or a child, all were fled into Wales, and but one man apprehended; all that circuit of rude barbarous people carried headlong into these desperate courses by priests (whereof there is great store) and principal gentlemen, lords of towns and manors there. They are all fled into the woods, and there they will lurk until the assizes be past." Rumours of the searches on the part of the "justices of the peace," "with such aid" as the Bishop of Hereford "could give them," would reach Gothurst and provoke Sir Everard. They remind one of the remark made by Cardinal Bellarmine on the Gunpowder Plot :—[2] "I excuse not the crime, I loathe unnatural murders,

---

[1] S. P. Dom. James I., Vol. xiv. n. 52, June 22, 1605.

[2] Reply to the King's *Triplici nodo triplex cuneus.* See *The Month,* No. 366, p. 501.

I execrate conspiracies, but no one can deny that provocation was given."

The plan of campaign was doubtless discussed at great length at Gothurst during the early part of the month of October. Parliament was to meet at the beginning of November, and the great attempt was intended to be made about the 5th. No time, therefore, was to be lost in making provision for every contingency. Sir Everard was still anxious as to whether all the Catholic peers, and those peers who were friendly to Catholics, could, with any certainty, be induced to absent themselves from the House at the time of the explosion.

"Assure yourself," said Catesby to him, "that such of the nobility as are worth saving shall be preserved, and yet know not of the matter."[1] As to the remainder of the lords, he declared that he regarded them as "atheists, fools, and cowards, and that lusty bodies would be better for the commonwealth than they."[2] There was considerable wrangling as to which of the peers were to be saved, and there was some diversity of opinion on the question —whether this or that Protestant lord was well-enough disposed towards Catholics and their religion to be worth rescue. For instance, some would have it that the Earl of Northumberland was likely to

---

[1] Digby's Exam., 2nd Dec. 1605. S.P.O. Jardine's *Gunpowder Plot*, pp. 75-6.

[2] Keyes' Exam., 30th Nov. 1605. S.P.O. Jardine, p. 75.

become a Catholic ; but his relative, Percy the conspirator, said that [1] for matters of relligion " he " trobled not much himselfe."   Notwithstanding this statement, Percy earnestly begged that he might be one of the peers to be spared,[2] which was indeed only fair, considering that his rents were to be stolen for the purposes of the plot.   Francis Tresham pleaded for his two brothers-in-law, Stourton and Mounteagle, both of whom were Catholics ; Keyes for his great friend, Mordaunt ; Fawkes for Montague, several for Arundel, and so on.

As to the plan of proceedings, when the explosion should have taken place with success, the great principle was to be to rally the Catholic gentry with their servants and retainers for a general rising in a central district.   Gothurst was considered too far east for this purpose, and Warwickshire was selected as the base of operations for the volunteer Catholic army.   It was true that that army did not yet exist ; that the number of men at present initiated into the conspiracy was very small ; and that the spirit in which the Catholics would receive the news of the wholesale massacre of the King and his Parliament remained to be proved ; but Catesby and his confederates, Sir Everard apparently among the number, were very sanguine.

Catesby, the originator, organiser, and leader of the whole proceeding, was to have the management

---

[1] Cal. Sta. Pa., 1603-10, p. 262.   [2] Jardine, p. 74.

of the grand explosion and the conduct of matters in London immediately afterwards, while Digby was to have the charge of the rising in Warwickshire, where Catesby was to join him, as occasion might serve. As a nucleus of his hoped-for army, Sir Everard was to take so many of his retainers as he could muster, with a quantity of arms in carts, to Dunchurch, a place very near Rugby, and to invite a large number of his trustworthy friends, likely to join in the cause, to come there with their horses and servants for a great "hunting-match" on Dunsmoor Heath.

Country gentlemen in our own times have often wondered what this "hunting-match" could be. Possibly it may have been a coursing meeting. The foundation of the rules of coursing, in its modern sense, was the code drawn up by the Duke of Norfolk in the reign of Elizabeth,[1] and as Sir Everard had been a good deal at the Court of that Queen, and was devoted to field sports, it is not unreasonable to infer that the so-called "hunting-match" may have been ostensibly what we should call a coursing-meeting, with, perhaps, some hawking added. It was arranged that on the arrival of the guests invited to take part in it at Dunchurch, Sir Everard was to hint to them that a decisive blow of some sort was about to be struck in London, although they were not to be enlightened as to its

---

[1] *The Greyhound*, by Hugh Dalziel, 1887.

nature until the news should arrive of its success. On the receipt of this news, Digby was at once to despatch a party to seize the Princess Elizabeth at the house of her governor, Lord Harington—he had been created Baron Harington of Exton in 1603 —at his house near Coventry, and if Catesby should fail to secure the persons of the Prince of Wales or the Duke of York in the South, Digby was to proclaim her Queen. The little volunteer army in Warwickshire was then to seize the horses at Warwick Castle and the store of armour at Whewell Grange, Lord Windsor's house in Worcestershire, "and by that time," said Catesby, in unfolding his plan, "I hope some friends will come and take our parts."[1]

Sir Everard was not going to leave his wife and children at Gothurst, between the great rallying centre of his expected army in Warwickshire and the possible opposing army which, in case of failure, might approach from London. On the contrary, he was anxious to place them on the further side of Warwickshire, so that the band of Catholic warriors might lie between them and the source of danger; at the same time he wished to have them within easy reach; and, for this purpose, he hired or borrowed from Mr Throckmorton, a house called Coughton (containing many "secret recesses"[2]), near Alcester, and about

---

[1] R. Winter's Letter to the Lords. S.P.O. 21st Jan. 1605. Jardine, p. 73.

[2] *Records of the Eng. Prov. S. J.*, Vol. iv. p. 34, footnote.

twenty-five miles from the primary rallying point at Dunchurch.

Sir Everard said in his examination in Nov. 1605, that he " did borrow a howse of Mr Thomas Throckmorton for one moneth, purposing to take it longer, or to enquire out some other if that were not to be had, if " his " wife should like to live there." [1]

Being, in those days, a quadrangular house,[2] it could easily be defended in case of need. It is impossible that Sir Everard can have given Lady Digby the real reason for which he proposed to remove her there : the secret which he was keeping from her can scarcely have failed to cause some restraint between them, and it would be but natural that she should feel considerable uneasiness. Why, she would ask herself, should her husband, who had hitherto shared everything with her, now have something in hand which he was evidently concealing ?

Another inmate at Gothurst was in a state of great anxiety, namely Father Garnet. The exertions to which his lay companion, " Little John," was put, at his host's request, to increase the secret passages and make a hidden room, may have aroused his suspicions still further ; but, after all, Gothurst would be no more ramified with such places of concealment than certain other houses ; for instance, at Hendlip Hall, about four

---

[1] S. P. Domestic, James I., Vol. xvi. No. 94.

[2] Gorton's Topography, Vol. i. p. 518.   The house at present belongs to Sir N. W. Throckmorton, Bart.

miles from Worcester, a house to which Father Garnet
was to go within two months, to spend several weeks,
a house, moreover, of much the same date as Gothurst,
there was [1] " scarcely an apartment that" had "not
secret ways of going in or going out " ; some had " back
stair cases concealed in the walls ; others" " places of
retreat in their chimneys ; some " " trap-doors, and all"
presented " a picture of gloom, insecurity, and suspicion."   And well might the inmates of a Catholic family
live in " gloom, insecurity, and suspicion," in those
days of pursuivants, fines, hangings, and quarterings.

Father Gerard, who was a frequent visitor at
Gothurst, observed with surprise that Sir Everard
had a far larger number of horses than he had been
accustomed to keep ; [2] but, when it occurred to him
that this might be because he was, for some reason
or other, better off than before, he found that, on the
contrary, he had been selling his farm-stock, and
even some land, which puzzled him much, particularly
in so prudent and careful a man, and the more so
since he was aware that Sir Everard was going to
pay the fine required of recusants by the statute, and
was therefore in no danger of having his stock taken
from him compulsorily.

<hr>

[1] *Beauties of England*, Vol. xv., Part I., p. 184.   Jardine, p. 182.
Nash, in his *Worcestershire*, quotes from Ashmole MSS., Vol. 804, fol. 93,
the following :—"Eleven secret corners and conveyances were found
in the said house, all of them having books, massing stuff, and popish
trumpery in them, only two excepted."
[2] *Life of Father J. Gerard*, p. ccxxxvi.

Although Sir Everard Digby had been led by Catesby to believe that some of the Jesuit Fathers had given their approval to the Gunpowder Plot, and had special reasons, as we have seen, for imagining Father Garnet to be one of these, he does not appear to have thought that Father Gerard knew anything about the matter, or would have consented to it if he had known of it: for, on his arraignment, he declared that Father Gerard was ignorant of it, and that he had never mentioned it to him, [1] "alleging the reason," "because, he said, he feared lest" that Father "should dissuade him from it." So here we find him acting in opposition to his greatest friend—his "brother," as he called him—the priest who had received him into the Church, and was his chief spiritual adviser. A good Catholic might lawfully act in opposition to the opinion of his confessor or director in matters open to difference of view, especially when that opinion was only suspected, and had not been delivered; but on such an all-important question as this, he might have been expected to consult Gerard, although it must be remembered that he had been assured by Catesby that another Jesuit had approved of the plot.

There is one consideration on this subject which is of the highest importance, namely, that Garnet was the Provincial, that is to say the superior and the very

---

[1] Father Gerard's letter to the Bishop of Chalcedon. See *Life of Father Gerard*, p. ccxxxviii.

highest authority among the Jesuits in England, at that time, and therefore the Jesuit of all others most in communication with Rome, and most likely to know the mind of the General of his Order as well as that of the Holy Father himself.

During October, not only Catesby, but other conspirators visited Gothurst. Among these was Fawkes, the adventurer who was intended to be actual perpetrator of the terrible deed. He was not altogether ill-born, being a member of an at least respectable family in Yorkshire, his father having been Registrar and Advocate of the Consistory Court of York Minster.[1] He was thirty-five years old, and he had seen much of the world, having entered the Spanish army in Flanders and been at the taking of Calais by the Archduke Albert in 1596.[2] He was a man, too, who made some profession of devotion as a Catholic.[3] Father Greenway describes him as [4] " a man of great piety, of exemplary temperance, of mild and cheerful demeanour, an enemy of broils and disputes, a faithful friend, and remarkable for his punctual attendance upon religious observances." He had been to Spain, on the private embassy to Philip II. with Christopher Wright, and he had a brother then a barrister in one of the Inns of Court in London. Therefore he was not ill-fitted by his antecedents to be received as a guest at Gothurst, shrink as we may

[1] Jardine's G. P., p. 36.   [2] Beeton's Encyclopædia, Vol. i.
[3] Narrative of the Gunpowder Plot, by J. Gerard, pp. 59, 60.
[4] Jardine, p. 38.

from the idea of such a man being admitted to the house of the gentle Lady Digby.

This intending actor in a very dark deed arrived in dull, stormy, and gloomy weather. Much rain had fallen, and the dead leaves lay wet and dank about the gables and recesses of Gothurst. There were, then, none of the modern arrangements of hot-water pipes, or other contrivances for keeping out the cold in a large stone house, of which luxurious people avail themselves so freely in these days, and the long rooms must have felt chilly, on the October nights, beyond a certain radius from the piles of burning logs in the large open grates.

People talking secrets do not find the family or social circle round the fire a very convenient place in which to interchange their confidences, and Sir Everard Digby and Guy Fawkes had good reason one evening, when supper was ended, for withdrawing to a dark and distant corner to discuss the terrible scheme in which both were so deeply engrossed ; neither Sir Everard's wife nor his chaplain, nor Father Garnet, nor either of the ladies who were staying in the house, could be permitted to hear a word of their whisperings about the details and prospects of the fatal plot ; so the two conspirators were obliged to forego the warmth of the cheerful fire until their conversation should be ended.

A damp chill, in spite of the flickering light from the burning wood, seems to have suggested to the host the probable condition of a certain fireless cellar in

Westminster; for he muttered in a low tone to his guest [1] "that he was much afraid that the Powder in the cellar was grown dank, and that some new must be provided, lest that should not take fire," words which show that, having once yielded to the temptations of Catesby, the ill-fated youth had thrown himself heart and soul into the diabolical conspiracy.   The biographer of Sir Everard Digby may well wish that he had never been guilty of any such speech.

[1] *Gunpowder Treason*, Barlow, p. 68.

CHAPTER X.

Both Catesby and Fawkes left Gothurst as October wore on ; so also did any other conspirators who may have visited it. Most of them betook themselves to White Webbs, a desolate, half-timbered house, with "many trap-doors and passages,"[1] on Enfield Chase, to the north of London, about ten miles from the cellar where their gunpowder lay.

This house had been taken, a long time before this, by Anne Vaux, and was rented by her[2] as a convenient place near London for the meeting of priests and the Catholic laity. Unfortunately, it had gradually got more into the hands of her relatives, who found it useful for other purposes. These relatives were Catesby and Tresham.

At one time White Webbs had been inhabited almost exclusively by Jesuits, being used as a centre for the renovation of vows, religious retreats, and conferences upon the affairs of their missions.[3] In his examination,[4] Father Garnet said "that it was a

[1] Cal. Sta. Pa. Dom., 1603-10, p. 256.   [2] *Ib.*, 1603-10, p. 297.
[3] *Records S. J.*, Vol. iv. p. 83, footnote.
[4] S. P. Dom.   James I., Vol. xix. n. 16

spacious house fitt to receave so great a company that should resort to him thither ; there being two bedds placed in a chamber, but thinketh there have not been above the number of 14 Jesuits at one time there."   Disastrously for himself and his order, he was obliged to confess [1] that " Catesby and Wynter, or Mr Catesby alone, came to him to White Webbs and tould this exam[t.] that there was a plott in hand for the Cath[e] cause against the King and the State," assuring him that it was something quite " lawfull " ; but that he had " dissuaded him," and that " he promised to surceasse."

It was no secret that White Webbs had been one of the principal meeting-places of the Jesuits ; therefore, after they had given up going there, and it had got into the hands of Catesby and his band of conspirators, the Government, not altogether unnaturally, supposed that the Jesuits had purposely assigned it to the plotters as a convenient place from which to carry out their dread design.

This, however, was not the case ; for, in October 1605, Father Garnet had intended to have gone thither, but finding that Catesby and his friends had established themselves in the house, most likely with the purpose of carrying out the " plott in hand," which he so greatly feared, he did not dare to go there,[2] " and so accepted the offer of Sir Everard to

---

[1] S. P. Dom. James I., Vol. xix. n. 44.
[2] *Father Garnet and the Gunpowder Plot*, p. 22.

be his tenants at Coughton." He felt the more anxious to go to Coughton because Catesby had promised to come there on the 31st;[1] and he says, " I assuredly, if they had come, had entered into the matter, and perhaps might have hindered all." As the modern Jesuit, Father Pollen, says, " to be able to do this he would, of course, have to ask Catesby to allow him to open the matter, but of success in this, considering that Catesby had of his own accord offered to tell him, he did not much doubt, and, perhaps to make the negotiations easier, he had ordered Greenway to be there too." The pity is that he had not " entered into the matter " earlier. Nervous and horror-stricken, he had refused to allow Catesby to tell him the details, when he had reason for believing a plot to be brewing ; he was tongue-tied when he afterwards met Catesby, having heard those details in confession ; yet, after being for some time at Gothurst with Catesby, it was not until Catesby had left that he came to the conclusion that he might, and that it was highly desirable that he should, beg Catesby's leave to speak to him of a subject which had been transmitted to him through the confessional, at Catesby's desire.

A zealous Catholic like Sir Everard would be comforted by learning that an envoy had been privately despatched to Rome, to explain everything to the Pope, from the point of view of the conspirators, as soon as

---

[1] *Father Garnet and the Gunpowder Plot*, p. 23. See also Lingard, Vol. vii. chap. i.

the great event should have taken place. The person selected for this purpose was Sir Edward Baynham, a member of a good Gloucestershire family, and an intimate friend of Catesby's. He had started in September. Unluckily for himself, Father Garnet, on hearing that Baynham was going to Rome, as Catesby's messenger, had encouraged it, believing,[1] "that he had procured Baynham's mission in order to inform the Pope generally of the Plot, and that this was the reason why he so confidently expected from his Holiness a prohibition of the whole business." Father Garnet's approval of Baynham's mission was thus capable of quotation, or rather misquotation, to Sir Everard Digby, and would naturally confirm the reports of his full approval of the conspiracy, as previously cited by Catesby.

This mission of Baynham to Rome was destined to bring trouble upon the conspirators, Sir Everard among them. In the indictment afterwards made against them, was the following Count.[2] "That after the destruction of the King, the Queen, the Prince, and the Royal Issue Male, the Lords Spiritual and Temporal, the Knights and Burgesses; they should notifie the same to Foreign States; and therefore Sir *Edmund Bayham*, an attainted person of Treason, and stiling himself prince of the damned crew, should be sent, and make the same known to the Pope, and crave his aid;

---

[1] Garnet's letters to the fathers and brethren, Palm Sunday, after his trial. *Antilogia*, p. 141. Jardine, p. 319.

[2] *Gunpowder Treason*, p. 13.

an Ambassador fit, both for the message and persons, to be sent betwixt the Pope and the Devil."

The last week of October must have been a time of great anxiety to Sir Everard. His companions at Gothurst appear to have been his wife and his two little children, Mrs Vaux, her sister-in-law, Anne Vaux, and Father Garnet. In the meantime he was making his preparations for the pretended coursing-meeting at Dunchurch. He was arranging how the arms, armour, and ammunition were to be conveyed in carts, covered over with other things to conceal them, and he was getting his men and horses ready for the start. He was also making preparations for the journey of his wife, children, and guests to Coughton, and for this party, alone, a good many servants and horses were required.

It is highly improbable that Catesby and the other conspirators at White Webbs kept up communications with their friend and ally at Gothurst; so most likely he was spared the anxiety of the news that on Saturday, the 26th, Lord Mounteagle had received, when at supper, an anonymous letter, warning him to "devyse some exscuse" for absenting himself from the "parleament," and to "retyere" himself into the "contri" where he might "expect the event in safti for thoghe theare be no apparance of anni stir yet i saye they shall receyve a terribel blowe this parlea-ment and yet they shall not seie who hurts them

&c. " ;[1] and that Lord Mounteagle[2] ordered a man in his service to read this letter then and there before the party assembled. Most likely, too, Sir Everard did not learn till much later that when, early in the following week, Catesby and Winter heard of the delivery of this letter of warning, they suspected Tresham of being its author; that, on Wednesday, the 30th, they summoned him, after he had been down in Northamptonshire for about a week, to come at once to White Webbs, with the full intention of poignarding him on the spot, if they could convince themselves that he had been guilty of writing and sending the warning, and that he denied it, with such firmness and so many oaths, that they hesitated to assassinate him, while still doubting his sincerity.

On Tuesday, the 29th of October, Lady Digby, her children, guests, and servants, started for Coughton, a

---

[1] Lingard, Vol. vii. chap. i.

[2] It would be beyond my sphere, nor have I the space, to go into the vexed question of the authorship of this letter. Nor can I here inquire whether Mounteagle was privy to the plot. A very affectionate letter from Mounteagle to Catesby is given in *Archæologia*, Vol. xxviii. pp. 423-4, and with it are some interesting remarks by Mr Bruce upon this subject. He infers from some, at first sight, playful words about "the ellimentes of Aier and fyre," and "the fyre of your spirite," that Mounteagle referred to the Gunpowder Plot; and he suspects that in telling Catesby that he "accumptes thy person the only sone that must Ripene our harvest," Mounteagle implies that Catesby is the chief instigator of the great blow that is to deliver the Catholics from persecution. The letter invites Catesby to meet him at Bath, and Mr Bruce says, "Catesby went to Bath about Michaelmas 1605, it now appears, in consequence of the above invitation. Percy, and, as we may conclude, Lord Mounteagle, met him there." This must have been either immediately before, or immediately after, Catesby revealed the Plot to Sir Everard Digby. Mr Bruce thinks before.

journey of some fifty miles. In mentioning Coughton, it may be worth noticing how many of those whose names are more or less connected, even indirectly, with the story of the Gunpowder Plot were related to each other. The owner of Coughton, Thomas Throckmorton, was a cousin both of Catesby's and of Tresham's, although he never had anything to do with the conspiracy. He was also a cousin of the Vaux family, his grandmother having been a daughter of a Lord Vaux of Harrowden.

It being known that Father Garnet was to be at Coughton for All Hallows' Eve, All Saints' Day, and All Souls' Day, many Catholics in the neighbourhood came thither in order to attend mass and go to their religious duties.

The feast of All-Hallows used then to be kept with some solemnity, and it was Father Garnet's custom on such occasions to sing the mass,[1] where it was practicable and safe to do so, and also to preach. Lingard[2] thought that it was " plain that Garnet had acted very imprudently at Coughton, probably had suffered expressions to escape him which, though sufficiently obscure then, might now prove his acquaintance with the plot; for he writes to Anne Vaux, on March 4th, ' there is some talk here of a discourse made by me or Hall; I fear it is that which I made at Coughton.'—Autib. 144." He certainly recited

---

[1] *Father Garnet and the Gunpowder Plot*, p. 23.
[2] Hist. of Eng., Vol. vii. Appendix H.H.H.

the prayer for the conversion of England, which had been authorised for that purpose by Cardinal Allen; and, although it was used that day throughout the world, being taken from the office of the feast,[1] his doing so was afterwards used in evidence against him as an act of treason.   The words

> " Gentem auferte perfidam
> Credentium de finibus,
> Ut Christo laudes debitas
> Persolvamus alacriter." [2]

from a hymn in the Office, had certainly no reference to the Gunpowder Plot.

On Saturday, the second of November, Sir Everard was up early, superintending the arrangements for his start a day or two later, as well as the putting away of valuables at Gothurst, and the closing of the house in preparation for a long absence.   Already some of his horses and men had been sent on to Dunchurch, together with his greyhounds, which were all-important for appearance sake.

Possibly my readers may have experienced the sensation caused by the unexpected and very sudden arrival of a hitherto invariably welcome friend at a moment when his presence was not exactly convenient.   Now few men, if any, were so dear to Sir Everard as Father Gerard, and he used to be specially welcome when he occasionally rode to Gothurst early

[1] *Father Garnet and the Gunpowder Plot,* p. 23.
[2] See Jardine, p. 217.

in a morning to say a mass in its chapel; but when
Sir Everard saw "his brother," as he usually called
him, riding up to Gothurst on that particular
Saturday morning, and when he was told by the
Father that he had come to say his mass in his
chapel on this All Souls' Day, he wished, for the
first time, that his favourite guest had not taken
it into his head to come on that Saturday morning,
"of all Saturday mornings." He knew that all the
chapel furniture, as well as the chalices, vestments,
and other necessaries for saying mass, had been
carefully hidden away, with the exception of those
which had been sent on to Dunchurch with a view
to having mass said during his stay there. Besides,
everything was in a state of fuss and confusion in
anticipation of the start; and, as his family were to remain for some time at Coughton, the house was on the
point of being shut up. One reason why the presence
of Father Gerard might be particularly unwelcome
just then was that, about that time, Digby may
have been superintending the "great provision of
armour and shot, which he sent before him in a cart
with some trusty servants" to Dunchurch.[1]

When told that it would be impossible to have mass
at Gothurst that morning, Father Gerard, in addition
to his expression of disappointment—for All Souls' is
a Feast upon which no priest likes to miss saying
mass — may have shown signs of embarrassment;

---

[1] *Narrative of the G. P.*, by Father Gerard, p. 92.

for the presence of a stranger prevented his asking his host the reasons. As soon as an opportunity offered itself, Father Gerard beckoned to Sir Everard to follow him into a room in which they would be alone.[1] There he told him that he could not understand the sudden alteration in the arrangements of his house, the putting away of so many things as if a long absence was contemplated, the removal of the family to Coughton, the preparations for a journey to Dunchurch with such an unusual number of men and horses, and—now that he came to think of it—the sales of land and stock, of which Sir Everard had spoken to him not long ago, as if to raise money for some special purpose. All this, as an intimate friend, Father Gerard was in a position to say to his so-called " brother " ; and he ventured to go further and inquire whether he " had something in hand for the Catholic cause."

Sir Everard's answer was " No, there is nothing in hand that I know of, or can tell you of."

Father Gerard then replied that he had some reason to feel anxious on the subject, as Sir Everard was much too careful a man to injure his estate by leaving it understocked, and by selling any portion of it in order to purchase horses, hire men, and spend money in other ways, unless he had some great object in view for what he believed to be the good of the Catholic cause ; and, added the Father, " Look well

[1] *Life of Father J. Gerard*, p. ccxxxvi.-vii.

that you follow counsel in your proceedings, or else you may hurt both yourself and the cause.

Ah! if some such words as these had been addressed to him by Father Garnet at the time he first joined the conspiracy, how much misery he might have been saved.

Perhaps Father Gerard's persistence in suspecting and implying that Sir Everard had "something in hand," after he had avowed that he had "nothing" may have irritated him, for he replied, with dignity: "I respect the Catholic cause much more than my own commodity, as it should well appear whenever I undertake anything."

Father Gerard was not to be put off in this manner, and he asked once more, " whether there were anything to be done," and, if so, whether help was expected from any foreign power.

Sir Everard was becoming hard pressed, and raising one finger, he replied, " 1 will not adventure so much in hope thereof."

Distressed and anxious, Father Gerard then said— "I pray God you follow counsel in your doings. If there be any matter in hand, doth Mr Walley know of it?" Walley was the name by which Father Garnet, the Provincial of the Jesuits, was spoken of at that time.

Digby's answer was a curious one, unless Catesby had not told him the name of the particular Jesuit whose approval he pretended to have obtained. " In truth, I think he doth not."

Then, said Father Gerard, "In truth, Sir Everard Digby, if there should be anything in hand, and that you retire yourself and company into Warwickshire, as into a place of most safety, I should think you did not perform the part of a friend to some of your neighbours not far off, and persons that, as you know, deserve every respect, and to whom you have professed much friendship, that they are left behind, and have not any warning to make so much provision for their own safety as were needful in such a time, but to defend themselves from rogues."

Sir Everard, who must have sincerely wished that his friend had stayed away, replied—"I warrant you it shall not need."

At this assurance Father Gerard felt rather more satisfied, and shortly afterwards he rode away, much to the relief of his host, who at any other time would have pressed him to remain as his guest.

Sir Everard stayed at home over the Sunday— whether he rode to some other Catholic's house to hear Mass on that day does not appear—and on the Monday [1] he started for Dunchurch, accompanied by his page, William Ellis, Richard Day, "his receaver," and five servants.

He can scarcely have left Gothurst in the best of spirits, as he must have reflected that, for the first time, he had prevaricated and dissembled, if not actually lied, to the man he considered his best friend,

[1] S. P. Gunpowder Plot Book, Part I. No. 108.

the very priest who had received him into the Church;
that he had parted with him on a far from satisfactory
footing, and that he had been obliged to send him
away from his house without saying Mass on a day
of such importance to all good Catholics as that
devoted to the memory of and intercession for the
dead.

Besides these, he had other good reasons for
depression as he rode away from his beautiful home;
he must have known that, at best, he was starting
upon a very perilous enterprise; whether it succeeded
or failed, many of his party might fall on the field in
prosecuting it, if nothing worse happened to them;
and it may be that, as he caught a last glimpse of
Gothurst in the distance, the thought occurred to his
mind that he would never see it again.

The journey and his plans, however, would soon
distract his thoughts. The plot itself, too, would
occupy his mind above all other subjects. In each
of the conspirators it seems to have produced a sort
of intoxication. Stow says that,[1] "being drunke
with the same folly," Sir Everard Digby "went to
the appointed hunting at Don-church."

Then there were his arms and his followers to be
thought of and looked after. It is difficult in these
days to realise that, some three hundred years ago,
the servants, retainers, and to some extent the tenants,
of large landowners were expected to fight when

[1] Stow's *Annales*, p. 879.

required by their lords. It is true that the feudal system had then almost ceased to exist; but although vassalage had been considerably limited more than a hundred years earlier by Henry VII., it was not abolished by statute until more than fifty years after the time of which I am writing.

To carry ourselves back to that period, we have to imagine our gardeners, under-gardeners, grooms, stable-helpers, gamekeepers, and perhaps footmen, strapping on broad-swords, carrying pikes, putting on such armour as could be provided, and going forth to possible battle, some on foot, and some mounted on hacks, coach-horses, cart-horses, and ponies, not a few of which would be taken up from grass for the purpose.

In this particular instance, the motley troop, with the exception of the seven men accompanying Sir Everard, had been already sent on, ostensibly to assist at the coursing and, perhaps, hawking, which was to take place at Dunchurch, while some of them were to attend to the wants of the guests. As to Sir Everard's own journey, most of his attendants rode; but one of them, Richard Hollis, the under cook, walked, leading the "trunckehorse," on which his master's personal clothing was slung.[1] This trunk, wrote Sir Everard,[2] "had in it cloathes of mine, as, a white Sattin Dublet cut with

<hr>

[1] S. P. Dom. James I., Vol. xvii.; G. P. Book, Part II. n. 138.
[2] Sir E. Digby's Letters, p. 172.

purple, a Jerkin and Hoase of De-roy colour sattin, laid very thicke with Gold-lace, there were other garments in it of mine, with a new black Winter Gown of my wife's, there was also in the trunk £300 in money."

On reaching Dunchurch, Sir Everard took his supper alone,[1] and it is not likely that his reflections as he did so were of the calmest or the happiest.

Now that it takes considerably less than a couple of hours to travel from London to Rugby, it seems curious that no news of the difficulties of the conspirators at White Webbs should have reached those at Dunchurch ; but it would have been dangerous in the extreme to have sent a letter describing them, and neither of the principals concerned wished to go far from London until they had seen what would happen.

Their anxiety on Wednesday, the 30th of October, had been increased by Tresham's eagerness in urging Catesby to give up the plot, which he said was discovered, and to leave England, promising that he should always " live upon his purse " ;[2] and by his imploring Winter to begone, on Saturday, the 2nd of November. On the Saturday or the Sunday, Winter again met Tresham in Lincoln's Inn Walks, when the latter declared that they were all lost men, unless they saved themselves by instant flight. Through another source, Catesby and Winter learned, on the Sunday,

---

[1] S. P. Gunpowder Plot Book, Part I. No. 108.
[2] Tresham's Declaration, Nov. 13. S.P.O. Jardine's *G. P.*, 93.

that the letter of warning which had been received by
Lord Mounteagle had been shown to the king, who
considered the matter of the highest importance, but
enjoined the strictest secrecy. The leading conspir-
tors, therefore, were in a state of great consternation
on the Sunday, two days before the explosion was to
take place. Of all this, however, Sir Everard Digby
knew nothing.

Either late on the Monday night, or early on the
Tuesday morning, several of Sir Everard's friends
assembled at the Inn [1] where he was staying, at Dun-
church ; among these were Throckmorton,[2] Sir Robert
Digby of Coleshill, James Digby, George Digby,
Stephen Littleton and Humphrey Littleton. On the
Tuesday morning,[3] mass was said by Father Hart, a
Jesuit, who had been a secular priest, and had been
introduced to Fathers of the Society of Jesus by
Father Strange,[4] Sir Everard Digby's own chaplain.
The party, after breakfast, hunted or coursed, so that,
although the " hunting-match " was a mere cover for
other designs, it actually took place for one day.

It seems that Sir Everard took opportunities of confiding to his friends the news that a scheme was on
foot for asserting the rights of Catholics ; that active
measures of some sort were to be taken on their behalf
immediately in London, probably on the following day,

---

[1] S. P. Gunpowder Plot Book, Part II. No. 121.
[2] S. P. Gunpowder Plot Book, Part I. No. 108.
[3] *Cal. Sta. Pa.*, 1603-10, p. 263.
[4] *Records of the Eng. Prov. S. J.*, Series I. p. 169.

and that very possibly the sportsmen assembled at Dunchurch might receive a message, summoning them to arms about Thursday or Friday; to some he told more, and to some less, according to their dispositions and the spirit in which they received his information.

The sportsmen naturally conversed together upon the intelligence they had received, although a few of the more enlightened were to some extent tongue-tied, and the whole party gradually became in an anxious and excited state.[1] This was especially the case when they all met together at supper at the inn after hunting, and more particularly as they talked in groups over their tankards when supper was finished.

Sir Everard Digby, his relative, Sir Robert Digby, and one of the Littletons, withdrew from the rest of the party to play cards [2] together in a room by themselves.

A little distraction must have been very desirable for Sir Everard's mind in its state of tension. As we know, he was usually an excellent card-player, but we may doubt whether he played his best on this occasion. He believed that the horrible catastrophe was either at that moment taking place, had just taken place, or was to take place immediately. Perhaps, as he sat quietly playing cards, numbers of

---

[1] Jardine, p. 108.

[2] S. P. Dom. James I., Nov. 1605, Vol. xvi. No. 94.

men whom he had known personally, or at least by sight, had just been put to a horrible death, among them his king, who had knighted him. The poor princes, innocent boys, might be lying beside him, dead also, crushed and mangled. Many among the slain would be almost as innocent, so far as any desire to injure the Catholics was concerned. Of course, Digby had made up his mind that the explosion was a necessary and even a heroic undertaking; but, if bloodguiltiness there were in it, he could not help knowing that it rested on his own head. Can one help imagining that, while he played cards, he must have devoutly wished, now that it was too late, that he could prevent such a fearful slaughter, or that he had never heard of or conspired in the plot? Let us hope that the game of cards diverted such thoughts; yet who could blame him if, with such matters on his mind, he forgot to follow suit?

At any rate, while he shuffled the cards, grim realities would be apt to present themselves to his memory. When would he hear of the great event? It would only take place that afternoon or evening at soonest. Dunchurch was about eighty miles from London. Catesby would hardly despatch a messenger until he had something definite to relate as to the result of the catastrophe upon the minds of the populace, the officials, and the army; so it might be almost another twenty-four hours before Digby could receive the news; yet such an appalling massacre would be talked about, right and left, and the intelligence would be passed on from one place to another very rapidly; it was possible, therefore, that tidings—most likely meagre, exaggerated, and untrustworthy tidings—might reach Dunchurch, in some form or other, on the following morning. As the day wore on they might, perhaps, see Rookwood himself, or one of his servants entrusted with a letter, for he had placed relays of horses on the road between London and Dunchurch.[1] Or Percy or Christopher Wright might appear, as Sir Everard had sent a servant with a couple of horses to meet them at Hockliffe.[2]

But it was useless to disturb the mind as to the particular moment at which the news could arrive ; possibly there was not at present any to send ; therefore it would be wisest, Sir Everard might tell himself, to divert his mind with his game, to go early to bed, and get a good night's rest, so as to be fresh and ready for whatever might happen on the following day.

Suddenly there was a sound without of many and hurried footsteps ; the door opened, and in rushed Catesby, Percy, John Wright, Christopher Wright, Rookwood, and Winter, mud - bespattered, heavily armed, and with grave faces. Acton and Grant came in after them.

It was clear, at a glance, that something was

---

[1] Jardine, p. 105.　　　　　[2] *Ib.*, p. 106, footnote.

wrong; and Sir Everard looked eagerly to Catesby for information. Instead of speaking, Catesby took him by the arm and led him out of the room, saying nothing until he had found an empty chamber, which they both entered alone.

Exactly what was said to Sir Everard by Catesby can never be known; but what he had to tell him, if he chose to do so, was much as follows.

On the evening, or late in the afternoon, of the previous day (Monday, November 4th), Catesby, Rookwood, John and Christopher Wright, Thomas Winter, Percy, and Keyes, who formed the band of conspirators in and about London, received notice from Fawkes that the cellar in which their gunpowder was laid had just been visited by the Lord Chamberlain—the already mentioned Earl of Suffolk, and Lord Mounteagle. Catesby and John Wright immediately fled, and started for Dunchurch. Christopher Wright, Rookwood, Keyes, Winter, and Percy waited in London to observe what would happen. They hung about during the night, and at about four or five o'clock in the morning [1] they discovered that Fawkes had been arrested. Then Christopher Wright and Percy started for Dunchurch.

Only Rookwood, Winter, and Keyes now remained. They were staying in the same lodging, and they determined to wait and see what the morning would

[1] *Somer's Tracts*, Vol. ii. p. 105.

bring forth.[1] On going out early, they found the populace in a state of great consternation and terror.[2] "The news of Fawkes's apprehension, and exaggerated rumours of a frightful plot discovered, were spread in every direction." Guards and soldiers protected all the streets and roads leading to the palace, and no one, excepting officials, was permitted to pass them. The whole town was in a state of excitement. Keyes sprang on his horse and galloped after the other fugitives; but Rookwood, who had taken care to place relays of horses along the road to Dunchurch, remained longer, in order to carry the latest news to his fellow-conspirators in Warwickshire. At ten[3] o'clock it became evident that it would be dangerous to delay an instant longer, so he also mounted his horse and galloped away.

The last of all to fly was Thomas Winter.[4] Of his movements Catesby could have told Sir Everard nothing; but he left London very soon after Rookwood, and eventually joined his fellow-conspirators at Huddington.

When Rookwood had gone about three miles beyond Highgate, he overtook Keyes, and rode

[1] A man named Tatnell deposed that "he met 2 gentlemen that morning near Lincoln's Inn, and one said, 'God's woundes! we are wonderfully besett, and all ys marred.'" S. P. Dom. James I., Vol. xvi. ; G. P. Bk., No. 11.

[2] Jardine, p. 105.

[3] S. P. Dom. James I., Vol. xvii. n. 9. See also Vol. xvi. Nos. 11 and 13.

[4] Gardiner. *Hist. Eng.*, Vol. i. p. 257.

with him into Bedfordshire, where Keyes took a different road, as is conjectured by Jardine,[1] for "Lord Mordaunt's house at Turvey, where his wife resided." Somewhere in the neighbourhood of Brickhill, a place not far from Fenny Stratford, Rookwood overtook Percy, the two Wrights, and Catesby, after which these five rode together to Ashby St Leger, Lady Catesby's place in Northamptonshire, which was very near to Dunchurch. Roughly speaking, the course of the fugitives had been not very wide of the route of the London and North-Western railway from Euston to Rugby, and while all did it quickly, Rookwood's pace was exceptionally fast, as he rode about eighty miles between eleven in the morning and six in the evening, averaging more than eleven miles an hour, including stoppages to change horses. He himself stated that he[2] "rode thirty miles of one horse in two hours," and that "Percy and John Wright cast off their cloaks and threw them into the hedge to ride the more speedily."

The five fugitives entered Lady Catesby's house just as she and her party, which included Robert Winter and Acton, were sitting down to supper. The news of the arrest of Fawkes and the failure of the main design having been announced by the new arrivals, who, as Jardine says, were[3] "fatigued and

---

[1] *G. P.*, p. 106.
[2] *Rookwood's Examination*, Dec. 2, 1605. S.P.O. Jardine, *G. P.*, p. 106.
[3] P. 108.

covered with dirt,"—Father Gerard, again, in describing their ride, writes of[1] "the foulness of the winter ways"—no time was lost over the hurried meal, during which a short conference took place, ending in a decision that the whole party should ride off immediately to Dunchurch, taking with them all the arms that were in the house.

[1] *Narrative G. P.*, p. 106.

CHAPTER XI.

IT is to be lamented that Catesby, not content with giving an account of the failure of the plot to Sir Everard Digby, added to it a lie. In his examination,[1] Digby stated that Catesby "told him that now was the time for men to stirre in the Catholick cause, for though the sayd Ro. Katesbie had bin disappointed of his first intention, yet there was such a pudder bredd in the State by *ye death of the King and the Earle of Salisburie*, as if true Catholiques would now stirre, he doubted not but they might procure to them selves good conditions. Wherefore by all the bondes of frendshippe to him self and all which that cause might require at this examt[s.] handes, he urged this exam[t] to proceede in that businesse as him self and all that companie would do, and as he had great assurance all other Catholiques in those parts would do the like : telling me that there were two gentlemen in the companie, naming the Littletons, that would bring 1000 men the next day."

The King and Lord Salisbury both killed, and a promise of a thousand men from one family alone !

[1] S. P. Dom. James I., Vol. xvi. No. 94.

This was something to start with, even though the parliament had not been destroyed; and in the general "pudder" that had been "bredd," the Catholics might possibly succeed in obtaining good terms, if not the reins of government. So was Sir Everard persuaded by Catesby, who was not only a traitor to his country, but a deceiver of his friends.

The conspirators assumed that their names would be soon, if not already, known to the Government, as Fawkes would almost certainly be tortured until he revealed them; and, brave as he was, there was no saying whether he would be able to withstand the temptations of putting an end to his agonies on the rack by giving the names of his employers and accomplices.

Besides all this, Catesby pretended that their case was by no means hopeless. No Catholics were more discontented with the Government than those in Wales and the English counties which bordered on it; few, again, as a body, were more powerful. Let the party at Dunchurch, therefore, start at once, said Catesby, with their servants and retainers, ride through Warwickshire and Worcestershire into Wales, rallying the Catholic gentry with their followers to their standard as they went along; and, so soon as they should be in considerable numbers, let them proclaim a general insurrection of the Catholics of England. Were it once to be known that a Catholic army was established in the West, others would certainly be raised in different parts of the country.

One man of power and influence he felt sure he could count upon: this was Talbot[1] of Grafton—a place not far from Coughton. Talbot was a zealous Catholic; he was heir presumptive to the Earldom of Shrewsbury; and his wife was a daughter of the Sir William Petre who had been Secretary of State to Queen Mary. He would be the more likely to join them, as he had suffered imprisonment and penalties for his religion under Elizabeth. Another reason for hoping for his adherence was the fact that his son-in-law, Robert Winter, was already one of the sworn conspirators, and had slept at his house only two nights earlier. Percy also came in and said that he was certain "all forces in those parts about Mr Talbot would assist" them. This assurance evidently weighed considerably with Sir Everard; for he afterwards wrote[2]:—"We all thought if we could procure Mr Talbot to rise that . . . that was not little, because we had in our Company his Son-in-Law, who gave us some hope of, and did not much doubt of it."

Of one thing there could be no sort of question; if action was to be taken at all, it must be taken at once, and without the delay of a moment: time was everything; the rapid journey of the conspirators from London was already much in their favour, and

---

[1] S. P. Dom. James I., Vol. xvi. No. 94.
[2] *Papers or Letters of Sir E. Digby*, n. 9.

this advantage would be thrown away if there were to be any dallying or indecision. Grafton, Talbot's place, was about five and twenty miles from where they were then standing, and it would be of the utmost importance to reach it, or send an envoy there, early the next morning.

Before condemning Digby for proceeding further, now that the main plot had failed, we must remember that he had sworn to be faithful to the conspiracy, and that, in their present straits, it might have been as much as his life was worth to refuse to go on with Catesby and his fellows. We have seen how narrowly Tresham escaped Catesby's dagger.

There were others, however, not bound by any oath or promise, whose immediate support was required. The so-called hunting-party assembled at the inn must needs be enlisted in the service. Scraps of the terrible news had already been passed from one to the other; for many, if not most of them, were well acquainted with the fugitives from London, and were eagerly questioning them concerning particulars. Digby and Catesby found the party in a state of great excitement when they went to summon them formally to join in the insurrection.

To the surprise of Sir Everard Digby and the disgust of Catesby, instead of rallying as one man to the call to arms, almost as one man they refused, with horror, to have anything whatever to do with an enterprise which had begun with an attempt at wholesale massacre, and promised to end in the hanging, drawing, and quartering of all who had a share in it

Sir Everard's own uncle, Sir Robert Digby,[1] was the very first to charge the conspirators with being a band of traitors, and to order his men and horses to be got ready for immediate departure. With scarcely any exceptions, the other guests followed his example, not only condemning the treason, but also reproaching the traitors with having gravely injured the Catholic cause. To join in a legitimate warfare, even a civil warfare, was one thing; to acquiesce in an attempted murder, a murder on a gigantic scale, and to endeavour to profit by the terror brought about by that attempted murder, was quite another. And besides all this; if they complained of having been invited to hunt and hawk at Dunchurch on false pretences, who could blame them? No doubt they were very angry. Besides, they were but mortal, and to be suddenly disturbed and required to decide hastily upon a most serious question, involving immediate action, is more disagreeable during the process of digestion, just after the principal meal of the day, than at any other time; and as the country squires, who had come to Dunchurch to enjoy good sport, scrambled into their uncleaned, and very likely but half-dried

---

[1] He afterwards "assisted in taking prisoners" of some of the conspirators. S. P Dom. James I., Vol. xvi. ; G. P. Bk., n. 142.

riding-clothes, and went out into the dark, damp night, to mount their horses for long, dreary journeys over bad roads towards their homes, they cannot have felt in the best of tempers.

It may be worth noticing here, that Sir Robert was not the only member of the Digby family who gave the Government assistance in respect to the Gunpowder Plot.[1] "Lord Harrington, who had the care of the Princess Elizabeth, having received some intimation of an attempt to seize her, immediately sent up John Digby, a younger son of Sir George Digby, to court, with an account of all he knew; where the young gentleman told the tale so well as to acquire thereby the King's good graces, who not long after knighted, employed him in long negotiation in Spain, and Sep. 15th, 1622, created him Earl of Bristol. His son was the famous George Digby, &c." Accordingly, if the Gunpowder Plot marred the fortunes of one branch of the Digby family, it made those of another!

Sir Everard was as much astonished as he was dispirited at finding that the "powder-action," far from being approved of, was repudiated with horror by the friends whom he had assembled at Dunchurch. He had expected them to have looked at the matter in a very different light. He can scarcely have failed now to see that, even if the plot had succeeded, the Catholics, as a body, would have condemned it, and

[1] *Biographia Britannica,* Vol. iii. p. 184.

refused to profit by it. Still he was weak enough to yield to Catesby's urgent requests to proceed with the insurrection and to endeavour to raise forces in Warwickshire, Worcestershire, and Wales.

The band of conspirators, with the very few friends who chose to stay with them, then held a council of war; they were "prepared to stand in Armes and raise rebellion,"[1] and they determined to start at once on their journey, so as to enlist Mr Talbot to their support, as early as possible on the morrow, and give him the whole day to rally his numerous retainers round the standard of the little army of traitors and would-be murderers.

Although five of the party had just ridden eighty miles at considerable speed, they swung themselves into the saddle again for a long night's march. Even if the whole hunting-party had remained there would not have been a large body of horsemen; in all the number present at Dunchurch was only eighty;[2] but some of the friends who had refused to have anything to do with the expedition were influential men, who could soon have raised substantial troops, even from among their own retainers. The party that actually started from Dunchurch under the command of the conspirators, according to Sir Everard Digby,[3] "were not above fiftie horse."

---

[1] Stow's *Annales*, p. 880.

[2] Examination of J. Fowes, S. P. Dom. James I., Vol. xvi. n. 19. Letter enclosed from the Sheriff and Justices of Warwickshire.

[3] S. P. Dom. James I., G. P. Bk., Part II. n. 135.   H.

It was a wretched little cavalcade : if it had anything military about it, it was more of a recruiting party than an army, and its stealthy creeping forth from the inn, that November night, in darkness and dejection, was very different from the triumphant dash of the entire " hunting-party " upon Combe Abbey, to seize the Princess Elizabeth and take her from the keeping of Lord Harington, which had been laid down in the programme. The discovery of the plot, the arrest of Fawkes, and the seizure of the gunpowder was bad enough ; and now, the refusal of the trusted, influential, and powerful Catholic landowners who had been assembled at Dunchurch to have hand or part in what they considered a detestable rebellion, added tenfold to the disappointment of Sir Everard and his companions.

The road of the rebels lay through Warwick, and it was remembered that there, in the stable of a poor horse-breaker of cavalry re-mounts, they would be able to supply themselves with fresh horses. Even two of the leading conspirators—I wish I could say that Sir Everard Digby had been one of them—winced at this act of felony ! Rookwood, as he subsequently admitted in examination,[1] " meant not to adventure himself in stealing any " horses, as he had already fifteen or sixteen ; and Robert Winter[2] tried to persuade Catesby " to let it alone, alleging that it would

[1] Jardine, p. 111, footnote.
[2] S. P., Robert Winter's Confession, 21 Jan, 1605-6.

make a great uproar in the country, and that once done," they "might not rest anywhere, the country would so rise about" them.

Catesby's reply was ominous. "Some of us may not look back."

"But others," said Winter, "I hope, may, and therefore, I pray you, let this alone."

Then Catesby spoke words in ill accordance with those which he had used to encourage Digby before leaving Dunchurch. "What! hast thou any hope, Robin? I assure thee there is none that knoweth of this action but shall perish."

On reaching Warwick, they left the trunk-horses with their attendants[1] at the entrance to the town, in case their intended raid should lead to any scrimmage or retaliation; and then they proceeded to the horse-breakers' stable and stole nine or ten horses. This took about half-an-hour, and when the robbery had been accomplished, they sent back for the trunk-horses and proceeded on their night-journey.

It was not far from Warwick to Norbrook, the house of John Grant, one of the conspirators. Here they made a brief halt, and, on entering the hall, they found two tables furnished with muskets and armour.[2] After taking a very short rest—William Handy, one of Sir Everard's servants, says half-an-hour;[3] but

---

[1] See the examination of Richard Hollis, S. P. Gunpowder Treason, 1605, Part II. No. 138.

[2] S. P. Gunpowder Plot Book, Part II. No. 121.   [3] *Ib.*

Jardine says an hour or two,[1] and Richard Hollis, a servant of Sir Everard's, says, " some howres," [2]—the cavalcade again started on its dark nocturnal march. The intention of its leaders was to ride to Huddington, near Droitwich, the house of Robert Winter; and on the way thither, to send a messenger a little to the right of their road, with a letter to Father Garnet at Coughton, explaining the desperate position in which they were placed. On arriving at Huddington, their host was to be sent to his father-in-law, Talbot of Grafton, to inform him of all that had happened, and to urge him to join the insurrection with as many men as he could muster.

Some time after sunrise, which does not take place at that time of the year till after seven o'clock, they drew near Alcester, and despatched their messenger to Coughton. The man chosen was Catesby's servant, Thomas Bates, the only menial who was a sworn conspirator. Besides the letter to Father Garnet, he was entrusted with one for Lady Digby, written by her husband.

The most trying part of Sir Everard Digby's long and gloomy ride must have been to pass within a couple of miles of his wife and children, as he went through Alcester in the early morning, without going to see them. Well-horsed, as he was, it might almost appear that he could have made time to visit

---

[1] P. 111.   [2] S. P. Gunpowder Plot Book, Part II. No. 138.

them for at least a few minutes, and then ridden on to Huddington, where the expedition was to make a long halt.　Did he hesitate to go to Coughton through fear of Catesby, or was he afraid to trust himself in the presence of his wife ?

When Bates arrived at Coughton, he was taken at once to Father Garnet, who was in the hall,[1] and he handed the letter to the priest, who opened it and read it in silence.

I will give Father Garnet's own description[2] of this letter, which "was subscribed by Sir E. Digby and Catesbye."　"The effect of this letter was to excuse their rashness, and required my assistance in Wales, and persuade me to make a party, saying that if I had scrupulosity or desire to free myself or my Order from blame and let them now perish, I should follow after myselfe and all Catholics."

While Father Garnet was reading the letter, Father Greenway came in and asked what was the matter. Thereupon Father Garnet read the letter in the hearing of Bates, and said to Greenway, "They would have blown up the Parliament House, and were discovered and we all utterly undone."　Father Greenway replied that in that case "there was no tarrying for himself and Garnet."　Then Bates begged Father Greenway to

---

[1] For accounts of Bates's visit to Coughton, see Bates's Examination, Jan. 13, 1605-6 ; Hall's Confession, Mar. 6, 1605-6 ; and Jardine's G. P., pp. 167-8.

[2] S. P. Dom. James I., Vol. xviii. n. 87 ; Exam. of H. Garnet, Feb. 13, 1605-6.　See Records S. J., Vol. iv. p. 146.

go with him to Catesby, his master, if he really wished
to help him. Father Greenway answered that he
"would not forbear to go unto him though it were
to suffer a thousand deaths, but that it would overthrow the state of the whole society of the Jesuits'
order."

When Father Garnet had read the letter to Father
Greenway, the latter exclaimed, " All Catholics are
undone."

Father Garnet, in an intercepted letter, gives a
pathetic account of the effect of her husband's letter
upon Lady Digby.[1] " My Lady Digby came. What
did she? Alas! what, but cry."

He tells us, too, the answer which he gave to the
messenger, Bates. " That I marvelled they would
enter into such wicked actions and not be ruled by the
advice of friends and order of His Holiness generally
given to all, and that I could not meddle but wished
them to give over, and if I could do anything in such
a matter (as I neither could nor would) it were in vain
now to attempt it."

Then the two fathers drew aside and talked together
for half-an-hour, while Bates walked up and down the
hall. After this, Father Greenway went to prepare
himself for his journey, and presently came out with
Bates, mounted a horse, and rode with him to
Huddington in order to see his penitent, Catesby.

Father Greenway's riding companion was not only

____

[1] "Father Garnet and the Gunpowder Plot," Pollen, p. 23.

one of the conspirators, but had helped [1] "in making provision of their powder." He confessed in prison the whole matter of his having been sent by Catesby, his master, with a letter to Father Garnet at Coughton, and that Father Greenway had accompanied him from that house to Huddington in order to visit Catesby.

We must return to Sir Everard, as he rode from Alcester to Huddington. One of his servants, named Hardy, came up to him, during this part of his journey, and asked him [2] what was to become "of him and the rest of his poore servants," who, as he pitifully protested, had not been "privy to this bloudy faction." Such a question, although it did not savour of mutiny, showed an inclination to defection, and must have added considerably to his master's discouragement. The answer which he gave to it was as follows:—"I believe you were not;" *i.e.*, privy to the plot; "but now there is no remedy." The servant then let out that it was not solely on his own account that he had asked the question; for he went on to implore his master to yield himself to the king's mercy; whereupon Sir Everard said sharply that he would permit no servant to utter such words in his presence.

Catesby and his band of warriors, brigands, horse-stealers, professors of physical force, or whatever else the reader may please to call them, reached Huddington

---

[1] *Narrative of the Gunpowder Plot*, Gerard, p. 84.
[2] S. P. Gunpowder Plot Book, Part II. No. 121.

about two o'clock on the Wednesday afternoon.[1] The
first thing they did was to place sentinels round the
house,[2] which was rendered suitable for defence by
its moat.[3] Then they proceeded to take their first
long rest, that is to say, until early on the following
morning, a sorely needed period of refreshment and
repose, especially for those who had ridden the whole
way from London. Where so large a party can have
been entertained and lodged at Huddington, it is
difficult to understand, as the house, which is now
used as a farm, rich as it is in carved oak, is not, and
probably never was, a large one.

During the first few hours of their stay, however, the
leading conspirators were awaiting the return of the
envoy from Grafton with too much anxiety to be able
to sleep or take their ease. Almost everything hung
upon the reply of Talbot. The assistance of the
large number of men and horses which it was in
his power to supply was of the utmost importance
at that very critical moment, and on his influence
and example might depend the attitude of all the
Catholic gentry in Worcestershire, as well as in
several of the counties adjoining it.

Just as it was beginning to grow dark, two horse-

---

[1] The G. P., Jardine, p. 111.

[2] S. P. Gunpowder Plot Book, Part II. n. 121.

[3] "The mansion-house, which is moated round, but now in a very
ruinous condition, having been much neglected ever since the gunpowder treason in 1606, in which plot the Winters were deeply concerned." *Nash's Worcestershire*, Vol. i. p. 592.

men rode up to the door of Huddington, and the ambassadors, Robert Winter and Stephen Littleton, entered the house. Sir Everard Digby and Catesby eagerly went up to them and asked the result of their embassy; but, before they had had time to reply, it was evident from the expression of their faces that they brought bad news. On reaching Grafton, said Winter, they found that the report of the Gunpowder Plot and its failure had arrived there before them. Their approach had been observed, perhaps watched for, and, as they rode up to the curious " L "-shaped house, with its gothic chapel at one end of it, Sir John Talbot himself stood at its arched doorway,[1] with a frown upon his countenance.[2] As soon as they were within earshot, he forbade them to enter his house. He then told them that he had already heard of the plot, which he condemned in the strongest terms, together with all that had been, or were, connected with it, whether personal friends of his own or otherwise. He was a very zealous Catholic, and he regarded the whole conspiracy as one of the worst evils that could possibly have befallen the Catholics of England, since it would bring scandal upon their very name, and increase the persecutions which they suffered.

[1] " Like the gateway of the schools of Oxford, but of much more antient date." *Nash's Worcestershire*, Vol. i. p. 258.

[2] Possibly he may have remembered that a former owner of Grafton, Sir Humphrey Stafford, had been executed at Tyburn for treason, rather more than a century earlier.

When Robert Winter not only defended the plot but urged Sir John to join the band of Catholics who intènded to make a struggle for their freedom, his father-in-law threatened that, although he was a Catholic, a neighbour, and his son-in-law, he would have him arrested if he did not make off as quickly as his horse's legs could carry him.[1]

As soon as Robert Winter had finished his story, the conspirators were plunged into the deepest dejection. Not one of them would be more depressed by the bad news than Sir Everard Digby. The rest were all more or less of a wild adventurous spirit, and probably had realised sooner than he to what a desperate issue the conspiracy had already arrived ; but Sir Everard had been deceived by Catesby into believing the king and Salisbury to be dead, and until now he had clung to the hope that the best Catholics in England, when they heard of what had been attempted, would unite with himself and his companions in a holy war. Sir John Talbot was the type of Catholic by whose side he had hoped to fight for the faith, a man full of zeal and unflinching energy for the Catholic cause, as well as an honourable English gentleman. It was chiefly on the guarantee of his adherence and assistance, too, that Sir Everard had consented to Catesby's entreaties to ride away from Dunchurch with the rest of the conspirators, and

[1] The greater part of Grafton was burned down about 1710. *Nash,* Vol. i. p. 158.

attempt to raise the Catholics against the Government ; and now Sir John Talbot repudiated Sir Everard, his friends, and his actions.

A more gloomy party than that at Huddington can rarely have been assembled at an English country house. The hostess, Robert Winter's wife, was indeed to be pitied. In her presence there was[1] "no talk of rebellion," as she afterwards declared ; but she must have known what was going forward, and have learned something of the disastrous failure of the appeal to her father, whose censure of her husband must have caused her the greatest pain. A few weeks later she was made to endure the distress of an examination before officials on the subject.[2]

In the course of the day, Father Greenway came to Huddington with Catesby's servant, Thomas Bates. Sir Everard does not appear to have seen him, for he wrote[3] :—" They said Mr Greenway came to Huddington when we were there and had speech of Mr" [probably Catesby], "but I told them it was more than I took note of, and that I did not know him very well."

Catesby, however, received Father Greenway with delight. On first seeing him, he exclaimed that " Here at least was a gentleman who would live and

<hr>

[1] Cal. Sta. Pa. Dom., 1603-10, p. 245.
[2] S. P. Gunpowder Plot Book, n. 43.
[3] *Sir E. D.'s Letters*, paper 3.

die with them." [1]   But Greenway seems to have paid
them a very short visit; and he was evidently com-
missioned by Catesby to go to a neighbouring landlord
and enlist him to the cause; for he rode away the same
afternoon to Henlip, or Hindlip,[2] a house about four
miles off, belonging to Thomas Abington, or Habingdon,
a man famed for his hospitality to priests flying from
persecution.   On arriving at Hindlip, Father Greenway told Abington that he had [3] " brought them the
worst newes that ever they hade, and sayd they were
all undone "; that "ther were certayne gentlemen that
meant to have blown upp the Parliament house, and
that ther plot was discovered a day or two before, and
now ther were gathered together some forty horse at
Mr Wynter's house, meaning Catesbye, Percye, Digby,
and others, and tould them," *i.e.*, Abington and his
houschold, " their throates would be cutt unlesse they
presently wente to joyne with them."   Abington
replied, " Alas, I am sorye;" but he said that he [4]

[1] Exam. of Bates, 13 Jan. 1606 ; G. P. Book, Gardiner's *Hist. Eng.*,
Declaration of Morgan, 10 Jan. ; G. P. Book ; Vol. i. p. 260.

[2] A very curious house, said to have been built by John Habington,
cofferer to Queen Elizabeth. *Nash's Worcestershire*, Vol. i. p. 585.   This
house has been pulled down, and a large modern mansion has been built
in its place by the Allsopp family, the head of which, Lord Hindlip,
takes his title from it.

[3] G. P. Book, Vol ii. n. 197.   Exam. of Oldcorne, Mar. 6, 1605, [6].

[4] Nevertheless, Abington was condemned to death, because Father
Garnet was found in his house, a few weeks later.   He was eventually
reprieved ; but his lands and goods were forfeited.   See *Narrative of the
G. P.*, Gerard, p. 268.   He was "confined to Worcestershire on account
of the Gunpowder Treason Plot," and became "The first Collector of
Antiquities for that County.   Died Oct. 1647, aged 87." *Nash's Wor-*

" would never ioyne with them in that matter, and chardged all his house to that purpose not to goe unto them."

Father Oldcorne, another Jesuit, was present at Hindlip[1] when this interview took place, and he also assured Father Greenway that[2] he would have nothing to do with the conspiracy or the insurrection. As we shall have little, if anything, more to do with Father Greenway, it may be worth observing here that he escaped from England[3] in "a small boat laden with dead pigs, of which cargo he passed as the owner," and that he lived thirty years afterwards. A ridiculous story was reported from Naples, in 1610, by Sir Edwin Rich, that Father Greenway (alias Beaumont) was plotting to send King James some poisoned clothes, which would be death to the wearer.[4]

While at Huddington, Sir Everard and most of the other conspirators probably went to confession to Father Hart, the priest who had said mass for them at Dunchurch ; for he was afterwards " charged with

cestershire, Vol i. Illustrations to p. 588. His wife, sister to Lord Mounteagle, " is supposed to have wrote the letter which discovered the Gunpowder Treason Plot ; " ib.

[1] Father Garnet was finally arrested at Hindlip, with several others. In their hiding-place their " maintenance had been by a quill or reed, through a whole in the chimney that backed another chimney into the gentlewoman's chamber, and by that passage cawdles, broths, and warm drinks had been conveyed in unto them." Ashmole MSS., Vol. 804, fol. 93, quoted by Nash, Vol. i. p. 586.

[2] Narrative of the G. P., Gerard, p. 268.

[3] *Troubles of our Catholic Forefathers*, by Father John Morris, S. J., First Series, pp. 143-4.

[4] S. P. Dom. James I., Vol. lvii. n. 92.

having heard the confessions and absolved the conspirators, two days after the discovery of the Plot," [1] and this is confirmed by Sir Everard's servant, Handy, who said [2] "that on Thursday morning about three of the clock all the said companie as servaunts as others heard masse, receaved the sacrament and were confessed, w$^{ch.}$ masse was said by a priest named Harte, a little man, whitely complexion and a little beard." If the conspirators really made full confessions with true sorrow for their terrible sins, on this occasion, nothing could have been better or more opportune. If not,—well, the less said the better! The same witness stated that on that Thursday morning, at about six o'clock, Sir Everard, who had had four fresh horses sent to him from Coughton,[3] and the rest of the party were again in the saddle, and the whole band started in a northerly direction for Whewell Grange, a house belonging to Lord Windsor, having added to the procession "a cart laden w$^{th.}$ trunckes, pikes, and other munition," from Huddington. On their way towards Whewell Grange "four of the principall gent." [4] rode in front of the procession, and four behind it "to kepe the company from starting away," *i.e.*, deserting.

They reached Lord Windsor's house,[5] about noon,

<hr>

[1] *Records S. J.*, Series I., p. 173.

[2] S. P. Gunpowder Treason, Part II. No. 121.

[3] S. P. Dom. James I., G. P. Bk., Part II. No. 135, D.   [4] *Ib.*

[5] Whewell, or Hewell Grange, had belonged to the Abbey of Bordesley, and had been given, soon after the dissolution of the monasteries, to Sir Andrew Windsor by Hen. VIII. in exchange for

and all dismounted, " saving some fewe whoe sate on
their horses to watch whoe should come unto the
howse." They then made their second raid. It was
not for horses, as at Warwick; this time they sought
for arms and armour, of which there was a large
store at Whewell Grange. They appear to have
met with no resistance, from which we may infer
that, to use a modern and vulgar phrase, " the
family were from home." When they had all armed
themselves, they put the remainder into a cart, while
they filled another with a quantity of powder. These
two carts then formed part of the procession. Sir
Everard Digby can scarcely have failed to feel shame
at the plunder of Whewell Grange. What had Lord
Windsor done that his house should be pillaged?
He had served his country as a sailor, and he
eventually became a Rear Admiral of the Fleet.
Why should his things be taken feloniously from
his home during his absence? His father had died
only seven months earlier, and the funeral hatchment
was most likely hanging over the doorway when
these thieves entered. While the robbers were
ransacking the house — I fear that Sir Everard
Digby was among them—some of the neighbouring
peasants and villagers came up, out of curiosity, to
see what was going on. As he came out of the

the manor of Stanwell in Middlesex. A new house was built at
Whewell about 1712. " Here is a pleasant park having hills gently
swelling, and a lake of clear water measuring above 30 acres." *Nash's
Worcestershire*, Vol ii. p. 423.

house, Catesby saw from twenty to thirty of them standing about.[1]

" Will you come with us ? " said he.

" Maybe we would, if we knew what you mean to do," was the reply.

" We are for God and the country !" said Catesby.

Then one of the men, who was leaning with his back against a wall, struck the ground with his stick and cried, " We are for the King James, as well as for God and the country, and we will not go against his will."

And now, with their arms, armour, gunpowder, and horses, which had been for the most part begged, borrowed, or stolen, the little party of filibusters started again, in a northerly direction, towards Holbeche House, Stephen Littleton's place in Staffordshire. Although more soldierlike in appearance, owing to their armour—their want now was not of armour, but of men to wear it—they felt much less martial at heart than on leaving Dunchurch two days earlier. They were greatly discouraged at finding that no volunteers rallied to their ranks ; that, when they rode up to the houses of any of the Catholic gentry, they were invariably driven with reproaches and ignominy from their doors as the greatest enemies of the Catholic cause, which they were told they had

[1] Thomas Maunder's Examination, Nov. 1605, and Ellis's Examination, Nov. 21, 1605. S. P. Dom. James I., Gunpowder Plot Bk., n. 62 and 108.

brought into disrepute by their misguided and iniquitous zeal.

[1] "Notwithstanding of their fair shews and pretence of their Catholick cause," says Bishop Barlow, "no creature, man or woman, through all that countrey would once so much as give them willingly a cup of drink, or any sort of comfort or support, but with execrations detested them." This not only chilled the hearts of the leaders, but also alarmed their followers, who saw them leaving one large Catholic house after another crestfallen in expression and without a single recruit in their train. To add to their depression, the roads were bad, and in many places deep with mud, and the weather was stormy and very wet.[2] Instead of increasing, as Sir Everard and his friends had hoped and expected, their numbers steadily diminished, and they were soon reduced to thirty-six or less.[3] Their men still further lagged behind and disappeared, and the leaders of the expedition threatened those who remained that the next man who attempted to desert should be instantly shot. When they rested, Sir Everard and his companions took it in turn to watch their men with a loaded pistol, determined to make an example of the first deserter they could get a shot at. When they rode on, they endeavoured to be equally vigilant ; but with such a straggling, wearied, undisciplined cavalcade, in a

[1] *Gunpowder Treason*, p. 67.   [2] Jardine, 112.
[3] Gardiner's Hist. Eng., Vol. i. p. 261.

wooded country like Worcestershire, on a dark and misty November afternoon, it was impossible to prevent men from sneaking away unperceived, and the desertions hourly continued.

Sir Everard's spirits drooped more and more. "Not one man came to take our part, though we expected so many,"[1] he says. As to the common people in the villages and the small towns through which the irregular train passed, they merely stood and gazed at them without showing the least inclination to join them.

In the course of the day (Thursday, Nov. 7th), Sir Everard and his allies had a fresh cause of anxiety. On looking back, one of them descried a small body of horsemen in the distance. Filled with hope, thinking that it consisted of Catholics from the neighbourhood coming to join them, they halted, to enable the riders to come up, but, to their disappointment, the other party pulled up also. This was suspicious, and still more so when the mysterious group moved slowly after them on their starting again. Evidently the horsemen in their rear were watching their movements with no friendly intentions. To the conspirators, their distant but ever following figures must have produced sensations not unlike those caused to worn-out travellers by the appearance of vultures in the desert. So long as it was light, they kept catching occasional glimpses of them, and, worst of

---

[1] Digby's Examination. S.P.O. James I. Dom., 2 Dec. 1605.

all, the band of "shadowers" was increasing in numbers and venturing nearer and nearer. The conspirators and their followers were not in actual flight; indeed, they professed to be recruiting for their "army"; but they were none the less steadily, if slowly, pursued by a body of horsemen exceeding their own in numbers, though not so well armed.

It would be difficult to imagine anything more wretched than the little band of conspirators as they wended their way through the Warwickshire, Worcestershire, and Staffordshire lanes and villages. Fagged and haggard were the men, on jaded and weary steeds, and their helmets, pikes, and pistols gave them an almost comical appearance of martial masquerade. The cart - loads of unused armour and weapons were terribly suggestive of failure, and the conspirators' appeals to the able-bodied men, who stood gazing at them from the doors of wayside inns and from village cross - roads, were met either with insult, laughter, or stolid indifference.

To a man like Sir Everard Digby, who had been accustomed to meet with respect, honour, and deference wherever he went, all this must have been exceptionally galling, and it would be made the more bitter by his observing that several of his companions were passing through a part of the country where they were well known and once honoured. He had expected to be received with cheers and enthusiasm at every Catholic house on his route for his attempt to better the condition of his co-religionists, and to see squires, yeomen, and peasants either hurrying to horse and to arms, or imploring for a headpiece and a sword or halberd from the store in the waggons of the little train; and what did he find?—the door of every Catholic house shut against him, or only opened for an outpouring of reproaches and repudiations; the Catholics, from the highest to the lowest, shaking their heads at him and bidding him begone; and his carts of arms, armour, and gunpowder eyed with anger, scorn, and derision. Instead of regarding him as the best friend of their cause, the Catholic squires treated him as if he were its worst enemy; and, as they turned their backs upon himself and his friends and his followers, they gave him to understand that they considered the "powder-action," which he protested was intended for the relief of the professors of the ancient faith, one of the most madly-conceived, iniquitous, and prejudicial projects ever undertaken by people bearing the name of Christians.

When we think of Sir Everard Digby accoutred and armed as if he were the leader of an army numbered by thousands, but actually surrounded by little more than a couple of dozen bedraggled and disheartened horsemen, all heavily, indeed over-armed, yet weary and unmilitary-looking to the last degree, himself haggard and anxious in countenance, yet vainly endeavouring to keep up a martial, knightly, and prosperous bearing, under conditions that rendered any such attempt ridiculous, we are inevitably reminded of that famous character of fiction, Don Quixote de la Mancha.

CHAPTER XII.

Mᴜᴄʜ time had been lost on the Thursday afternoon, in going hither and thither, on either side of the
route, in the vain hope of persuading the Catholic
knights and squires, who lived in the neighbourhood,
to join the insurgents ; even after dark Digby and his
allies continued these fruitless endeavours, in defiance
of the band of horsemen that was dogging their footsteps at some distance in the rear; and it was nearly
ten o'clock at night [1] before the rapidly diminishing
and draggled party reached its destination at
Holbeche House, the home of Stephen Littleton.

Holbeche was a large and handsome Elizabethan
mansion [2] standing a little way over the South Border
of Staffordshire; about four miles to the north of
Stourbridge, and a trifle less to the West of Dudley,
on what are now the outskirts of the great coal and
iron district known as the " black country."   It was a
relief to find a resting-place of any sort ; and, if the
sensations of the conspirators and their followers had
much in common with wild beasts tracked to their

[1] S. P. Gunpowder Treason, Part I. n. 108 ; Exam. of Wm. Ellis, 20
Nov. 1605.

[2] Jardine's G.P., p. 70.

lairs, or foxes run to ground, they were, at any rate, within walls which would afford them a temporary protection, and enable them to take a little of the rest and refreshment which they now so much required.

They had not, however, much leisure for repose. They may have learned that the ominous band of horsemen, which had persistently shadowed their progress, had consisted of Sir Richard Walsh, the Sheriff of Worcestershire, a number of country gentlemen who had rallied to his assistance, and a *posse comitatus*. Although no enemy was any longer in sight, they knew that their position had been ascertained, that spies were probably on the watch for any attempted movement on their part, and that they were to all intents and purposes besieged. Worn out as they were with fatigue and anxiety, they set to work, therefore, to prepare the house to withstand an assault,[1] and spent most of the night thus occupied; so they cannot have had much sleep.

At last Sir Everard Digby had completely lost heart. Worse still, he felt that he had been deceived. "He began to suspect that" the stories which Catesby and Percy had told him of the assistance which Talbot and the Littletons would bring, were not so much mistakes as untruths "devised to engage him in theyr desperate cases."[2] During the night he still cherished the hope that some strong forces might come to their aid, a hope

---

[1] Jardine, p. 114.
[2] S. P. Dom. James I., Nov. 1605, Vol. 16. n. 94.

which he would hardly have entertained unless it had been encouraged by Catesby and the other conspirators ; but when the day began to dawn and it was evident there were no " succors coming thyther," he " discryed the falshood of it."

Whether he informed Catesby of his determination to throw up the whole undertaking does not appear. He may have made the excuse of going away to try to raise men for their help, or of ascertaining whether there were any symptoms of an approaching attack from without. To proclaim himself a deserter from the cause to Catesby would have been to risk a dangerous interview, in which the clinking of swords or the crack of a pistol would be likely to be heard above the interchange of bitter words ; and judging from Catesby's and Winter's intentions in a certain interview with Tresham, it was more than possible that a sudden stab with a dagger might have given a practical demonstration of Catesby's opinion of renegades.

" About daie light," [1] on the Friday morning, he sent his page, William Ellis, and another of his servants, named Michael Rapior, on before him, and presently followed them, accompanied by the rest of his men, with the deliberate intention " to have yealded him self," and I cannot but suspect that he did so without telling Catesby.

He overtook Ellis and Rapior within a mile of Hol-

[1] S. P. Gunpowder Treason, 1605, I. n. 108 ; W. Ellis.

beche, and, telling his servants how desperate he believed their case to be, he made them all a present of their horses and whatever money belonging to him they happened to have upon them ; he then freed them from his service and advised them to make their escape as best they could.[1]   William Ellis and one other, however, " said they would never leave him, but against their will."   Sir Everard made up his mind to go to " Sir Foulk Greville " and surrender himself, and he began to ask everybody whom he met on the road the way to his house.[2] As Sir Fulke Greville [3] had already obtained Warwick Castle, and was probably living there, Sir Everard must have expected to have a long ride before him.

The three horsemen had been observed by some of the scouts who had been watching Holbeche House, and they gave the alarm to the body of men which had collected for the purpose of either attacking or hunting down the conspirators ; the consequence was

[1] *Narrative of the G. P.*, Gerard, p. 110. See also an account of the money Sir E. D. had taken with him ; *ib.*, p. 92,—" above £1000 in ready coin, as his servants since have averred, that did escape, and one of them delivered up great part of the money to the king's officers so soon as he saw his master had fallen into the lapse."

[2] Exam. of Sir E. D.

[3] " Sir Fulke Greville, a man of letters, and a distinguished courtier in the reigns of Elizabeth and James I., who, at the coronation of the latter prince, was made a Knight of the Bath, and soon after was called from being Treasurer of the Navy to be Chancellor of the Exchequer, and was sworn of the privy council. In the 2nd of King James's reign he obtained a grant of Warwick Castle and other dependencies about it, and was elevated to the peerage, 29 Jan. 1620-1, by the title of Lord Brooke, &c." *Burke's Peerage*, 1886, p. 1390. Sir Fulke Greville is represented by the present Earl of Warwick.

that Sir Everard, his page, and his servant had not proceeded more than a few miles when they heard shouts in the distance behind them, and on looking round, perceived that they were being pursued by that motley, but much-dreaded, force known as the " hue and cry."

To say nothing of the indignity of being captured by a yelling mob, it would be infinitely more dangerous than a voluntary submission to some recognised authority ; for this reason, Digby, with his two attendants, tried to escape, and, as they were riding three excellent horses, they had great hopes of succeeding in doing so.

Nor were these hopes altogether groundless ; for, when they began to gallop, they soon widened the distance between themselves and their pursuers ; but they observed that the peasants and wayfarers whom they passed turned round to stare at them, which showed that their route would be pointed out to the " hue-and-cry." As Father Gerard says, " it was not possible for them to pass or go unknown, especially Sir Everard Digby, being so noted a man for his stature and personage, and withal so well appointed as he was." [1] He thought it wisest, therefore, to go into a large wood, and to hide there until the " hue-and-cry " should have passed. In this fortune favoured them, for, on turning along a bye-path from the main track in the wood, they saw a dry pit, and down into this they rode.

[1] *Narrative of the G. P.*, p. 110.

They had not been very long concealed in it when they heard the distant thud of galloping horses, and every now and then the shouting of their riders. Nearer and nearer came the sounds, and, just as they grew loudest, to his great delight Digby heard them beginning to decrease in force, which showed that the galloping mob had passed his retreat and was going on an objectless errand.

Presently the sounds ceased altogether, and Sir Everard and his two companions were on the point of emerging from their ambush, when they fancied they heard the footsteps of two horses proceeding at a walk. A voice confirmed them in this opinion. Once more there was silence, and once again there were sounds of horses' feet and men's voices.

Suddenly a cry of " Here he is ; here he is ! "[1] showed that they were discovered. The baffled hunters had turned back to try to trace the hoof-marks of the fugitives' horses on either side of the rough roadway through the wood, and the wet, muddy weather had enabled them to succeed in this attempt. In that moment of extreme peril, Sir Everard showed plenty of courage. " Here he is, indeed ! " said he ; " what then ? "

Looking up, he saw about ten or twelve horsemen standing about the entrance to the pit ; and believing that the main body of the " hue-and-cry " were scattered about the wood searching in different

[1] *Narrative of the G. P.*, p. 111.

directions, he hoped to be able to force his way
through the small group which he saw above;
accordingly he " advanced his horse in the manner
of curvetting (which he was expert in) and thought
to have borne them over, and so to break from them."

As the event proved, they were quite unprepared
for the shock of his charge, and, thrown into confusion, they were unable to prevent him from forcing
his way safely through their midst; but as soon as
he had done so, he found himself surrounded by more
than a hundred horsemen, trotting up from different
directions.   Perceiving that escape was now impossible, he " willingly yielded himself to the likeliest
man of the company," and was immediately made
a prisoner.

Would it have been more becoming to have sold
his life dearly and to have died on the field by shot,
pike, or sword, than to have surrendered to that ill-
mounted, ill-armed, and irregular band of squireens,
yeomen, and tradesmen, with the certainty of the
disgraceful gallows and the quartering hatchet before
him ? The reasons for his acting otherwise, given
by Father Gerard, are at least logical. He had a
desire, he says,[1] " to have some time before his
death for his better preparation, and withal " he
hoped " to have done some service to the Catholic
cause by word, sith he saw he could not do it by
the sword."

[1] P. 111.

P

I have been unable to find any details as to what befel Sir Everard between his arrest and his long, wearying, and humiliating ride of nearly a hundred and twenty miles to London. Bound a prisoner on his horse, and guarded by armed men on all sides, he would be an object of curiosity and derision in every town, village, and hamlet through which he passed. He would be taken through Warwickshire, which had been the scene of his fruitless attempt to raise an insurrection during the two previous days; probably, through many places well known in happier times in Northamptonshire; through yet more familiar localities in Buckinghamshire, where he had hitherto been hailed with raised hats and genial smiles; and even, perhaps, within a few miles of his beloved Gothurst itself. When he entered Middlesex, the nearer he came to London, the greater would be the angry demonstrations of hostility on the part of the crowds that turned out to see the traitor and conspirator as he was conducted towards the Tower to take his trial for high treason. There may have been a few sympathisers among the mob, such as the man who was heard to whisper that " It had been brave sport, yf it had gone forward " ;[1] but such remarks would not be made loud enough to reach the ears of Digby.

The shame of that journey must have been intense to a man constituted like Sir Everard, and it may

[1] S. P. Dom. James I., Vol. xvi. n. 29, 1.

have been increased by the reflection that he had
forsaken his friends, with the intention of surrender-
ing `himself; and that, although they had certainly
deceived him, he was in some sense a deserter from
their ranks, at the moment of their extremity, as
well as a traitor to his king.

Unquestionably his greatest sorrow of all was to
think of his wife and children at Coughton. The
unfortunate Lady Digby had sent a servant, named
James Garvey,[1] "in search of his master, when he
was apprehended"; for "Sir Everard had horses at
Coughton." Although she would doubtless think it
a comparatively minor matter, the rude fact was soon
forced upon her that, if her husband were attainted of
high treason, all his estates would be confiscated, and
she presently learned that the lawyers were already
wrangling over the technical question whether her
own property at Gothurst, which was settled on Sir
Everard and his children, would not have to go too.
The Crown lawyers claimed that it would, and they
issued a notice that no part of it, or its revenues,
must be touched by Lady Digby, or anyone else,
until after her husband's trial. She was, therefore,
immediately placed in a position of pecuniary embarrassment and want.

Although it is an oft-told tale, and does not directly
concern the subject of my biography, my story might
seem incomplete if I were to say nothing of those

[1] Cal. Sta. Pa. Dom., 1603-10, p. 248.

whom Sir Everard had left behind him, when he rode away from Holbeche.

According to Jardine, two of the company at Holbeche, besides Sir Everard, deserted that house on the Friday morning. One was the host, Stephen Littleton. It should be remembered that he had not been a sworn conspirator in the Gunpowder Plot, and that it would seem hard that he should bear the penalty of sheltering his friends who had been concerned in it. As a matter of fact, this was exactly what he had to do; for he was executed for this very offence and, curiously enough, another too good-natured man, of the name of Perkises, was executed in his turn for sheltering him. The other fugitive was Robert Winter, who was afterwards captured and executed.

Sir Everard and his men had not long left Holbeche, when Catesby, Rookwood, and Grant endeavoured to dry some of the gunpowder from Whewell, which had got "dank" in the open cart on its journey the previous afternoon, upon a platter over a large fire. As might have been expected, it ignited and exploded, severely burning several of them.

Even Catesby now lost heart, expressed his fears that God disapproved of their proceedings,[1] and said that here he meant to remain and die. The other conspirators said they would do the same, and they

---

[1] Stephen Littleton's Confession—Rookwood's Examination—Jardine, p. 115.

seem now, for the first time, to some extent, to have realised the enormity of their sin. They perceived "God to be against them; all prayed before the picture of Our Lady, and confessed that the act was so bloody as they desired God to forgive them." Then, says Father Gerard,[1] "They all fell earnestly to their prayers, the Litanies and such like (as some of the company affirmed that escaped taking, being none of the conspirators, but such as joined with them in the country); they also spent an hour in meditation." It is satisfactory to know that they showed some contrition for their terrible iniquity and tried to make their peace with God; and, being Catholics, they would know what to do to this end.

At eleven o'clock, the High Sheriff appeared with a large force and surrounded the house. Thomas Winter went out into the court-yard and was shot in the shoulder by an arrow from a cross-bow, just as Catesby, who followed him, exclaimed, "Stand by me, Tom, and we will die together." The two brothers, John and Christopher Wright, followed him, and both were mortally wounded. Rookwood, who had been severely burned by the explosion of gunpowder, was shot through the arm by a bullet from a musket and wounded in the body by a pike. Catesby and Percy stood back to back and were both shot through the body. Catesby died shortly afterwards in the house, after declaring "that the plot and practice of

---

[1] *Narrative of the Gunpowder Plot*, p. 109.

this treason was only his, and that all others were but his assistants, chosen by himself to that purpose, and that the honour thereof belonged only to himself." Percy died the next day.

As soon as Catesby and Percy had fallen, the attacking party rushed into the court-yard, overpowered the feeble resistance offered to them, and made prisoners of the whole party.

The besiegers of Holbeche House were little more orderly than the hue and cry which had chased Sir Everard Digby.   Sir Thos. Lawley, who was assisting the Sheriff of Worcestershire, wrote afterward to Salisbury[1]:—" I hasted to revive Catesby and Percy and the two Wrights, who lay deadly wounded on the ground, thinking by the recovery of them to have done unto his Majesty better service than by suffering them to die.   But such was the extreme disorder of the baser sort, that while I with my men took up one of the languishing traitors, the rude people stripped the rest naked ; and their wounds being many and grievous, and no surgeon at hand, they became incurable and so died."

In a very short time, Sir Everard Digby, Rookwood, Thomas Winter, John Grant, Robert Keyes, Francis and Tresham were all safely lodged in the Tower, besides the earliest conspirator arrested—Guy Fawkes.

One of the first things that Sir Everard did after being brought to London was to beg as a special

[1] Additional MSS., British Museum, No. 617, p. 565.

favour to be permitted to see the king [1]—a boon most unlikely to be granted—" intending to lay down the causes so plainly which had moved them to this attempt," namely the Gunpowder Plot, " and withal how dangerous it was for His Majesty to take the course he did, as that he hoped to persuade at least some mitigation, if not toleration, for Catholics." Of course he was informed that no such favour would be shown him ; but that he would very shortly be examined by the Lords of the Council, when an opportunity would be given to him of making a statement.

The news of the popular indignation at the Gunpowder Plot must have added greatly to Digby's sorrows. On Sunday, November 10th,[2] " a solemn thanksgiving was offered in all the churches." He would hear, too, that on the night of the very day that the explosion was to have taken place, church-bells were ringing, and bonfires were blazing in all directions as a testimony of the public rejoicing at the failure of the plot.[3] Even[4] " the Spanish Ambassador made bonfires, and threw money amongst the people."

More galling still was the ever-increasing evidence of the horror of the English Catholics and their angry disclaimers of having had anything to do with, or any sympathy for, such a nefarious scheme.

" If, after the discovery," says Tierney,[5] " the pope

---

[1] *Narrative of the G. P.*, Gerard, p. 111.
[2] Gardiner's *Hist. Eng.*, Vol. i. p. 266.
[3] S. P. Dom. James I., Vol. xvi. n. 23.   [4] Stow's *Annales*, p. 880.
[5] Notes to Dodds' Church *Hist. of Eng.*, Vol. iv. p. 64.

himself abstained from issuing a formal condemnation of the conspiracy, Blackwell, at least, his delegate and representative in England, instantly came forward to stigmatize it as a 'detestable device,' an 'intolerable, uncharitable, scandalous, and desperate fact.' No sooner had the proclamation for the apprehension of the conspirators announced the intelligence that Catholics were implicated in it, than he addressed a letter to the clergy and laity of his flock (Nov. 7), reminding them of the criminality of all forcible attempts against the government, and exhorting them to manifest their respect for the decisions of the church, the clergy by inculcating, the laity by practising, that patient submission to the laws, which alone could 'please God, mollify man, and increase their merits and their glory in the world to come.'" Reports of this letter would be received by Sir Everard on his arrival in London.

The Archpriest's manifesto was most opportune ; for about the time he was writing it, Ben Jonson, the poet, who had been a Catholic for seven years,[1] was writing to Salisbury that some say they must consult the Archpriest ; but that he, Ben Jonson, thinks [2] "they are all so enweaved in it as it will make 500 gent. lesse of the religion within this weeke." He also got up in the Council Chamber at Whitehall,[3] denounced the plot on

---

[1] Dixon's *Her Majesty's Tower*, Vol. ii. p. 191.
[2] S. P., James I., Dom., Vol. xvi. n. 30.
[3] Dixon's *Her Majesty's Tower*, Vol. ii. p. 191.

behalf of the Catholics of England, and offered his services in hunting down the gang of miscreants that had brought this discredit on his Church.

"Three weeks later," continues Tierney, the Arch-priest "repeated his admonition in still stronger terms. He reminded his people of his former letter, assured them that 'no violent attempt against the king or his government could be other than a most grievous and heinous offence to God'; and concluded by declaring that, as the pope had already condemned all such unlawful proceedings, so he, by the authority of the pope, now strictly forbad Catholics, under pain of ecclesiastical censures, 'to attempt any practise or action, tending to the prejudice' of the throne, or to behave themselves in any manner but such 'as became dutiful subjects and religious Catholics, to their king, his counsellors, and officers.'"

With a copy of the first of these two letters [1] before me, I am struck by one sentence which lays down a golden rule concerning political plots. "Moreover, our divines do say that it is not lawful for private subjects, by private authority, to take arms against their lawful king, albeit he become a tyrant."

How bitterly Sir Everard Digby felt the dis-approval of the Catholics may be judged from one of his letters to his wife, written in the Tower. [2] "But now let me tell you, what a grief it hath been to me,

---

[1] See S. P. Dom. James I., Vol. xvi. n. 21.

[2] Letters of Sir E. D. (p. 170), No. 1.

to hear that so much condemned which I did believe would have been otherwise thought on by Catholicks ; there is no other cause but this, which hath made me desire life, for when I came into prison, death would have been a welcome friend unto me, and was most desired ; but when I heard how Catholicks and Priests thought of the matter, and that it should be a great sin that should be in the *Cause* of my end, it called my conscience in doubt of my very best actions and intentions in question : for I knew that my self might easily be deceived in such a business, therefore I protest unto you that the doubts I had of my own good state, which only proceeded from the censure of others, caused more bitterness of grief in me than all the miseries that ever I suffered, and only this caused me wish life till I might meet with a ghostly friend. For some good space I could do nothing, but with tears ask pardon at God's hands for all my errors, both in actions and intentions in this business, and in my whole life, which the censure of this, contrary to my expectance, caused me to doubt ; I did humbly beseech that my death, might satisfie for my offence, which I should and shall offer most gladly to the Giver of Life. I assure you as I hope in God that the love of all my estate and worldly happiness did never trouble me, nor the love of it since my imprisonment did ever move me to wish life. But if that I may live to make satisfaction to God and the world, where I have given any scandal, I shall not grieve if I should never look Living Creature in the face again, and besides that deprivation endure all worldly misery."[1]

Sir Everard was examined in the Tower several times; first, on two successive days, November 19th and 20th, he was questioned at some length, before Nottingham, Suffolk, Devonshire, Northampton, Salisbury, Mar, Dunbar, and Coke. A good deal of his evidence has already been quoted. On the first day, he only admitted that Catesby[2] "did comfort him with future hopes and told him that he doubted not but there would be a course effected for theyr good," and that it was not until Tuesday, the 5th of November, that "Mr Catesbie acquainted him with the practice of y^e treason of y^e blowing up the Parlam$^{t.}$ howse," when he "gave him some inkling what had bin the plott of undermining the Parlament howse, to blow it up; and on Wednesday told him more at large &c.," naming "who had bin the miners."

On the following day, however, "he beinge shewed by the L^s his follye and faulte in denyinge that wch was so manyfest and beinge toulde that both Tho. Wynter had speach w^h him of the pticulars, concerninge the plot of the powder to blow upp the K. in the Parliament house, and being confronted wth Mr Faucks who charged him to have discoursed wth

---

[1] In the Tower, he wrote to his wife with lemon juice on slips of paper as opportunity offered. These were kept as precious relics by his family. See *Biographia Britannica*, Vol. iii. p. 1608.

[2] S. P. Dom. James i, Vol. xvi. n. 94, 95.

him thereof abowte a weeke before the 5th of November at his house in Buck.shyer," he confessed more freely. Fawkes had been tortured,[1] and most likely, when he charged Sir Everard in this way, he did it in order to escape being tortured again. So many of the conspirators were now known by the others to be in the Tower, and each was so much afraid of what the others might have confessed, that they became terrified and confessed freely when examined. Neither of them knew which of his companions had been tortured in order to induce him to incriminate his friends; and each feared that he might, at any moment, be himself laid upon the rack.

[1] The King wrote :—'The gentler tortours are to be first usid unto him, *et sic per gradus ad ima tenditur*, and so God speede youre goode rke." S. P., James I., Dom., Vol. xvi. n. 17, Nov. 6.

CHAPTER XIII

Sir Everard says, in a letter from the Tower,[1] that, at one of his examinations, "they did in a Fashion offer me the torture, which I wil rather indure then hurt any body"; but it was only a threat; for, although torture was used to priests and Jesuits in connection with the Gunpowder Plot, it does not[2] appear to have been brought to bear upon any of the actual conspirators except Guy Fawkes. Lord Dunfermline, however, strongly urged Salisbury to expose them to it.[3] "Recommends that the prisoners be confined apart, in darkness, and examined by torch-light, and that the tortures be slow and at intervals, as being the most effectual." On the other hand, a tract, printed in 1606,[4] says of the conspirators, that "in the time of their imprison-

[1] *Letters of Sir E. D.*, Paper 7.

[2] A modern Jesuit thinks otherwise (see *The Month*, No. 367, p. 8), quoting Cecil's letter to Favat (Brit. Museum MSS. Add. 6178. fol. 625). "Most of the prisoners have wilfully forsworn that the priests knew anything in particular, and obstinately refuse to be accusers of them, *yea, what torture soever they be put to.*" Cecil may have referred to Fawkes only when he mentioned torture; but the Jesuit Father may be right, and he gives other evidence in support of his theory.

[3] Cal. Sta. Pa. Dom., 1603-10, p. 258.

[4] *Somer's Tracts*, Vol. ii. p. 113.

ment, they rather feasted with their sins, than fasted with sorrow for them ; were richly apparelled, fared deliciously, and took tobacco out of measure, with a seeming carelessness of their crime."

Sir Everard had not been many days in the Tower before the Government had a search made at Harrow-den, the house of his young friend, Lord Vaux, whose mother was suspected of having been privy to the plot. Great hopes were entertained of finding here Digby's great friend, Father Gerard, who also lay under suspicion of having been concerned in it.[1] "The house was beset with at least 300 men, and those well appointed." "They searched for two or three days continually, and searched with candles in cellars and several dark corners. They searched every cabinet and box in her [Mrs Vaux's] own closet, for letters, &c." A letter to Salisbury stated[2] that Mrs Vaux "gave up all her keys; all the rooms, especially his closet, narrowly searched, but no papers found. She and the young Lord strongly deny all knowledge of the treason; the house still guarded." Brother Foley says[3] "that house was strictly searched and watched for nine days, with the especial hope of seizing Father Gerard. Though he escaped, the pious lady of the house was herself carried off to London." She was severely examined

---

[1] *Narrative of the G. P.*, Gerard, p. 139.
[2] Cal. Sta. Pa. Dom., 1603-10, p. 256.
[3] *Records, S. J.*, Series I. p. 527.

before the Privy Council; and Sir Everard Digby was pressed to say whether he had not been very lately in her company—indeed, it was on this point that "they did in a Fashion offer" him "the torture"—but, although she admitted, in her examination,[1] that Sir Everard Digby, Robert Catesby, and "Greene and Darcy, priests," had been visitors at her house, and, when she refused to say where Father Gerard was, she was told she must die,[2] nothing could be proved against her and she was liberated.

It must have been a great comfort to Lady Digby to receive the scraps of paper inscribed with lemon juice from her husband. It is easy to imagine the eagerness and care with which she would hold them before the fire in order to develope their writing, with anxiety to make every letter legible and fear lest the paper should become scorched. Sir Everard calls her his "Dearest"; but, in letters which might possibly fall into hands for which they were not intended, it would have been out of place to make much display of affection, and the only exhibition of that kind is to be found in a poem which will be quoted later.

In her straits for money, she applied, and not altogether without success, to Salisbury; for we find her writing to him thus :—[3]

---

[1] Cal. Sta. Pa. Dom., 1003-10, p. 259.   [2] *Records*, S. J., Vol. iv. p. 9.
[3] S. P. Dom. James I., 1606, Vol. 18, n. 36.

" Right Ho^{ble.}—Your comfortable favours towards
me proseding from your noblle disposition in ordering a means for my relefe (being plunged in distresse)
by aucthoritie of yours and the rest of the Lords
letters to the Sherife of Buck. incytith me to yeld
and duly too acknowleg by thes my most humble
thankes; for wch favor I shall ever ho^r your Lo^p
and praye to the —— allmighti for your greatest
hapines and with all humbllenes remayne to

" Your ho^r devoted

"Mary Digby."

As usual, in a lady's letter, the pith is in the
postscript.

" *Pos.* Being most fearfull to ofend you ho^r yet
enforced out of the dutifull love towards my wofull
husband, I humbly beg pardon to desier your Lo^ps
consent and furtharance for such an unspeakable
hapines as that out of your worthy and noblle disposition you would purchase merci for my husband's
life, for wch you should tie us our posteritie to you
and your howse for ever and I hope his ofence
agaynst his Matie is not so haynous in that excrable
plot, as is sayd to be contrived by som others, which
in my hart I cannot conceve his natuer to give
consente for such an ackt to be committed."

[Endorsed] " To the Right Hono^{ble.} the Earlle of
Salsbery, Principall Secretary to the King's most
excelent Matie.

Lady Digby did not find Lord Salisbury's orders for

her relief so availing in practice as in theory; for, a little later, she wrote to him again. I will not weary my readers by giving her exact spelling—such words as " pertickellers," for particulars, " shreife," for sheriff, " reseved," for received, and " howsold " for household, soon become troublesome and vexatious—but I will endeavour to transcribe her letter according to modern orthography and punctuation.

[1] " MARY DIGBY TO LORD SALISBURY.

Right Honourable Lord.—My poor and perplexed estate enforceth me to be an humble petitioner to your good Lordship. I was most fearful and loth to trouble your honour so long as I had any hopes of redress without it ; but finding none elsewhere, makes me presume to present these unto your honour. I confidently believe your lordship doth think that, upon yours with others of the Lords of his majesty ——— —— council, your letters to the Sheriff of Buckinghamshire in my behalf (for which I humbly give thanks), hath given ease and relief unto my present wants ; but truly my lord it is nothing so, for all which he hath done, since he received that letter, is but that he hath returned, near from whence he had taken, part of the household stuff which he had carried away and there keepeth it ; but will not let anything be delivered to my use ; notwithstanding I procured the Lord Treasurer's warrant to him, for the delivery of divers things most needful for my present use ; for

[1] S. P. Dom. James I., Vol. xviii. n. 37.

which I was to put in sureties for their return, when they should be justly demanded, which was by bond and drawn according to the Lord Treasurer his own direction, which was, as the sheriff said, too favourable for me, and therefore did refuse it ; such strange and hard proceedings doth he still continue against me (the particulars thereof were too tedious to relate unto your lordship) that, without your honour's good assistance, I shall receive no part of such good favours as your lordship meant unto me. Never, since my grievous calamities, I have received no one penny, but am forced to borrow, both for my own present spending, and to furnish Mr Digby with those things he wants, and as hath been called to me for by the lieutenant of the Tower, which borrowed money I must forthwith repay ; and the cause why I can receive none, according to the allowance which was granted for me, is because this sheriff will not pay the money into the exchequer which he hath received for such goods which he sold of Mr Digby's, which is between 200 and 300 pounds, and hath said he would keep it in his hands till he were allowed for the charge he was at, for the carrying the goods " [some words here are mutilated] "and bringing of them back again. My hope in your Lordship's pity to my distress promiseth me to find relief for these my complaints, for which I will ever remain your honour's most thankful—

" MARY DIGBY.

" *Postscript.*— Right honourable,—Though it be no part of my letter, yet is it a very far greater part of my humble desire to your Lordship whereby, I cannot but beg your pitiful commiseration to incline and further his majesty's mercy for my woeful husband, which if your Lordship extend such a charitable act, we and all what is ours will ever be your honour's.

The "goods which he sold of Mr Digby's," mentioned in the letter may be assumed to have been the contents of the trunk, carried by his "trunk-horse," and inventoried in a letter[1] written from the Tower.

It is probable that Lady Digby wrote to her husband, expressing herself powerless to "conceive his nature to give consent for such an act" as the Gunpowder Plot ; for he wrote to her from the Tower excusing himself.[2]

" Let me tell you, that if I had thought there had been the least sin in the Plot, I would not have been of it for all the world : and no other cause drew me to hazard my Fortune and Life, but zeal to God's Religion. For my keeping it secret, it was caused by certain belief, that those which were best able to judge of the lawfulness of it,"—by these he evidently means the Jesuit Fathers—"had been acquainted with it, and given way to it. More reasons I had to persuade me to this belief than I dare utter, which I will never,

---

[1] *Letters of Sir E. D.*, paper 22.
[2] *Letters of Sir E. D.* (p. 169) No. 1.

to the suspicion of any, though I should go to the Rack for it, and as I did not know it directly that it was approved by such so did I hold it in my Conscience the best not to know any more if I might." He seems to have intended to convey that he had been practically certain that the Jesuit Fathers had given their approval but was anxious to be able to say that he did not actually know this.

In another letter,[1] he says " My dearest, the —— —— I take at the uncharitable taking of these matters, will make me say more than I ever thought to have done. For if this design had taken place, there could have been no doubt of other Success : for that night, before any other could have brought the news, we should have known it by Mr Catesby, who should have proclaimed the Heir-Apparent at Charing-Cross, as he came out of Town ; to which purpose there was a Proclamation Drawn," etc. The absurdity of attaching any value to a proclamation by such a comparatively insignificant individual as Catesby does not appear to have occurred to him !

After describing the plans laid for securing the young Duke and the Princess Elizabeth, he goes on to say " there were also courses taken for the satisfying of the people if the first had taken effect, as the speedy notice of Liberty and Freedom from all manner of Slavery, as the ceasing of Wardships and all Monopolies, which with change would have been more plausible to

---

[1] (P. 177), No. 9.

the people, if the first had been, than is now. There was also a course taken to have given present notice to all Princes, and to *Associate* them with an Oath answerable to the League in France." Whether "all Princes" would have felt inclined "to associate" themselves "with an Oath" at the request of a band of assassins may be questioned.

Sir Everard, as well as Lady Digby, wrote to Salisbury ; but his letters asked for fewer favours.

" If your Lordship," he wrote,[1] " and the State think it fit to deal severely with the Catholics, within brief there will be massacres, rebellions, and desperate attempts against the King and State. For it is a general received reason among Catholics, that there is not that expecting and suffering course now to be run that was in the Queen's time, who was the last of her line, and last in expectance to run violent courses against Catholics ; for then it was hoped that the King that now is, would have been at least free from persecuting, as his promise was before coming into this realm, and as divers his promises have been since his coming. All these promises every man sees broken." At the same time, he said that he [2] " will undertake to secure the Pope's promise not to excommunicate the King, if he will deal mildly with Catholics." As to plots against the king and the government, something of the

[1] I use Jardine's modern rendering of this particular letter, in *Criminal Trials*, Vol. ii. p. 24. But the actual letter may be found among the S. P. Dom. James I., Vol. xvii., n. 9.

[2] Cal. Sta. Pa. Dom., 1603-10, p. 206.

kind, he declares, would have been contrived sooner, if the priests had not hindered it.

An earlier letter written by him from the Tower,[1] is thus summarized :—" Sir Everard Digby to Salisbury. Is willing to tell all he knows, but can remember nothing more than he has already confessed, except that Catesby intended to send the Earls of Westmoreland and Derby to raise forces in the North, and would send information to France, Spain, Italy, etc., of their success. Begs that the King will have compassion on his family."

Meanwhile examinations were constantly going on, not only of the prisoners in the Tower, but also of other persons, with regard to the Gunpowder Plot, and the correspondence on the subject was very large. Lord Salisbury wrote to the Lord Chancellor of Scotland,[2] assuring him that he " would rather die than be slack in searching the dregs of " the plot " to the bottom." Lady Markham wrote to Salisbury, that[3] the " Plot hath taken deep and dangerous root " ; that many will not believe " that holy and good man," Father Gerard, had anything to do with it ; and that Sir Everard Digby is the man from whom he must endeavour to obtain particulars about Walley—i.e., Father Garnet. Mrs Vaux was examined on the eighteenth of November, and she made no secret of Sir Everard having been a visitor at her house. Lady Lovel admitted knowing

---

[1] Cal. Sta. Pa. Dom., 1603-10, p. 261.
[2] Cal. Sta. Pa. Dom., 1603-10, p. 265.   [3] *Ib.*, p. 259.

both Sir Everard and Catesby, though slightly. To have been a friend of Digby's was now very dangerous. Servants and retainers of the conspirators were arrested in Worcestershire and Warwickshire, and there examined.

Sir Everard must have envied Tresham his fate, when he heard that he had died in the Tower, especially as he was allowed to have his wife to attend him in his illness; although his death was caused by a painful disease.[1] Sir William Waad, the Lieutenant of the Tower, had a consultation of three doctors—not from motives of mercy, but in order that, "by great care and good providence," he might "die of that kind of death he most" deserved, and, in spite of his disappointment, Waad seems to have felt a grain of satisfaction, when writing to Salisbury to announce his death,[2] in stating that he died "with very great pain." His death took place only four days before that appointed for the trial, and, whatever may have been his sufferings, who can doubt that Sir Everard would gladly have changed places with him.

In his solitude in the Tower, Sir Everard wrote the following lines which, if considerably lacking in merit from a poetical and critical point of view, have some interest on account of their pitiful, though calm and dignified tone, as well as the affection which they

---

[1] Jardine's *Gunpowder Plot*, p. 124. *N.B.*—By many people, Tresham's death was attributed to poison.—See *The Month*, No. 366, p. 493. Jardine's *G. P.*, p. 127, and Goodman's Court of King James, p. 107.

[2] S. P. Dom. James I., 23 Dec. 1605.

exhibit towards his wife and his children ; and, as the Protestant Bishop Barlow, in his preface to their publication in 1678, says, "though they be not excellent, yet have" they " a good tincture of Piety and devotion in them."

☩

Come grief, possess that place thy Harbingers have
    seen,
And think most fit to entertain thyself :
Bring with thee all thy Troops, and sorrow's longest
    Teem
Of followers, that wail for worldly pelf :
Here shall they see a Wight more lamentable,
Than all the troop that seem most miserable.

For here they may discry, if perfect search be made,
The substance of that shadow causing woe :
An unkind Frost, that caused hopeful Sprouts to fade;
Not only mine, but other's grief did grow
By my misdeed, which grieves me most of all,
That I should be chief cause of other's fall.

For private loss to grieve, when others have no cause
Of sorrow, is unmeet for worthy mind ;
For who but knows, that each man's sinful life still
    draws
More just revenge than he on earth can find.
But to undo desert and innocence,
Is, to my mind, grief's chiefest pestilence.

I grieve not to look back into my former state,
Though different that were from present case ;
I moan not future haps, though forced death with
    hate
Of all the world were blustred in my face :
But oh I grieve to think that ever I
Have been a means of others misery.

When on my little Babes I think, as I do oft,
I cannot chuse but then let fall some tears ;
Me-thinks I hear the little Pratler, with words soft,
Ask, Where is Father that did promise Pears,
And other knacks, which I did never see,
Nor Father neither, since he promised me.

'Tis true, my Babe, thou never saw'st thy Father since,
Nor art thou ever like to see again :
That stopping Father into mischief which will pinch
The tender Bud, and give thee cause to plain
His hard dysaster ; that must punish thee,
Who art from guilt as any creature free.

But oh ! when she that bare thee, Babe, comes to my
    mind,
Then do I stand as drunk with bitterest woe,
To think that she, whose worth were such to all,
    should find
Such usage hard, and I to cause the blow,
Of her such sufferance, that doth pierce my heart,
And gives full grief to every other part.

Hence comes the cause, that each tear striveth to be
    first,
As if I meant to stint them of their course,
No salted meats : that done you know my heart would
    burst
With violent assaults of your great force :
But when I stay you, 'tis for that I fear,
Your gushing so will leave me ne'er a tear.

But ah ! this doubt, grief says I never need to fear
For she will undertake t'afford me store ;
Who in all her knowledge never cause of woe did hear
That gall'd her deeper or gave witness more
Of earth's hard usage, that does punish those
That guiltless be, with Fortune's cruellest blows.

Though further cause of more than utterable grief,
As other's loss I could dilate at large,
Which I am cause of, yet her suffering being chief
Of all their woes, that sail in this deep Barge
Of sorrow's Sea : I cannot but reflect
Hereon more deeply, and with more respect.

On which dear object when I look with grieved mind,
Such store of pities see I plead her case,
As hardest hearts cause of compassion there would find ;
To hear what could be said before that face
Which I have wrong'd in causing so to weep ;
The grief whereof constrains my pen to sleep.

The trial of the prisoners was long delayed; quite ten weeks passed between their capture and their sentence; but, as Mr Hepworth Dixon puts it,[1] they were, in fact, "undergoing a course of daily trial by Northampton in the Tower." In the so-called gunpowder plot room, in the Lieutenant's House, with its panelled walls, and high, wide window, they underwent "a thousand interrogatories from Coke, a thousand hostilities from Waad, and a thousand treacheries from Forsett. This Forsett was one of Northampton's spies; a useful and despicable wretch, whom his master employed in overhearing and reporting the private conversations of prisoners with each other."

Coke himself, in his speech at the trial, referred to the long delay in bringing the prisoners to the bar, saying[2] "There have been already twenty and three several days spent in Examinations." And he summarized the good results of the delay thus[3]:— "*Veritas Temporis filia*, Truth is the daughter of Time, especially in this case; wherein by timely and often Examinations, First, matters of greatest moment have been lately found out. Secondly, some known Offenders, and those capital, but lately apprehended. Thirdly, sundry of the principal and Arch-traytors before unknown, now manifested, as the Jesuits. Fourthly—" but he might have abridged this statement into these few words—We hoped to worm some evidence out of the prisoners against Catholic priests.

---

[1] *Her Majesty's Tower*, Vol. ii. p. 193.
[2] *Gunpowder Treason*, p. (16).   [3] *Ib.*

CHAPTER XIV.

SIR EVERARD appears to have received several kind communications, whilst in the Tower, from Father Gerard, if we may judge from some of his remarks concerning "my brother" in his letters to Lady Digby.

For instance, we find him writing[1] :—"Let my Brother see this, or know its Contents, tell him I love his sweet comforts as my greatest Jewel in this Place"; in another,[2] "I give my Brother many thanks for his sweet comforts, and assure him that now I desire death; for the more I think on God's mercy the more I hope in my own case: though others have censured our Intentions otherwise than I understood them to be, and though the Act be thought so wicked by those of Judgment, yet I hope that my understanding it otherwise, with my Sorrow for my Error, will find acceptance at God's hands." In another he sends a warning to him,[3] "Howsoever my Brother is informed, I am sure they fear him for knowledge of the Plot, for at every examination I am told that he did give the Sacrament to five at

---

[1] *Sir E. D.'s Letters*, No. 1. [2] *Ib.*, No. 4. [3] *Ib.*, No. 5.

252

one time." And once again,[1] he says :—"Tell my Brother I do honour him as befits me, but I did not think I could have increased so much, loving him more as his charitable Lessons *would* make me."

But if Father Gerard had sent very consoling messages to Sir Everard in his imprisonment ; on one occasion—it was within a few days of the trial— he wrote him a formal letter, which he sent to Lord Salisbury and the Duke of Lenox, asking them to give it to Sir Everard and hear what he might say in answer to it. To Salisbury himself he wrote another letter, in the course of which he said[2] :— " Sir Everard Digby can testify for me, how ignorant I was of any such matter" [as the Gunpowder Plot], " but two days before that unnatural parricide should have been practised. I have, for full trial thereof, enclosed a letter unto him, which I humbly beseech may be delivered, &c."

At the same time he wrote to the Duke of Lenox, " My humble petition therefore is, that a witness be asked his knowledge who is well able.to clear me if he will, and I hope he will not be so unjust in this time of his own danger as to conceal so needful a proof being so demanded of him. Sir Everard Digby doth well know how far I was from knowledge of any such matter but two days before the treason

---

[1] *Sir E. D.'s Letters*, No. 6.

[2] S. P. Dom. James I., Vol. xviii. n. 35. But I avail myself of the endering in " Life of Fr. J. Gerard," pp. ccxxxi-ccxxxvii.

was known to all men. I have therefore written a letter unto him, to require his testimony of that which passed between him and me at that time. Wherein, if I may have your lordship's furtherance to have just trial made of the truth whilst yet he liveth, I shall ever esteem myself most deeply bound, &c., &c."

This letter to Sir Everard, which, of course, would be read first by Salisbury and Lenox, began :—" Sir Everard Digby,—I presume so much of your sincerity both to God and man, that I cannot fear you will be loath to utter your knowledge for the clearing of one that is innocent from a most unjust accusation importing both loss of life to him that is accused, and of good name also, which he much more esteemeth."

Then he says that upon some false information, given, he supposes, "by some base fellows, desirous to save their lives by the loss of their honesty,"—this looks as if he suspected some of the conspirators in the Gunpowder Plot, imprisoned in the Tower—a "proclamation has been issued against myself and my superior"—this would be Father Garnet—" and one other of the Society," probably Father Oldcorne, " as against three notorious practisers, with divers of the principal conspirators in this late most odious treason of destroying the King's Majesty and all in the Parliament House with powder. And myself am put in the first place, as the first or chiefest offender therein."

He calls God to witness that he knew nothing of the plot until it became known publicly; but, he says, "to give more full proof of my innocency to those who also may doubt my words, I take witness to yourself whether you, upon your certain knowledge cannot clear me." At first he would not appeal to Sir Everard because, as he says, "I would not take knowledge of any personal acquaintance with you, especially at your own house, not knowing how far you were to be vouched for your life, and therefore would not add unto your danger,"—*i.e.*, by showing that he knew and had harboured a priest. "But now that it appears by your confession and trial in the country that you stand at the King's mercy for greater matters than your acquaintance with a Priest, I hope you will not be loath, I should publish that which cannot hurt you, and may help myself in a matter of such importance. And as I know you could never like to stoop to so base and unworthy a humour as to flatter or dissemble with any man, so much less can I fear that now (being in the case you are in) you can ever think it fit to dissemble with God, or not to utter your every knowledge, being required as from him, and in behalf of truth. Therefore I desire you will bear witness of the truth which followeth (if it be true that I affirm of my demand to you, growing upon my ignorance in the matter then in hand) as you expect truth and mercy at God's hand hereafter. First, I desire you to bear witness, whether, coming to your house upon All Souls' Day last—" and then he questions him upon the details, described in a former chapter, of what took place at Gothurst upon All Souls' Day, which are mainly taken from this letter.

He ends by saying, " And thus clear I was from the knowledge of that Plot against the Parliament House, whereof, notwithstanding, I am accused and proclaimed to be a practiser with the principal conspirators. But I refer me to God and your conscience, who are able to clear me, and I challenge the conscience of any one that certainly expecteth death, and desireth to die in the fear of God and with hope of His salvation, to accuse me of it if he can. God, of His mercy, grant unto us all grace to see and do His will, and to live and die His servants, for they only are and shall be happy for ever.—Your companion in tribulation though not in the cause,   JOHN GERARD."

Considering the bosom friendship that existed between Gerard and Digby, and the high opinion of the honourable character expressed, in his writings, by the former of the latter, these tremendous exhortations to speak the truth in his favour look a little superfluous. They may have been intended rather for the eyes of Salisbury and Lennox than for those of Digby; for anything which could show an excessive familiarity between Digby and Gerard might have been suspicious evidence against the latter.

There is a postscript, again, which seems written as a suggestion for what Digby should say. " I hope you will also witness with me that you have ever seen me much averted from such violent courses, and hopeful rather of help by favour than force. And, indeed, if I had not now been satisfied by your assurance that there was nothing in hand, it should presently have appeared how much I had misliked any forcible attempts, the counsel of Christ and the commandment of our superiors requiring the contrary, and that in patience we should possess our souls."

To give him his due, Sir Everard Digby spoke boldly in Father Gerard's favour at his trial. Five-and-twenty years later, Father Gerard wrote, in a letter to Dr Smith, Bishop of Chalcedon,[1] " Sir Everard Digby, who of all the others, for many reasons, was most suspected of having possibly revealed the secret to me, protested in open Court and declared that he had often been instigated to say I knew something of the Plot, but that he had always answered in the negative, alleging the reason why he had never disclosed it to me, because, he said, he feared lest I should dissuade him from it. Therefore the greater part of the Privy Councillors considered my innocence established, &c."

Six months later, Father Fitzherbert, Rector of the English College of Rome, wrote concerning Father Gerard to the same bishop [2] " he was fully cleared of

---

[1] *Life of Father J. Gerard*, p. ccxxxviii.
[2] Bartoli's *Inghilterra*, pp. 510, 512.

it " [the Gunpowder Plot] " by the public and solemn testimony of the delinquents themselves, namely, of Sir Everard Digby (with whom he was known to be most familiar and confident), who publicly protested at his arraignment that he did never acquaint him with their design, being assured that he would not like of it, but dissuade him from it; and of this I can show good testimony by letters from London written hither at the time."

Probably owing, in the main, to Sir Everard's declarations of his innocence, Father Gerard was allowed to escape from England, and he survived the Gunpowder Plot thirty-one years. It must not be supposed, however, that he had never suffered for the faith in this country; for he had been terribly tortured, some years before the Gunpowder Plot, in the Tower, from which he escaped.

(Topcliffe's description [1] of " Jhon Gerrarde y⁰ Jhezcwᵗ preest that escaip out of the Tower " may be worthy of a passing notice. " Of a good stature sumwhat higheʳ than Sʳ Tho. Layton and upright in his paysse and countcnance sum what stayring in his look or Eyes Currilde heire by Nature and blackyshe and not apt to have much heire on his bearde. I thincke his noose sum what wide and turninge Upp Blubarde Lipps turninge outwards Especially the over Lipps most Uppwards toward the Noose Kewryoos in speetche If he do now contynewe his custome And in

---

[1] S. P. Dom. Elizabeth, Vol. 165 n. 21.

his speetche he flourrethe and smyles much and a falteringe or Lispinge or dooblinge of his Tonge in his speeche."

On the very day that Father Gerard's letter for Sir Everard Digby seems to have been delivered to Lord Salisbury, January 23rd, Sir Everard himself wrote a long letter to his two little sons, the eldest of which was not yet three years old. The writing of it must have caused him much pain ; probably, also, many tears. The most remarkable thing about it is that he does not enter upon the question of the cause of his death. As his sons would certainly hear of the manner and reason of it, it might have been well to have spoken plainly on the subject. Nevertheless, there is something dignified in his assumption of the position of a parent, in giving good advice to his children, without recounting those personal faults and follies, which he might, perhaps, consider it no part of the duty of a father to confess to his sons.

✠

"Jesus Maria.[1]

"There be many reasons (my dear children) that might disswade me from putting Pen to Paper in this Kind, and onely one which urgeth me to undertake this poor and fruitless pains. Wherefore to tell you what inciteth me to it, is my want of

---

[1] Papers or Letters of Sir Everard Digby. Appendix to the Gunpowder Treason, by Thomas, Bp. of Lincoln, p. 181.

other means to shew my Fatherly affection to each
of you (which is so far from uttering, as my mind
is willing to accept of poor means, rather than none
to bewray my disposition) if I would have been
checked from the performance of these lines, by
number and probabilities of reasons; I might then
have called to mind the unlikelihood, that these
would ever have come to your view; with the
malice of the world to me, which (I do imagine)
will not fail to endeavour to possess you with a
loathness to hear of anything that comes from me:
as also I might, and do think, on my own disability
in advising, with many other disswasive reasons,
which my former recited single stirrer-up hath
banished. Wherefore to begin with both and each
of you, I send you by these my Fatherly and last
blessing; which I have not failed to ask at God's
hands on my knees, that he will grant to descend
so effectually on you (that his holy grace accompanying it) it may work in you the performance
(on your part) of God's sweet and just commandments and on his part to you, the Guerdon that
his mercy inricheth his servants with all. Let this
end (God's service I mean) be the chief and onely
contentious strife between you, which with all
vehemency and desire each of you may strive to
attain soonest. Let this be the mark which your
thoughts and actions may still level at; for here
is the chiefest Prise, to recompense the best de-

server. Believe me in this (my Sons) that though my unripe years afford me not general experience, yet my variety of courses in the world (and God's grace to illumine me) may sufficiently warrant the verity of this principle. If you make this your chief business (as you ought to do, and for which end onely you were sent into the world) I doubt not but God will send you better means for your particular directions, than either the brevity of a Letter or my ability can discharge. So that in this I will say no more, but pray that you may live as I hope to die, which is in the perfect obedience of the Catholick and onely saving Church.

" I cannot but a little touch, what I could wish you did, and I hope will do to all sorts of people ; it is a lesson I could never learn well my self, but perhaps see more what is convenient for others, than that I were ever able to shew the force of wholesome counsel and good instructions in my own life.

" Above all things in the world, seek to obey and follow your Mother's will and pleasure ; who as she hath been the best wife to me that ever man enjoyed, so can she not fail to shew her self equal to the best Mother, if you deserve not the contrary. If it please God to send her life (though you have nothing else), I shall leave you enough : and on the contrary, if I could leave you ten times more than my self ever had, yet she being taken from you, I should think

you but poor. It is not (my Sons) abundance of
riches that makes a man happy but a virtuous life ;
and as they are blessings from God, and cause of
happiness to a man that useth them well, so are they
cause of misery to most men even in this world.

" You may read of divers men, who whiles they
lived in private state, deserved the fame of all that
knew them ; but so soon as prosperous fortune, and
higher degrees, had taken possession of them, they
seemed not to be the same men, but grew into scorn
of all the world. For example *Galba* whiles he lived
in *Spain* as a private man, and, as it were, banished
his Countrey, by a Charge that procured in him great
pains and care ; he was so well liked, that upon the
death of *Nero* the Emperor, he was Elected in his
room but was no sooner in that Place, than he was
plucked out of it again by violent death, as a man
unfit for such a Charge, by reason of his alteration
which that Dignity wrought in him. You may see
also in *Otho* who succeeded him, that all the while
of his prosperity, he lived a most dissolute life and
odious to all men ; but he was no sooner touched
with adversity, but he grew to a brave and worthy
resolution, making choice rather (not out of desperation) of his own death, than that by his life the
Common-weal should be disturbed. And though I
cannot but disallow the manner of his death (by
reason he knew not God truly) yet is it plain, that
adversity brought him to that worthy mind, which

contemned life in regard of his Countrey's good ; and which was so contrary to that mind that prosperity had misled in him. If then adverse Fortune were so powerful more than prosperity on Pagans and Misbelievers, to procure in them worthy minds ; what may we expect the force of it should be in Christians, whose first Captain (not out of necessity, but free choice) made manifest to the world, by his own painful foot steps that there is no other perfect and certain way to true happiness.

"He hath not onely staid here in demonstration of his verity, but hath sent to all those (who, the world knows, he highliest esteemed, and best loved) nothing but variety of misery in this life, with cruel and forced death ; the which thing truest wisdom esteems as the best tokens of Love from so powerful a Sender, and as the best and certainest way to bring a man to perfect happiness.

" I speak not this to conclude, that no man is happy but those which run this strict and best course. But to tell you (my Children) that if the world seek and prevail to cut you off from enjoying my Estate and Patrimony in this world, yet you should not think your selves more unhappy therein : for God, it may be, doth see, that there is some other course more fit for you ; or that this would give great hazard to your Soul's health, which he taketh away, by removing the occasion.

"But, howsoever you find your selves in fortunes of

this world, use them to God's best pleasure, and think yourselves but Bailiffs of such things for an uncertain time. If they be few or poor, your fear of making a good accompt may be the lesser; and know, that God can send more and richer, if it be requisite for his glory and your good; if they be many or great, so much the more care you ought to take in governing your selves, lest God, as holding you unworthy such a charge, by taking them from you, or you from them, do also punish you with eternal misery for abusing his benefits. You shall the better learn to make true use and reckoning of these vanities, if with due obedience you do hearken to your mother's wholesome counsel; and what want you shall find in my instructions, you may see better declared to you by looking on her life, which though I cannot give assurance for any thing to be done in future times yet can I not but very stedfastly believe, that the same Lord will give perseverance in virtue, where he hath laid so strong a foundation for his spiritual building, and where there is such an humble and resigned will to the pleasure of her Lord and Maker.

"The next part of my charge shall be, in your mutual carriage the one to the other; in which, all reasons to move you to perfect accord, and entire love, do present themselves unto you, as the obligation of Christianity, the tie of natural and nearest consanguinity, and the equality, or very small difference of Age. There is in none of these any thing wanting, that may be an impediment to truest Friendship, nor anything to be added to them (for procuring your mutual and heartiest love) but your own consent and particular desert each to other. Since then there is all cause in each of you for this love, do not deprive yourselves of that earthly happiness, which God, Nature, and Time offereth unto you ; but if you think that the benefit which accord and friendship bringeth, be not sufficient to enkindle this love (which God forbid you should) yet let the consideration of the misery which the contrary worketh in all degrees, stay your mind from dislike.

As no man in any Age, but may see great happiness to have been attained by good agreement of Friends, Kinsmen, and Brethren ; so wanteth there not too many examples of such, as by hate and dis-cord have frustrated strong hopes sowed in peace, and brought to nothing great Fortunes ; besides the incurring God's displeasure, which still comes accompanied with perpetual misery. If you look into Divine Writ, you shall find, that this was the cause of " *Abel* " and " *Cain's* " misery, which the least hard hap that came to either of them, was to be murdered by his Brother.

" If you look into Humane Stories, you need search no further to behold a most pitiful object than the two sons of ' Phillip,' king of ' Macedon,' whose dislike each to other was so deeply rooted, that at length it burst forth to open complaints, the one of the other to good old 'Phillip' who seeing it, could not be put off from a publick hearing, called both his sons (Demetrius and Perseus) and in both their hearing made a most effectual speech of concord unto them; but finding that it would not take effect, gave them free leave to wound his heart with their unnatural accusations, the one against the other; which staid not there, by the unjust hastning of their Father's sudden death, but caused the murther of one of them, with the utter overthrow of that commonwealth, and the misery of the survivor. These things (I hope) will not be so necessary for your use, as they are hurtless to know, and effectual where need requires.

"Besides these examples, and fore-recited obligations, let me joyn a Father's charge which ought not to be lightly esteemed in so just a cause. Let me tell you my son *Kenelm*, that you ought to be both a Father and a Brother to your unprovided for Brother, and think, that what I am hindred from performing to him by short life, and voluntary tie of my Land to you; so much account your self bound to do him, both in Brotherly affection to him, and in natural duty to me. And you, my son *John*, know I send you as Fatherly a Blessing, as if I had also given you a great Patrimony; and that if my life had permitted, I would have done my endeavour that way. If you find any-thing in that kind to come from your Brother, take it the more thankfully; but if that you do not, let it not lessen your love to him, who ought not to be loved by you for his Fortune or Bounty, but for himself. I am sorry that I am cut off by time from saying so much as I did intend at the first; but since I may not, I will commend in my Prayers your instruction and guidance to the Giver of all goodness, who ever bless and keep you.—Your affectionate Father,

"EVE DIGBY—

"From my Prison this
of Jan. 1605."

CHAPTER XV.

On Monday, the 27th of January 1606, Sir Everard Digby, Robert and Thomas Winter, Guy Fawkes, John Grant, Ambrose Rookwood, Robert Keyes, and Thomas Bates, were taken from their cells in the Tower, led to a barge, and conveyed up the river to Westminster to be put on their trial in the celebrated hall, which stands on the site of the banquetting room of William Rufus. They were to stand before their accusers on soil already famous, and destined to become yet more famous for important trials. Here, three hundred years earlier, Sir William Wallace had been condemned to death. Here, only about eighty years before their own time came, both Anne Boleyn and Sir Thomas More had been tried and sentenced. In this splendid building, Wentworth, Earl of Strafford, and King Charles the First were destined to be condemned to the block. In the following century, sentence of death was here to be passed upon the rebel lords of 1745; here too, still later, Warren Hastings and Lord Melville were to be impeached.

Sir Everard Digby and his fellow-prisoners reached Westminster about half-an-hour before the time fixed for the trial, and they were taken to the Star Chamber to await the arrival of their judges. The following is a contemporary account of their appearance and behaviour while there.

[1] " It was strange to note their carriage, even in their very countenances : some hanging down the head, as if their hearts were full of doggedness, and others forcing a stern look, as if they would fear " [" that is *frighten. Footnote.*"] " death with a frown, never seeming to pray, except it were by the dozen upon their beads, and taking tobacco, as if hanging were no trouble to them ; saying nothing but in commendation of their conceited religion, craving mercy of neither God nor the king for their offences, and making their consciences, as it were, as wide as the world ; and to the very gates of hell, to be the cause of their hellish courses, to make a work meritorious."

This writer clearly did not go to the trial prepared to be pleased with the prisoners. If they looked down, they were " dogged " and ought to have been looking up ; if they looked up, they were " forcing a stern look," and ought to have been looking down : if they were not praying, they should have been praying, and if they were praying, yea, even praying " by the dozen," they should have not have been

[1] Somers' Tracts, Vol. xi. p. 113.

praying ; if they smoked, it was because they did not mind being hanged ; if they talked of nothing but religion, it was because they did not desire God's mercy, and one thing was certain—that their prayers and their religion and all things about them, to their very consciences, were " hellish."

Sir John Harrington was another unadmiring spectator.

[1] " I have seen some of the chief" [conspirators], he says, " and think they bear an evil mark in their foreheads, for more terrible countenances never were looked upon."

Another writer takes a different view, at any rate in the case of Sir Everard Digby. As that prisoner was being brought up for trial, says Father Gerard,[2] " (not in the best case to make show of himself as you may imagine), yet some of the chiefest in the Court seeing him out of a window brought in that manner, lamented him much, and said he was the goodliest man in the whole Court."

On entering Westminster Hall, the prisoners were made to ascend a scaffold placed in front of the judges. The Queen and the Prince were seated in a concealed chamber from which they could see, but could not be seen ; and it was reported that the King also was somewhere present.[3] The crowd was enormous. Although a special part of the hall had

1 *Nugæ Antiquæ*, Vol. i. p. 373.   2 *Narrative of the G. P.*, p. 88.
3 Letter from Sir E. Hoby to Sir T. Edmondes.

been assigned to members of parliament who might wish to attend the trial, they were so[1] "pestered with others not of the House," that one member complained, and a committee was afterwards appointed to enquire into the matter.

Sir Everard Digby was arraigned under a separate indictment from that of the other prisoners, and he was tried by himself after them; but he stood by them throughout the trial. The first indictment was very long. After a much spun-out preamble, it stated that the prisoners "traiterously[2] among themselves did conclude and agree, with Gun-powder, as it were with one blast, suddenly, traiterously, and barbarously to blow up and tear in pieces our said Sovereign Lord the King, the Excellent, Virtuous, and gracious Queen Anne his dearest Wife, the most Noble Prince Henry their Eldest Son, the future Hope and Joy of England, and the Lords Spiritual and Temporal; the Reverend Judges of the Realm, the Knights, Citizens, and Burgesses of Parliament, and divers other faithful Subjects and Servants of the King in the said Parliament," &c., "and all of them, without any respect of Majesty, Dignity, Degree, Sex, Age, or Place, most barbarously, and more than beastly, traiterously and suddenly, to destroy and swallow up."

---

[1] Journals of the House of Commons, Jan. 28 1605-6. *Criminal Trials*. Jardine, p. 115, footnote.

[2] *Gunpowder Treason*, Bp. Barlow, p. (3)

The prisoners under this indictment pleaded " *Not Guilty*; and put themselves upon God and the Country."

Sir Edward Philips, Sergeant at Law, then got upon his legs. The matter before the Court, he said, was one of Treason;[1] "but of such horrour, and monstrous nature, that before now,

The Tongue of Man never delivered,

The Ear of Man never heard,

The Heart of Man never conceited,

Nor the Malice of Hellish or Earthly Devil never practised."

And, if it were "abominable to murder the least," and if "to touch God's annointed," were to oppose God himself, "Then how much more than too monstrous" was it "to murder and subvert

Such a King,

Such a Queen,

Such a Prince,

Such a Progeny,

Such a State,

Such a Government,

So compleat and absolute;

That God approves :

The World admires :

All true English Hearts honour and reverence :

The Pope and his Disciples onely envies and maligns."

The Sergeant, after dwelling briefly on the chief

<hr>

[1] *Gunpowder Treason*, Bp. Barlow, p. (9).

points of the indictment, and describing the objects of the conspiracy and the plan of the conspirators, sat down to make way for the principal counsel for the prosecution, His Majesty's Attorney-General, Sir Edward Coke.

Coke, the enemy of Bacon, was now about fifty-five, and he had filled the post of Attorney-General for nine years. Sir Everard Digby and his fellow-prisoners knew that they had little mercy to expect at his hands. The asperity which he had shown in prosecuting Essex, five years earlier, and the personal animosity which he had exhibited, still later, in his sarcastic speech at the trial of Raleigh, when he had wound up with the phrase, "Thou hast an English face but a Spanish heart," were notorious, and he was certain to make such a trial as that of the conspirators in the Gunpowder Plot the occasion of a great forensic display. It so happened that his speeches at this trial and that of Father Garnet, which presently followed it, brought his career as an advocate to a close; for within a year he was appointed Chief-Justice of Common Pleas.

Undoubtedly, his speeches at the trial of Sir Everard Digby and his accomplices added to his fame; but Jardine[1] called one of them "a long and laboured harangue," and other historians thought him guilty of [2] "unnecessary cruelty in the torture and gratuitous" insolence which he exhibited towards

------

[1] P. 141.   [2] See *Ency. Brit.*, Eighth Ed., Vol. vii. p. 95.

the accused. The glaring eyes, which we see represented in his portrait, would be an unpleasant prospect for Sir Everard as he listened to his cruel words ; but whatever tenderness a biographer may feel for his subject, and whatever dislike a Catholic may entertain to the Protestant bigotry of Sir Edward Coke, it ought not to be forgotten that, according to his lights, he was an honest, if a hard and an unmerciful man, that some ten years later he himself fell into disgrace and suffered imprisonment in the Tower, rather than yield on a point of principle, and that, vindictive as he could be in prosecuting a prisoner, one of his enemies—Lord Chancellor Egerton—said that his greatest fault was his " excessive popularity."

Although he began his speech by saying that the Gunpowder Plot had been the greatest treason ever conceived against the greatest king that ever lived, he had presently a complimentary word or two to say as to the origins and previous lives of some of the conspirators. With an air of great truthfulness and fairness he said :—[1] " It is by some given out that they are such men as admit just exception, either desperate in estate, or base, or not settled in their wits ; such as are *sine religione, sine sede, sine fide, sine re, et sine spe*—without religion, without habitation, without credit, without means, without hope. But (that no man, though never so wicked,

[1] *Criminal Trials*, Jardine, p. 127 *seq.*

may be wronged) true it is, they were gentlemen of good houses, of excellent parts, howsoever most perniciously seduced, abused, corrupted, and jesuited, of very competent fortunes and estates."

After having said these comparatively gentle words concerning the laity, he launched forth in declamation against "those of the spirituality," not one of whom was actually on his trial. "It is falsely said," he cried, "that there is never a religious man in this action; for I never yet knew a treason without a Romish priest; but in this there are very many Jesuits, who are known to have dealt and passed through the whole action." He then named four of these, beginning with Father Garnet, "besides their cursory men," the first of which was Father Gerard. "The studies and practises of this sect principally consisted in two D's, to wit, in deposing of kings and disposing of kingdoms." Having thundered away at Jesuits and priests to his heart's content, he exclaimed that "the Romish Catholicks" had put themselves under "Gunpowder Law, fit for Justices of Hell."

"Note," said he, with great vehemence, "that gunpowder was the invention of a Friar, one of that Romish Rabble."[1] "All friars, religions, and priests were bad"; but "the principal offenders are

---

[1] So it is commonly said; but Mr Tomlinson, in his article on Gunpowder in the *Ency. Brit.*, Vol. xi. p. 150, ed. 1856, says that it was known, in some form at least, in the year 355 B.C.

the seducing Jesuits, men that use the reverence of Religion, yea, even the most Sacred and Blessed name of JESUS as a mantle to cover their impiety, blasphemy, treason, and rebellion, and all manner of wickedness."

No speech in those days was considered perfect without a few words of astrology, so he called the attention of the Court to the remarkable fact "that it was in the entering of the Sun into the Tropick of *Capricorn*, when they " [the conspirators] "began their mine ; noting that by mincing they should descend, and by hanging ascend."

In the latter part of his pompous harangue, there was a passage which must have been very unpleasant hearing to the prisoners, however interesting to the rest of the audience.[1]

"The conclusion shall be from the admirable clemency and moderation of the King, in that howsoever these traitors have exceeded all others their predecessors in mischief, and *Crescente, malitia crescere debuit, etc., Pœna* ; yet neither will the King exceed the usual punishment of Law, nor invent any new torture or torment for them, but is graciously pleased to afford them an ordinary course of trial, as an ordinary punishment, much inferior to their offence."   Nor was this reference to a "new torture" a mere figure of rhetoric on the part of the Attorney - General ; for a few days

---

[1] *Gunpowder Treason*, by Thomas, Bp. of Lincoln, pp. (48)-(50).

earlier,[1] in both houses of Parliament, a proposal had been made to petition the King "to stay judgment until Parliament should have time to consider some extraordinary mode of punishment, which might surpass in horror even the scenes which usually occurred at the execution of traitors." To their credit be it spoken, this suggestion was negatived by both Lords and Commons.

"And surely," continued Coke, "worthy of observation is the punishment by law provided for High Treason, which we call *Crimen læsæ Majestatis*. For first after a traitor hath had his fair trial, and is convicted and attainted, he shall have his judgment to be drawn to the place of execution from his prison, as being not worthy any more to tread upon the face of the earth, whereof he was made. Also for that he hath been retrograde to Nature, therefore is he drawn backwards at a horse-tail. And whereas God hath made the head of man the highest and most supreme part, as being his chief grace and ornament: *Pronáque cum spectent Animalia cætera terram, Os homini sublime dedit;* he must be drawn with his head declining downward, and lying so near the ground as may be, being thought unfit to take benefit of the common air. For which cause also he shall be strangled, being hanged up by the neck between heaven and earth, as deemed unworthy of both, or either; as likewise,

[1] Gardiner's Hist. of Eng., Vol. i. p. 286 ; and see 3 Jac. I. cap. 1.

that the eyes of men may behold, and their hearts contemn him. Then is he to be cut down alive, and to have —— cut off, and burnt before his face, as being unworthily begotten, and unfit to leave any generation after him ; his bowels and inlayed parts taken out and burnt, who inwardly conceived and harboured in his heart such horrible Treason. After, to have his head cut off, which had imagined the mischief. And lastly, his body to be quartered, and the quarters set up in some high and eminent place, to the view and detestation of men, and to become a prey for the Fouls of the Air."

Considering that the prisoners had not yet been found guilty, and that even had they been, it was no business of his to pass sentence on them, this pointless and objectless description of their probable fate was as gratuitous as it was cruel on the part of the Attorney-General.

With the prisoners, other than Sir Everard Digby, I have nothing to do, and it will suffice to say, that, at the conclusion of the Attorney-General's speech, the depositions of their examinations in the Tower —" the voluntary confessions of all the said several traitors in writings subscribed with their own proper hands " — were then read aloud. These are very interesting, and have already been partially used in framing the story in the preceding pages. They are humble and penitent in tone, and as a specimen of this apparent penitence I will quote the opening of one of the longest, namely that by Thomas Winter.[1]

"My most honorable Lordes.—Not out of hope to obtayne pardon, for speakinge of my temporall past, I may say the fault is greater than can be forgiven, nor affectinge hereby the title of a good subject, for I must redeeme my countrey from as great a danger as I have hazarded the bringinge her into, before I can purchase any such opinion ; only at your Ho. Commans I will breifely sett downe my owne accusation, and how farr I have proceeded in this busyness wch I shall the faythfuller doe since I see such courses are not pleasinge to Allmighty God, and that all or the most material parts have been allready confessed."

At the conclusion of the public reading of these confessions, the Lord Chief Justice made some remarks to the jury, and then directed them to consider of their verdict ; upon "which they retired into a separate place."[2]

Sir Everard Digby was then arraigned by himself upon a separate indictment issued by Sir Christopher Yelverton and other special commissioners of Oyer & Terminer, on the 16th of January, at Wellingborough, in Northamptonshire, and delivered to the same commission in Middlesex that had tried the other prisoners. It charged him with High Treason in conspiring the death of the king, with conferring with

---

[1] S. P. Dom. James I., G. P. Book, Part II. n. 114.
[2] *Criminal Trials*, Jardine, Vol. ii. pp. 138 and 169.

Catesby in Northamptonshire concerning the Gunpowder Plot, assenting to the design, and taking the oath of secrecy.

As soon as the indictment was read, Sir Everard began to make a speech; but was interrupted by being told that he must first plead, either guilty or not guilty, and that then he would be allowed to say what he liked.

He at once confessed that he was guilty of the treason; and then he spoke of the motives which had led him to it.[1] The first of these was neither ambition, nor discontent, nor ill-will towards any member of Parliament, but his intense friendship and affection for Robert Catesby, whose influence over him was so great that he could not help risking his own property and his life at his bidding. The second motive was the cause of religion, on behalf of which he was glad to endanger " his estate, his life, his name, his memory, his posterity, and all worldly and earthly felicity whatsoever." His third motive was prompted by the broken promises to Catholics, and had as its object the prevention of the harder laws which they feared and professed to have solid reasons for fearing, from the new Parliament; as " that Recusant's Wives, and women, should be liable to the Mulct as well as their husbands and men." And further, that " it was supposed, that it should be made a *Præmunire* onely to be a Catholick."

---

[1] *Gunpowder Treason*, by Thomas, Bp. of Lincoln, p. (55) *seq.*

Having stated the motives of his crime, he proceeded to make his petitions—[1] "That sithens his offence was confined and contained within himself, that the punishment also of the same might extend only to himself, and not be transferred either to his Wife, Children, Sisters, or others : and therefore for his Wife he humbly craved, that she might enjoy her Joynture, his Son the benefit of an Entail made long before any thought of this action ; his Sisters, their just and due portions which were in his hands ; his Creditors, their rightful Debts ; which that he might more justly set down under his hand, he requested, that before his death, his Man (who was better acquainted both with the men and the particulars than himself) might be licensed to come unto him. Then prayed he pardon of the King and Ll. for his guilt, and lastly, he entreated to be beheaded, desiring all men to forgive him, and that his death might satisfie them for his trespass."

The daylight was waning quickly in the great hall of Westminster, on that short January day, when Sir Edward Coke, the Attorney-General, rose from his seat, at the conclusion of Sir Everard Digby's dignified but distressed speech. He had already shown refinement of cruelty in treating the prisoners to a detailed description of the horrors of the death that was awaiting them, and he was now again ready to inflict as much pain as possible.

[1] *Gunpowder Treason*, by Thomas, Bp. of Lincoln, p. (56).

As to Sir Everard's friendship with Catesby, he said, it was "mere folly, and wicked Conspiracy"; his religion was "Error and Heresie"; his promises —it does not appear that he had made any—were "idle and vain presumptions"; "as also his fears, false alarms, Concerning Wives that were Recusants." "If a man married one," great reason there is, "that he or they should pay for it"; but if a wife "were no Recusant at the time of Marriage"—as had been the case with Lady Digby, although he did not mention her by name—"and yet afterwards he suffer her to be corrupted and seduced, by admitting Priests and Romanists into his house"—Roger Lee and Father Gerard, for instance, Sir Everard might understand him to imply—"good reason that he, be he Papist or Protestant, should pay for his negligence and misgovernment."

Next he dealt with Sir Everard's petitions on behalf of his wife, children, sisters, &c., and on this point he became eloquent.[1] "Oh how he doth now put on the bowels of Nature and Compassion in the perils of his private and domesticated estate! But before, when the publick state of his Countrey, when the King, the Queen, the tender Princes, the Nobles, the whole Kingdom, were designed to a perpetual destruction, Where was then this piety, this Religious affection?" "All Nature, all Humanity, all respect of Laws both Divine and Humane, were quite

---

[1] *Gunpowder Treason*, by Thomas, Bp. of Lincoln, p. (57).

abandoned; then there was no conscience made to extirpate the whole Nation, and all for a pretended zeal to the Catholick Religion, and the justification of so detestable and damnable a Fact."

Here Sir Everard Digby interrupted the great lawyer with the remark that he had not justified the fact, but had confessed that he deserved the vilest death; and that all he had done was to seek mercy, "and some moderation of justice."

As to moderation of justice, replied the Attorney-General, how could a man expect or ask for it who had acted in direct opposition to all mercy and all justice? And had he not already had most ample and most undeserved moderation shown to him? Verily he ought "to admire the great moderation and mercy of the King, in that, for so exorbitant a crime, no new torture answerable thereunto was devised to be inflicted upon him." Was it not sufficient consolation to him to reflect upon his good fortune in this respect? Sir Everard had talked about his wife and children. Well! did he forget how he had said "that for the Catholick Cause he was content to neglect the ruine of himself, his Wife, his Estate, and all "? Oh! he should be made content enough on this point. Here was an appropriate text for him :—" Let his Wife be a widow, and his Children vagabonds, let his posterity be destroyed, and in the next generation let his name be quite put out." Then Sir Edward Coke spoke directly to Sir Everard, and said :—" For the paying of your

Creditors, it is equal and just, but yet fit the King be first satisfied and paid, to whom you owe so much, as that all you have is too little : yet these things must be left to the pleasure of his Majesty, and the course of Justice and Law." Fortunately for Sir Everard, " in respect for the time (for it grew now dark) " the Attorney General spoke " very briefly."

One of the nine Commissioners, appointed to try the prisoners, now addressed Sir Everard. His words came with more force, perhaps it might be said with more cruel force, because he was himself a Catholic. This was Henry Howard, Earl of Northampton, younger brother of the Duke of Norfolk, and second son of Henry Howard, Earl of Surrey, who had been beheaded on Tower Hill, nearly sixty years earlier, in the reign of Henry VIII. This Commissioner had espoused the cause of Mary, Queen of Scots,[1] and he was rather ostentatiously put forward at this trial, and afterwards at that of Father Garnet, to prove his loyalty and to counteract the jealousy and suspicion which had been caused by the appointment of a man of his religion[2] to the Wardenship of the Cinque Ports. Banks wrote of him,[3] " other authors represent him as the most contemptible and despicable of mankind ; a wretch, that it causes astonishment to reflect, that he was the son of the generous, the noble, and

---

[1] Froude's Hist. of Eng., Vol. xi. p. 74.

[2] *Criminal Trials*, Jardine, Vol. xi. p. 172, footnote.

[3] I quote from Burke's *Dormant and Extinct Peerages*, p. 285.

accomplished Earl of Surrey.[1]   He was a learned man, but a pedant, dark and mysterious, and consequently far from possessing masterly abilities.   He was the grossest of flatterers, &c."

Northampton began his speech as follows :—

[2] " You must not hold it strange, Sir Everard Digby, though at this time being pressed in duty, Conscience and Truth, I do not suffer you to wander in the Laberinth of your own idle conceits without opposition, to seduce others, as your self have been seduced, by false Principles ; or to convey your self by charms of imputation, by clouds of errour, and by shifts of lately devised 'Equivocation'; out of that streight wherein your late secure and happy fortune hath been unluckily entangled ; but yet justly surprised, by the rage and revenge of your own rash humors.   If in this crime (more horrible than any man is able to express) I could lament the estate of any person upon earth, I could pity you, but thank your self and your bad counsellours, for leading you into a Crime of such a kind ; as no less benummeth in all faithfull, true and honest men, the tenderness of affection, than it did in you, the sense of all humanity.   That you were once well thought of, and esteemed by the late Queen, I can witness, having heard her speak of you with that grace which might have encouraged a true gentleman to have run a

----

[1] Henry, Earl of Surrey, was the first English writer of blank verse and sonnets.   *Beeton's Encyclopædia.*

[2] *Gunpowder Treason,* p. 59.

better course : Nay, I will add further, that there was a time, wherein you were as well affected to the king our master's expectation, though perhaps upon false rumours and reports, that he would have yielded satisfaction to your unprobable and vast desires : but the seed that wanted moisture (as our Saviour Himself reporteth) took no deep root : that zeal which hath no other end or object than the pleasing of it self, is quickly spent : and Trajan, that worthy and wise Emperour, had reason to hold himself discharged of all debts to those, that had offended more by prevarication, than they could deserve by industry."

The main contention of his long and wordy speech was to refute the charge of broken promises to his co-religionists brought by Sir Everard Digby in his description of his motives. It was well-known that the Catholics considered the king guilty of perfidy on this point, and that they based their accusation chiefly upon the reports of Father Watson's celebrated interview with James in Scotland, a matter with which I dealt in an early chapter. Northampton denied that James had ever encouraged the Catholics to expect any favour.

He made a strong point of Percy's having asserted that the king had promised toleration to the Catholics; asking why, if this were really the case, Percy, at the beginning of the king's reign, thought it worth while to employ Guy Fawkes and others to plot against the king in Spain ? He wound up by praying for Sir Everard's repentance in this world and his forgiveness in the next.

Then Lord Salisbury spoke. He began by acknowledging his own connection, by marriage, with Sir Everard, and then he proceeded, with even greater zeal than Northampton, to imply that the prisoner's plea of broken promises to Catholics would be understood to mean bad faith on the part of the king ; and it was thought by some that Sir Everard would have had his sentence commuted for beheading, had it not been for what Salisbury now said.[1]   After defending the king from all imputation of faithlessness towards his Catholic subjects, Salisbury referred to Sir Everard's personal guilt, and dwelt upon Guy Fawkes's evidence that, at Gothurst, he had expresssd a fear lest the gunpowder stored beneath the houses of Parliament, might, during the wet weather in October, have "grown dank."

When Salisbury had finished, Sergeant Philips got up and "prayed the judgment of the court upon the verdict of the Jury against the seven first prisoners, and against Sir Everard Digby upon his own confession."   Each prisoner was then formally asked what he had to say why judgment of death should not be pronounced against him. Finally Lord Chief Justice Popham described and defended the laws made by Queen Elizabeth against

---

[1] *Narrative of the G. P.*, Gerard, p. 216.

priests, recusants, and receivers and harbourers of priests, [1] which seems to have been a little wide of the subject of the crime of the prisoners, and then he solemnly pronounced the usual sentence for high treason upon all the eight men who stood convicted before him.

Then Sir Everard bowed towards the commissioners who had tried him and said :—"If I may but hear any of your Lordships say you forgive me, I shall go more cheerfully to the gallows."

They all immediately replied :—"God forgive you, and we do."

And thus, late in the evening, this memorable trial ended, and the prisoners were conveyed by torches to their barge; then they were rowed down the river to the Tower, and led through the dark "Traitor's Gate" to their cells.

[1] *Criminal Trials*, Jardine, Vol. ii. p. 181.

CHAPTER XVI.

Sir Everard Digby was only allowed two clear days between his trial and his execution to prepare for death. He was not permitted to see his young wife or his little sons, nor was he granted the consolation of the services of a priest. Short as was the time he had yet to live, it must have hung heavily on his hands. Fortunately he had lived much with Jesuits, who would doubtless have instructed him in their admirable system of meditation; but "the exercise of the memory," which it includes, can hardly have afforded him much consolation under the circumstances. To add to his depression, it was at the time of year when there are but few hours of daylight, and the artificial light permitted in a prisoner's room in the Tower would certainly be very meagre, and little more than sufficient to render the ghastly gloom of the dungeon-walls more manifest. Very early, too, all prisoners' lights would be put out, and terrible then must have been the dreariness of the long nights and the dark mornings, until the sun rose at about a quarter to eight o'clock. It is easy to imagine him dreaming of his happy home at

Gothurst, and fancying himself walking with his wife in its garden, or playing with his little children by its great hall fireside, or entertaining his guests at its long banquetting-table, and suddenly waking with a start, to find himself in darkness, on a hard bed, with a rough, cold wall beside him, and to remember that he was a condemned traitor in the Tower of London; and then, perhaps, lying awake to reflect upon the brilliant opportunities of happiness, prosperity, and usefulness with which he had started in his short life, and the misery in which he was about to end it. Nor does it require any great effort of the imagination to see him falling, from sheer weariness, into a fitful, feverish sleep, and, as he turned and tossed, frequently dreaming of the horrors of his impending execution, as they had been so lately described in his presence by the Attorney-General.

When, in the morning, he rose to obtain consolation from devotion, how likely that the heavy drowsiness or headache resulting from a wretched night would make him feel utterly helpless as he tried to pray or meditate; or that, distracted by the memories of his misfortunes, and the terrible thought of the destitution to which his wife and family might be exposed—for he seems to have died in doubt whether Gothurst, as well as his estates inherited from his father, would not be confiscated—he would be unable to fix his attention upon spiritual matters.

During the interval preceding his death Sir Everard wrote the following lines. Criticise them as you please; call them doggrel if you will; but at least respect them as the words of a broken-hearted and dying man.

✠

JESUS MARIA.

Who's that which knocks ? Oh stay, my Lord, I come :
   I know that call, since first it made me know
My self, which makes me now with joy to run,
   Lest He be gone that can my duty show.
     Jesu, my Lord, I know Thee by the Cross
     Thou offer'st me, but not unto my loss.

Come in, my Lord, whose presence most I crave,
   And shew Thy will unto my longing mind ;
From punishments of sin Thy servant save,
   Though he hath been to Thy deserts unkind.
     Jesu forgive, and strengthen so my mind,
     That rooted virtues thou in me maist find.

Stay still, my Lord, else will they fade away,
   As Marigold that mourns for absent Sun :
Thou know'st thou plantest in a barren clay
   That choaks in Winter all that up is come ;
     I do not fear thy Summers wished for heat
     My tears shall water where thy shine doth threat.

However deeply Sir Everard Digby may have sinned, he knew how to make his peace with God when death approached him. He had a definite religion to depend on, he had no need to consider which of many widely divergent views held by the professors of one nominal church was the most probable. It is true that he was deprived of those consoling rites which the Catholic Church provides for her children when on the threshold of death ; he had none of the "soothing charm" of "the words of peace and blessing"[1] uttered by the confessor in absolution ; he was not strengthened for the perilous journey from this life to the next by the sacred viaticum, but he knew that, where these privileges could not be obtained, a hearty desire for them, with a good act of contrition, might obtain many of their blessings and all that was necessary for salvation.

From a theological point of view, it was a happy thing that he knew the plot in which he had been implicated to be all but universally condemned by his co-religionists. If many of them had defended it, and he had heard that there were two parties, one extenuating the conspiracy and another anathematising it, he might have clung to the belief that he had done nothing wrong, and that "rending of the heart" conducive to true contrition might have been wanting.

He had sinned deeply ; let us hope that deep was his sorrow. Yet is not this the moment—the moment when we are supposing him in the deepest

[1] See Cardinal Newman in *Present Position of Catholics*, p. 351.

degradation of spirit for his iniquities—at which we may best say a kind word for him?

Hitherto I have written little in palliation of his crime; perhaps the very fact of his having professed my own religion may have made me more careful to say nothing that might have the appearance of minimising his guilt; nor, in the few more pages that I have still to write, do I intend to plead that his sentence ought to have been commuted on account of any extenuating circumstances. Unquestionably he deserved to die, but I beg to commend his memory to the mercy of my readers.

Let others speak for him. The Protestant Bishop Barlow, in his book on the Gunpowder Plot, which so severely condemns all concerned in it, says [1] :—" This Gentleman was verily persuaded of the lawfulness of this Design, and did engage in it out of a sincere, but ignorant zeal for the advancement, as he thought, of the true Religion." These are the words of a hostile historian: the following—some of which have been quoted earlier—are those of a friend [2] :—" He was so much and so generally lamented, and is so much esteemed and praised by all sorts in England, both Catholics and others, although neither side can or do approve this last outrageous and exorbitant attempt against our King and country, wherein a man otherwise so worthy, was so unworthily lost and cast away

---

[1] *Gunpowder Treason*, Appendix.
[2] *Narrative of the G. P.*, Gerard, p. 91.

to the great grief of all that knew him, and especially
of all that loved him.   And truly it was hard to do
the one and not the other."   An unfriendly critic,
Scott, in a footnote to the *Somers' Tracts*,[1] says that
Sir Everard "was a man of unblemished reputation
until this hellish conspiracy."   Yet another, Caulfield,
says of him,[2] "Digby himself was as highly esteemed
and beloved as any man in England"; and one more
hostile writer, Jardine, says[3]:—"There is abundant
evidence that Sir Everard Digby joined in the enterprise under the full persuasion that in so doing he
was rendering good service to his church and pro-
moting the cause of true religion."

Testimonies to his character would be incomplete
without any from a woman.   Here is one from a
Protestant to the back-bone, Miss Aikin:—[4] "His
youth, his personal graces, the constancy which he
had exhibited whilst he believed himself a martyr
in a good cause, the deep sorrow which he testified
on becoming sensible of his error, seemed to have
moved all hearts with pity and even admiration;
and if so detestable a villainy as the powder plot
may be permitted to have a hero, Everard Digby
was undoubtedly the man."

Lastly, he must be allowed to have his share in the
fair and considerate pleadings of the greatest of all

[1] Vol. ii. p. 116.
[2] *History of the G. P.*, by James Caulfield, 1804, p. 56.
[3] *Gunpowder Plot*, p. 153.
[4] *Memoirs of the Court of James I.*, Vol. i. p. 254.

historians of the Stuart period, on behalf of the conspirators in the Gunpowder Plot. Dr Samuel Rawson Gardiner writes :—[1] " Atrocious as the whole undertaking was, great as must have been the moral obliquity of their minds before they could have conceived such a project, there was at least nothing mean or selfish about them. They had boldly risked their lives for what they honestly believed to be the cause of God and of their country." A few lines further on he says, " if the criminality of their design was hidden from the eyes of the plotters, it was not from any ambitious thoughts of the consequences of success to themselves." Presently he adds, " As far as we can judge, they would have been ready, as soon as the wrongs of which they complained had been redressed, to sink back again into obscurity." And finally, after dwelling upon their difficulty in seeing "their atrocious crime in the light in which we see it," he declares his opinion that, just at last, at least some of them saw "their acts as they really were," and "with such thoughts as these on their minds," "passed away from the world which they had wronged to the presence of Him who had seen their guilt and their repentance alike."

It is well, however, to be just as well as generous, and if it be impossible to consider the fine, handsome youth, of four and twenty, awaiting execution in the Tower of London, without feelings of compassion ;

[1] History of England, Vol. i. pp. 263-4.

we should none the less remember that Sir Everard
Digby's co-religionists have other reasons for sorrow
in connection with him.   Instead of benefiting
the Catholic cause in his country by the enterprise
which he assisted with his influence, his wealth,
his time, and his personal services, he did it
the most serious mischief conceivable; we must
keep before our minds, therefore, the fact, that to
Catholics he should appear, not so much an unhappy failure, as a most active, if most uninten-
tional, aggressor.   Although King James himself
declared that the English Catholics, as a body,
were neither implicated in, nor approvers of the
Gunpowder Plot; although the Archpriest condemned it formally a day or two after its discovery; although Father Gerard and other Jesuits
distinctly and categorically disclaimed all connection
with it, and although the Pope himself addressed
two letters to King James, expressing his unqualified
horror of it, the idea was never dispelled that it
was a Popish and Jesuitical design.   For many
years, English people were ready to believe any
absurd tale of Catholic conspiracy, such as [1] "Rome's
Master-piece : or, The Grand Conspiracy of the Pope
and his Jesuited Instruments," in 1640, and the
pretended plot to assassinate Charles II. in 1678,
for which, on the perjured evidence of Titus Oates

---

[1] See Wharton's *Laud's History*, &c., p. 567.

and others,[1] "about eighteen Roman Catholics were accused, and upon false testimony convicted and executed ; among them the aged Viscount Stafford." Ballads, such as that which begins as follows, describing this so-called and non-existent conspiracy, were eagerly purchased in the streets.

[2] "Good People, I pray you, give ear unto me,
　　A Story so strange you have never been told,
　How the *Jesuit, Devil,* and *Pope* did agree
　　Our *State* to destroy, and *Religion so old.*
　　　To *murder* our *King,*
　　　A most horrible thing, &c."

Nor did the prejudices against Catholics raised by the Gunpowder Plot, early in the seventeenth century, die out at the end of it. Even now there remains a traditional superstition in this country that it was planned by the Jesuits, admired by the majority of English Catholics, and secretly connived at by the Pope and the Sacred College. For generations, English schoolboys have believed that Roman Catholics are people who would blow up every Protestant with gunpowder if they could. So indelible has been the prejudice created against Catholics by the misdoings of a mere handful of conspirators in the Gunpowder Plot, that the large number of English Catholic squires, baronets, and

---

[1] Haydn's *Dictionary of Dates,* 1892, p. 696.
[2] *A New Narrative of the Popish Plot, showing the Cunning Contrivance thereof.*

noblemen, who squandered their estates and their patrimony, and even gave their lives, for their king, in the reigns of Charles I. and Charles II., failed to eradicate the popular notion that all Catholics were disloyal. The meetings at White Webbs and Gothurst gave rise to the idea that the private house of every Catholic served as a rendezvous for plotters, and every seminary as a nest of traitors; the fact that Catesby and Digby had Jesuit friends has made Protestants believe that every Jesuit would commit a murder if he thought it would serve the cause of his religion; and the fact that they had priests in their houses has led to the impression that, wherever there is a domestic Catholic chaplain, mischief is certain to be brewing. Worst of all, when Protestants are told of "an excellent Catholic," a man who goes to confession and communion every week, a man of irreproachable character both in private and in public life, a man of high position, great wealth, charming manners, and popularity among Protestants as well as Catholics, they can point, as they have been able to point for nearly three hundred years, to the history of Sir Everard Digby, as an example of what even such a man would be "obliged to do" were "his priest" so to order him.

Thus much for the moral effect produced by the efforts of Sir Everard Digby and his friends for the benefit of the English Catholics; the material effect may be described in a few words. It was, instead of relieving them from oppression, to cause the laws and disabilities under which they suffered to be redoubled. When they reflect upon all these things, can Catholics recall the memory of Sir Everard Digby with no other feelings than those of pity? Surely, if any class of men have cause to execrate the memory of every conspirator in the Gunpowder Plot, it is not the Protestants but the Catholics.

None the less may it be doubted, whether, among misguided men, there is a character in history more to be pitied than Sir Everard Digby. Whatever his faults, whatever his errors, whatever the mischief he wrought to the cause for which he was ready to give his life, he never seems to have been guilty of a selfish action; if he was disloyal to his country, he believed that he was serving its best interests; if he mistook atrocious murder for legitimate warfare, it was with the hope of restoring his fellow-countrymen to the faith of their forefathers.

*   *   *   *   *   *

The inhabitants of London were to have two thoroughly happy days; there was to be a great execution on Thursday and another on Friday. Four traitors were to be hanged, drawn, and quartered on either day.

On Thursday, the 30th of January 1606, Sir Everard Digby was taken from his prison in the Tower to a doorway in front of which four horses were each harnessed to a separate wattled hurdle lying on the ground. He found three of his fellow-conspirators awaiting him—his late host, Robert Winter of Huddington, the courageous, but rough and pugnacious, John Grant of Norbrook, and—there being no respect of persons on the scaffold—Thomas Bates, Catesby's servant.

Ordered to lie down on his back, with his head towards the horse's tail, Sir Everard was tightly bound to the hurdle, and when all the four condemned men had been treated in the same manner, the procession started on its doleful journey. To be dragged through the muddy streets of London, to be splashed and saturated with their slush and filth, and to be bruised and shaken over the rough stones as the hurdle rose and fell over them, must have been as disagreeable as it was degrading ; and the mile or more from the Tower to the place of execution—the west of St Paul's Cathedral—was a long distance over which to be submitted to such an ordeal. To add to the sensations of disgrace, the streets were crowded, and nearly every window in Cheapside was filled with people watching the prisoners passing to their doom.

Every pains had been taken to render the execution as imposing as possible. A large number of soldiers accompanied the procession, and the Lord Mayor had issued an order to the Alderman of each ward of the city, ordering him to [1] " cause one able

---

[1] Repertories in the Town Clerk's Office. *Criminal Trials.* Jardine, Vol. xi. pp. 181-2.

and sufficient person, with a halbard in his hand, to stand at the door of every several dwelling-house in the open street in the way that the traitors were to be drawn towards the place of execution, from seven in the morning until the return of the sheriff." This was partly with a view to add dignity and importance to the terrible function, and partly to provide against tumult or raids by the mob.

When the shadow of St Paul's Cathedral fell upon his hurdle, Sir Everard knew that he was very near the scene of his execution ; the crowd became greater at every step of the horse that was dragging him, and he had scarcely passed the great church before he found himself in a narrow lane formed by a densely packed mass of people, kept apart by a line of soldiers on either side.

Suddenly the horse that was drawing his hurdle stopped, and, on looking up, he saw the ghastly gallows by his side. There, also, was the long, low, thick table, or block, on which the quartering would take place ; there, too, were the preparations for the fire in which certain portions of his body would be burnt before it went out.

He was liberated from the hurdle. Stiff and mud-bespattered, he got up and was led towards the gallows. He was then informed that he was to be the first to suffer. Many officials were present. The protestant clergy came forward and offered their services. He courteously refused them ; but turning to the crowd, he begged the assistance and prayers of all good Catholics.[1] Even his enemies admitted that as he stood on the scaffold, he was [2] " a man of a goodly personage and a manly aspect," although " his colour grew pale," as well it might, after having been dragged on his back for a mile over the streets of that period ; nor could a man be expected to carry much colour on his face immediately before being put to a horrible death in cold blood.

After saying a few prayers, he again turned to the people, and one of the officials asked him to acknowledge his treason before he died.   He then made a short speech.

[3] " Sir Everard Digby " says Stow, " protested from the bottome of his heart, he asked forgivenesse of God, the King, the Queene, the Prince, and all the Parliament, and if that hee had knowne it at first to have ben so foule a treason, he would not have concealed it to have gayned a world, requiring the people to witnesse he died penitent and sorrowfull for this vile Treason, and confident to be saved in the merits of his sweet Saviour Jesus, etc."

Still, he declared most solemnly [4] that while he was quite willing to die for his offence, he had not been impelled to commit the treason by feelings of ill-will towards any living creature, or a desire for self-advancement or worldly gains.   His sole motive had

---

[1] Narrative G. P., Gerard, p. 217. [2] Somers' Tracts, Vol. ii. p. 114.
[3] Stow's *Annales*, p. 882.
[4] Narrative of the G. P., Gerard, p. 217.

been to put an end to the persecutions of Catholics, to benefit human souls, and to serve the cause of religion. The action itself he acknowledged to have been sinful ; the intentions which prompted it he protested to have been pure.

"His speech was not long,"[1] and, when it was ended he knelt down, made the sign of the Cross, and said some prayers in a low voice in Latin, "often bowing his head to the ground," says Stow, "mumbling to himself," and "refusing to have any prayers of any but of the Romish Catholics," says the hostile historian in the *Somers' Tracts*, he "fell to his prayers with such devotion as moved all the beholders," states his friend Father Gerard, who goes on to say :— "And when he had done, he stood up and saluted all the noblemen and gentlemen that stood upon the scaffold, every one according to his estate, to the noblemen with a lower *congé*, to others with more show of equality, but to all in so friendly and so cheerful a manner, as they afterwards said, he seemed so free from fear of death, as that he showed no feeling at all of any passion therein, but took his leave of them as he was wont to do when he went from the Court or out of the city to his own house in the country ; yet he showed so great devotion of mind, so much fervour and humility in his prayers, and so great confidence in God, as that very many said[2] they made no doubt but his soul was

[1] Somers' Tracts.

[2] A footnote says, "Here wants something. *In another hand, erased in Original.*"

happy, and wished themselves might die in the like state of mind."

The hangman now came up to assist him in his preparations for execution. Before going to the gallows for hanging and quartering, the condemned man was stripped, with the exception of his shirt. This humiliating process having been completed, with his hands bound, Sir Everard accompanied the executioner to the foot of the ladder, and saying, " Oh ! Jesu, Jesu, save me and keep me," he ascended it, as also did the hangman.

I should like to let the curtain fall here ; but, were I to do so, my story would be incomplete.

The punishment of hanging, drawing, and quartering was so horrible, that it was often mitigated by allowing the victim to hang until he was dead. This might well have been done in the case of Sir Everard Digby. To be hung, partially naked, knowing that his body would afterwards be hacked to pieces in the most disgraceful manner before the eyes of an immense concourse of people, should have been considered a sufficient punishment. But no ! Not even was he permitted to be to some extent stupefied by being half-strangled. The executioner had no sooner turned him off the ladder than he cut the rope.[1] Sir Everard " fell on his face and bruised his forehead." Then followed a scene of vivisection and butchery,[2]

[1] *Narrative G. P.*, Gerard, p. 218.

[2] Wood, in his *Athenæ Oxonienses*, Vol. ii. p. 354, says, " when the Executioner pluck't out his Heart (when his Body was to be quartered),

which would not be tolerated in these days if the subject were a sheep or an ox. Yet even on the awful block, Sir Everard never betrayed his dignity;[1] and, condemn his offences as we may, we cannot fairly refuse to give him credit for having died like a good Christian, a courteous gentleman, and a courageous Englishman.

*   *   *   *   *   *

No biographer ever felt more genuine sorrow for his subject than have I for Sir Everard Digby. My sympathy for him has been the greater because he was, like myself, a convert to the Roman Catholic Church; because both he and I were received into that Church by Fathers of the Society of Jesus; because, both in his house and in mine, Jesuits have very frequently been welcomed as guests, and because in my private chapel, as in his, they have often acted as chaplains. Moreover, an additional bond between Sir Everard Digby and myself is the fact that he was my ancestor. Nevertheless, I hope that I have not allowed any of these accidents of faith or family to induce me wilfully to conceal an incident important to his history, to gloss over a mistake that he committed, to put a dishonest construction upon one of his actions, or to say an untrue word either about

and according to the manner held it up, saying, *Here is the Heart of a Traytor, Sir Everard* made answer, *Thou liest.* This a most famous Author ["*Franc.* Lord *Bacon*," says a footnote], mentions, but tells us not his Name, in his *Historia Vitæ et Mortis.*

[1] Narrative G. P., Gerard, p. 218.

himself, or any other character that has been introduced among these pages. Like his own life, my attempt at recounting it may be disfigured by mistaken zeal, false inferences, and rash conclusions; or possibly my authorities, like his friends, may have led me into error; if so, before laying down my pen, like Sir Everard Digby, before laying down his life, let me admit the offence, but declare that it was prompted by no unworthy motive.

A LIST OF

KEGAN PAUL, TRENCH, TRÜBNER, & CO.'S

PUBLICATIONS.

SIZES OF BOOKS.

A book is folio (fol.); quarto (4to.); octavo (8vo.); twelve mo (12mo.); sixteen mo (16mo.); eighteen mo (18mo.); thirty-two mo (32mo.), &c., according to the number of leaves or foldings of a printed sheet, whether the sheet be foolscap, crown, demy, medium, royal, super-royal, or imperial, and irrespective of the thickness of the volume. The following are *approximate* outside measurements in inches of the more common sizes.

	height		*breadth*			*height*		*breadth*
32mo. = royal 32mo.	$5\frac{1}{4}$	×	$3\frac{3}{4}$	P-8vo. = post 8vo.	8	×	$5\frac{1}{4}$
16mo. = demy 16mo.	$5\frac{1}{2}$	×	$4\frac{1}{2}$	LP-8vo. = large post 8vo.	$8\frac{1}{2}$	×	6
18mo. = royal 18mo.	6	×	$4\frac{1}{4}$	8vo. = demy 8vo.	9	×	6
fcp. = fcp. 8vo.	$6\frac{3}{4}$	×	$4\frac{1}{2}$	M-8vo. = medium 8vo.	$9\frac{1}{2}$	×	6
cr. = demy 12mo.	$7\frac{1}{4}$	×	$4\frac{1}{2}$	SR-8vo. = super-royal 8vo.	10	×	$6\frac{1}{2}$
cr. = small crown 8vo.	$7\frac{1}{4}$	×	5	IMP-8vo. = imperial 8vo.	12	×	$8\frac{1}{2}$
cr. = crown 8vo.	$7\frac{1}{2}$	×	$5\frac{1}{4}$				
cr. = large crown 8vo.	$8\frac{1}{4}$	×	$5\frac{1}{2}$				

Printed and folded in the reverse way—the breadth being greater than the height—the size is described as "oblong" 8vo., "oblong" 4to. &c.

Paternoster House,
Charing Cross Road,
August 21, 1893.

A LIST OF

KEGAN PAUL, TRENCH, TRÜBNER, & CO.'S PUBLICATIONS.

NOTE.—*Books are arranged in alphabetical order under the names or pseudonyms of author, translator, or editor. Biographies 'by the author of' are placed under the name of the subject. Anonymous works and 'selections' will be found under the first word of the title. The letters I.S.S. denote that the work forms a volume of the International Scientific Series.*

A. K. H. B., From a Quiet Place : some Discourses. Cr. 8vo. 5*s.*

ABEL, CARL, Linguistic Essays. Post 8vo. 9*s.* (*Trübner's Oriental Series.*)
    Slavic and Latin : Lectures on Comparative Lexicography. Post 8vo. 5*s.*

ABERCROMBY, Hon. RALPH, Weather : a popular Exposition of the Nature of Weather Changes from day to day. With 96 Figures. Second Edition. Cr. 8vo. 5*s.* (*I.S.S.*)

ABRAHAMS, L. B., Manual of Scripture History for Jewish Schools and Families. With Map. - Eleventh Edition. Cr. 8vo. 1*s.* 6*d.*

ACLAND, Sir HENRY, Bart., Science in Secondary Schools. Cr. 8vo. 1*s.* 6*d.*

ACLAND, Hon. Mrs. W., Love in a Life. 2 vols. Cr. 8vo. 21*s.*

ADAMS, ESTELLE, Sea Song and River Rhyme, from Chaucer to Tennyson. With 12 Etchings. Large cr. 8vo. 10*s.* 6*d.*

ADAMS, Mrs. LEITH, The Peyton Romance. 3 vols. £1. 11*s.* 6*d.*

ADAMS, W. H. DAVENPORT, The White King ; or, Charles the First, and Men and Women, Life and Manners, &c., in the first half of the 17th Century. 2 vols. 8vo. 21*s.*

ÆSCHYLUS. The Seven Plays in English Verse. Translated by Prof. LEWIS CAMPBELL. Cr. 8vo. 7*s.* 6*d.*

AHLWARDT, W., The Diváns of the Six Ancient Arabic Poets—Ennábiga, 'Antara, Tharafa, Zuhair, 'Alquama, and Imruulquais. With a complete list of the various readings of the text. 8vo. 12*s.*

AHN, F., Grammar of the Dutch Language. Fifth Edition, revised and enlarged. 12mo. 3*s.* 6*d.*
    Grammar of the German Language. New Edition. Cr. 8vo. 3*s.* 6*d.*
    Method of Learning German. 12mo. 3*s.* Key, 8*d.*
    Manual of German Conversation ; or, Vade Mecum for English Travellers. Second Edition. 12mo. 1*s.* 6*d.*
    Method of Learning French. First and Second Courses. 12mo. 3*s.* ; separately, 1*s.* 6*d.* each.
    Method of Learning French. Third Course. 12mo. 1*s.* 6*d.*
    Method of Learning Italian. 12mo. 3*s.* 6*d.*
    Latin Grammar for Beginners. Thirteenth Edition. Cr. 8vo. 3*s.*

AINSWORTH, W. F., Personal Narrative of the Euphrates Expedition. With Map. 2 vols. Demy 8vo. 30*s.*

AIZLEWOOD, J. W., Echo and Narcissus. Cr. 8vo. 2s. 6d.

Albanaise Grammaire, à l'usage de ceux qui désirent apprendre cette langue sans l'aide d'un maître. Par P. W. Cr. 8vo. 7s. 6d.

ALBÊRÛNÎ'S India: an Account of the Religion, Philosophy, Literature, Geography, Chronology, Astronomy, Customs, Laws, and Astrology of India, about A.D. 1030. Arabic text, edited by Prof. E. SACHAU. 4to. £3. 3s.

ALEXANDER, Major-Gen. G. G., Confucius, the Great Teacher. Cr. 8vo. 6s.

ALEXANDER, S., Moral Order and Progress: an Analysis of Ethical Conceptions. Second Edition. Post 8vo. 14s. (*Philosophical Library.*)

ALEXANDER, WILLIAM, D.D., Bishop of Derry, St. Augustine's Holiday, and other Poems. Cr. 8vo. 6s.

 The Great Question, and other Sermons. Cr. 8vo. 6s.

ALEXANDROW, A., Complete English-Russian and Russian-English Dictionary. 2 vols. 8vo. £2.

ALLEN, C. F. ROMILLY, Book of Chinese Poetry. Being the collection of Ballads, Sagas, Hymns, and other Pieces known as the Shih Ching, metrically translated. 8vo. 16s.

ALLEN, GRANT, The Colour-Sense: its Origin and Development. An Essay in Comparative Psychology. Second Edition. Post 8vo. 10s. 6d. (*Philosophical Library.*)

ALLEN, MARY L., Luncheon Dishes; comprising Menus in French and English, as well as Suggestions for Arrangement and Decoration of Table. Fcp. 8vo. cloth, 1s. 6d. ; paper covers, 1s.

 Five-o'clock Tea. Containing Receipts for Cakes, Savoury Sandwiches, &c. Eleventh Thousand. Fcp. 8vo. 1s. 6d.; paper covers, 1s.

ALLIBONE, S. A., Dictionary of English Literature and British and American Authors, from the Earliest Accounts to the Latter Half of the 19th Century. 3 vols. Roy. 8vo. £5. 8s SUPPLEMENT, 2 vols. roy. 8vo. (1891), £3. 3s.

ALTHAUS, JULIUS, The Spas of Europe. 8vo. 7s. 6d.

AMOS, Professor Sheldon, History and Principles of the Civil Law of Rome: an Aid to the Study of Scientific and Comparative Jurisprudence. 8vo. 16s.

 Science of Law. Seventh Edition. Cr. 8vo. 5s. (*I.S.S.*)

 Science of Politics. Third Edition. Cr. 8vo. 5s. (*I.S.S.*)

ANDERSON, DAVID, 'Scenes' in the Commons. Cr. 8vo. 5s.

ANDERSON, J., English Intercourse with Siam in the Seventeenth Century. Post 8vo. 15s. (*Trübner's Oriental Series.*)

ANDERSON, WILLIAM, Practical Mercantile Correspondence: a Collection of Modern Letters of Business, with Notes. Thirtieth Edition, revised. Cr. 8vo. 3s. 6d.

Antiquarian Magazine and Bibliographer, The. Edited by EDWARD WALFORD and G. W. REDWAY. Complete in 12 vols. 8vo. £3 net.

APEL, H., Prose Specimens for Translation into German. With copious Vocabularies and Explanations. Cr. 8vo. 4s. 6d.

APPLETON, J. H., and SAYCE, A. H., Dr. Appleton: his Life and Literary Relics. Post 8vo. 10s. 6d. (*Philosophical Library.*)

ARAGO, ÉTIENNE, Les Aristocraties: a Comedy in Verse. Second Edition. 12mo. 4s.

ARBUTHNOT, Sir A. J., Major-Gen. Sir Thomas Munro: a Memoir. Cr. 8vo. 3s. 6d.

ARCHER, WILLIAM, William Charles Macready. Cr. 8vo. 2*s*. 6*d*. (*Eminent Actors.*)

ARDEN, A. H., Progressive Grammar of Common Tamil. 5*s*.

ARISTOTLE, The Nicomachean Ethics. Translated by F. H. PETERS. Third Edition. Cr. 8vo. 6*s*.

ARNOLD, Sir EDWIN, Grammar of the Turkish Language. With Dialogues and Vocabulary. Pott 8vo. 2*s*. 6*d*.

Death—and Afterwards. Reprinted from the *Fortnightly Review* of August 1885, with a Supplement. Eleventh Edition. Cr. 8vo. cloth, 1*s*. 6*d*.; paper covers, 1*s*.

In My Lady's Praise: Poems Old and New, written to the honour of Fanny, Lady Arnold. Fourth Edition. Imperial 16mo. parchment, 3*s*. 6*d*.

India Revisited. With 32 Full-page Illustrations. Second Edition. Cr. 8vo. 6*s*.

Indian Idylls. From the Sanskrit of the Mahâbhârata. Second Edition. Cr. 8vo. 6*s*.

Indian Poetry. Containing 'The Indian Song of Songs' from the Sanskrit, two books from 'The Iliad of India,' and other Oriental Poems. Sixth Edition. 6*s*. (*Trübner's Oriental Series.*)

Lotus and Jewel. Containing 'In an Indian Temple,' 'A Casket of Gems,' 'A Queen's Revenge,' with other Poems. Third Edition. Cr. 8vo. 6*s*.

Pearls of the Faith, or Islam's Rosary. Being the Ninety-Nine Beautiful Names of Allah. Sixth Edition. Cr. 8vo. 6*s*.

Poems, National and Non-Oriental, with some new Pieces. Second Edition. Cr. 8vo. 6*s*.

The Light of Asia, or The Great Renunciation. Being the Life and Teaching of Gautama. Presentation Edition. With Illustrations and Portrait. Sm. 4to. 21*s*. Library Edition, cr. 8vo. 6*s*. Elzevir Edition, 6*s*. Cheap Edition (*Lotos Series*), cloth or half-parchment, 3*s*. 6*d*.

The Secret of Death: being a Version of the Katha Upanishad, from the Sanskrit. Fifth Edition. Cr. 8vo. 6*s*.

The Song Celestial, or Bhagavad-Gîtâ, from the Sanskrit. Fifth Edition. Cr. 8vo. 5*s*.

With Sa'di in the Garden, or The Book of Love: being the 'Ishk,' or third chapter of the 'Bostân' of the Persian poet Sa'di, embodied in a Dialogue. Fourth Edition. Cr. 8vo. 6*s*.

Poetical Works. Uniform Edition, comprising—The Light of Asia, Lotus and Jewel, Indian Poetry, Pearls of the Faith, Indian Idylls, The Secret of Death, The Song Celestial, With Sa'di in the Garden. 8 vols. Cr. 8vo. 48*s*.

ARNOLD, THOMAS, and SCANNELL, T. B., Catholic Dictionary. An account of the Doctrine, Discipline, Rites, Ceremonies, &c., of the Catholic Church. Fourth Edition, revised and enlarged. 8vo. 21*s*.

ASTON, W. G., Grammar of the Japanese Spoken Language. Fourth Edition. Cr. 8vo. 12*s*.

Grammar of the Japanese Written Language. Second Edition. 8vo. 28*s*.

AUBERTIN, J. J., A Flight to Mexico. With 7 Full-page Illustrations and a Railway Map. Cr. 8vo. 7*s*. 6*d*.

Six Months in Cape Colony and Natal. With Illustrations and Map. Cr. 8vo. 6*s*.

A Fight with Distances. With Illustrations and Maps. Cr. 8vo. 7*s*. 6*d*.

Wanderings and Wonderings. With Portrait, Map, and 7 Illustrations. Cr. 8vo. 8*s*. 6*d*.

AUGIER, ÉMILE, Diane : a Drama in Verse. Third Edition. 12mo. 2*s.* 6*d.*

AVELING, F. W., The Classic Birthday Book. 8vo. cloth, 8*s.* 6*d.* ; paste grain, 15*s.* ; tree calf, 21*s.*

AXON, W. E. A., The Mechanic's Friend. A Collection of Receipts and Practical Suggestions relating to Aquaria, Bronzing, Cements, Drawing, Dyes, Electricity, Gilding, Glass-working, &c. Numerous Woodcuts. Second Edition. Cr. 8vo. 3*s.* 6*d.*

AZARIAS, Brother, Aristotle and the Christian Church : an Essay. Sm. cr. 8vo. 3*s.* 6*d.*

BADER, CHARLES, Natural and Morbid Changes of the Human Eye, and their Treatment. 8vo. 16*s.* Atlas of Plates, in portfolio. Medium 8vo. 21*s.* Text and Atlas together, £1. 12*s.*

BADHAM, F. P., Formation of the Gospels. Second Edition, revised and enlarged. Cr. 8vo. 5*s.*

BAGEHOT, WALTER, The English Constitution. Seventh Edition. Cr. 8vo. 7*s.* 6*d.*
    Lombard Street. A Description of the Money Market. Tenth Edition. With Notes, bringing the work up to the present time, by E. JOHNSTONE. Cr. 8vo. 7*s.* 6*d.*
    Essays on Parliamentary Reform. Cr. 8vo. 5*s.*
    On the Depreciation of Silver, and Topics connected with it. 8vo. 5*s.*
    Physics and Politics; or, Thoughts on the Application of the Principles of 'Natural Selection' and 'Inheritance' to Political Society. Ninth Edition. Cr. 8vo. 5*s.* (*I.S.S.*)

BAGENAL, PHILIP H., American Irish and their Influence on Irish Politics. Cr. 8vo. 5*s.*

BAGOT, ALAN, Accidents in Mines : their Causes and Prevention. Cr. 8vo. 6*s.*
    Principles of Colliery Ventilation. Second Edition, greatly enlarged. Cr. 8vo. 5*s.*
    Principles of Civil Engineering as applied to Agriculture and Estate Management. Cr. 8vo. 7*s.* 6*d.*

BAIN, ALEX., Education as a Science. Seventh Edition. Cr. 8vo. 5*s.* (*I.S.S.*)
    Mind and Body. The Theories of their Relation. With 4 Illustrations. Eighth Edition. Cr. 8vo. 5*s.* (*I.S.S.*)

BAKER, Major EDEN, R.A., Preliminary Tactics. An Introduction to the Study of War. For the use of Junior Officers. Cr. 8vo. 6*s.*

BAKER, IRA, Treatise on Masonry Construction. Royal 8vo. 21*s.*

BAKER, Sir SHERSTON, Bart., Laws relating to Quarantine. Cr. 8vo. 12*s.* 6*d.*
    Halleck's International Law. Third Edition, thoroughly revised by Sir SHERSTON BAKER, Bart. 2 vols. Demy 8vo. 38*s.*

BALDWIN, Capt. J. H., Large and Small Game of Bengal and the North-Western Provinces of India. With 20 Illustrations. Sm. 4to. 10*s.* 6*d.*

BALFOUR, F. H., Leaves from my Chinese Scrap-Book. Post 8vo. 7*s.* 6*d.*

BALKWILL, F. H., The Testimony of the Teeth to Man's Place in Nature. With Illustrations. Cr. 8vo. 6*s.*

BALL, JOHN, Notes of a Naturalist in South America. With Map. Cr. 8vo. 8*s.* 6*d.*

BALL, Sir ROBERT, The Cause of an Ice Age. Cr. 8vo. 2*s.* 6*d.* (*Modern Science Series.*)

BALL, V., Diamonds, Coal, and Gold of India : their Mode of Occurrence and Distribution. Fcp. 8vo. 5*s.*

BALLANTYNE, J. R., Elements of Hindi and Braj Bhakha Grammar. Compiled for the East India College at Haileybury. Second Edition. Cr. 8vo. 5*s.*

BALLANTYNE, J. R., First Lessons in Sanskrit Grammar. Fifth Edition. 8vo. 3*s.* 6*d.*

Sankhya Aphorisms of Kapila. With Illustrative Extracts from the Commentaries. Third Edition. Post 8vo. 16*s.* (*Trübner's Oriental Series.*)

BALLIN, ADA S. and F. L., Hebrew Grammar. With Exercises selected from the Bible. Cr. 8vo. 7*s.* 6*d.*

BANCROFT, H. H., Popular History of the Mexican People. 8vo. 15*s.*

BANKS, Mrs. G. LINNÆUS, God's Providence House. Cr. 8vo. 6*s.*

BARING-GOULD, S., Germany, Present and Past. New and Cheaper Edition. Large cr. 8vo. 7*s.* 6*d.*

BARLOW, J. W., The Ultimatum of Pessimism. An Ethical Study. 8vo. 6*s.*

BARNES, WILLIAM, Poems of Rural Life in the Dorset Dialect. New Edition. Cr. 8vo. 6*s.*

BARRIÈRE, THEODORE, and CAPENDU, ERNEST, Les Faux Bonshommes. A Comedy. 12mo. 4*s.*

BARTH, A., Religions of India. Translated by the Rev. J. WOOD. Third Edition. Post 8vo. 16*s.* (*Trübner's Oriental Series.*)

BARTLETT, J. R., Dictionary of Americanisms : a Glossary of Words and Phrases colloquially used in the United States. Fourth Edition. 8vo. 21*s.*

BASU, K. P., Students' Mathematical Companion. Containing Problems in Arithmetic, Algebra, Geometry, and Mensuration, for Students of the Indian Universities. Cr. 8vo. 6*s.*

BASTIAN, H. CHARLTON, The Brain as an Organ of Mind. With 184 Illustrations. Fourth Edition. Cr. 8vo. 5*s.* (*I.S.S.*)

BAUGHAN, ROSA, The Influence of the Stars : a Treatise on Astrology, Chiromancy, and Physiognomy. Second Edition. 8vo. 5*s.*

BAUR, FERDINAND, Philological Introduction to Greek and Latin for Students. Translated and adapted from the German by C. KEGAN PAUL and E. D. STONE. Third Edition. Cr. 8vo. 6*s.*

BAYNES, Canon H. R., Home Songs for Quiet Hours. Fourth and Cheaper Edition. Fcp. 8vo. 2*s.* 6*d.*

BEAL, S., Catena of Buddhist Scriptures. From the Chinese. 8vo. 15*s.*

Romantic Legend of Sakya Buddha. From the Chinese-Sanskrit. Cr. 8vo. 12*s.*

Life of Hiuen-Tsiang. By the Shamans HWUI LI and YEN-TSUNG. With an Account of the Works of I-Tsing. Post 8vo. 10*s.* (*Trübner's Oriental Series.*)

Si-Yu-Ki : Buddhist Records of the Western World. Translated from the Chinese of HIUEN-TSIANG (A.D. 629). With Map. 2 vols. post 8vo. 24*s.* (*Trübner's Oriental Series.*)

Texts from the Buddhist Canon, commonly known as Dhammapada. Translated from the Chinese. Post 8vo. 7*s.* 6*d.* (*Trübner's Oriental Series.*)

BEAMES, JOHN, Outlines of Indian Philology. With a Map showing the Distribution of Indian languages. Enlarged Edition. Cr. 8vo. 5*s.*

Comparative Grammar of the Modern Aryan Languages of India : Hindi, Panjabi, Sindhi, Gujarati, Marathi, Oriya, and Bengali. 3 vols. 8vo. 16*s.* each.

BEARD, CHARLES, Martin Luther and the Reformation in Germany. 8vo. 16*s.*

BELL, A. M., Elocutionary Manual. Fifth Edition Revised. 12mo. 7*s.* 6*d.*

BELLASIS, EDWARD, Cardinal Newman as a Musician. Sewed, 1*s.* 6*d.*

BELLOWS, JOHN, French and English Dictionary for the Pocket. Containing the French-English and English-French Divisions on the same page; Conjugating all the Verbs ; Distinguishing the Genders by Different Types ; giving Numerous Aids to Pronunciation, &c. Fifty-third Thousand of the Second Edition. 32mo. morocco tuck, 12*s.* 6*d.*; roan, 10*s.* 6*d.*

Tous les Verbes. Conjugations of all the Verbs in French and English. Second Edition. With Tables of Weights, Measures, &c. 32mo. 6*d.*

BENEDEN, P. J. van, Animal Parasites and Messmates. With 83 Illustrations. Fourth Edition. Cr. 8vo. 5s. (*I.S.S.*)

BENEDIX, RODERICK, Der Vetter. Comedy in Three Acts. 12mo. 2s. 6d.

BENFEY, THEODOR, Grammar of the Sanskrit Language. For the Use of Early Students. Second Edition. Roy. 8vo. 10s. 6d.

BENSON, A. C., William Laud, sometime Archbishop of Canterbury. With Portrait. Cr. 8vo. 6s.

BENSON, MARY ELEANOR, At Sundry Times and in Divers Manners. With Portrait and Memoir. 2 vols. cr. 8vo. 10s. 6d.

BENTHAM, JEREMY, Theory of Legislation. Translated from the French of Étienne Dumont by R. HILDRETH. Seventh Edition. Post 8vo. 7s. 6d.

'BERNARD,' From World to Cloister; or, My Novitiate. Cr. 8vo. 5s.

BERNSTEIN, Prof., The Five Senses of Man. With 91 Illustrations. Fifth Edition. Cr. 8vo. 5s. (*I.S.S.*)

BERTIN, GEORGE, Abridged Grammar of the Languages of the Cuneiform Inscriptions. Cr. 8vo. 5s.

BEVAN, THEODORE F., Toil, Travel, and Discovery in British New Guinea. With 5 Maps. Large cr. 8vo. 7s. 6d.

BHIKSHU, SUBHADRA, Buddhist Catechism. 12mo. 2s.

BIDDULPH, C. E., Four Months in Persia. 8vo. 3s. 6d.

BILLER, EMMA, Ulli: the Story of a Neglected Girl. Translated from the German by A. B. DAISY ROST. Cr. 8vo. 6s.

Bible Folk Lore: a Study in Comparative Mythology. Cr. 8vo. 10s. 6d.

BINET, A., and FERE, C., Animal Magnetism. Second Edition. Cr. 8vo. 5s. (*I.S.S.*)

BIRD, ROBERT, Jesus, the Carpenter of Nazareth. Seventh Edition, revised. Cr. 8vo. 5s. Also in Two Parts, price 2s. 6d. each.

BISHOP, M. C., The Prison Life of Marie Antoinette and her Children, the Dauphin and the Duchesse D'Angoulême. New and Revised Edition. With Portrait. Cr. 8vo. 6s.

BLADES, W., Biography and Typography of William Caxton, England's First Printer. 8vo. hand-made paper, imitation old bevelled binding, £1. 1s.; Cheap Edition, cr. 8vo. 5s.

Account of the German Morality Play, entitled, 'Depositio Cornuti Typographici.' As performed in the 17th or 18th Centuries. With facsimile illustrations. Sm. 4to. 7s. 6d.

BLAKE, WILLIAM, Selections from the Writings of. Edited, with Introduction, by LAURENCE HOUSMAN. With Frontispiece. Elzevir 8vo. Parchment, 6s.; vellum, 7s. 6d. (*Parchment Library.*)

BLASERNA, Prof. P., Theory of Sound in its Relation to Music. With numerous Illustrations. Fourth Edition. Cr. 8vo. 5s. (*I.S.S.*)

BLEEK, W. H. I., Reynard the Fox in South Africa, or, Hottentot Fables and Tales. Post 8vo. 3s. 6d.

BLOGG, H. B., Life of Francis Duncan. With Introduction by the BISHOP OF CHESTER. Cr. 8vo. 3s. 6d.

BLOOMFIELD, The Lady, Reminiscences of Court and Diplomatic Life. New and Cheaper Edition, with Frontispiece. Cr. 8vo. 6s.

BLUMHARDT, J. F., Charitabali, The; or, Instructive Biography. By ISVARA-CHANDRA VIDYASAGARA. With Vocabulary of all the Words occurring in the Text. 12mo. 5s. Vocabulary only, 2s. 6d.

BLUNT, WILFRID SCAWEN, The Wind and the Whirlwind. 8vo. 1s. 6d.

The Love Sonnets of Proteus. Fifth Edition. Elzevir 8vo. 5s.

In Vinculis. With Portrait. Elzevir 8vo. 5s.

A New Pilgrimage, and other Poems. Elzevir 8vo. 5s.

Esther, Love Lyrics, and Natalia's Resurrection. 7s. 6d.

BLYTH, E. KELL, Life of William Ellis, founder of the Birkbeck Schools. Second Edition. 8vo. 10*s.* 6*d.*

BODEMANN, TH. and **KARL, Bruno :** a Treatise on the Assaying of Lead, Copper, Silver, Gold, and Mercury. Translated by W. A. GOODYEAR. Illustrated with Plates. Cr. 8vo. 6*s.* 6*d.*

BOGER, Mrs. E., Myths, Scenes, and Worthies of Somerset. Cr. 8vo. 10*s.* 6*d.*

BOJESEN, MARIA, Guide to the Danish Language. 12mo. 5*s.*

BOSANQUET, BERNARD, Introduction to Hegel's Philosophy of Fine Art. Cr. 8vo. 5*s.*

BOWDEN, Fr. CHARLES HENRY, Life of B. John Juvenal Ancina. 8vo. 9*s.*

BOWEN, H. C., Studies in English. For the use of Modern Schools. Tenth thousand. Sm. cr. 8vo. 1*s.* 6*d.*

English Grammar for Beginners. Fcp. 8vo. 1*s.*

Simple English Poems. English Literature for Junior Classes, 3s. Parts I. II. and III. 6*d.* each. Part IV. 1*s.*

BOYD, P., Nágánanda ; or, the Joy of the Snake World. From the Sanskrit of Sri-Harsha-Deva. Cr. 8vo. 4*s.* 6*d.*

BRACKENBURY, Major-General, Field Works : their Technical Construction and Tactical Application. 2 vols. Sm. cr. 8vo. 12*s.* (*Military Handbooks.*)

BRADLEY, F. H., The Principles of Logic. 8vo. 16*s.*

BRADSHAW'S Guide. Dictionary of Mineral Waters, Climatic Health Resorts, Sea Baths, and Hydropathic Establishments. With a Map. 2*s.* 6*d.*

Brave Men's Footsteps : a Book of Example and Anecdote for Young People. By the editor of 'Men who have Risen' Illustrations by C. DOYLE. Ninth Edition. Cr. 8vo. 2*s.* 6*d.*

BRENTANO, LUJO, History and Development of Gilds, and the Origin of Trade Unions. 8vo. 3*s.* 6*d.*

BRETSCHNEIDER, E., Mediæval Researches from Eastern Asiatic Sources : Fragments towards the Knowledge of the Geography and History of Central and Western Asia, from the 13th to the 17th century, with 2 Maps. 2 vols. Post 8vo. 21*s.* (*Trübner's Oriental Series.*)

BRETTE, P. H., THOMAS, F., French Examination Papers set at the University of London. Part I. Matriculation, and the General Examination for Women. Cr. 8vo. 3*s.* 6*d.* Key, 5*s.* Part II. First B.A. Examinations for Honours and D. Litt. Examinations. Cr. 8vo. 7*s.*

BRIDGETT, T. E., Blunders and Forgeries : Historical Essays. Cr. 8vo. 6*s.*

History of the Holy Eucharist in Great Britain. 2 vols. 8vo. 18*s.*

BROOKE, Rev. STOPFORD A., The Fight of Faith : Sermons preached on various occasions. Sixth Edition, cr. 8vo. 5*s.*

The Spirit of the Christian Life. Fourth Edition. Cr. 8vo. 5*s.*

Theology in the English Poets : Cowper, Coleridge, Wordsworth, and Burns. Sixth Edition. Post 8vo. 5*s.*

Christ in Modern Life. Eighteenth Edition. Cr. 8vo. 5*s.*

Sermons. Two Series. Thirteenth Edition. Cr. 8vo. 5*s.* each.

Life and Letters of F. W. Robertson. With Portrait. 2 vols. Cr. 8vo. 7*s.* 6*d.* Library Edition, 8vo. with portrait, 12*s.* Popular Edition, cr. 8vo. 6*s.*

BROWN, C. P., Sanskrit Prosody and Numerical Symbols Explained. 8vo. 3*s.* 6*d.*

BROWN, HORATIO F., Venetian Studies. Cr. 8vo. 7*s.* 6*d.*

BROWN, Rev. J. BALDWIN, The Higher Life : its Reality, Experience, and Destiny. Seventh Edition. Cr. 8vo. 5*s.*

Doctrine of Annihilation in the Light of the Gospel of Love. Fourth Edition. Cr. 8vo. 2*s.* 6*d.*

The Christian Policy of Life : a Book for Young Men of Business. Third Edition. Cr. 8vo. 3*s.* 6*d.*

BROWN, J. C., People of Finland in Archaic Times. Cr. 8vo. 5s.

BROWN, J. P., The Dervishes; or, Oriental Spiritualism. With 24 Illustrations. Cr. 8vo. 14s.

BROWNE, EDGAR A., How to Use the Ophthalmoscope. Third Edition. Cr. 8vo. 3s. 6d.

BROWNING, OSCAR, Introduction to the History of Educational Theories. Second Edition. 3s. 6d. (*Education Library.*)

BRUGMANN, KARL, Comparative Grammar of the Indo-Germanic Languages. 3 vols. 8vo. Vol. I. Introduction and Phonology, 18s. Vol. II. Morphology (Stem-Formation and Inflexion), Part 1, 16s. Vol. III. 12s. 6d.

BRUN, L. LE, Materials for Translating English into French. Seventh Edition. Post 8vo. 4s. 6d.

BRYANT, SOPHIE, Celtic Ireland. With 3 Maps. Cr. 8vo. 5s.

BRYANT, W. CULLEN, Poems. Cheap Edition. Sm. 8vo. 3s. 6d.

BRYCE, J., Handbook of Home Rule: being Articles on the Irish Question. Second Edition. Cr. 8vo, 1s. 6d. ; paper covers, 1s.

Two Centuries of Irish History. 8vo. 16s.

BUDGE, E. A., History of Esarhaddon (Son of Sennacherib), King of Assyria, B.C. 681–668. Translated from the Cuneiform Inscriptions in the British Museum. Post 8vo. 10s. 6d. (*Trübner's Oriental Series.*)

Archaic Classics: Assyrian Texts, being Extracts from the Annals of Shalmaneser II., Sennacherib, and Assur-Bani-Pal, with Philological Notes. Sm. 4to. 7s. 6d.

BUNGE, Prof. G., Text-Book of Physiological and Pathological Chemistry, for Physicians and Students. Translated from the German by L. C. WOOLDRIDGE. 8vo. 16s.

BUNSEN, ERNEST DE, Islam ; or, True Christianity. Crown 8vo. 5s.

BURGESS, JAMES, The Buddhist Cave-Temples and their Inscriptions, containing Views, Plans, Sections, and Elevation of Façades of Cave-temples ; Drawings of Architectural and Mythological Sculptures ; Facsimiles of Inscriptions, &c. ; with Descriptive and Explanatory Text, and Translations of Inscriptions. With 86 Plates and Woodcuts. Royal 4to. half-bound, £3. 3s. [*Archæological Survey of Western India.*]

Elura Cave-Temples and the Brahmanical and Jaina Caves in Western India. With 66 Plates and Woodcuts. Royal 4to. half-bound, £3. 3s. [*Archæological Survey of Western India.*]

Reports of the Amaravati and Jaggayyapeta Buddhist Stupas, containing numerous Collotype and other Illustrations of Buddhist Sculpture and Architecture, &c., in South-eastern India ; Facsimiles of Inscriptions, &c., with Descriptive and Explanatory Text ; together with Transcriptions, Translations, and Elucidations of the Dhauli and Jaugada Inscriptions of Asoka. With numerous Plates and Woodcuts. Royal 4to. half-bound, £4. 4s. [*Archæological Survey of Southern India.*]

BURNELL, A. C., Elements of South Indian Palæography, from the 4th to the 17th century: an Introduction to the Study of South Indian Inscriptions and MSS. Enlarged Edition. With Map and 35 Plates. 4to. £2. 12s. 6d.

The Ordinances of Manu. Translated from the Sanskrit, with Introduction by the late A. C. BURNELL. Completed and Edited by E. W. HOPKINS. Post 8vo. 12s. (*Trübner's Oriental Series.*)

BURNEY, Capt., R.N., The Young Seaman's Manual and Rigger's Guide. Tenth Edition, revised and corrected. With 200 Illustrations and 16 Sheets of Signals. Cr. 8vo. 7s. 6d.

BURNS, ROBERT, Selected Poems of. With an Introduction by ANDREW LANG. Elzevir 8vo. vellum, 7s. 6d. ; parchment or cloth, 6s. (*Parchment Library.*)

BUTLER, F., Spanish Teacher and Colloquial Phrase-Book. 18mo. half-roan, 2s. 6d.

BUXTON, Major, Elements of Military Administration. First part : Permanent System of Administration. Small cr. 8vo. 7s. 6d. (*Military Handbooks.*)

BYRNE, Dean JAMES, General Principles of the Structure of Language. 2 vols. Second and Revised Edition. 8vo. 36*s.*

Origin of Greek, Latin, and Gothic Roots. Second and Revised Edition. 8vo. 18*s.*

CABLE, G. W., Strange True Stories of Louisiana. 8vo. 7*s.* 6*d.*

CAIRD, MONA, The Wing of Azrael. Cr. 8vo. 6*s.*

CALDERON'S Dramas. Translated by DENIS FLORENCE MACCARTHY. Post 8vo. 10*s.*

CAMERINI, E., L'Eco Italiano : a Guide to Italian Conversation, with Vocabulary. 12mo. 4*s.* 6*d.*

CAMERON, Miss, Soups and Stews and Choice Ragoûts. Cr. 8vo. cloth, 1*s.* 6*d.*; paper covers, 1*s.*

CAMOENS' Lusiads. Portuguese Text, with Translation, by J. J. AUBERTIN. Second Edition. 2 vols. Cr. 8vo. 12*s.*

CAMPBELL, Prof. LEWIS, Sophocles. The Seven Plays in English Verse. Cr. 8vo. 7*s.* 6*d.*

Æschylus. The Seven Plays in English Verse. Cr. 8vo. 7*s.* 6*d.*

Candid Examination of Theism. By PHYSICUS. Second Edition, post 8vo. 7*s.* 6*d.* (*Philosophical Library.*)

CANDOLLE, ALPHONSE DE, Origin of Cultivated Plants. Second Edition. Cr. 8vo. 5*s.* (*I.S.S.*)

CARLYLE, THOMAS, Sartor Resartus. Elzevir 8vo. vellum, 7*s.* 6*d.* ; parchment or cloth, 6*s.* (*Parchment Library.*)

CARPENTER, R. L., Personal and Social Christianity : Sermons and Addresses by the late RUSSELL LANT CARPENTER. With a Short Memoir by FRANCES E. COOKE. Edited by J. ESTLIN CARPENTER. Cr. 8vo. 6*s.*

CARPENTER, W. B., Principles of Mental Physiology, with their Applications to the Training and Discipline of the Mind, and the Study of its Morbid Conditions. Illustrated. Sixth Edition. 8vo. 12*s.*

Nature and Man. With a Memorial Sketch by J. ESTLIN CARPENTER. Portrait. Large cr. 8vo. 8*s.* 6*d.*

CARREÑO, Metodo para aprender a Leer, escribir y hablar el Inglés segun el sistema de Ollendorff. 8vo. 4*s.* 6*d.* Key, 3*s.*

CARRINGTON, H., Of the Imitation of Christ. By THOMAS À KEMPIS. A Metrical Version. Cr. 8vo. 5*s.*

CASSAL, CHARLES, Glossary of Idioms, Gallicisms, and other Difficulties contained in the Senior Course of the 'Modern French Reader.' Cr. 8vo. 2*s.* 6*d.*

CASSAL, CH., and KARCHER, THEODORE. Modern French Reader. Junior Course. Nineteenth Edition. Cr. 8vo. 2*s.* 6*d.* Senior Course. Seventh Edition. Cr. 8vo. 4*s.* Senior Course and Glossary in 1 vol. Cr. 8vo. 6*s.*

Little French Reader : extracted from the ' Modern French Reader.' Third Edition. Cr. 8vo. 2*s.*

CATLIN, GEORGE, O-Kee-Pa : a Religious Ceremony ; and other Customs of the Mandans. With 13 coloured Illustrations. Small 4to. 14*s.*

The Lifted and Subsided Rocks of America, with their Influence on the Oceanic, Atmospheric, and Land Currents, and the Distribution of Races. With 2 Maps. Cr. 8vo. 6*s.* 6*d.*

Shut your Mouth and Save your Life. With 29 Illustrations. Ninth Edition, Cr. 8vo. 2*s.* 6*d.*

CHAMBERLAIN, Prof. B. H., Classical Poetry of the Japanese. Post 8vo. 7*s.* 6*d.* (*Trübner's Oriental Series.*)

Simplified Japanese Grammar. Cr. 8vo. 5*s.*

Romanised Japanese Reader. Consisting of Japanese Anecdotes and Maxims, with English Translations and Notes. 12mo. 6*s.*

Handbook of Colloquial Japanese. 8vo. 12*s.* 6*d.*

Things Japanese. Second, Revised Edition. Cr. 8vo. 8*s.* 6*d.*

CHAMBERS, J. D., Theological and Philosophical Works of Hermes Trismegistus, Christian Neoplatonist. Translated from the Greek. 8vo. 7s. 6d.

CHAUCER, G., Canterbury Tales. Edited by A. W. POLLARD. 2 vols. Elzevir 8vo. vellum, 15s. ; parchment or cloth, 12s. (*Parchment Library.*)

CHEYNE, Canon T. K., The Prophecies of Isaiah. With Notes and Dissertations. 2 vols. Fifth Edition, Revised. 8vo. 25s.

Job and Solomon ; or, The Wisdom of the Old Testament. 8vo. 12s. 6d.

The Book of Psalms ; or, the Praises of Israel. With Commentary. 8vo. 16s.

The Book of Psalms. Elzevir 8vo. vellum, 7s. 6d. ; parchment or cloth, 6s. (*Parchment Library.*)

The Origin and Religious Contents of the Psalter. The Bampton Lectures, 1889. 8vo. 16s.

CHICHELE, Mary, Doing and Undoing. Cr. 8vo. 4s. 6d.

CHILDERS, R. C., Pali-English Dictionary, with Sanskrit Equivalents. Imp. 8vo. £3. 3s.

CHRISTIAN, JOHN, Behar Proverbs, Classified and arranged according to subject matter, with Notes. Post 8vo. 10s. 6d. (*Trübner's Oriental Series.*)

Civil War (American), Campaigns of the. 12 vols., and Supplement. With Maps and Plans. 12mo. 5s. each vol. **Navy in the Civil War.** 3 vols. 5s. each.

CLAIRAUT, Elements of Geometry. Translated by Dr. KAINES. With 145 Figures. Cr. 8vo. 4s. 6d.

CLAPPERTON, JANE HUME, Scientific Meliorism and the Evolution of Happiness. Large cr. 8vo. 8s. 6d.

CLARKE, HENRY W., History of Tithes from Abraham to Queen Victoria. Cr. 8vo 5s.

CLARKE, JAMES FREEMAN, Ten Great Religions : an Essay in Comparative Theology. 2 vols. 8vo. 10s. 6d. each.

CLERY, Gen. C. FRANCIS, Minor Tactics. With 26 Maps and Plans. Eleventh Edition, revised. Cr. 8vo. 9s.

CLIFF, MARIA, Poems on True Incidents, and other Poems. Cr. 8vo. 3s. 6d.

CLIFFORD, W. KINGDON, Common Sense of the Exact Sciences. Second Edition. With 100 Figures. Cr. 8vo. 5s. (*I.S.S.*)

CLODD, EDWARD, Childhood of the World : a Simple Account of Man in early times. Ninth Edition. Cr. 8vo. 3s. Special Edition for Schools, 1s.

Childhood of Religions. Including a simple account of the birth and growth of Myths and Legends. Ninth Edition. Cr. 8vo. 5s. Special Edition for Schools, 1s. 6d.

Jesus of Nazareth. With a brief Sketch of Jewish History to the time of His birth. Second Edition. Revised throughout and partly re-written. Sm. cr. 8vo. 6s. Special Edition for Schools, in 2 parts, 1s. 6d. each.

COGHLAN, J. COLE, D.D., The Modern Pharisee and other Sermons. Edited by the Very Rev. H. H. DICKINSON, D.D. New and Cheaper Edition. Cr. 8vo. 7s. 6d.

COLERIDGE. Memoir and Letters of Sara Coleridge. Edited by her Daughter. Cheap Edition. With Portrait. Cr. 8vo. 7s. 6d.

COLLETTE, C. H., Life, Times, and Writings of Thomas Cranmer, D.D., the First Reforming Archbishop of Canterbury. 8vo. 7s. 6d.

Pope Joan. An Historical Study, from the Greek of Rhoïdis. 12mo. 2s. 6d.

COLLINS, MABEL, Through the Gates of Gold : a Fragment of Thought. Sm. 8vo. 4s. 6d.

Light on the Path. Fcp. 8vo. 1s. 6d.

COMPTON, A. G., First Lessons in Metal-Working. Cr. 8vo. 6s. 6d.

COMPTON, C. G., Scot Free: a Novel. Cr. 8vo. 6s.

COMTE, AUGUSTE, Catechism of Positive Religion, from the French, by R. CONGREVE. Third Edition, revised and corrected. Cr. 8vo. 2s. 6d.

Eight Circulars of Auguste Comte. Fcp. 8vo. 1s. 6d.

Appeal to Conservatives. Cr. 8vo. 2s. 6d.

Positive Philosophy of Auguste Comte, translated and condensed by HARRIET MARTINEAU. 2 vols. New and Cheaper Edition. Large post 8vo. 15s.

Subjective Synthesis; or, Universal System of the Conceptions adapted to the Normal State of Humanity. Vol. I., containing the System of Positive Logic. 8vo. paper covers, 2s. 6d.

CONTE, JOSEPH LE, Sight: an Exposition of the Principles of Monocular and Binocular Vision. Second Edition. With 132 Illustrations. Cr. 8vo. 5s. (*I.S.S.*)

CONTOPOULOS, N., Lexicon of Modern Greek-English and English-Modern Greek. 2 vols. 8vo. 27s.

Modern-Greek and English Dialogues and Correspondence. Fcp. 8vo. 2s. 6d.

CONWAY, M. D., Emerson at Home and Abroad. With Portrait. Post 8vo, 10s. 6d. (*Philosophical Library.*)

CONWAY, R. S., Verner's Law in Italy: an Essay in the History of the Indo-European sibilants. 8vo. 5s.

COOK, KENINGALE, The Fathers of Jesus. A Study of the Lineage of the Christian Doctrine and Traditions. 2 vols. 8vo. 28s.

COOK, LOUISA S., Geometrical Psychology; or, The Science of Representation. An Abstract of the Theories and Diagrams of B. W. Betts. 16 Plates. 8vo. 7s. 6d.

COOKE, M. C., British Edible Fungi: how to distinguish and how to cook them. With Coloured Figures of upwards of Forty Species. Cr. 8vo. 7s. 6d.

Fungi: their Nature, Influences, Uses, &c. Edited by Rev. M. J. BERKELEY. With numerous Illustrations. Fourth Edition. Cr. 8vo. 5s. (*I.S.S.*)

Introduction to Fresh-Water Algæ. With an Enumeration of all the British Species. With 13 Plates. Cr. 8vo. 5s. (*I.S.S.*)

COOKE, Prof. J. P., New Chemistry. With 31 Illustrations. Ninth Edition. Cr. 8vo. 5s. (*I.S.S.*)

Laboratory Practice. A Series of Experiments on the Fundamental Principles of Chemistry. Cr. 8vo. 5s.

CORDERY, J. G., Homer's Iliad. Greek Text, with Translation. 2 vols. 8vo. 14s. Translation only, cr. 8vo. 5s.

CORY, W., Guide to Modern English History. Part I. 1815-1830. 8vo. 9s. Part II. 1830-1835, 8vo. 15s.

COTTA, BERNHARD von, Geology and History. A Popular Exposition of all that is known of the Earth and its Inhabitants in Prehistoric Times. 12mo. 2s.

COTTON, LOUISE, Palmistry and its Practical Uses. With 12 Plates. Second Edition. Cr. 8vo. 2s. 6d.

COWELL, E. B., Short Introduction to the Ordinary Prakrit of the Sanskrit Dramas. Cr. 8vo. 3s. 6d.

Prakrita-Prakasa; or, The Prakrit Grammar of Vararuchi, with the Commentary (Manorama) of Bhamaba. 8vo. 14s.

COWELL, E. B., and **GOUGH, A. E., The Sarva-Darsana-Samgraha;** or, Review of the Different Systems of Hindu Philosophy. Post 8vo. 10s. 6d. (*Trübner's Oriental Series.*)

COWIE, Bishop, Our Last Year in New Zealand, 1887. Cr. 8vo. 7s. 6d.

COX, SAMUEL, D.D., Commentary on the Book of Job. With a Translation. Second Edition. 8vo. 15s.

Salvator Mundi; or, Is Christ the Saviour of all Men? Fourteenth Edition. Cr. 8vo. 2s. 6d.

The Larger Hope: A Sequel to 'Salvator Mundi.' Second Edition. 16mo. 1s.

COX, SAMUEL, D.D., The Genesis of Evil, and other Sermons, mainly Expository. Fourth Edition. Cr. 8vo. 6s.

Balaam : an Exposition and a Study. Cr. 8vo. 5s.

Miracles : an Argument and a Challenge. Cr. 8vo. 2s. 6d.

COX, Sir G. W., Bart., Mythology of the Aryan Nations. New Edition. 8vo. 16s.

Tales of Ancient Greece. New Edition. Sm. cr. 8vo. 6s.

Tales of the Gods and Heroes. Sm. cr. 8vc. 3s. 6d

Manual of Mythology in the Form of Question and Answer. New Edition. Fcap. 8vo. 3s.

Introduction to the Science of Comparative Mythology and Folk-lore. Second Edition. Cr. 8vo. 7s. 6d.

COX, Sir G. W., Bart., and JONES, E. H., Popular Romances of the Middle Ages. Third Edition. Cr. 8vo. 6s.

CRAVEN, Mrs., A Year's Meditations. Cr. 8vo. 6s.

CRAVEN, T., English-Hindustani and Hindustani-English Dictionary. New Edition. 18mo. 4s. 6d.

CRAWFURD, OSWALD, Portugal, Old and New. With Illustrations and Maps. New and Cheaper Edition. Cr. 8vo. 6s.

CRUISE, F. R., Notes of a Visit to the Scenes in which the Life of Thomas à Kempis was spent. With numerous Illustrations. 8vo. 12s.

CUNNINGHAM, Major-Gen. ALEX., Ancient Geography of India. I. The Buddhist Period, including the Campaigns of Alexander and the Travels of Hwen-Thsang. With 13 Maps. 8vo. £1. 8s.

CURTEIS, Canon, Bishop Selwyn of New Zealand and of Lichfield : a Sketch of his Life and Work, with further gleanings from his Letters, Sermons, and Speeches. Large cr. 8vo. 7s. 6d.

CUST, R. N., Linguistic and Oriental Essays. Post 8vo. First Series, 10s. 6d. ; Second Series, with 6 Maps, 21s. ; Third Series, with Portrait, 21s. (*Trübner's Oriental Series.*)

DANA, E. S., Text-Book of Mineralogy. With Treatise on Crystallography and Physical Mineralogy. Third Edition, with 800 Woodcuts and Plate. 8vo. 15s.

DANA, J. D., Text-Book of Geology, for Schools. Illustrated. Cr. 8vo. 10s.

Manual of Geology. Illustrated by a Chart of the World, and 1,000 Figures. 8vo. 21s.

The Geological Story Briefly Told. Illustrated. 12mo. 7s. 6d.

DANA, J. D., and BRUSH, G. J., System of Mineralogy. Sixth Edition, entirely rewritten and enlarged. Roy. 8vo. £3. 3s.

Manual of Mineralogy and Petrography. Fourth Edition. Numerous Woodcuts. Cr. 8vo. 8s. 6d.

DANTE'S Treatise 'De Vulgari Eloquentiâ.' Translated, with Notes, by A. G. F. HOWELL. 3s. 6d.

The Banquet (Il Convito). Translated by KATHARINE HILLARD. Cr. 8vo. 7s. 6d.

DARMESTETER, ARSENE, Life of Words as the Symbols of Ideas. Cr. 8vo. 4s. 6d.

D'ASSIER, ADOLPHE, Posthumous Humanity : a Study of Phantoms. From the French by H. S. OLCOTT. With Appendix. Cr. 8vo. 7s. 6d.

DAVIDS, T. W. RHYS, Buddhist Birth-Stories; or, Jataka Tales. The oldest Collection of Folk-lore extant. Being the Jātakatthavannanā. Translated from the Pali Text of V. FAUSBOLL. Post 8vo. 18s. (*Trübner's Oriental Series.*)

The Numismata Orientalia. Part VI. The Ancient Coins and Measures of Ceylon. With 1 Plate. Royal 4to. Paper wrapper, 10s.

DAVIDSON, SAMUEL, D.D., Canon of the Bible : its Formation, History, and Fluctuations. Third Edition. Sm. Cr. 8vo. 5s.

Doctrine of Last Things. Sm. Cr. 8vo. 3s. 6d.

DAVIDSON, T., Compendium of the Philosophical System of Antonio Rosmini-Serbati. Second Edition, 8vo. 10s. 6d.

DAVIES, G. CHRISTOPHER, Rambles and Adventures of Our School Field Club. With 4 Illustrations. New and Cheaper Edition. Cr. 8vo. 3s. 6d.

DAVIES, J., Sânkhya Kârikâ of Iswara Krishna: an Exposition of the System of Kapila. Post 8vo. 6s. (*Trübner's Oriental Series.*)

    The Bhagavad Gîtâ; or, the Sacred Lay. Translated, with Notes, from the Sanskrit. Third Edition. Post 8vo. 6s. (*Trübner's Oriental Series.*)

DAVITT, MICHAEL, Speech before the Special Commission. Cr. 8vo. 5s.

DAWSON, GEORGE, Prayers. First Series, Edited by his WIFE. Eleventh Edition. Sm. 8vo. 3s. 6d.

    Prayers. Second Series. Edited by GEORGE ST. CLAIR. Second Edition. Sm. 8vo. 3s. 6d.

    Sermons on Disputed Points and Special Occasions. Edited by his WIFE. Fifth Edition. Sm. 8vo. 3s. 6d.

    Sermons on Daily Life and Duty. Edited by his WIFE. Fifth Edition. Sm. 8vo. 3s. 6d.

    The Authentic Gospel. Sermons. Edited by GEORGE ST. CLAIR. Fourth Edition. Sm. 8vo. 3s. 6d.

    Every-Day Counsels. Edited by GEORGE ST. CLAIR. Cr. 8vo. 6s.

    Biographical Lectures. Edited by GEORGE ST. CLAIR. Third Edition. Large cr. 8vo. 7s. 6d.

    Shakespeare; and other Lectures. Edited by GEORGE ST. CLAIR. Large Cr. 8vo. 7s. 6d.

DAWSON, Sir J. W., Geological History of Plants. With 80 Illustrations. Cr. 8vo. 5s. (*I.S.S.*)

DEAN, TERESA H., How to be Beautiful: Nature Unmasked. A Book for every Woman. Fcp. 8vo. 2s. 6d.

DELBRUCK, B., Introduction to the Study of Language: the History and Methods of Comparative Philology of the Indo-European Languages. 8vo. 5s.

DENNIS, J., Collection of English Sonnets. Sm. Cr. 8vo. 2s. 6d.

DENNYS, N. B., Folk-Lore of China, and its Affinities with that of the Aryan and Semitic Races. 8vo. 10s. 6d.

DENVIR, JOHN, The Irish in Britain, from the Earliest Times to the Fall and Death of Parnell. Cr. 8vo. 6s.

DEWEY, JOHN, Psychology. Large Cr. 8vo. 5s. 6d.

DEWEY, J. H., The Way, the Truth, and the Life: a Handbook of Christian Theosophy, Healing and Psychic Culture. 10s. 6d.

DIDON, Father, Jesus Christ. Cheaper Edition. 2 vols. 8vo. 12s.

DILLON, W., Life of John Mitchel. With Portrait. 2 vols. 8vo. 21s.

DOBSON, AUSTIN, Old World Idylls, and other Verses. With Frontispiece. Eleventh Edition. Elzevir 8vo. 6s.

    At the Sign of the Lyre. With Frontispiece. Eighth Edition. Elzevir 8vo. 6s.

    The Ballad of Beau Brocade; and other Poems of the Eighteenth Century. With Fifty Illustrations by Hugh Thomson. Cr. 8vo. 5s.

DOMVILE, Lady M., Life of Alphonse de Lamartine. Large Cr. 8vo. 7s. 6d.

D'ORSEY, A. J. D., Grammar of Portuguese and English. Adapted to Ollendorff's System. Fourth Edition. 12mo. 7s.

    Colloquial Portuguese; or, the Words and Phrases of Every-day Life. Fourth Edition. Cr. 8vo. 3s. 6d.

Doubter's Doubt about Science and Religion, A. Cr. 8vo. 3s. 6d.

DOUGLAS, Prof. R. K., Chinese Language and Literature. Cr. 8vo. 5s.

    The Life of Jenghiz Khan. Translated from the Chinese. Cr. 8vo. 5s.

DOWDEN, EDWARD, Shakspere : a Critical Study of His Mind and Art. Tenth Edition. Large post 8vo. 12s.

Shakspere's Sonnets. With Introduction and Notes. Large post 8vo. 7s. 6d.

Shakspere's Sonnets. Edited, with Frontispiece after the Death Mask. Elzevir 8vo. vellum, 7s. 6d. ; parchment or cloth, 6s. (*Parchment Library.*)

Studies in Literature. 1789–1877. Fifth Edition. Large post 8vo. 6s.

Transcripts and Studies. Large post 8vo. 12s.

Life of Percy Bysshe Shelley. With Portraits. 2 vols. 8vo. 36s.

DOWNING, C., Fruits and Fruit Trees of America : or, the Culture and Management of Fruit Trees generally. Illustrated. 8vo. 25s.

DOWSON, JOHN, Grammar of the Urdū or Hindūstānī Language. Second Edition. Cr. 8vo. 10s. 6d.

Hindūstānī Exercise Book. Passages and Extracts for Translation into Hindūstānī. Cr. 8vo. 2s. 6d.

Classical Dictionary of Hindu Mythology and History, Geography and Literature. Post 8vo. 16s. (*Trübner's Oriental Series.*)

DRAPER, J. W., The Conflict between Religion and Science. 21st Edition. Cr. 8vo. 5s. (*I.S.S.*)

DRAYSON, Major-General, Untrodden Ground in Astronomy and Geology. With Numerous Figures. 8vo. 14s.

DRUMMOND. Maria Drummond : a Sketch. Pott 8vo. 2s.

DUFF, E. GORDON, Early Printed Books. With Frontispiece and Ten Plates. Post 8vo. 6s. net. (*Books about Books.*)

DUFFY, Sir C. GAVAN, Thomas Davis : the Memoirs of an Irish Patriot, 1840–46. 8vo. 12s.

DUKA, THEODORE, Life and Works of Alexander Csoma de Körös between 1819 and 1842. With a Short Notice of all his Works and Essays, from Original Documents. Post 8vo. 9s. (*Trübner's Oriental Series.*)

DUNN, H. P., Infant Health : the Physiology and Hygiene of Early Life. Sm. Cr. 8vo. 3s. 6d.

DURUY, VICTOR, History of Greece. With Introduction by Prof. J. P. Mahaffy. 8 vols. Super royal 8vo. £8. 8s.

DUSAR, P. FRIEDRICH, Grammar of the German Language. With Exercises. 2nd Edition. Cr. 8vo. 4s. 6d.

Grammatical Course of the German Language. 3rd Edition. Cr. 8vo. 3s. 6d.

DUTT, ROMESH CHUNDER, History of Civilisation in Ancient India, based on Sanskrit literature. Cr. 8vo. Vol. I. Vedic and Epic Ages, 8s. Vol. II. Rationalistic Age, 8s. Vol. III. Buddhist and Pauranik Ages, 8s.

DUTT, TORU, Ancient Ballads and Legends of Hindustan. With an Introductory Memoir by Edmund Gosse. 18mo. cloth extra, gilt top, 5s.

EASTWICK, E. B., The Gulistan ; or, Rose Garden of Shekh Mushliu-'d-Din Sadi of Shiraz. Translated from the Atish Kadah. 2nd Edition. Post 8vo. 10s. 6d. (*Trübner's Oriental Series.*)

EDGREN, H., Compendious Sanskrit Grammar. With a Brief Sketch of Scenic Prakrit. Cr. 8vo. 10s. 6d.

EDKINS, J., D.D., Religion in China. Containing a Brief Account of the Three Religions of the Chinese. 3rd Edition. Post 8vo. 7s. 6d. (*Philosophical Library and Trübner's Oriental Series.*)

Chinese Buddhism : Sketches Historical and Critical. Post 8vo. 18s. (*Trübner's Oriental Series.*)

EDMONDS, HERBERT, Well-spent Lives : a Series of Modern Biographies. New and Cheaper Edition. Cr. 8vo. 3s. 6d.

EGER, GUSTAV, Technological Dictionary in the English and German Languages. 2 vols. roy. 8vo. £1. 7s.

Eighteenth Century Essays. Edited by AUSTIN DOBSON. With Frontispiece. Elzevir 8vo. vellum, 7s. 6d. ; parchment or cloth, 6s. (*Parchment Library.*) Cheap Edition, fcap. 8vo. 1s. 6d.

EITEL, E. J., Buddhism : its Historical, Theoretical, and Popular Aspects. Third Edition, revised, 8vo. 5s.

    Handbook for the Student of Chinese Buddhism. Second Edition. Cr. 8vo. 18s.

Electricity in Daily Life : a Popular Account of its Application to Every-day Uses. With 125 Illustrations. Sq. 8vo. 9s.

ELLIOTT, EBENEZER, Poems. Edited by his Son, the Rev. EDWIN ELLIOTT, of St. John's, Antigua. 2 vols. crown 8vo. 18s.

ELLIOTT, F. R., Handbook for Fruit Growers. Illustrated. Sq. 16mo. 5s.

    Handbook of Practical Landscape Gardening. Illustrated. 8vo. 7s. 6d.

ELLIOT, Sir H. M., History, Folk-lore, and Distribution of the Races of the North-Western Provinces of India. Edited by J. BEAMES. With 3 Coloured Maps. 2 vols. 8vo. £1. 16s.

    History of India, as told by its own Historians: the Muhammadan Period. From the Posthumous Papers of the late Sir H. M. ELLIOT. Revised and continued by Professor JOHN DOWSON. 8 vols. 8vo. £4. 8s.

ELLIOT, Sir W., Coins of Southern India. With Map and Plates. Roy. 4to. 25s. (*Numismata Orientalia.*)

ELLIS, W. ASHTON, Wagner Sketches : 1849. A Vindication. Cr. 8vo. cloth, 2s. 6d. ; paper, 2s.

    Richard Wagner's Prose Works. Translated by W. A. ELLIS. Vol. I. The Art Work of the Future. 8vo. 12s. 6d.

ELTON, CHARLES and MARY, The Great Book Collectors. With 10 Illustrations. Post 8vo. 6s. net. (*Books about Books.*)

Encyclopædia Americana. 4 vols. 4to. £8. 8s.

English Comic Dramatists. Edited by OSWALD CRAWFURD. Elzevir 8vo. vellum, 7s. 6d. ; parchment or cloth, 6s. (*Parchment Library.*)

English Lyrics. Elzevir 8vo. vellum, 7s. 6d.; parchment or cloth, 6s. (*Parchment Library.*)

English Odes. Edited by E. GOSSE. With Frontispiece. Elzevir 8vo. vellum, 7s. 6d.; parchment or cloth, 6s. (*Parchment Library.*)

English Sacred Lyrics. Elzevir 8vo. vellum, 7s. 6d.; parchment or cloth, 6s. (*Parchment Library.*)

English Poets (Living). With Frontispiece by WALTER CRANE. Second Edition. Large cr. 8vo. Printed on hand-made paper, vellum, 15s. ; cloth, 12s.

English Verse. CHAUCER TO BURNS. TRANSLATIONS. LYRICS OF THE NINETEENTH CENTURY. DRAMATIC SCENES AND CHARACTERS. BALLADS AND ROMANCES. Edited by W. J. LINTON and R. H. STODDARD. 5 vols. cr. 8vo. 5s. each.

EYTON, ROBERT, The Apostles' Creed : Sermons. Cr. 8vo. 3s. 6d.

    The True Life, and Other Sermons. Cr. 8vo. 7s. 6d.

    The Lord's Prayer : Sermons. Cr. 8vo. 3s. 6d.

    A Rash Investment : Sermon on Salvation Army Scheme of Social Reform. Fcp. 8vo. 1s.

    The Search for God, and other Sermons. Cr. 8vo 3s. 6d.

FABER, E., The Mind of Mencius; or, Political Economy founded upon Moral Philosophy. A systematic digest of the doctrines of the Chinese philosopher, Mencius. Original text Classified and Translated. Post 8vo. 10s. 6d. (*Trübner's Oriental Series.*)

FAUSBOLL, V., The Jataka, together with its Commentary: being Tales of the Anterior Birth of Gotama Buddha. 5 vols. 8vo. 28s. each.

FERGUSSON, T., Chinese Researches: Chinese Chronology and Cycles. Cr. 8vo. 10s. 6d.

FEUERBACH, L., Essence of Christianity. From the German, by MARIAN EVANS. Second Edition. Post 8vo. 7s. 6d. (*Philosophical Library.*)

FICHTE, J. GOTTLIEB, New Exposition of the Science of Knowledge. Translated by A. E. KROEGER. 8vo. 6s.

    Science of Knowledge. From the German, by A. E. KROEGER. With an Introduction by Prof. W. T. HARRIS. Post 8vo. 10s. 6d. (*Philosophical Library.*)

    Science of Rights. From the German by A. E. KROEGER. With an Introduction by Prof. W. T. HARRIS. Post 8vo. 12s. 6d. (*Philosophical Library.*)

    Popular Works: The Nature of the Scholar; The Vocation of the Scholar; The Vocation of Man; The Doctrine of Religion; Characteristics of the Present Age; Outlines of the Doctrine of Knowledge. With a Memoir by W. SMITH. Post 8vo. 2 vols. 21s. (*Philosophical Library.*)

FINN, ALEXANDER, Persian for Travellers. Oblong 32mo. 5s.

FITZARTHUR, T., The Worth of Human Testimony. Fcp. 8vo. 2s.

FITZGERALD, R. D., Australian Orchids. Part I., 7 Plates; Part II., 10 Plates; Part III., 10 Plates; Part IV., 10 Plates; Part V., 10 Plates; Part VI., 10 Plates. Each Part, coloured, 21s.; plain, 10s. 6d. Part VII., 10 Plates. Vol. II., Part I., 10 Plates. Each, coloured, 25s.

FITZPATRICK, W. J., Life of the Very Rev. T. N. Burke. With Portrait. 2 vols. 8vo. 30s.

FLETCHER, J. S., Andrewlina. Cr. 8vo. cloth, 1s. 6d.; paper covers, 1s.

    The Winding Way. Cr. 8vo. 6s.

FLINN, D. EDGAR, Ireland: its Health Resorts and Watering Places. With Frontispiece and Maps. 8vo. 5s.

FLOWER, W. H., The Horse: a Study in Natural History. Cr. 8vo. 2s. 6d. (*Modern Science Series.*)

FORNANDER, A., Account of the Polynesian Race: its Origin and Migrations, and the Ancient History of the Hawaian People. Post 8vo. Vol. I., 7s. 6d. Vol. II., 10s. 6d. Vol. III., 9s. (*Philosophical Library.*)

FORNEY, MATTHIAS N., Catechism of the Locomotive. Second Edition, revised and enlarged. Fcp. 4to. 18s.

FRASER, Sir WILLIAM, Bart., Disraeli and His Day. Second Edition. Post 8vo. 9s.

FRAZAR, DOUGLAS, Practical Boat Sailing: a Treatise on Management of Small Boats and Yachts. Sm. cr. 4s. 6d.

FREEBOROUGH, E., and RANKEN, C. E., Chess Openings, Ancient and Modern. Revised and Corrected up to the Present Time from the best Authorities. Large post 8vo. 7s. 6d.

FREEBOROUGH, E., Chess Endings. A Companion to 'Chess Openings, Ancient and Modern.' Edited and Arranged. Large post 8vo. 7s. 6d.

FREEMAN, E. A., Lectures to American Audiences. I. The English People in its Three Homes. II. Practical Bearings of General European History. Post 8vo. 8s. 6d.

French Jansenists. By the Author of 'Spanish Mystics' and 'Many Voices.' Cr. 8vo. 6s.

French Lyrics. Edited by GEORGE SAINTSBURY. With Frontispiece. Elzevir 8vo. vellum, 7s. 6d.; parchment or cloth, 6s. (*Parchment Library.*)

FREWEN, MORETON, The Economic Crisis. Cr. 8vo. 4*s.* 6*d.*

FRIEDLÄNDER, M., Text-Book of Jewish Religion. Third Edition, revised. Cr. 8vo. 1*s.* 6*d.*

The Jewish Religion. Cr. 8vo. 5*s.*

FRIEDRICH, P., Progressive German Reader. With copious Notes. Cr. 8vo. 4*s.* 6*d.*

FRITH, I., Life of Giordano Bruno, the Nolan. Revised by Prof. MORIZ CARRIERE. With Portrait. Post 8vo. 14*s.* (*Philosophical Library.*)

FRŒMBLING, F. OTTO, Graduated German Reader : a Selection from the most popular writers. With a Vocabulary. Twelfth Edition. 12mo. 3*s.* 6*d.*

Graduated Exercises for Translation into German : Extracts from the best English Authors, with Idiomatic Notes. Cr. 8vo. 4*s.* 6*d.* ; without Notes, 4*s.*

GALL, Capt. H. R., Tactical Questions and Answers on the Infantry Drill Book 1892. Third Edition. Cr. 8vo. 1*s.* 6*d.*

GARDINER, LINDA, His Heritage. With Frontispiece. Cr. 8vo. 6*s.*

GARDNER, PERCY, The Numismata Orientalia. Part V. The Parthian Coinage. With 8 Plates. Royal 4to. Paper wrapper, 18*s.*

GARLANDA, FEDERICO, The Fortunes of Words. Cr. 8vo. 5*s.*

The Philosophy of Words : a popular introduction to the Science of Language. Cr. 8vo. 5*s.*

GASTER, M., Greeko-Slavonic Literature, and its Relation to the Folk-lore of Europe during the Middle Ages. Large Post 8vo. 7*s.* 6*d.*

GAY, JOHN, Fables. Edited by AUSTIN DOBSON. With Portrait. Elzevir 8vo. vellum, 7*s.* 6*d.* ; parchment or cloth, 6*s.* (*Parchment Library.*)

GEIGER, LAZARUS, Contributions to the History of the Development of the Human Race. From the German by D. ASHER. Post 8vo. 6*s.* (*Philosophical Library.*)

GELDART, E. M., Guide to Modern Greek. Post 8vo. 7*s.* 6*d.* Key, 2*s.* 6*d.*

Simplified Grammar of Modern Greek. Cr. 8vo. 2*s.* 6*d.*

GEORGE, HENRY, Progress and Poverty : an Inquiry into the Causes of Industrial Depressions, and of Increase of Want with Increase of Wealth ; the Remedy. Fifth Edition. Post 8vo. 7*s.* 6*d.* Cabinet Edition, cr. 8vo. 2*s.* 6*d.* Cheap Edition, limp cloth, 1*s.* 6*d.* ; paper covers, 1*s.*

Protection or Free Trade : an Examination of the Tariff Question, with especial regard to the interests of labour. Second Edition. Cr. 8vo. 5*s.* Cheap Edition, limp cloth, 1*s.* 6*d.* ; paper covers, 1*s.*

Social Problems. Fourth Thousand. Cr. 8vo. 5*s.* Cheap Edition, limp cloth, 1*s.* 6*d.* ; paper covers, 1*s.*

A Perplexed Philosopher : being an Examination of Mr. HERBERT SPENCER'S various utterances on the Land Question, &c. Cr. 8vo. 5*s.*

GERARD, E. and D., A Sensitive Plant : a Novel. With Frontispiece. Cr. 8vo. 6*s.*

GIBB, E. J. W., The History of the Forty Vezirs ; or, The Story of the Forty Morns and Eves. Translated from the Turkish. Cr. 8vo. 10*s.* 6*d.*

GILBERT. Autobiography, and other Memorials of Mrs. Gilbert. Edited by JOSIAH GILBERT. Fifth Edition. Cr. 8vo. 7*s.* 6*d.*

GLANVILL, JOSEPH, Scepsis Scientifica. Edited, with Introductory Essay, by JOHN OWEN. Elzevir 8vo. 6*s.*

GLAZEBROOK, R. T., Laws and Properties of Matter. Cr. 8vo. 2*s.* 6*d.* (*Modern Science.*)

GLOVER, F., Exempla Latina : a First Construing Book, with Notes, Lexicon, and an Introduction to Analysis of Sentences. Second Edition, Fcp. 8vo. 2*s.*

GOETHE'S Faust. Translated from the German by JOHN ANSTER. With an Introduction by BURDETT MASON. With illustrations (18 in black and white, 10 in colour) by FRANK M. GREGORY. Grand folio, £3. 3s.

GOLDSMITH, Oliver, Vicar of Wakefield. Edited by AUSTIN DOBSON. Elzevir 8vo. vellum, 7s. 6d. ; parchment or cloth, 6s. (*Parchment Library.*)

GOMME, G. L., Ethnology in Folklore. Cr. 8vo. 2s. 6d. (*Modern Science.*)

GOOCH, Diaries of Sir Daniel Gooch, Bart. With an Introductory Notice by Sir THEODORE MARTIN, K.C.B. With 2 Portraits and an Illustration. Cr. 8vo. 6s.

GOODENOUGH. Memoir of Commodore J. G. Goodenough. Edited by his Widow. With Portrait. Third Edition. Cr. 8vo. 5s.

GORDON, Major-General C. G., Journals at Khartoum. Printed from the original MS. With Introduction and Notes by A. EGMONT HAKE. Portrait, 2 Maps, and 30 Illustrations. 8vo. 21s. Cheap Edition, 6s.

> **Last Journal :** a Facsimile of the last Journal received in England from General Gordon, reproduced by Photo-lithography. Imp. 4to. £3. 3s.

GORDON, Sir H. W., Events in the Life of General Gordon, from the Day of his Birth to the Day of his Death. With Maps and Illustrations. Second Edition. 8vo. 7s. 6d.

Gospel according to Matthew, Mark, and Luke (The). Elzevir 8vo. vellum, 7s. 6d. ; parchment or cloth, 6s. (*Parchment Library.*)

GOSSE, EDMUND, Seventeenth Century Studies : a Contribution to the History of English Poetry. 8vo. 10s. 6d.

> **New Poems.** Cr. 8vo. 7s. 6d.

> **Firdausi in Exile,** and other Poems. Second Edition. Elzevir 8vo. gilt top, 6s.

> **On Viol and Flute :** Lyrical Poems. With Frontispiece by L. ALMA TADEMA, and Tailpiece by HAMO THORNYCROFT. Elzevir 8vo. 6s.

> **Life of Philip Henry Gosse.** By his Son. 8vo. 15s.

GOSSIP, G. H. D., The Chess-Player's Text-Book : an Elementary Treatise on the Game of Chess. Numerous Diagrams. 16mo. 2s.

GOUGH, A. E., Philosophy of the Upanishads. Post 8vo. 9s. (*Trübner's Oriental Series.*)

GOUGH, EDWARD, The Bible True from the Beginning : a Commentary on all those portions of Scripture that are most questioned and assailed. Vols. I. to V. 8vo. 16s. each.

GOWER, Lord RONALD, Bric-à-Brac. Being some Photoprints illustrating Art Objects at Gower Lodge, Windsor. With Letterpress descriptions. Super roy. 8vo. 15s.; extra binding, 21s.

> **Last Days of Marie Antoinette :** an Historical Sketch. With Portrait and Facsimiles. Fcap. 4to. 10s. 6d.

> **Notes of a Tour from Brindisi to Yokohama, 1883-1884.** Fcp. 8vo. 2s. 6d.

> **Rupert of the Rhine :** a Biographical Sketch of the Life of Prince Rupert. With 3 Portraits. Cr. 8vo. buckram, 6s.

> **Stafford House Letters.** With 2 Portraits. 8vo. 10s. 6d.

GRAHAM, JEAN CARLYLE, Songs, Measures, Metrical Lines. Cr. 8vo. 5s.

GRAHAM, WILLIAM, The Creed of Science : Religious, Moral, and Social. Second Edition, revised. Cr. 8vo. 6s.

> **The Social Problem, in its Economic, Moral and Political Aspects.** 8vo. 14s.

> **Socialism New and Old.** Second Edition. Cr. 8vo. 5s. (*I.S.S.*)

GRAY, J., Ancient Proverbs and Maxims from Burmese Sources ; or, The Niti Literature of Burma. Post 8vo. 6s. (*Trübner's Oriental Series.*)

GRAY, MAXWELL, Silence of Dean Maitland. Eighth Edition. With Frontispiece. Cr. 8vo. 6*s.*

The Reproach of Annesley. Fifth Edition. With Frontispiece. Cr. 8vo. 6*s.*

In the Heart of the Storm. With Frontispiece by GORDON BROWNE. Cr. 8vo. 6*s.*

Westminster Chimes, and other Poems. Sm. 8vo. 5*s.*

GREEN, F. W. EDRIDGE, Colour Blindness and Colour Perception. With 3 Coloured Plates. Cr. 8vo. 5*s.* (*I.S.S.*)

GREG, R. P., Comparative Philology of the Old and New Worlds in Relation to Archaic Speech. With copious Vocabularies. Super royal 8vo. £1. 11*s.* 6*d.*

GREG, W. R., Literary and Social Judgments. Fourth Edition. 2 vols. Cr. 8vo. 15*s.*

The Creed of Christendom. Eighth Edition. 2 vols. post 8vo. 15*s.* (*Philosophical Library*).

Enigmas of Life. Seventeenth Edition. Post 8vo. 10*s.* 6*d.* (*Philosophical Library*).

Enigmas of Life. With a Prefatory Memoir. Edited by his WIFE. Nineteenth Edition. Cr. 8vo. 6*s.*

Political Problems for our Age and Country. 8vo. 10*s.* 6*d.*

Miscellaneous Essays. Two Series. Cr. 8vo. 7*s.* 6*d.* each.

GREY, ROWLAND, In Sunny Switzerland : a Tale of Six Weeks. Second Edition. Sm. 8vo. 5*s.*

Lindenblumen, and other Stories. Sm. 8vo. 5*s.*

By Virtue of His Office. Cr. 8vo. 6*s.*

Jacob's Letter, and other Stories. Cr. 8vo. 5*s.*

GRIFFIN, Sir Lepel, The Rajas of the Punjab : History of the Principal States in the Punjab, and their Political Relations with the British Government. Royal 8vo. 21*s.*

GRIFFIS, W. E., The Mikado's Empire. Book I. History of Japan from B.C. 660 to A.D. 1872. Book II. Personal Experiences, Observations, and Studies in Japan, 1870-1874. Second Edition, illustrated. 8vo. 20*s.*

Japanese Fairy World : Stories from the Wonder-Lore of Japan. With 12 Plates. Square 16mo. 3*s.* 6*d.*

GRIFFITH, R. T. H., Birth of the War-God : a Poem from the Sanskrit of KÁLIDASÁ. Second Edition. Post 8vo. 5*s.* (*Trübner's Oriental Series*).

Yúsef and Zulaikha : a Poem by JAMI. Translated from the Persian into English verse. Post 8vo. 8*s.* 6*d.* (*Trübner's Oriental Series.*)

GRIMLEY, H. N., The Prayer of Humanity : Sermons on the Lord's Prayer. Cr. 8vo. 3*s.* 6*d.*

Tremadoc Sermons, chiefly on the Spiritual Body, the Unseen World, and the Divine Humanity. Fourth Edition. Cr. 8vo. 6*s.*

The Temple of Humanity, and other Sermons. Cr. 8vo. 6*s.*

GRIMSHAW, R., Engine Runner's Catechism. A Sequel to the Author's ' Steam Engine Catechism.' Illustrated. 18mo. 8*s.* 6*d.*

GUBERNATIS, ANGELO DE, Zoological Mythology ; or, The Legends of Animals. 2 vols. 8vo. £1. 8*s.*

GUICCIARDINI, FRANCESCO, Counsels and Reflections. Translated by N. H. Thomson. Cr. 8vo. 6*s.*

GURNEY, ALFRED, The Vision of the Eucharist, and other Poems. Cr. 8vo. 5*s.*

A Christmas Faggot. Sm. 8vo. 5*s.*

Voices from the Holy Sepulchre, and other Poems. Cr. 8vo. 5*s.*

Wagner's Parsifal : a Study. Second Edition. Fcp. 8vo. 1*s.* 6*d.*

Our Catholic Inheritance in the Larger Hope. Cr. 8vo. 1*s.* 6*d.*

The Story of a Friendship. Cr. 8vo. 5*s.*

HADDON, CAROLINE, The Larger Life : Studies in Hinton's Ethics. Cr. 8vo. 5*s.*

HAECKEL, Prof. ERNST, The History of Creation. New Edition. Translation revised by Professor E. RAY LANKESTER, with 20 plates and numerous figures. Fourth Edition. 2 vols. Large post 8vo. 32s.

The History of the Evolution of Man. With numerous Illustrations. 2 vols. Post 8vo. 32s.

A Visit to Ceylon. Post 8vo. 7s. 6d.

Freedom in Science and Teaching. With a Prefatory Note by Prof. T. H. HUXLEY. Cr. 8vo. 5s.

HAGGARD, H. RIDER, Cetywayo and His White Neighbours; or, Remarks on Recent Events in Zululand, Natal, and the Transvaal. Fourth Edition. Cr. 8vo. 6s.

HAGGARD, W. H., and LE STRANGE, G., The Vazir of Lankuran: a Persian Play. With a Grammatical Introduction, Translation, Notes, and Vocabulary. Cr. 8vo. 10s. 6d.

HAHN, T., Tsuni- ‖ Goam, the Supreme Being of the Khoi-Khoi. Post 8vo. 7s. 6d. (*Trübner's Oriental Series.*)

HALL, H. E., Leadership, not Lordship. Cr. 8vo. 2s.

HALLECK'S International Law; or, Rules Regulating the Intercourse of States in Peace and War. Third Edition, thoroughly revised by Sir SHERSTON BAKER, Bart. 2 vols. 8vo. 38s.

HALLOCK, CHARLES, The Sportsman's Gazetteer and General Guide to the Game Animals, Birds, and Fishes of North America. Maps and Portrait. Cr. 8vo. 15s.

HAMILTON. Memoirs of Arthur Hamilton, B.A., of Trinity College, Cambridge. Cr. 8vo. 6s.

HARDY, W. J., Book Plates. With Frontispiece and 36 Illustrations of Book Plates. Post 8vo. 6s. net. (*Books about Books.*)

HARRISON, CLIFFORD, In Hours of Leisure. Second Edition. Cr. 8vo. 5s.

HARRISON, Col. R., Officer's Memorandum Book for Peace and War. Fourth Edition, revised. Oblong 32mo. red basil, with pencil, 3s. 6d.

HARRISON, J. A., and BASKERVILL, W., Handy Dictionary of Anglo-Saxon Poetry. Sq. 8vo. 12s.

HART, J. W. T., Autobiography of Judas Iscariot. A Character Study. Cr. 8vo. 3s. 6d.

HARTMANN, EDUARD von, Philosophy of the Unconscious. Translated by W. C. COUPLAND. 3 vols. Post 8vo. 31s. 6d. (*Philosophical Library.*)

HARTMANN, FRANZ, Magic, White and Black; or, The Science of Finite and Infinite Life. Fourth Edition, revised. Cr. 8vo. 6s.

The Life of Paracelsus, and the Substance of his Teachings. Post 8vo. 10s. 6d.

Life and Doctrines of Jacob Boehme: an Introduction to the Study of his Works. Post 8vo. 10s. 6d.

HARTMANN, R., Anthropoid Apes. With 63 Illustrations. Second Edition. Cr. 8vo. 5s. (*I.S.S.*)

HARVEY, W. F., Simplified Grammar of the Spanish Language. Cr. 8vo. 3s. 6d.

HAUG, M., Essays on the Sacred Language, Writings. and Religion of the Parsis. Third Edition. Edited and Enlarged by E. W. WEST. Post 8vo. 16s. (*Trübner's Oriental Series.*)

HAWEIS, H. R., Current Coin. Materialism—The Devil—Crime—Drunkenness—Pauperism—Emotion—Recreation—The Sabbath. Sixth Edition. Cr. 8vo. 5s.

Arrows in the Air. Fifth Edition. Cr. 8vo. 5s.

Speech in Season. Sixth Edition. Cr. 8vo. 5s.

Thoughts for the Times. Fourteenth Edition. Cr. 8vo. 5s.

Unsectarian Family Prayers. Fourth Edition. Fcp. 8vo. 1s. 6d.

HAWTHORNE, NATHANIEL, Works. Complete in 12 vols. Large post 8vo. 7s. 6d each. (Scarlet Letter. New Illustrated Edition. Post 8vo. 10s. 6d.)

HEAD, BARCLAY V., The Numismata Orientalia. Part III. The Coinage of Lydia and Persia, from the Earliest Times to the Fall of the Dynasty of the Achæmenidæ. With 3 Plates. Royal 4to. Paper wrapper, 10s. 6d.

HEALES, Major ALFRED, The Architecture of the Churches of Denmark. 8vo. 14s.

HEATH, FRANCIS GEORGE, Autumnal Leaves. With 12 Coloured Plates. Third and Cheaper Edition. 8vo. 6s.

    Sylvan Winter. With 70 Illustrations. 14s.

HEATH, RICHARD, Edgar Quinet : His Early Life and Writings. With Portraits, Illustrations, and an Autograph Letter. Post 8vo. 12s. 6d. (*Philosophical Library.*)

HEGEL. Lectures on the History of Philosophy. Translated by E. S. HALDANE. 3 vols. Vol. I. 12s.

    The Introduction to Hegel's Philosophy of Fine Art, translated by BERNARD BOSANQUET. Cr. 8vo. 5s.

HEIDENHAIN, RUDOLPH, Hypnotism, or Animal Magnetism. With Preface by G. J. ROMANES. Second Edition. Sm. 8vo. 2s. 6d.

HEILPRIN, Prof. A., Bermuda Islands. 8vo. 18s.

    Geographical and Geological Distribution of Animals. With Frontispiece. Cr. 8vo. 5s. (*I.S.S.*)

HEINE, H., Religion and Philosophy in Germany. Translated by J. SNODGRASS. Post 8vo. 6s. (*Philosophical Library.*)

HENDRIKS, DOM LAWRENCE, The London Charterhouse : its Monks and its Martyrs. Illustrated. 8vo. 15s.

HENSLOW, Prof. G., Origin of Floral Structures through Insect and other Agencies. With 88 Illustrations. Cr. 8vo. 5s.

HEPBURN, J. C., Japanese and English Dictionary. Second Edition. Imp. 8vo. half-roan, 18s.

    Japanese-English and English-Japanese Dictionary. Third Edition. Royal 8vo. half-morocco, cloth sides, 30s. Pocket Edition, square 16mo. 14s.

HERMES TRISMEGISTUS, Works. Translated by J. D. CHAMBERS. Post 8vo. 7s. 6d.

    The Virgin of the World. Translated and Edited by the Authors of 'The Perfect Way.' Illustrations. 4to. imitation parchment, 10s. 6d.

HERSHON, P. J., Talmudic Miscellany ; or, One Thousand and One Extracts from the Talmud, the Midrashim, and the Kabbalah. Post 8vo. 14s. (*Trübner's Oriental Series.*)

HILLEBRAND, KARL, France and the French in the Second Half of the 19th Century. From the third German Edition. Post 8vo. 10s. 6d.

HINTON. Life and Letters of James Hinton. With an Introduction by Sir W. W. GULL, and Portrait engraved on steel by C. H. JEENS. Sixth Edition. Cr. 8vo. 8s. 6d.

    Philosophy and Religion. Selections from the Manuscripts of the late James Hinton. Edited by CAROLINE HADDON. Second Edition. Cr. 8vo. 5s.

    The Law-Breaker and **The Coming of the Law.** Edited by MARGARET HINTON. Cr. 8vo. 6s.

    The Mystery of Pain. New Edition. Fcp. 8vo. 1s.

HIRSCHFELD, H., Arabic Chrestomathy in Hebrew Characters. With a Glossary. 8vo. 7s. 6d.

HODGSON, B. H., Essays on the Languages, Literature, and Religion of Nepal and Tibet. Roy. 8vo. 14s.

    Essays relating to Indian Subjects. 2 vols. Post 8vo. 28s. (*Trübner's Oriental Series.*)

HODGSON, J. E., Academy Lectures. Cr. 8vo. 7s. 6d.

HOLBOROW, A., Evolution and Scripture; with an Inquiry into the nature of the Scriptures and Inspiration. Cr. 8vo. 4s. 6d.

HOLMES-FORBES, A. W., The Science of Beauty : an Analytical Inquiry into the Laws of Æsthetics. Second Edition. Post 8vo. 3s. 6d.

HOLMES, OLIVER WENDELL, John Lothrop Motley : a Memoir. Cr. 8vo. 6s.
    Life of Ralph Waldo Emerson. With Portrait. English Copyright Edition. Cr. 8vo. 6s.

HOLTHAM, E. G., Eight Years in Japan, 1873-1881. With 3 Maps. Large Cr. 8vo. 9s.

HOMER'S Iliad. Greek Text, with Translation by J. G. CORDERY. 2 vols. 8vo. 14s. Translation only, cr. 8vo. 5s.

HOOPER, MARY, Little Dinners : How to Serve them with Elegance and Economy. Twenty-second Edition. Cr. 8vo. 2s. 6d.
    Cookery for Invalids, Persons of Delicate Digestion, and Children. Fifth Edition. Cr. 8vo. 2s. 6d.
    Every-day Meals : being Economical and Wholesome Recipes for Breakfast, Luncheon, and Supper. Seventh Edition. Cr. 8vo. 2s. 6d.

HOPKINS, ELLICE, Work amongst Working Men. Sixth Edition. Cr. 8vo. 3s. 6d.

HORATIUS FLACCUS, Q., Opera. Edited by F. A. CORNISH. With Frontispiece. Elzevir 8vo. vellum, 7s. 6d. ; parchment or cloth, 6s. (*Parchment Library.*)

HORNADAY, W. T., Two Years in a Jungle. With Illustrations. 8vo. 21s.
    Taxidermy and Zoological Collecting; with Chapters on Collecting and Preserving Insects, by W. J. HOLLAND, D.D. With 24 Plates and 85 Illustrations. 8vo. 10s. 6d.

HOSPITALIER, E., The Modern Applications of Electricity. Translated and Enlarged by JULIUS MAIER. Second Edition, revised, with many Additions and Numerous Illustrations. 2 vols. 8vo. 25s.

HOWARD, H. C., Christabel (concluded), with other Poems. Cr. 8vo. 2s. 6d.

HOWE, HENRY MARION, The Metallurgy of Steel. Vol. I. Second Edition, revised and enlarged. Royal 4to. £2. 12s. 6d.

HULME, F. EDWARD, Mathematical Drawing Instruments, and How to Use Them. With Illustrations. Fifth Edition, imperial 16mo, 3s. 6d.

HUMBOLDT, Baron W. von, The Sphere and Duties of Government. From the German by J. COULTHARD. Post 8vo, 5s.

HUNTER, HAY, and **WHYTE, WALTER. My Ducats and My Daughter.** With Frontispiece. Cr. 8vo. 6s.

HUSMANN, G., American Grape Growing and Wine Making. Illustrated. 12mo. 7s. 6d.

HUTCHINSON, A. B., The Mind of Mencius ; or, Political Economy founded upon Moral Philosophy. A Systematic Digest of the Doctrines of the Chinese Philosopher Mencius. Translated from the German of FABER, with Additional Notes. Post 8vo. 10s. 6d. (*Trübner's Oriental Series.*)

HUTCHINSON, Colonel, and **MACGREGOR, Major, Military Sketching and Reconnaissance.** Fifth Edition, with 16 Plates. Sm. cr. 8vo. 4s. (*Military Handbooks.*)

HUXLEY, Prof. T. H., The Crayfish : an Introduction to the Study of Zoology. With 82 Illustrations. Fifth Edition. Cr. 8vo. 5s. (*I.S.S.*)

IHNE, W., Latin Grammar for Beginners. Ahn's System. 12mo. 3s.

IM THURN, EVERARD F., Among the Indians of Guiana : Sketches, Chiefly Anthropologic, from the Interior of British Guiana. With 53 Illustrations and a Map. 8vo. 18s.

INGELOW, JEAN, Off the Skelligs: a Novel. With Frontispiece. Cr. 8vo. 6s.

INMAN, JAMES, Nautical Tables. Designed for the use of British Seamen. New Edition, revised and enlarged. 8vo. 16s.

IVANOFF'S Russian Grammar. Sixteenth Edition. Translated, Enlarged, and Arranged for use of Students by Major W. E. GOWAN. 8vo. 6s.

JACOB, G. A., Manual of Hindu Pantheism: the Vedântasâra. Third Edition, post 8vo. 6s. (*Trübner's Oriental Series.*)

JAPP, ALEXANDER H., Days with Industrials: Adventures and Experiences among Curious Industries. With Illustrations. Cr. 8vo. 6s.

JÄSCHKE, H. A., Tibetan Grammar. Prepared by Dr. H. WENZELL. Second Edition. Cr. 8vo. 5s.

JEAFFRESON, HERBERT H., Magnificat: a Course of Sermons. With Frontispiece. Cr. 8vo. 2s. 6d.

JENKINS, E., A Modern Paladin: Contemporary Manners. Cr. 8vo. 5s.

JENKINS, E., and RAYMOND, J., Architect's Legal Handbook. Fourth Edition, revised. Cr. 8vo. 6s.

JENKINS, JABEZ, Vest-Pocket Lexicon. An English Dictionary of all except Familiar Words, including the principal Scientific and Technical Terms. 64mo. roan, 1s. 6d.; cloth, 1s.

JENKINS, Canon R. C., Heraldry, English and Foreign. With a Dictionary of Heraldic Terms and 156 Illustrations. Sm. 8vo. 3s. 6d.

JENNINGS, HARGRAVE, The Indian Religions; or, Results of the Mysterious Buddhism. 8vo. 10s. 6d.

JESSOP, C. MOORE, Past and Future; or, Fable and Fact. Cr. 8vo. 5s.

JEVONS, W. STANLEY, Money and the Mechanism of Exchange. Ninth Edition. Cr. 8vo. 5s. (*I.S.S.*)

JOEL, L., Consul's Manual, and Shipowner's and Shipmaster's Practical Guide in their Transactions Abroad. 8vo. 12s.

Johns Hopkins University Studies in History and Politics. Edited by HERBERT B. ADAMS. Nine Annual Series, and nine Extra Volumes. 8vo. £10. 10s. Also sold separately.

JOHNSON, J. B., Theory and Practice of Surveying. Designed for use of Students in Engineering. Illustrated. Second Edition. 8vo. 15s.

JOHNSON, S. W., How Crops Feed: a Treatise on the Atmosphere and the Soil as related to Nutrition of Plants. Illustrated. Cr. 8vo. 10s.

    How Crops Grow: a Treatise on the Chemical Composition, Structure, and Life of the Plant. Illustrated. Cr. 8vo. 10s.

JOHNSON, SAMUEL, Oriental Religions and their Relation to Universal Religion—Persia. 8vo. 18s.

    Oriental Religions and their Relation to Universal Religion—India. 2 vols. 21s. (*Philosophical Library.*)

JOHNSTON, H. H., The Kilima-njaro Expedition: a Record of Scientific Exploration in Eastern Equatorial Africa. With 6 Maps and 80 Illustrations. 8vo. 21s.

    History of a Slave. With 47 Illustrations. Square 8vo. 6s.

JOLLY, JULIUS, Naradiya Dharma-Sastra: or, The Institutes of Narada. Translated from the Sanskrit. Cr. 8vo. 10s. 6d.

    Manava-Dharma-Castra: the Code of Manu. Original Sanskrit Text. With Critical Notes. Post 8vo. 10s. 6d. (*Trübner's Oriental Series.*)

JOLY, N., Man before Metals. With 148 Illustrations. Fourth Edition. Cr. 8vo. 5s. (*I.S.S.*)

JONCOURT, Madame MARIE DE, Wholesome Cookery. Fifth Edition. Cr. 8vo. cloth, 1s. 6d. ; paper covers, 1s.

JUDD, Prof. J. W., Volcanoes: what they are and what they teach. With 96 Illustrations on Wood. Fourth Edition. Cr. 8vo. 5s. (*I.S.S.*)

Kalender of Shepherdes. Facsimile Reprint. With Introduction and Glossary by Dr. H. Oskar Sommer. £2. 2s. net.

KARCHER, THÉODORE, Questionnaire Français: Questions on French Grammar, Idiomatic Difficulties, and Military Expressions. Fourth Edition. Cr. 8vo. 4s. 6d. ; interleaved with writing paper, 5s. 6d.

KARMARSCH, KARL, Technological Dictionary. Fourth Edition, revised. Imp. 8vo. 3 vols.
> Vol. 1.—German-English-French, 12s.
> Vol. 2.—English-German-French, 12s.
> Vol. 3.—French-German-English, 15s.

KAUFMANN, M., Socialism: its Nature, its Dangers, and its Remedies considered. Cr. 8vo. 7s. 6d.

Utopias; or, Schemes of Social Improvement, from Sir Thomas More to Karl Marx. Cr. 8vo. 5s.

Christian Socialism. Cr. 8vo. 4s. 6d.

KAY, JOSEPH, Free Trade in Land. Edited by his Widow. With Preface by Right Hon. John Bright. Seventh Edition. Cr. 8vo. 5s. Cheap Edition. Cloth, 1s. 6d.; paper covers, 1s.

KEATS, JOHN, Poetical Works. Edited by W. T. Arnold. Large Cr. 8vo. choicely printed on hand-made paper, with etched portrait, vellum, 15s. ; parchment or cloth, 12s. Cheap edition, crown 8vo, cloth, 3s. 6d.

KEBLE, J., Christian Year. With Portrait. Elzevir 8vo. vellum, 7s. 6d. ; parchment or cloth, 6s. (*Parchment Library.*)

KELKE, W. H. H., An Epitome of English Grammar. For the Use of Students. Adapted to London Matriculation Course. Cr. 8vo. 4s. 6d.

KELLOGG, G. H., Grammar of the Hindi Language. Second Edition, revised and enlarged. 8vo. 18s.

KEMPIS, THOMAS À, The Imitation of Christ. Revised Translation. Elzevir 8vo. (*Parchment Library*), vellum, 7s. 6d. ; parchment or cloth, 6s. Red line Edition, fcp. 8vo. 2s. 6d. Cabinet Edition, sm. 8vo. 1s. 6d. ; cloth limp, 1s. Miniature Edition, 32mo. with red lines, 1s. 6d. ; without red lines, 1s.

A Metrical Version. By H. Carrington. Cr. 8vo. 5s.

De Imitatione Christi. Latin Text, Rhythmically Arranged, with Translation on Opposite Pages. Cr. 8vo. 7s. 6d.

KETTLEWELL, S., Thomas à Kempis and the Brothers of Common Life. With Portrait. Cr. 8vo. 7s. 6d.

KHAYYÁM, OMAR, The Quatrains of. Persian Text, with an English Verse Translation. Post 8vo. 10s. 6d. Translation only, 5s. (*Trübner's Oriental Series.*)

KIDD, JOSEPH, Laws of Therapeutics. Second Edition. Cr. 8vo. 6s.

KINAHAN, G. H., Valleys and their Relation to Fissures, Fractures, and Faults. Cr. 8vo. 7s. 6d.

KING, Mrs. HAMILTON, The Disciples. Eleventh Edition. Elzevir 8vo. 6s. Fourteenth Edition. Sm. 8vo. 5s.

A Book of Dreams. Third Edition. Cr. 8vo. 3s. 6d.

Sermon in the Hospital (from 'The Disciples'). Fifth Edition. Fcp. 8vo. 1s. Cheap Edition, 3d.

Ballads of the North, and other Poems. Cr. 8vo. 5s.

KINGSFORD, ANNA, The Perfect Way in Diet: a Treatise advocating a Return to the Natural and Ancient Food of our Race. Sixth Edition. Sm. 8vo. 2s.

Spiritual Hermeneutics of Astrology and Holy Writ. Illustrated. 4to. parchment, 10s. 6d.

KINGSFORD, ANNA, and MAITLAND, EDWARD, The Virgin of the World of Hermes Mercurius Trismegistus, rendered into English. 4to. imit. parchment, 10s. 6d.

KINGSFORD, W., History of Canada. 5 vols. 8vo. 15s. each.

KISTNA, OTTO, Buddha and His Doctrines: a Bibliographical Essay. 4to. 2s. 6d.

KITTON, FRED. G., John Leech, Artist and Humourist: a Biographical Sketch. 18mo. 1s.

KNOWLES, J. HINTON, Folk-Tales of Kashmir. Post 8vo. 16s. (*Trübner's Oriental Series.*)

KNOX, A. A., The New Playground; or, Wanderings in Algeria. New and Cheaper Edition. Large cr. 8vo. 6s.

KOLBE, F. W., A Language-Study based on Bantu: an Inquiry into the Laws of Root-formation. 8vo. 6s.

KRAMER, J., Pocket Dictionary of the Dutch Language. Fifth Edition. 16mo. 4s.

KRAPF, L., Dictionary of the Suahili Language. 8vo. 30s.

KRAUS, J., Carlsbad: its Thermal Springs and Baths, and how to use them. Fourth Edition, revised and enlarged. Cr. 8vo. 6s. 6d.

KUNZ, G. F., Gems and Precious Stones of North America. Illustrated with 8 Coloured Plates and numerous Engravings. Super-royal 8vo. £2. 12s. 6d.

LAGRANGE, F., Physiology of Bodily Exercise. Second Edition. Cr. 8vo. 5s. (*I.S.S.*)

LANDON, JOSEPH, School Management; including a General View of the Work of Education, Organisation, and Discipline. Seventh Edition. Cr. 8vo. 6s. (*Education Library.*)

LANE, E. W., Selections from the Koran. New Edition, with Introduction by STANLEY LANE-POOLE. Post 8vo. 9s. (*Trübner's Oriental Series.*)

LANG, ANDREW, In the Wrong Paradise, and other Stories. Cr. 8vo. 6s.
Ballades in Blue China. Elzevir 8vo. 5s.
Rhymes à la Mode. With Frontispiece. Fourth Edition. Elzevir 8vo. 5s.
Lost Leaders. Cr. 8vo. 5s. Second Edition.

LANGE, Prof. F. A., History of Materialism, and Criticism of its present importance. Authorised Translation by ERNEST C. THOMAS. Fourth Edition. 3 vols. Post 8vo. 10s. 6d. each. (*Philosophical Library.*)

LANGE, F. K. W., Germania: a German Reading-book. Part I. Anthology of Prose and Poetry, with vocabulary. Part II. Essays on German History and Institutions. 8vo. 2 vols. 5s. 6d. ; separately, 3s. 6d. each.

LANGSTROTH on the Hive and Honey Bee. Revised and Enlarged Edition. With numerous Illustrations. 8vo. 9s.

LARMOYER, M. de, Practical French Grammar. Cr. 8vo. New Edition, in one vol. 3s. 6d. Two Parts, 2s. 6d. each.

LARSEN, A., Dano-Norwegian Dictionary. Cr. 8vo. 10s. 6d.

LAURIE, S. S., Rise and Early Constitution of Universities. With a Survey of Mediæval Education. Cr. 8vo. 6s.

LEE, G., Manual of Politics. Sm. cr. 8vo. 2s. 6d.

LEE, MATTHEW HENRY, Diaries and Letters of Philip Henry, M.A., o Broad Oak, Flintshire. Cr. 8vo. 7s. 6d.

LEFEVRE, Right Hon. G. SHAW, Peel and O'Connell. 8vo. 10s. 6d.

> **Incidents of Coercion**: a Journal of Visits to Ireland. Third Edition. Cr. 8vo. limp cloth, 1s. 6d. ; paper covers, 1s.

> **Irish Members and English Gaolers.** Cr. 8vo. limp cloth, 1s 6d. ; paper covers, 1s.

> **Combination and Coercion in Ireland**: Sequel to 'Incidents of Coercion.' Cr. 8vo. cloth, 1s. 6d. ; paper covers, 1s.

LEFFMANN, HENRY, and **BEAM, W., Examination of Water for Sanitary and Technical Purposes.** Second Edition, revised and enlarged. With Illustrations. Cr. 8vo. 5s.

Legend of Maandoo, The: a Poem. With Fifteen Collotype Plates. Second Edition. 8vo. 10s. 6d.

LEGGE, J., Chinese Classics. Translated into English. Popular Edition. Cr. 8vo.
> Vol. I.   Life and Teachings of Confucius. 6th edition, 10s. 6d.
> Vol. II.   Works of Mencius, 12s.
> Vol. III.   She-King, or Book of Poetry, 12s.

LELAND, C. G., Breitmann Ballads. The only Authorised Edition. Including Nineteen Original Ballads, illustrating his Travels in Europe. Cr. 8vo. 6s. Cheap Edition, 3s. 6d. (*Lotos Series.*)

> **Gaudeamus**: Humorous Poems from the German of JOSEPH VICTOR SCHEFFEL and others. 16mo. 3s. 6d.

> **English Gipsies and their Language.** Second Edition. Cr. 8vo. 7s. 6d.

> **Fu-Sang**; or, The Discovery of America by Chinese Buddhist Priests in the 5th Century. Cr. 8vo. 7s. 6d.

> **Pidgin-English Sing-Song**; or, Songs and Stories in the China-English Dialect. Third Edition. Cr. 8vo. 5s.

> **The Gipsies.** Cr. 8vo. 10s. 6d.

LEOPARDI, GIACOMO, Essays and Dialogues. Translated by CHARLES EDWARDES, with Biographical Sketch. Post 8vo. 7s. 6d. (*Philosophical Library.*)

LESLEY, J. P., Man's Origin and Destiny. Sketches from the Platform of the Physical Sciences. Second Edition. Cr. 8vo. 7s. 6d.

LESSING, GOTTHOLD E., Education of the Human Race. From the German by F. W. Robertson. Fcp. 8vo. 2s. 6d.

LEVI, Prof. LEONE, International Law, with Materials for a Code of International Law. Cr. 8vo. 5s. (*I.S.S.*)

LEWES, GEORGE HENRY, Problems of Life and Mind. 8vo.
> Series I. Foundations of a Creed. 2 vols. 28s.
> Series III. The Study of Psychology. 2 vols. 22s. 6d.

> **The Physical Basis of Mind.** With Illustrations. New Edition, with Prefatory Note by Prof. J. SULLY. Large post 8vo. 10s. 6d.

Life's Greatest Possibility: an Essay on Spiritual Realism. Fcp. 8vo. 2s. 6d.

Light on the Path. For the Personal Use of those who are Ignorant of the Eastern Wisdom. Written down by M. C. Fcp. 8vo. 1s. 6d.

LILLIE, ARTHUR, Popular Life of Buddha. Containing an Answer to the Hibbert Lectures of 1881. With Illustrations. Cr. 8vo. 6s.

> **Buddhism in Christendom**; or, Jesus the Essene. With Illustrations. 8vo. 15s.

LILLY, W. S., Characteristics from the Writings of Cardinal Newman. Selections from his various Works. Ninth Edition. With Portrait. Cr. 8vo. 6s.

LINTON, W. J., Rare Poems of the 16th and 17th Centuries. Cr. 8vo. 5s.

LINTON, W. J., and STODDARD, R. H., English Verse. CHAUCER TO BURNS— TRANSLATIONS—LYRICS OF THE NINETEENTH CENTURY—DRAMATIC SCENES AND CHARACTERS—BALLADS AND ROMANCES. 5 vols. Cr. 8vo. 5*s.* each.

LIOY, DIODATO, The Philosophy of Right, with special reference to the Principles and Development of Law. Translated from the Italian by W. HASTIE, B.D. 2 vols. Post 8vo. 21*s.* (*Philosophical Library.*)

LOCHER, CARL, Explanation of Organ Stops. With Hints for Effective Combinations. 8vo. 5*s.*

LOCKER, F., London Lyrics. Twelfth Edition. With Portrait. Elzevir 8vo. 5*s.*

LOCKYER, J. NORMAN, Studies in Spectrum Analysis. With 6 Photographic Illustrations of Spectra, and numerous Engravings on Wood. Fourth Edition. Cr. 8vo. 6*s.* 6*d.* (*I.S.S.*)

LOMMEL, Dr. EUGENE, Nature of Light. With a General Account of Physical Optics. With 188 Illustrations and a Table of Spectra in Chromo-lithography. Fifth Edition. Cr. 8vo. 5*s.* (*I.S.S.*)

LONG, J., Eastern Proverbs and Emblems, illustrating Old Truths. Post 8vo. 6*s.* (*Trübner's Oriental Series.*)

LONGFELLOW. Life of H. Wadsworth Longfellow. By HIS BROTHER. With Portraits and Illustrations. 3 vols. 8vo. 42*s.*

LONSDALE, MARGARET, Sister Dora: a Biography. With Portrait. Thirtieth Edition. Small 8vo. 2*s.* 6*d.*

LOVAT, Lady, Seeds and Sheaves: Thoughts for Incurables. Cr. 8vo. 5*s.*

LOWDER. Charles Lowder: a Biography. By the Author of 'St. Teresa.' Twelfth Edition. With Portrait. Cr. 8vo. 3*s.* 6*d.*

LOWE, R. W., Thomas Betterton. Cr. 8vo. 2*s.* 6*d.* (*Eminent Actors.*)

LOWELL, JAMES RUSSELL, Biglow Papers. Edited by THOMAS HUGHES, Q.C. Fcp. 8vo. 2*s.* 6*d.*

LUBBOCK, Sir JOHN, Ants, Bees, and Wasps: a Record of Observations on the Habits of the Social Hymenoptera. With 5 Chromo-lithographic Plates. Tenth Edition. Cr. 8vo. 5*s.* (*I.S.S.*)

    On the Senses, Instincts, and Intelligence of Animals. With Special Reference to Insects. With 118 Illustrations. Third Edition. Cr. 8vo. 5*s.* (*I.S.S.*)

    A Contribution to our Knowledge of Seedlings. With nearly 700 figures in text. 2 vols. 8vo. 36*s.* net.

LÜCKES, EVA C. E., Lectures on General Nursing, Delivered to the Probationers of the London Hospital Training School for Nurses. Fourth Edition. Cr. 8vo. 2*s.* 6*d.*

LUKIN, J., Amateur Mechanics' Workshop: Plain and Concise Directions for the Manipulation of Wood and Metals. Sixth Edition. Numerous Woodcuts. 8vo. 6*s.*

    The Lathe and Its Uses: or, Instruction in the Art of Turning Wood and Metal. Seventh Edition. Illustrated. 8vo. 10*s.* 6*d.*

    Amongst Machines: a Description of Various Mechanical Appliances Used in the Manufacture of Wood, Metal, &c. A Book for Boys. Third Edition. With 64 Engravings. Cr. 8vo. 3*s.* 6*d.*

    The Boy Engineers: What They Did, and How They Did It. A Book for Boys. With 30 Engravings. Third Edition. Imp. 16mo. 3*s.* 6*d.*

    The Young Mechanic: a Book for Boys. Containing Directions for the Use of all Kinds of Tools, and for the Construction of Steam-engines and Mechanical Models, including the Art of Turning in Wood and Metal. Seventh Edition. With 70 Engravings. Cr. 8vo. 3*s.* 6*d.*

LUYS, J., The Brain and Its Functions. With Illustrations. Third Edition. Cr. 8vo. 5*s.* (*I.S.S.*)

LYALL, Sir ALFRED, Verses written in India. Second Edition. Elzevir 8vo. gilt top, 5*s*.

LYTTON, Earl of, Life, Letters, and Literary Remains of Edward Bulwer, Lord Lytton. With Portraits, Illustrations, and Facsimiles. 8vo. 2 vols. 32*s*.

Lucile. Illustrated. 16mo. 4*s*. 6*d*.

MACAULAY'S Essays on Men and Books: Lord Clive, Milton, Earl of Chatham, Lord Byron. Edited by ALEX. H. JAPP. Pott 8vo. 3*s*. 6*d*. (*Lotos Series.*)

MacCARTHY, DENIS FLORENCE, Calderon's Dramas. Translated by. Post 8vo. 10*s*.

MACDONALD, GEORGE, Malcolm. With Portrait of the Author engraved on Steel. Cr. 8vo. 6*s*. New and cheaper Edition, 3*s*. 6*d*.

    Castle Warlock. With Frontispiece. Cr. 8vo. 6*s*. New and cheaper Edition, 3*s*. 6*d*.

    There and Back. With Frontispiece. 6*s*.

    Donal Grant. With Frontispiece. Cr. 8vo. 6*s*. New and cheaper Edition, 3*s*. 6*d*.

    Home Again. With Frontispiece. Cr. 8vo. 6*s*.

    The Marquis of Lossie. With Frontispiece. Cr. 8vo. 6*s*. New and cheaper Edition, 3*s*. 6*d*.

    St. George and St. Michael. With Frontispiece. Cr. 8vo. 6*s*. New and cheaper Edition, 3*s*. 6*d*.

    What's Mine's Mine. With Frontispiece. Cr. 8vo. 6*s*. New and cheaper Edition, 3*s*. 6*d*.

    Annals of a Quiet Neighbourhood. With Frontispiece. Cr. 8vo. 6*s*. New and cheaper Edition, 3*s*. 6*d*.

    The Seaboard Parish: a Sequel to 'Annals of a Quiet Neighbourhood.' With Frontispiece. Cr. 8vo. 6*s*. New and cheaper Edition, 3*s*. 6*d*.

    Wilfrid Cumbermede: an Autobiographical Story. With Frontispiece. Cr. 8vo. 6*s*. New and cheaper Edition, 3*s*. 6*d*.

    Thomas Wingfold, Curate. With Frontispiece. Cr. 8vo. 6*s*. New and cheaper Edition, 3*s*. 6*d*.

    Paul Faber, Surgeon. With Frontispiece. Cr. 8vo. 6*s*. New and Cheaper Edition, 3*s*. 6*d*.

    The Elect Lady. With Frontispiece. Cr. 8vo. 6*s*.

    Flight of the Shadow. With Frontispiece. Cr. 8vo. 6*s*.

McGRATH, TERENCE, Pictures from Ireland. New Edition. Cr. 8vo. 2*s*.

MACHIAVELLI, NICCOLÒ, Discourses on the First Decade of Titus Livius. From the Italian by N. HILL THOMPSON. Large cr. 8vo. 12*s*.

MACKAY, DONALD J., Bishop Forbes: a Memoir. With Portrait and Map. Cr. 8vo. 7*s*. 6*d*.

MACKAY, ERIC, A Lover's Litanies, and other Poems. With Portrait of Author. 3*s*. 6*d*. (*Lotos Series.*)

MAC KENNA, S. J., Plucky Fellows: a Book for Boys. With 6 Illustrations. Fifth Edition. Cr. 8vo. 3*s*. 6*d*.

MACKONOCHIE. Alexander Heriot Mackonochie: a Memoir. By E. A. T. Edited, with Preface, by E. F. RUSSELL. With Portrait and Views. Large cr. 8vo. 7*s*. 6*d*. Cheap Edition, cr. 8vo. 3*s*. 6*d*.

MACMASTER, J., The Divine Purpose of Capital Punishment. Cr. 8vo. 6*s*.

MACNEILL, J. G. SWIFT, How the Union was Carried. Cr. 8vo. cloth, 1*s*. 6*d*.; paper covers, 1*s*.

MADAN, FALCONER, Books in Manuscript. With 8 Plates. Post 8vo. 6*s*. net. (*Books about Books.*)

MADDEN, F. W., Coins of the Jews; being a History of the Jewish Coinage and Money in the Old and New Testaments. With 279 Woodcuts and a Plate of Alphabets. Roy. 4to. £2. 2*s*.

    The Numismata Orientalia. Vol. II. Coins of the Jews. Being a History of the Jewish Coinage and Money in the Old and New Testaments. With 279 Woodcuts and Plate. Royal 4to. £2.

MAGNUS, Lady, About the Jews since Bible times. Sm. Cr. 8vo, 6s.

MAGNUS, Sir PHILIP, Industrial Education. Cr. 8vo. 6s. (*Education Library.*)

MAGUIRE, W. R., Domestic Sanitary Drainage and Plumbing. 8vo. 12s.

MAHAFFY, Prof., Old Greek Education. Second Edition. Cr. 8vo. 3s. 6d. (*Education Library.*)

MAIMONIDES, Guide of the Perplexed. Translated and annotated by M. FRIED-LÄNDER. 3 vols. post 8vo. 31s. 6d. (*Philosophical Library.*)

MAISEY, Gen. F. C., Sanchi and Its Remains. With Introductory Note by Maj.-Gen. Sir ALEX. CUNNINGHAM, K.C.I.E. With 40 Plates. Royal 4to. £2. 10s.

MALET, LUCAS, Little Peter : a Christmas Morality for Children of any Age. With numerous Illustrations. Fourth Thousand. Imp. 16mo. 5s.

    Colonel Enderby's Wife. With Frontispiece. Cr. 8vo. 6s.

    A Counsel of Perfection. With Frontispiece. Cr. 8vo. 6s.

MALLET, Right Hon. Sir LOUIS, Free Exchange. Papers on Political and Economical Subjects, including Chapters on the Law of Value and Unearned Increment. Edited by BERNARD MALLET. 8vo. 12s.

MANNING. Towards Evening : Selections from the Writings of CARDINAL MANNING. Fifth Edition. With Facsimile. 16mo. 2s.

Many Voices. Extracts from Religious Writers of Christendom from the 1st to the 16th Century. With Biographical Sketches. Cr. 8vo. 6s.

MARCHANT, W. T., In Praise of Ale : Songs, Ballads, Epigrams, and Anecdotes. Cr. 8vo. 10s. 6d.

MAREY, Prof. E. J., Animal Mechanism : a Treatise on Terrestrial and Aërial Locomotion. With 117 Illustrations. Third Edition. Cr. 8vo. 5s. (*I.S.S.*)

MARKHAM, Capt. ALBERT HASTINGS, R.N., The Great Frozen Sea : a Personal Narrative of the Voyage of the *Alert* during the Arctic Expedition of 1875-6. With Illustrations and Maps. Sixth and Cheaper Edition. Cr. 8vo. 6s.

MARSDEN, J. PENNINGTON, The Personal History of Jim Duncan : a Chronicle of Small Beer. 3 vols. 31s. 6d.

MARSDEN, WILLIAM, Numismata Orientalia Illustrata. 57 Plates of Oriental Coins, from the Collection of the late WILLIAM MARSDEN, F.R.S., engraved from drawings made under his directions. 4to. 31s. 6d.

MARTIN, G. A., The Family Horse : its Stabling, Care, and Feeding. Cr. 8vo 3s. 6d.

MARTINEAU, GERTRUDE, Outline Lessons on Morals. Sm. cr. 8vo. 3s. 6d.

MARTINEAU, HARRIET, The Positive Philosophy of Auguste Comte. Translated and condensed. New and cheaper Edition. 2 vols. Large post 8vo.

MARTINEAU, JAMES, Essays, Philosophical and Theological. 2 vols. cr. 8vo. £1. 4s.

MASON, CHARLOTTE M., Home Education : a Course of Lectures to Ladies. Cr. 8vo. 3s. 6d.

MASON, Capt. F. H., Life and Public Service of James A. Garfield, President U.S.A. With a Preface by BRET HARTE. Portrait. Cr. 8vo. 2s. 6d.

MATHER, G., and BLAGG, C. J., Bishop Rawle : a Memoir. Large cr. 8vo. 7s. 6d.

MATHERS, S. L. M., The Key of Solomon the King. Translated from ancient MSS. in the British Museum. With Plates. Cr. 4to. 25s.

    The Kabbalah Unveiled. Containing the Three Books of the Zohar, translated from the Chaldee and Hebrew Text. Post 8vo. 10s. 6d.

    The Tarot : its Occult Signification, use in Fortune-telling, and method of Play. With pack of 78 Tarot Cards, 5s. ; without the Cards, 1s. 6d.

MATUCE, H. OGRAM, A Wanderer. Cr. 8vo. 5s.

MAUDSLEY, H., Body and Will: an Essay concerning Will, in its Metaphysical, Physiological, and Pathological Aspects. 8vo. 12s.

   Natural Causes and Supernatural Seemings. Second Edition. Cr. 8vo. 6s.

   Responsibility in Mental Disease. Fourth Edition. Cr. 8vo. 5s. (*I.S.S.*)

MAXWELL, W. E., Manual of the Malay Language. Second Edition. Cr. 8vo. 7s. 6d.

MEAD, C. M., D.D., Supernatural Revelation: an Essay concerning the basis of the Christian Faith. Royal 8vo. 14s.

MEAKIN, J. E. BUDGETT, Introduction to the Arabic of Morocco. English-Arabic Vocabulary, Grammar, Notes, &c. Fcp. 8vo. 6s.

Meditations on Death and Eternity. Translated from the German by FREDERICA ROWAN. Published by Her Majesty's gracious permission. Cr. 8vo. 6s.

Meditations on Life and its Religious Duties. Translated from the German by FREDERICA ROWAN. Published by Her Majesty's gracious permission. Cr. 8vo. 6s.

MENDELSSOHN'S Letters to Ignaz and Charlotte Moscheles. Translated by FELIX MOSCHELES. Numerous Illustrations and Facsimiles. 8vo. 12s.

MERRILL, G. P., Stones for Building and Decoration. Royal 8vo. 21s.

MEYER, G. HERMANN von, Organs of Speech and their Application in the Formation of Articulate Sounds. With 47 Illustrations. Cr. 8vo. 5s. (*I.S.S.*)

MEYNELL, WILFRID, John Henry Newman, the Founder of Modern Anglicanism, and a Cardinal of the Roman Church. Cr. 8vo. 2s. 6d.

MILL, JOHN STUART, Auguste Comte and Positivism. Fourth Edition. Post 8vo. 3s. 6d. (*Philosophical Library.*)

MILLER, EDWARD, The History and Doctrines of Irvingism; or, The So-called Catholic and Apostolic Church. 2 vols. Large post 8vo. 15s.

MILLER, ELLEN E., Alone Through Syria. With Introduction by Prof. A. H. SAYCE. With 8 Illustrations. Second Edition. Cr. 8vo. 5s.

MILLHOUSE, JOHN, Italian Dictionary. 2 vols. 8vo. 12s.

   Manual of Italian Conversation. 18mo. 2s.

MILLS, HERBERT, Poverty and the State; or, Work for the Unemployed. Cr. 8vo. 6s. ; cheap edition, limp cloth, 1s. 6d. ; paper covers, 1s.

MILNE, J., Earthquakes and other Earth Movements. With 38 Figures. Third and Revised Edition. Cr. 8vo. 5s. (*I.S.S.*)

MILTON, JOHN, Prose Writings. Edited by E. MYERS. Elzevir 8vo. vellum, 7s. 6d. ; parchment or cloth, 6s. (*Parchment Library.*)

   Poetical Works. 2 vols. elzevir 8vo. vellum, 15s. ; parchment or cloth, 12s. (*Parchment Library.*)

   Sonnets. Edited by MARK PATTISON. With Portrait. Elzevir 8vo. vellum, 7s. 6d. ; parchment or cloth, 6s. (*Parchment Library.*)

MITCHELL, LUCY M., History of Ancient Sculpture. With Numerous Illustrations. Super-royal 8vo. 42s.

MIVART, ST. GEORGE, On Truth. 8vo. 16s.

   Origin of Human Reason. 8vo. 10s. 6d.

MOLTKE, Count Von, Notes of Travel. Cr. 8vo. 2s. 6d.

MONCEL, Count DU, The Telephone, the Microphone, and the Phonograph. With 74 Illustrations. 3rd Edition. Sm. 8vo. 5s.

MONIER-WILLIAMS, Sir M., Modern India and the Indians: a Series of Impressions, Notes, and Essays. Fifth Edition. Post 8vo. 14s. (*Trübner's Oriental Series.*)

MOORE, AUBREY L., Essays, Scientific and Philosophical. With Memoir of the Author. Cr. 8vo. 6s.

Lectures and Papers on the History of the Reformation in England and on the Continent. 8vo. 16s.

Science and the Faith: Essays on Apologetic Subjects. Third Edition. Cr. 8vo. 6s.

MOORE, T. W., Treatise and Handbook of Orange Culture in Florida, Louisiana, and California. Fourth Edition Enlarged. 18mo. 5s.

MORFILL, W. R., Simplified Grammar of the Polish Language. Cr. 8vo. 3s. 6d.

Simplified Serbian Grammar. Crown 8vo. 4s. 6d.

MORFIT, CAMPBELL, Manufacture of Soaps. With Illustrations. 8vo. £2. 12s. 6d.

Pure Fertilizers, and the Chemical Conversion of Rock Guanos, &c., into various Valuable Products. With 28 Plates. 8vo. £4. 4s.

MORISON, J. COTTER, The Service of Man: an Essay towards the Religion of the Future. Cr. 8vo. 5s.

MORRIS. Diary and Letters of Gouverneur Morris, Minister of the U.S. to France. With Portraits. 2 vols. 8vo. 30s.

MORRIS, HENRY, Simplified Grammar of the Telugu Language. With Map of India showing Telugu Country. Cr. 8vo. 10s. 6d.

MORRIS, LEWIS, Poetical Works. New and Cheaper Edition. 5 vols. fcap. 8vo. 5s. each.

Songs of Two Worlds. Fourteenth Edition. Fcap. 8vo. 5s.

Gwen, and the Ode of Life. Ninth Edition. Fcap. 8vo. 5s.

Songs Unsung, and Gycia. Fifth Edition. Fcap. 8vo. 5s.

Songs of Britain. Fourth Edition. Fcap. 8vo. 5s.

A Vision of Saints. Fourth Edition. Fcap. 8vo. 6s.

Poetical Works. Eighth Thousand. In 1 vol. cr. 8vo. 6s. Cloth extra, gilt edges, 7s. 6d.

The Epic of Hades. Thirty-fifth Thousand. Fcap. 8vo. 5s.

The Epic of Hades. With 16 Autotype Illustrations, after the Drawings of the late GEORGE R. CHAPMAN. 4to. cloth extra, gilt edges, 21s.

The Epic of Hades. Presentation Edition. 4to. cloth extra, gilt edges, 10s. 6d. Elzevir Edition, 6s.

Ode on the Marriage of H.R.H. the Duke of York and H.S.H. Princess Victoria Mary of Teck, July 6, 1893. Royal 4to. hand-made paper, 1s. 6d. net.

Birthday Book. Edited by S. S. COPEMAN. With Frontispiece. 32mo. cloth extra, gilt edges, 2s. ; cloth limp, 1s. 6d.

MORSE, E. S., First Book of Zoology. With numerous Illustrations. New Edition. Cr. 8vo. 2s. 6d.

MORSELLI, Prof. H., Suicide: an Essay on Comparative Moral Statistics. Second Edition, with Diagrams. Cr. 8vo. 5s. (*I.S.S.*)

MOSENTHAL, J. De, and HARTING, JAMES E., Ostriches and Ostrich Farming. Second Edition. With 8 full-page Illustrations and 20 woodcuts, royal 8vo. 10s. 6d.

MUIR, JOHN, Original Sanskrit Texts, on the Origin and History of the People of India. 5 vols. 8vo.

Mythical and Legendary Accounts of the Origin of Caste. Third Edition. £1. 1s. Also issued as a volume of *Trübner's Oriental Series,* at the same price.

The Trans-Himalayan Origin of the Hindus. Second Edition. £1. 1s.

C

MUIR, JOHN, The Vedas. Second Edition. 16s.

Comparison of the Vedic with the Principal Indian Deities. Second Edition. £1. 1s.

Cosmogony, Mythology, &c., of the Indians in the Vedic Age. Third Edition. £1. 1s.

Metrical Translations from Sanskrit Writers. Post 8vo. 14s. (*Trübner's Oriental Series.*)

MULHALL, M. G. & E. T., Handbook of the River Plate, comprising the Argentine Republic, Uruguay, and Paraguay. With Railway Map. Sixth Edition. Cr. 8vo. 6s.

MULHOLLAND, ROSA, Marcella Grace : an Irish Novel. Cr. 8vo. 6s.

A Fair Emigrant. With Frontispiece. Cr. 8vo. 6s.

MÜLLER, E., Simplified Grammar of the Pali Language. Cr. 8vo. 7s. 6d.

MÜLLER, F. MAX, Outline Dictionary, for the Use of Missionaries, Explorers, and Students of Language. 12mo. morocco, 7s. 6d.

Sacred Hymns of the Brahmins, as preserved in the oldest Collection of Religious Poetry, the Rig-Veda-Sanhita. Vol. I. Hymns to the Maruts, or the Storm-Gods. 8vo. 12s. 6d.

Hymns of the Rig-Veda, in the Sanhita and Pada Texts. 2 vols. Second Edition. 8vo. £1. 1s.

Munchausen's Travels and Surprising Adventures. Illustrated by ALFRED CROWQUILL. 3s. 6d. (*Lotos Series.*)

My Lawyer ; or, the People's Legal Adviser. A Concise Abridgement of and Popular Guide to the Laws of England. By a BARRISTER-AT-LAW. Second Edition. Cr. 8vo. 6s. 6d.

NARADIYA DHARMA-SASTRA ; or, The Institutes of Narada. Translated by Dr. JULIUS JOLLY. Cr. 8vo. 10s. 6d.

NEWHOUSE, S., Trapper's Guide ; a Manual of Instructions for Capturing all Kinds of Fur-bearing Animals, and Curing their Skins, &c. Eighth, Revised Edition. 8vo. 5s.

NEWMAN. Characteristics from the Writings of Cardinal Newman. Selections from his various Works, arranged by W. S. LILLY. Ninth Edition. With Portrait. Cr. 8vo. 6s.

*** Portrait of the late Cardinal Newman, mounted for framing, 2s. 6d.

NEWMAN, F. W., Miscellanies. 8vo. Vol. I., Chiefly Addresses, Academical and Historical, 7s. 6d.

A Handbook of Modern Arabic. Post 8vo. 6s.

NICOLS, ARTHUR, Chapters from the Physical History of the Earth : an Introduction to Geology and Palæontology. With numerous Illustrations. Cr. 8vo. 5s.

NILSSON, L. G., WIDMARK, P. F., and **COLLIN, A. Z., Swedish Dictionary.** New Edition. 8vo. 16s.

NOEL, Hon. RODEN, A Modern Faust, and other Poems. Sm. cr. 8vo. 5s.

Essays on Poetry and Poets. 8vo. 12s.

NOIRIT, JULES, French Course in Ten Lessons. Cr. 8vo. 1s. 6d.

French Grammatical Questions, for the use of Gentlemen preparing for the Army, Civil Service, Oxford Examinations, &c. Cr. 8vo. 1s. ; interleaved, 1s. 6d.

NOPS, M., Class Lessons on Euclid. Cr. 8vo. 2s. 6d.

NORTHALL, G. F., English Folk Rhymes. A Collection of Traditional Verses relating to Places and Persons, Customs, Superstitions, &c. Cr. 8vo. 10s. 6d.

Notes on Cavalry Tactics, Organisation, &c. By a CAVALRY OFFICER. With Diagrams. 8vo. 12*s.*

NUGENT'S French Pocket Dictionary. 24mo. 3*s.*

Numismata Orientalia (The), Royal 4to. in Paper Wrapper. Part I. Ancient Indian Weights, by E. THOMAS, with a Plate and Map, 9*s.* 6*d.* Part II. Coins of the Urtuki Turkumáns, by S. LANE POOLE, with 6 Plates, 9*s.* Part III. Coinage of Lydia and Persia, by BARCLAY V. HEAD, with 3 Plates, 10*s.* 6*d.* Part IV. Coins of the Tuluni Dynasty, by E. T. ROGERS, with 1 Plate, 5*s.* Part V. Parthian Coinage, by PERCY GARDNER, with 8 Plates, 18*s.* Part VI. Ancient Coins and Measures of Ceylon, by T. W. RHYS DAVIDS, with 1 Plate, 10*s.*

Vol. I. containing Six Parts, as specified above, half-bound, £3. 13*s.* 6*d.*

Vol. II. **Coins of the Jews**: being a History of the Jewish Coinage in the Old and New Testaments. By F. W. MADDEN. With 279 Woodcuts and Plate. Royal 4to. £2.

Vol. III. Part I. **The Coins of Arakan, of Pegu, and of Burma.** By Lieut.-General Sir ARTHUR PHAYRE. Also contains the Indian Balhara, and the Arabian Intercourse with India in the Ninth and following Centuries. By EDWARD THOMAS. With 5 Illustrations. Royal 4to. 8*s.* 6*d.*

Vol. III. Part II. **The Coins of Southern India.** By Sir W. ELLIOT. With Map and Plates. Royal 4to. 25*s.*

OATES, FRANK, Matabele Land and the Victoria Falls: a Naturalist's Wanderings in the Interior of South Africa. Edited by C. G. OATES. With numerous Illustrations and 4 Maps. Second Edition. 8vo. 21*s.*

O'BRIEN, R. BARRY, Irish Wrongs and English Remedies, with other Essays. Cr. 8vo. 5*s.*

Home Ruler's Manual. Cr. 8vo. cloth, 1*s.* 6*d.* ; paper covers, 1*s.*

Life and Letters of Thomas Drummond, Under-Secretary in Ireland, 1835-40. 8vo. 14*s.*

O'CLERY, The, The Making of Italy, 1856-70. With Sketch Maps. 8vo. 16*s.*

O'CONNELL, Mrs. MORGAN J., The Last Colonel of the Irish Brigade, Count O'Connell, and Old Irish Life at Home and Abroad, 1745-1833. 2 vols. 8vo. 25*s.*

O'CONNOR, EVANGELINE, Index to Shakspere's Works. Cr. 8vo. 5*s.*

O'HAGAN, JOHN, Joan of Arc: an Historical Essay. Cr. 8vo. 3*s.* 6*d.*

OLCOTT, Colonel, Posthumous Humanity: a Study of Phantoms, from the French of Adolphe D'Assier. With Appendix and Notes. Cr. 8vo. 7*s.* 6*d.*

Theosophy, Religion, and Occult Science, with Glossary of Eastern words. Cr. 8vo. 7*s.* 6*d.*

OLLENDORFF. Metodo para aprender a Leer, escribir y hablar el Inglés, segun el sistema de Ollendorff. 8vo. 7*s.* 6*d.* Key, 4*s.*

Metodo para aprender a Leer, escribir y hablar el Frances, segun el sistema de Ollendorff. Cr. 8vo. 6*s.* Key, 3*s.* 6*d.*

OMAN, F. G., Swedish Dictionary. Cr. 8vo. 8*s.*

O'MEARA, KATHLEEN, Henri Perreyve and his Counsels to the Sick. Sm. cr. 8vo. 5*s.*

One-and-a-Half in Norway. By EITHER and BOTH. Sm. cr. 8vo. 3*s.* 6*d.*

OTTÉ E. C., Dano-Norwegian Grammar: a Manual for Students of Danish, based on the Ollendorffian System. Third Edition. Cr. 8vo. 7*s.* 6*d.* Key, 3*s.*

Simplified Grammar of the Danish Language. Cr. 8vo. 2*s.* 6*d.*

Simplified Grammar of the Swedish Language. Cr. 8vo. 2*s.* 6*d.*

OWEN, ROBERT DALE, Footfalls on the Boundary of another World. With Narrative Illustrations. Post 8vo. 7s. 6d.

Debatable Land between this World and the Next. With Illustrative Narrations. Second Edition. Cr. 8vo. 7s. 6d.

Threading My Way: Twenty-seven Years of Autobiography. Cr. 8vo. 7s. 6d.

PACKARD, A. S., The Labrador Coast. A Journal of two Summer Cruises to that Region. With Maps and Illustrations. 8vo. 18s.

PALGRAVE, W. GIFFORD, Hermann Agha: an Eastern Narrative. Third Edition. Cr. 8vo. 6s.

PALMER, E. H., English-Persian Dictionary. With Simplified Grammar of the Persian Language. Royal 16mo. 10s. 6d.

Persian-English Dictionary. Second Edition. Royal 16mo. 10s. 6d.

Simplified Grammar of Hindustani, Persian, and Arabic. Second Edition. Cr. 8vo. 5s.

Papers relating to Indo-China. Reprinted from Dalrymple's 'Oriental Repertory,' 'Asiatic Researches,' and the 'Journal' of the Asiatic Society of Bengal. Post 8vo. 2 vols. 21s.

> MISCELLANEOUS ESSAYS ON SUBJECTS CONNECTED WITH THE MALAY PENINSULA AND THE INDIAN ARCHIPELAGO. From the Journals of the Royal Asiatic, Royal Geographical Societies, &c. Edited by R. ROST. With 5 Plates and a Map. Second Series, 2 vols. 25s. (*Trübner's Oriental Series.*)

PARAVICINI, FRANCES de, Early History of Balliol College. 8vo. 12s.

PARKER, G. W., Concise Grammar of the Malagasy Language. Cr. 8vo. 5s.

PARKER, THEODORE, Discourse on Matters pertaining to Religion. People's Edition. Cr. 8vo. cloth, 2s. ; paper covers, 1s. 6d.

Collected Works of Theodore Parker, Minister of the Twenty-eighth Congregational Society at Boston, U.S. 14 vols. Cr. 8vo. 6s. each.

PARRY, EDWARD ABBOTT, Charles Macklin. Cr. 8vo. 2s. 6d. (*Eminent Actors.*)

PARRY, E. GAMBIER, Biography of Reynell Taylor, C.B., C.S.I. With Portrait and Map. 8vo. 14s.

PARSLOE, JOSEPH, Our Railways: Sketches, Historical and Descriptive. With Information as to Fares and Rates, &c. Cr. 8vo. 6s.

PASCAL, BLAISE, Thoughts. Translated by C. KEGAN PAUL. Large cr. 8vo. Parchment, 12s. ; vellum, 15s. Cheap edition. Cr. 8vo. 6s.

PATON, A. A., History of the Egyptian Revolution, from the Period of the Mamelukes to the Death of Mohammed Ali. Second Edition. 2 vols. 8vo. 7s. 6d.

PAUL, ALEXANDER, Short Parliaments. History of National Demand for Frequent General Elections. Sm. cr. 8vo. 3s. 6d.

PAUL, C. KEGAN, Faith and Unfaith, and other Essays. Cr. 8vo. 7s. 6d.

Biographical Sketches. Second Edition. Cr. 8vo. 7s. 6d.

Confessio Viatoris. Fcp. 8vo. 2s.

Thoughts of Blaise Pascal. Translated. Large cr. 8vo. Parchment, 12s. ; vellum, 15s. Cheap Edition, cr. 8vo. 6s.

Paul of Tarsus. By the Author of 'Rabbi Jeshua.' Cr. 8vo. 4s. 6d.

PAULI, REINHOLD, Simon de Montfort, Earl of Leicester, the Creator of the House of Commons. Cr. 8vo. 6s.

PEMBERTON, T. EDGAR, Charles Dickens and the Stage: a Record of his Connection with the Drama. Cr. 8vo. 6s.

PERRY, ARTHUR LATHAM, Principles of Political Economy. Large post 8vo. 9s.

PESCHEL, OSCAR, The Races of Man and their Geographical Distribution. Second Edition. Large cr. 8vo. 9s.

PETTIGREW, J. B., Animal Locomotion; or, Walking, Swimming, and Flying. With 130 Illustrations. Third Edition. Cr. 8vo. 5*s*. (*I.S.S.*)

PHAYRE, Lieut.-Gen. Sir A., History of Burma. Including Burma Proper, Pegu, Taungu, Tenasserim, and Arakan, from the Earliest Time to the end of the First War with British India. Post 8vo. 14*s*. (*Trübner's Oriental Series.*)

PHAYRE, Lieut.-Gen. Sir A., and **THOMAS, E., Coins of Arakan, of Pegu, and of Burma.** With 5 Illustrations. Royal 4to. 8*s*. 6*d*. (*Numismata Orientalia.*)

PHILLIPS, Col. A. N., Hindustani Idioms. With Vocabulary and Explanatory Notes. Cr. 8vo. 5*s*.

PHILLIPS, W., Manual of British Discomycetes. With Descriptions of all the Species of Fungi hitherto found in Britain included in the Family, and Illustrations of the Genera. Cr. 8vo. 5*s*. (*I.S.S.*)

'PHYSICUS,' Candid Examination of Theism. Third Edition. Post 8vo. 7*s*. 6*d*. (*Philosophical Library.*)

PICARD, A., Pocket Dictionary of the Dutch Language. Fifth Edition. 16mo. 10*s*.

PICKFORD, JOHN, Maha-vira-Charita; or, the Adventures of the Great Hero Rama. From the Sanskrit of BHAVABHÜTI. Cr. 8vo. 5*s*.

PIESSE, C. H., Chemistry in the Brewing Room: a Course of Lessons to Practical Brewers. Fcp. 8vo. 5*s*.

PILCHER, J. E., First Aid in Illness and Injury. With 174 Illustrations. Cr. 8vo. 6*s*.

PLOWRIGHT, C. B., British Uredineæ and Ustilagineæ. With Illustrations. 8vo. 10*s*. 6*d*.

PLUMPTRE, C. J., Lectures on Elocution, delivered at King's College. Fourth Edition. Post 8vo. 15*s*.

POE, EDGAR ALLAN, Poems. Edited by ANDREW LANG. With Frontispiece. Elzevir 8vo. vellum, 7*s*. 6*d*. ; parchment or cloth, 6*s*. (*Parchment Library.*)

   The Raven. With Commentary by JOHN H. INGRAM. Cr. 8vo. parchment, 6*s*.

POLE, W., Philosophy of Music. Lectures delivered at the Royal Institution. Third Edition. Post 8vo. 7*s*. 6*d*. (*Philosophical Library.*)

POLLEN, JOHN, Rhymes from the Russian. Translations from the best Russian Poets. Cr. 8vo. 3*s*. 6*a*.

PONSARD, F., Charlotte Corday: a Tragedy. Edited by Professor C. CASSAL. Fourth Edition. 12mo. 2*s*. 6*d*.

   L'Honneur et l'Argent: a Comedy. Edited by Professor C. CASSAL. Fourth Edition. 12mo. 3*s*. 6*d*.

PONTOPIDDAN, HENRIK, The Apothecary's Daughters. Translated from the Danish by GORDIUS NIELSEN. Cr. 8vo. 3*s*. 6*d*.

POOLE, STANLEY LANE, The Numismata Orientalia. Part II. Coins of the Urtuki Turkumáns. With 6 Plates. Royal 4to. Paper wrapper, 9*s*.

POOLE, W. F., Index to Periodical Literature. Revised Edition. Royal 8vo. £3. 13*s*. 6*d*. net. FIRST SUPPLEMENT, 1882 to 1887. Royal 8vo. £2 net. SECOND SUPPLEMENT, 1887 to 1892. Royal 8vo. £2 net.

POSNETT, H. M., Comparative Literature. Crown 8vo. 5*s*. (*I.S.S.*)

POULTON, E. B., Colours of Animals: their Meaning and Use, especially considered in the case of Insects. With Coloured Frontispiece and 66 Illustrations in Text. Cr. 8vo. 5*s*. (*I.S.S.*)

Practical Guides, to see all that ought to be seen in the shortest period and at the least expense. 113th Thousand, Illustrated. Sm. 8vo. paper covers. France, Belgium, Holland, and the Rhine, 1*s*. Italian Lakes, 1*s*. Wintering Places of the South, 2*s*. Switzerland, Savoy, and North Italy, 2*s*. 6*d*. General Continental Guide, 5*s*. Geneva, 1*s*. Paris, 1*s*. Bernese Oberland, 1*s*. Italy, 4*s*.

PRATT, GEORGE, Grammar and Dictionary of the Samoan Language. Second Edition. Cr. 8vo. 18*s.*

PRATT, Lieut.-Colonel S. C., Field Artillery: its Equipment, Organisation, and Tactics. Fourth Edition. Sm. cr. 8vo. 6*s.* (*Military Handbooks.*)

Military Law: its Procedure and Practice. Seventh revised Edition. Sm. cr. 8vo. 4*s.* 6*d.* (*Military Handbooks.*)

PREL, CARL DU, Philosophy of Mysticism. Translated from the German by C. C. MASSEY. 2 vols. 8vo. cloth, 25*s.*

PRICE, Prof. BONAMY, Chapters on Practical Political Economy. New Edition. Cr. 8vo. 5*s.*

PRIG, The Prigment: 'The Life of a Prig,' 'Prig's Bede,' 'How to Make a Saint,' 'Black is White.' Second Edition. In 1 vol. Cr. 8vo. 5*s.*

A Romance of the Recusants. Cr. 8vo. 5*s.*

Dulce Domum. Fcap. 8vo. 5*s.*

Black is White; or, Continuity Continued. Second Edition. Fcp. 8vo. 3*s.* 6*d.*

Prig's Bede: the Venerable Bede Expurgated, Expounded, and Exposed. Second Edition. Fcp. 8vo. 3*s.* 6*d.*

Riches or Ruin. Fcp. 8vo. 3*s.* 6*d.*

Egosophy. Fcp. 8vo. 3*s.* 6*d.*

PRIOR, MATTHEW, Selected Poems. Edited by AUSTIN DOBSON. Elzevir 8vo. vellum, 7*s.* 6*d.*; parchment or cloth, 6*s.* (*Parchment Library.*)

PROTHERO, G. W., Henry Bradshaw: a Memoir, with Portrait and Facsimile. 8vo. 16*s.*

Psalms of the West. Second Edition. Sm. 8vo. 1*s.* 6*d.*

Pulpit Commentary, The (Old Testament Series). Edited by the Very Rev. Dean H. D. M. SPENCE, D.D., and the Rev. J. S. EXELL. Super royal 8vo.

Genesis, by the Rev. T. WHITELAW, D.D.; Homilies by the Very Rev. J. F. MONTGOMERY, D.D., Rev. Prof. R. A. REDFORD, Rev. F. HASTINGS, Rev. W. ROBERTS; Introduction to the Study of the Old Testament, by Ven. Archdeacon FARRAR, D.D.; Introductions to the Pentateuch, by the Right Rev. H. COTTERILL, D.D., and Rev. T. WHITELAW, D.D. Ninth Edition. 15*s.*

Exodus, by the Rev. Canon RAWLINSON; Homilies by the Rev. J. ORR, D.D., Rev. D. YOUNG, Rev. C. A. GOODHART, Rev. J. URQUHART, and the Rev. H. T. ROBJOHNS. Fifth Edition. 2 vols. 9*s.* each.

Leviticus, by the Rev. Prebendary MEYRICK; Introductions by the Rev. R. COLLINS, Rev. Professor A. CAVE; Homilies by the Rev. Prof. REDFORD, Rev. J. A. MACDONALD, Rev. W. CLARKSON, Rev. S. R. ALDRIDGE, and Rev. McCHEYNE EDGAR. Fifth Edition. 15*s.*

Numbers, by the Rev. R. WINTERBOTHAM; Homilies by the Rev. Prof. W. BINNIE, D.D., Rev. E. S. PROUT, Rev. D. YOUNG, Rev. J. WAITE; Introduction by the Rev. THOMAS WHITELAW, D.D. Fifth Edition. 15*s.*

Deuteronomy, by the Rev. W. L. ALEXANDER, D.D.; Homilies by the Rev. C. CLEMANCE, D.D., Rev. J. ORR, D.D., Rev. R. M. EDGAR, Rev. J. D. DAVIES. Fourth Edition. 15*s.*

Joshua, by the Rev. J. J. LIAS; Homilies by the Rev. S. R. ALDRIDGE, Rev. R. GLOVER, Rev. E. DE PRESSENSÉ, D.D., Rev. J. WAITE, Rev. W. F. ADENEY; Introduction by the Rev. A. PLUMMER, D.D. Sixth Edition. 12*s.* 6*d.*

Judges and Ruth, by the Bishop of BATH and WELLS, and Rev. J. MORISON, D.D.; Homilies by the Rev. A. F. MUIR, Rev. W. F. ADENEY, Rev. W. M. STATHAM, and Rev. Prof. J. THOMSON. Fifth Edition. 10*s.* 6*d.*

1 and 2 Samuel, by the Very Rev. R. PAYNE SMITH, D.D.; Homilies by the Rev. DONALD FRASER, D.D., Rev. Prof. CHAPMAN, Rev. B. DALE, and Rev. G. WOOD. Seventh Edition. 2 vols. 15*s.* each.

Pulpit Commentary, The (Old Testament Series)—

1 Kings, by the Rev. JOSEPH HAMMOND ; Homilies by the Rev. E. DE PRESSENSÉ, D.D., Rev. J. WAITE, Rev. A. ROWLAND, Rev. J. A. MACDONALD, and Rev. J. URQUHART. Fifth Edition. 15s.

2 Kings, by the Rev. Canon RAWLINSON ; Homilies by the Rev. J. ORR, D.D., Rev. D. THOMAS, D.D., and Rev. C. H. IRWIN. Second Edition. 15s.

1 Chronicles, by the Rev. Prof. P. C. BARKER ; Homilies by the Rev. Prof J. R. THOMSON, Rev. R. TUCK, Rev. W. CLARKSON, Rev. F. WHITFIELD, and Rev. RICHARD GLOVER. Second Edition. 15s.

2 Chronicles, by the Rev. PHILIP C. BARKER; Homilies by the Rev. W. CLARKSON and Rev. T. WHITELAW, D.D. Second Edition. 15s.

Ezra, Nehemiah, and Esther, by the Rev. Canon G. RAWLINSO Homilies, by the Rev. Prof. J. R. THOMSON, Rev. Prof. R. A. REDFORD, Rev. W. S. LEWIS, Rev. J. A. MACDONALD, Rev. A. MACKENNAL, Rev. W. CLARKSON, Rev. F. HASTINGS, Rev. W. DINWIDDIE, Rev. Prof. ROWLANDS, Rev. G. WOOD, Rev. Prof. P. C. BARKER, and the Rev. J. S. EXELL. Seventh Edition. 12s. 6d.

Job, by the Rev. Canon G. RAWLINSON. Homilies by the Rev. T. WHITELAW, D.D., the Rev. Prof. E. JOHNSON, the Rev. Prof. W. F. ADENEY, and the Rev. R. GREEN. 21s.

Proverbs, by the Rev. W. J. DEANE and the Rev. S. T. TAYLOR-TASWELL. Homilies by the Rev. Prof. W. F. ADENEY, the Rev. Prof. E. JOHNSON, and the Rev. W. CLARKSON. Second Edition. 15s.

Ecclesiastes and Song of Solomon, by the Rev. W. J. DEANE and Rev. Prof. R. A. REDFORD. Homilies by the Rev. T. WHITELAW, D.D., Rev. B. C. CAFFIN, Rev. Prof. J. R. THOMSON, Rev. S. CONWAY, Rev. D. DAVIES, Rev. W. CLARKSON, and Rev. J. WILLCOCK. 21s.

Isaiah, by the Rev. Canon G. RAWLINSON ; Homilies by the Rev. Prof. E. JOHNSON, Rev. W. CLARKSON, Rev. W. M. STATHAM, and Rev. R. TUCK. Third Edition. 2 vols. 15s. each.

Jeremiah and Lamentations, by the Rev. Canon T. K. CHEYNE, D.D. ; Homilies by the Rev. Prof. J. R. THOMSON, Rev. W. F. ADENEY, Rev. A. F. MUIR, Rev. S. CONWAY, Rev. D. YOUNG, Rev. J. WAITE. 2 vols. Fourth Edition. 15s. each.

Ezekiel, by the Very Rev. E. H. PLUMPTRE, D.D. Homilies by the Rev. Prof. W. F. ADENEY, the Rev. Prof. J. R. THOMSON, the Rev. J. D. DAVIES, the Rev. W. JONES, and the Rev. W. CLARKSON. Introduction by the Rev. T. WHITELAW, D.D. 2 vols. 12s. 6d. each.

Hosea and Joel, by the Rev. Prof. J. J. GIVEN, D.D. ; Homilies by the Rev. Prof. J. R. THOMSON, Rev. A. ROWLAND, Rev. C. JERDAN, Rev. J. ORR, D.D., and Rev. D. THOMAS, D.D. Second Edition. 15s.

Amos, Obadiah, Jonah, and Micah, by the Rev. W. J. DEANE; Homilies by the Rev. J. EDGAR HENRY, Rev. Prof. J. R. THOMSON, Rev. S. D. HILLMAN, Rev. A. ROWLAND, Rev. D. THOMAS, Rev. A. C. THISELTON, Rev. E. S. PROUT, Rev. G. T. COSTER, Rev. W. G. BLAIKIE. 15s.

Pulpit Commentary, The (New Testament Series). Edited by the Very Rev. H. D. M. SPENCE, D.D., and Rev. JOSEPH S. EXELL.

St. Matthew, by the Rev. A. L. WILLIAMS. Homilies by the Rev. B. C. CAFFIN, Rev. Prof. W. F. ADENEY, Rev. P. C. BARKER, Rev. M. DODS, D.D., Rev. J. A. MACDONALD, and Rev. R. TUCK.

St. Mark, by the Very Rev. Dean E. BICKERSTETH, D.D. ; Homilies by the Rev. Prof. J. R. THOMSON, Rev. Prof. J. J. GIVEN, D.D., Rev. Prof. E. JOHNSON, Rev. A. ROWLAND, Rev. A. F. MUIR, and Rev. R. GREEN. Sixth Edition. 2 vols. 10s. 6d. each.

St. Luke, by the Very Rev. Dean H. D. M. SPENCE; Homilies by the Rev. J. MARSHALL LANG, D.D., Rev. W. CLARKSON, and Rev. R. M. EDGAR. Second Edition. 2 vols. 10s. 6d. each.

St. John, by the Rev. Prof. H. R. REYNOLDS, D.D. ; Homilies by the Rev. Prof. T. CROSKERY, D.D., Rev. Prof. J. R. THOMSON, Rev. D. YOUNG, Rev. B. THOMAS, and Rev. G. BROWN. Third Edition. 2 vols. 15s. each.

Pulpit Commentary, The (New Testament Series)—

The Acts of the Apostles, by the Right Rev. Bishop of BATH and WELLS; Homilies by the Rev. Prof. P. C. BARKER, Rev. Prof. E. JOHNSON, Rev. Prof. R. A. REDFORD, Rev. R. TUCK, Rev. W. CLARKSON. Fifth Edition. 2 vols. 10s. 6d. each.

Romans, by the Rev. J. BARMBY; Homilies by Rev. Prof. J. R. THOMSON, Rev. C. H. IRWIN, Rev. T. F. LOCKYER, Rev. S. R. ALDRIDGE, and Rev. R. M. EDGAR. 15s.

Corinthians and Galatians, by the Ven. Archdeacon FARRAR, D.D., and Rev. Prebendary E. HUXTABLE; Homilies by the Rev. Ex-Chancellor LIPSCOMB, Rev. DAVID THOMAS, D.D., Rev. DONALD FRASER, D.D., Rev. R. TUCK, Rev. E. HURNDALL, Rev. Prof. J. R. THOMSON, Rev. R. FINLAYSON, Rev. W. F. ADENEY, Rev. R. M. EDGAR, and Rev. T. CROSKERY, D.D. 2 vols. Vol I., containing I. Corinthians, Fifth Edition, 15s. Vol. II., containing Corinthians and Galatians, Second Edition, 21s.

Ephesians, Philippians, and Colossians, by the Rev. Prof. W. G. BLAIKIE, D.D., Rev. B. C. CAFFIN, and Rev. G. G. FINDLAY; Homilies by the Rev. D. THOMAS, D.D., Rev. R. M. EDGAR, Rev. R. FINLAYSON, Rev. W. F. ADENEY, Rev. Prof. T. CROSKERY, D.D., Rev. E. S. PROUT, Rev. Canon VERNON HUTTON, and Rev. U. R. THOMAS, D.D. Third Edition. 21s.

Thessalonians, Timothy, Titus, and Philemon, by the Right Rev. Bishop of BATH and WELLS, Rev. Dr. GLOAG, and Rev. Dr. EALES; Homilies by the Rev. B. C. CAFFIN, Rev. R. FINLAYSON, Rev. Prof. T. CROSKERY, D.D., Rev. W. F. ADENEY, Rev. W. M. STATHAM, and Rev. D. THOMAS, D.D. Second Edition. 15s.

Hebrews and James, by the Rev. J. BARMBY, and Rev. Prebendary E. C. S. GIBSON; Homilies by the Rev. C. JERDAN and Rev. Prebendary E. C. S. GIBSON, Rev. W. JONES, Rev. C. NEW, Rev. D. YOUNG, Rev. J. S. BRIGHT, and Rev. T. F. LOCKYER. Third Edition. 15s.

Peter, John, and Jude, by the Rev. B. C. CAFFIN, Rev. A. PLUMMER, D.D., and Rev. Prof. S. D. F. SALMOND, D.D.; Homilies by the Rev. A. MACLAREN, D.D., Rev. C. CLEMANCE, D.D., Rev. Prof. J. R. THOMSON, Rev. C. NEW, Rev. U. R. THOMAS, Rev. R. FINLAYSON, Rev. W. JONES, Rev. Prof. T. CROSKERY, D.D., and Rev. J. S. BRIGHT, D.D. Second Edition. 15s.

Revelation. Introduction by the Rev. T. RANDELL, principal of Bede College, Durham. Exposition by the Rev. A. PLUMMER, D.D., assisted by Rev. T. RANDELL and A. T. BOTT. Homilies by the Rev. C. CLEMANCE, D.D., Rev. S. CONWAY, Rev. R. GREEN, and Rev. D. THOMAS, D.D. Second Edition. 15s.

PUSEY. Sermons for the Church's Seasons from Advent to Trinity. Selected from the published Sermons of the late EDWARD BOUVERIE PUSEY, D.D. Cr. 8vo. 5s.

PYE, W., Surgical Handicraft: a Manual of Surgical Manipulations, &c. With 235 Illustrations. Third Edition, Revised and Edited by T. H. R. CROWLE. Cr. 8vo. 10s. 6d.

Elementary Bandaging and Surgical Dressing, for the use of Dressers and Nurses. Twelfth Thousand. 18mo. 2s.

Public Schools (Our): Eton, Harrow, Winchester, Rugby, Westminster, Marlborough, and The Charterhouse. Cr. 8vo. 6s.

QUATREFAGES, Prof. A. de, The Human Species. Fifth Edition. Cr. 8vo. 5s. (*I.S.S.*)

QUINCEY, DE, Confessions of an English Opium Eater. Edited by RICHARD GARNETT. Elzevir 8vo. vellum, 7s. 6d.; parchment or cloth, 6s. (*Parchment Library.*)

RALSTON, W. R. S., Tibetan Tales, derived from Indian Sources. Done into English from the German of F. ANTON VON SCHIEFNER. Post 8vo. 14s. (*Trübner's Oriental Series.*)

Rare Poems of the 16th and 17th Centuries. Edited by W. J. LINTON. Cr. 8vo. 5*s.*

RASK, ERASMUS, Grammar of the Anglo-Saxon Tongue. From the Danish, by B. THORPE. Third Edition. Post 8vo, 5*s.* 6*d.*

READE, WINWOOD, The Martyrdom of Man. Fourteenth Edition. Cr. 8vo. 7*s.* 6*d.*

REANEY, Mrs. G. S., Waking and Working; or, From Girlhood to Womanhood. New and Cheaper Edition, with Frontispiece. Cr. 8vo. 3*s.* 6*d.*

 Blessing and Blessed : a Sketch of Girl Life. New and Cheaper Edition. Cr. 8vo. 3*s.* 6*d.*

 Rose Gurney's Discovery : a Story for Girls, dedicated to their Mothers. Cr. 8vo. 3*s.* 6*d.*

 English Girls : their Place and Power. With Preface by the Rev. R. W. DALE. Fifth Edition. Fcp. 8vo. 2*s.* 6*d.*

 Just Anyone, and other Stories. With 3 Illustrations. 16mo. 1*s.* 6*d.*

 Sunbeam Willie, and other Stories. With 3 Illustrations. 16mo. 1*s.* 6*d.*

 Sunshine Jenny, and other Stories. With 3 Illustrations. 16mo. 1*s.* 6*d.*

REDHOUSE, J. W., Simplified Grammar of the Ottoman-Turkish Language. Cr. 8vo. 10*s.* 6*d.*

 Turkish Vade-Mecum of Ottoman Colloquial Language. English-Turkish and Turkish-English, the whole in English Characters, the Pronunciation being fully indicated. Third Edition. 32mo. 6*s.*

 The Mesnevi (usually known as the Mesnevîyi Sherîf, or Holy Mesnevî) of Mevlânâ (Our Lord) Jelâlu'd-Din Muhammed Er-Rûmi. Illustrated by a selection of Characteristic Anecdotes. Post 8vo. £1. 1*s.* (*Trübner's Oriental Series.*)

 History, System, and Varieties of Turkish Poetry. Illustrated by Selections in the original English Paraphrase. 8vo. 2*s.* 6*d.*

 Tentative Chronological Synopsis of the History of Arabia and its Neighbours, from B.C. 500,000 (?) to A.D. 679. 8vo. 2*s.*

REES, J. D., H.R.H. The Duke of Clarence and Avondale in Southern India. With a Narrative of Elephant Catching in Mysore, by G. P. SANDERSON. With Map, Portraits, and Illustrations. Medium 8vo. 31*s.* 6*d.*

Lord Connemara's Tours in India, 1886-1890. 8vo. 15*s.*

RENAN, ERNEST, Age and Antiquity of the Book of Nabathæan Agriculture. Cr. 8vo. 3*s.* 6*d.*

 Life of Jesus. Cr. 8vo. 1*s.* 6*d.* ; paper covers, 1*s.*

 The Apostles. Cr. 8vo. 1*s.* 6*d.* ; paper covers, 1*s.*

RENDELL, J. M., Handbook of the Island of Madeira. With Plan and Map. Second Edition. Fcp. 8vo. 1*s.* 6*d.*

REYNOLDS, J. W., The Supernatural in Nature : a Verification by Free Use of Science. Third Edition, Revised and Enlarged. 8vo. 14*s.*

 Mystery of the Universe our Common Faith. 8vo. 14*s.*

 Mystery of Miracles. Third Edition, Enlarged. Cr. 8vo. 6*s.*

 The World to Come : Immortality a Physical Fact. Cr. 8vo. 6*s.*

REYNOLDS, Sir JOSHUA, Discourses. Edited by E. GOSSE. Elzevir 8vo. vellum, 7*s.* 6*d.* ; parchment or cloth, 6*s.* (*Parchment Library.*)

RHOIDIS, EMMANUEL, Pope Joan : an Historical Study. From the Greek by C. H. COLLETTE. 12mo. 2*s.* 6*d.*

RHYS, JOHN, Lectures on Welsh Philology. Second Edition. Cr. 8vo. 15*s.*

RIBOT, Prof. Th., Diseases of Memory: an Essay in the Positive Psychology. Third Edition. Cr. 8vo. 5s. (*I.S.S.*)

Heredity: a Psychological Study of its Phenomena, Laws, Causes, and Consequences. Second Edition. Large cr. 8vo. 9s.

English Psychology. Cr. 8vo. 7s. 6d.

RICHARD, Ap, Marriage and Divorce. Including the Religious, Practical, and Political Aspects of the Question. Cr. 8vo. 5s.

RICHARDSON, AUSTIN, 'What are the Catholic Claims?' With Introduction by Rev. LUKE RIVINGTON. Cr. 8vo. 3s. 6d.

RICHARDSON, M. T., Practical Blacksmithing. With 400 Illustrations. 4 vols. Cr. 8vo. 5s. each.

Practical Horse-shoer. With 170 Illustrations. Cr. 8vo. 5s.

RICHTER, Prof. VICTOR von, Text-book of Inorganic Chemistry. Authorised Translation. By EDGAR F. SMITH. Third American Edition, from the Fifth German Edition. Cr. 8vo. 8s. 6d.

Chemistry of the Carbon Compounds; or, Organic Chemistry. Authorised Translation. By EDGAR F. SMITH. Second American Edition, from the Sixth German Edition. Cr. 8vo. 20s.

RIOLA, HENRY, How to learn Russian: a Manual for Students. Based upon the Ollendorffian System. Fourth Edition. Cr. 8vo. 12s. Key, 5s.

Russian Reader. With Vocabulary. Cr. 8vo. 10s. 6d.

RIVINGTON, LUKE, Authority; or, A Plain Reason for Joining the Church of Rome. Sixth Edition. Cr. 8vo. 3s. 6d.

Dependence; or, The Insecurity of the Anglican Position. Cr. 8vo. 5s.

The English Martyrs. Sewed, 6d.

The Church Visible. Sewed, 6d.

The Appeal to History: a Letter to the Bishop of Lincoln. Sewed, 6d.

ROBERTS, H., Grammar of the Khassi Language. Cr. 8vo. 10s. 6d.

ROBERTSON, F. W., Life and Letters. Edited by STOPFORD BROOKE.

I. Library Edition. With Portrait. 8vo. 12s.
II. Two vols. With Portrait. Cr. 8vo. 7s. 6d.
III. Popular Edition. Cr. 8vo. 6s.

Sermons. 5 vols. Sm. 8vo. 3s. 6d. each.

Notes on Genesis. New and Cheaper Edition. Sm. 8vo. 3s. 6d.

St. Paul's Epistles to the Corinthians: Expository Lectures. New Edition. Sm. 8vo. 5s.

Lectures and Addresses. With other Literary Remains. New Edition. Sm. 8vo. 5s.

Analysis of Tennyson's 'In Memoriam.' Dedicated by Permission to the Poet-Laureate. Fcp. 8vo. 2s.

Education of the Human Race. Translated from the German of GOTTHOLD EPHRAIM LESSING. Fcp. 8vo. 2s. 6d.

*** Portrait of the late Rev. F. W. Robertson, mounted for framing, 2s. 6d.

ROBINSON, A. MARY F., The Fortunate Lovers. Twenty-seven Novels of the Queen of Navarre. Frontispiece by G. P. JACOMB HOOD. Large cr. 8vo. 10s. 6d.

The Crowned Hippolytus. Sm. cr. 8vo. 5s.

ROBINSON, E. FORBES, The Early History of Coffee Houses in England. With Illustrations. Cr. 8vo. 6s.

ROCHE, A., French Grammar. Adopted by the Imperial Council of Public Instruction. Cr. 8vo. 3s.

Prose and Poetry, from English Authors. For Reading, Composition, and Translation. Second Edition. Fcp. 8vo. 2s. 6d.

ROCKHILL, W. W., Life of the Buddha and the Early History of his Order. Derived from Tibetan Works in the Bkah-Hgyur and the Bstan-Hgyur. Post 8vo. 9s. (*Trübner's Oriental Series.*)

UDANAVARGA: a Collection of Verses from the Buddhist Canon. Compiled by DHARMATRÂTA and Translated from the Tibetan. Post 8vo. 9s. (*Trübner's Oriental Series.*)

RODD, E. H., Birds of Cornwall and the Scilly Islands. Edited by J. E. HARTING. With Portrait and Map. 8vo. 14*s.*

ROGERS, E. T., The Numismata Orientalia. Part IV. The Coins of the Tulun Dynasty. With 1 Plate. Royal 4to. Paper wrapper, 5*s.*

ROGERS, WILLIAM, Reminiscences. Compiled by R. H. HADDEN. With Portrait. Cr. 8vo. 6*s.* ; Cheap Edition, 2*s.* 6*d.*

ROMANES, G. J., Mental Evolution in Animals. With Posthumous Essay on Instinct by CHARLES DARWIN. 8vo. 12*s.*

Mental Evolution in Man : Origin of the Human Faculty. 8vo. 14*s.*

Animal Intelligence. Fourth Edition. Cr. 8vo. 5*s.* (*I.S.S.*)

Jelly-Fish, Star-Fish, and Sea-Urchins : being a Research on Primitive Nervous Systems. With Illustrations. Second Edition. Cr. 8vo. 5*s.* (*I.S.S.*)

ROOD, OGDEN N., Colour : a Text-book of Modern Chromatics. With Applications to Art and Industry. With 130 Original Illustrations. Third Edition. Cr. 8vo. 5*s.* (*I.S.S.*)

ROOT, A. I., The A B C of Bee Culture. A Cyclopædia of everything pertaining to the care of the Honey Bee. Illustrated. Royal 8vo. 7*s.* 6*d.*

ROOSEVELT, BLANCHE, Victorien Sardou : a Personal Study. Fcp. 8vo. 3*s.* 6*d.*

ROOSEVELT, THEODORE, Hunting Trips of a Ranchman. With 26 Illustrations. Royal 8vo. 18*s.*

ROSENTHAL, Prof. J., General Physiology of Muscles and Nerves. Third Edition. With 75 Illustrations. Cr. 8vo. 5*s.* (*I.S.S.*)

ROSING, S., Danish Dictionary. Cr. 8vo. 8*s.* 6*d.*

ROSS, JANET, Italian Sketches. With 14 full-page Illustrations. Cr. 8vo. 7*s.* 6*d.*

ROSS, PERCY, A Professor of Alchemy. Cr. 8vo. 3*s.* 6*d.*

ROSS, Lieut.-Col. W. A., Alphabetical Manual of Blowpipe Analysis. Cr. 8vo. 5*s.*

Pyrology, or Fire Chemistry. Sm. 4to. 36*s.*

ROUTLEDGE, Canon C. F., History of St. Martin's Church, Canterbury. Cr. 8vo. 5*s.*

ROUTLEDGE, JAMES, English Rule and Native Opinion in India. 8vo. 10*s.* 6*d.*

ROWLEY, A. C., The Christ in the Two Testaments. With an Introduction by the BISHOP OF LINCOLN. Cr. 8vo. 2*s.*

RULE, MARTIN, Life and Times of St. Anselm, Archbishop of Canterbury and Primate of the Britains. 2 vols. 8vo. 32*s.*

ST. CLAIR, GEORGE, Buried Cities and Bible Countries. Second Edition. Large cr. 8vo. 7*s.* 6*d.*

SAINTSBURY G., Specimens of English Prose Style from Malory to Macaulay. Selected and Annotated. With Introductory Essay. Large cr. 8vo. Printed on hand-made paper. Vellum, 15*s.*; parchment antique or cloth, 12*s.*

SALAMAN, J. S., Trade Marks : their Registration and Protection. Cr. 8vo. 5*s.*

SALMONÉ, H. A., Arabic-English Dictionary, comprising about 120,000 Arabic Words, with English Index of about 50,000 Words. 2 vols. post 8vo. 36*s.*

SAMUELSON, JAMES, Bulgaria, Past and Present : Historical, Political, and Descriptive. With Map and numerous Illustrations. 8vo. 10*s.* 6*d.*

SANDWITH, F. M., Egypt as a Winter Resort. Cr. 8vo. 3*s.* 6*d.*

SANTIAGOE, DANIEL, Curry Cook's Assistant. Fcp. 8vo. 1s. 6d.; paper covers, 1s.

SAYCE, A. H., Introduction to the Science of Language. New and Cheaper Edition. 2 vols. cr. 8vo. 9s.

The Principles of Comparative Philology. Fourth Edition, revised and enlarged. Cr. 8vo. 10s. 6d.

SCANNELL, THOMAS B., and WILHELM, JOSEPH, D.D., Manual of Catholic Theology, based on SCHEEBEN's 'Dogmatik.' Vol. I. 15s.

SCHAW, Col. H., Defence and Attack of Positions and Localities. Fifth Edition. Cr. 8vo. 3s. 6d.

SCHLAGINTWEIT, EMIL, Buddhism in Tibet. Illustrated by Literary Documents and Objects of Religious Worship. With 20 Plates. 2 vols. roy. 8vo. and folio, £2. 2s.

SCHLEICHER, AUGUST, Comparative Grammar of the Indo-European, Sanskrit, Greek, and Latin Languages. From the Third German Edition by H. BENDALL. 8vo. 13s. 6d.

SCHLEIERMACHER, F., On Religion: Speeches to its Cultured Despisers. Translated, with Introduction, by J. OMAN. 8vo. 7s. 6d.

SCHMIDT, Prof. O., Doctrine of Descent and Darwinism. With 26 Illustrations. Seventh Edition. Cr. 8vo. 5s. (*I.S.S.*)

Mammalia in their Relation to Primeval Times. With 51 Woodcuts. Cr. 8vo. 5s. (*I.S.S.*)

SCHOOLING, J. HOLT, Handwriting and Expression: a Study of Written Gesture, with 150 Facsimile Reproductions of the Handwritings of Men and Women of various Nationalities. Translated. 8vo. 6s.

SCHOPENHAUER, A., The World as Will and Idea. From the German by R. B. HALDANE and J. KEMP. Third Edition. 3 vols. post 8vo. £2. 12s. (*Philosophical Library.*)

SCHÜTZENBERGER, Prof., Fermentation. With 28 Illustrations. Fourth Edition. Cr. 8vo. 5s. (*I.S.S.*)

SCHWENDLER, LOUIS, Instructions for Testing Telegraph Lines. 2 vols. 8vo. 21s.

SCOONES, W. B., Four Centuries of English Letters: a Selection of 350 Letters by 150 Writers, from the period of the Paston Letters to the Present Time. Third Edition. Large cr. 8vo. 6s.

SCOTT, JAMES GEORGE, Burma as it Was, as it Is, and as it Will Be. Cheap Edition. Cr. 8vo. 2s. 6d.

SCOTT, ROBERT H., Elementary Meteorology. Fifth Edition. With numerous Illustrations. Cr. 8vo. 5s. (*I.S.S.*)

SEDDING, JOHN D., Gardencraft, Old and New. With Memorial Notice by the Rev. E. F. RUSSELL. 16 Illustrations. Second Edition. 8vo. 12s.

Art and Handicraft. Six Essays. 8vo. 7s. 6d.

SELBY, H. M., Shakespeare Classical Dictionary; or, Mythological Allusions in the Plays of Shakespeare explained. Fcap. 8vo. 1s.

SEMPER, KARL, Natural Conditions of Existence as they affect Animal Life. With 2 Maps and 106 Woodcuts. Fourth Edition. Cr. 8vo. 5s. (*I.S.S.*)

SERJEANT, W. C. ELDON, The Astrologer's Guide (Anima Astrologiæ). 8vo. 7s. 6d.

SEVERNE, FLORENCE, The Pillar House. With Frontispiece. Cr. 8vo. 6s.

SEYMOUR, W. DIGBY, Home Rule and State Supremacy. Cr. 8vo. 3s. 6d.

SHAKSPERE. WORKS. Avon Edition. In One Volume. With Glossarial Index. Super roy. 8vo. 7*s*. 6*d*.

Works. Avon Edition. 12 vols. Elzevir 8vo. (*Parchment Library*), vellum, 7*s*. 6*d*. per vol.; parchment or cloth, 6*s*. per vol.; Cheap Edition, 1*s*. 6*d*. per vol.

⁎ The Cheap Edition may also be had complete, 12 vols. in cloth box, 21*s*., or bound in 6 vols. 15*s*.

Works. New Variorum Edition. Edited by HORACE HOWARD FURNESS. Roy. 8vo. Vol. I. Romeo and Juliet, 18*s*. Vol. II. Macbeth, 18*s*. Vols. III. and IV. Hamlet, 2 vols. 36*s*. Vol. V. King Lear, 18*s*. Vol. VI. Othello, 18*s*. Vol. VII. Merchant of Venice, 18*s*. Vol. VIII. As You Like It, 18*s*.

Concordance to Shakspere's Poems. By Mrs. FURNESS. Roy. 8vo. 18*s*.

Sonnets. Edited by EDWARD DOWDEN. With Frontispiece. Elzevir 8vo. (*Parchment Library*), vellum, 7*s*. 6*d*.; parchment or cloth, 6*s*.

SHAW, FLORA L., Castle Blair : a Story of Youthful Days. Cr. 8vo. 3*s*. 6*d*.

SHAW, Lieut.-Col. WILKINSON, Elements of Modern Tactics practically applied to English Formations. Seventh Edition. With 31 Plates and Maps. Small cr. 8vo. 9*s*. (*Military Handbooks.*)

SHELLEY. Life of P. B. Shelley. By EDWARD DOWDEN, LL.D. With Portraits. 2 vols. 8vo. 36*s*.

Poems. Edited, with Preface, by RICHARD GARNETT. Frontispiece. Elzevir 8vo. vellum, 7*s*. 6*d*.; parchment or cloth, 6*s*. (*Parchment Library.*)

Select Letters. Edited by RICHARD GARNETT. Elzevir 8vo. vellum, 7*s*. 6*d*.; parchment or cloth, 6*s*. (*Parchment Library.*)

SHORE. Journal of Emily Shore. With Portrait and Facsimile. Cr. 8vo. 6*s*.

SIBREE, JAMES, The Great African Island, Madagascar : its Physical Geography, &c. With Maps and Illustrations. 8vo. 10*s*. 6*d*.

SIDGWICK, A., Fallacies : a View of Logic from the Practical Side. Second Edition. Cr. 8vo. 5*s*. (*I.S.S.*)

SIDNEY, Sir PHILIP, Knt., The Countess of Pembroke's Arcadia. Edited by H. OSKAR SOMMER. The original 4to. Edition (1590) in Photographic Facsimile, with Bibliographical Introduction. £2. 2*s*.

SIMCOX, EDITH, Episodes in the Lives of Men, Women, and Lovers. Cr. 8vo. 7*s*. 6*d*.

Natural Law : an Essay in Ethics. Second Edition. Post 8vo. 10*s*. 6*d*. (*Philosophical Library.*)

SIME, JAMES, Lessing : his Life and Writings. Second Edition, with Portraits. 2 vols. Post 8vo. 21*s*. (*Philosophical Library.*)

SIMONNÉ, Metodo para aprender a Leer Escribir y hablar el Frances, segun el verdadero sistema de Ollendorff. Cr. 8vo. 6*s*. Key, 3*s*. 6*d*.

SIMPSON, M. C. M., Letters and Recollections of Julius and Mary Mohl. With Portraits and 2 Illustrations. 8vo. 15*s*.

SINGER, I., Simplified Grammar of the Hungarian Language. Cr. 8vo. 4*s*. 6*d*.

SINNETT, A. P., The Occult World. Sixth Edition. Cr. 8vo. 3*s*. 6*d*.

Incidents in the Life of Madame Blavatsky. With Portrait. 8vo. 10*s*. 6*d*.

The Rationale of Mesmerism. Cr. 8vo. 3*s*. 6*d*.

Sister Augustine, Superior of the Sisters of Charity at the St. Johannis Hospital at Bonn. Translated by HANS THARAU. Cheap Edition. Large cr. 8vo. 4*s*. 6*d*.

SKINNER. James Skinner : a Memoir. By the Author of 'Charles Lowder.' With Preface by the Rev. Canon CARTER, and Portrait. Large cr. 8vo. 7*s*. 6*d*. Cheap Edition, cr. 8vo. 3*s*. 6*d*.

SMITH, A. H., Chinese Characteristics. 8vo. 7s. 6d.

SMITH, E., Foods. With numerous Illustrations. Ninth Edition. Cr. 8vo. 5s. (*I.S.S.*)

SMITH, EDGAR F., Electro-Chemical Analysis. With 25 Illustrations. Square 16mo. 5s.

SMITH, H. PERCY, Glossary of Terms and Phrases. Cheap Edition. Medium 8vo. 3s. 6d.

SMITH, HAMILTON, Hydraulics : the Flow of Water through Orifices, over Weirs, and through open Conduits and Pipes. With 17 plates. Royal 4to. 30s.

SMITH, HUNTINGTON, A Century of American Literature : Benjamin Franklin to James Russell Lowell. Cr. 8vo. 6s.

SMITH, JAMES C., The Distribution of the Produce. Cr. 8vo. 2s. 6d.

SMITH, L. A., The Music of the Waters : Sailors' Chanties and Working Songs of the Sea. Words and Music. 8vo. 12s.

SMITH, M., and HORNEMAN, H., Norwegian Grammar. With a Glossary for Tourists. Post 8vo. 2s.

SMYTH, R. BROUGH, The Aborigines of Victoria. Compiled for the Government. With Maps, Plates, and Woodcuts. 2 vols. royal 8vo. £3. 3s.

SOPHOCLES. The Seven Plays in English Verse. Translated by Prof. LEWIS CAMPBELL. Cr. 8vo. 7s. 6d.

Spanish Mystics. By the Editor of 'Many Voices.' Cr. 8vo. 5s.

Specimens of English Prose Style from Malory to Macaulay. Selected and Annotated. With an Introductory Essay by GEORGE SAINTSBURY. Large cr. 8vo, printed on hand-made paper, vellum, 15s. ; parchment antique or cloth, 12s.

SPENCER, HERBERT, Study of Sociology. Fifteenth Edition. Cr. 8vo. 5s. (*I.S.S.*)

SPINOZA. Life, Correspondence, and Ethics of Spinoza. By R. WILLIS. 8vo. 21s.

SPRAGUE, CHARLES E., Handbook of Volapuk, the International Language. Second Edition. Cr. 8vo. 5s.

STALLO, J. B., Concepts and Theories of Modern Physics. Third Edition. Cr. 8vo. 5s. (*I.S.S.*)

STANHOPE, The British Army and our Defensive Position in 1892. Preface by Rt. Hon. E. STANHOPE. Cr. 8vo. 1s.

STARCKE, C. N., The Primitive Family in its Origin and Development. Cr. 8vo. 5s. (*I.S.S.*)

STEBBING, T. R. R., The Naturalist of Cumbrae : a True Story, being the Life of David Robertson. Cr. 8vo. 6s.

A History of Crustacea. Recent Malacostraca. With numerous Illustrations. Cr. 8vo. 5s. (*I.S.S.*)

STEELE, TH., An Eastern Love-Story : Kusa Játakaya. Cr. 8vo. 6s.

STEVENSON, W. FLEMING, Hymns for the Church and Home. 32mo. 1s.

STEWART, BALFOUR, Conservation of Energy. With 14 Illustrations. Seventh Edition. Cr. 8vo. 5s. (*I.S.S.*)

STONE, J. M., Faithful unto Death : an Account of the Sufferings of the English Franciscans during the 16th and 17th centuries. With Preface by Rev. J. MORRIS, S.J. 8vo. 7s. 6d.

STORR, F., and TURNER, H., Canterbury Chimes ; or, Chaucer Tales Re-told to Children. With 6 Illustrations from the Ellesmere Manuscript. Third Edition. Fcap. 8vo. 3s. 6d.

STRACHEY, Sir JOHN, India. With Map. 8vo. 15s.

STRAHAN, S. A. K., Marriage and Disease. A Study of Heredity and the more important Family Degenerations. Cr. 8vo. 6s.

Stray Papers on Education, and Scenes from School Life. By B. H. Second Edition. Sm. cr. 8vo. 3s. 6d.

STRECKER, ADOLPH, Text-book of Organic Chemistry. Edited by Prof. WISLICENUS. Translated and Edited, with Extensive Additions, by W. R. HODGKINSON and A. J. GREENAWAY. Second and Cheaper Edition. 8vo. 12s. 6d.

STREET, J. C., The Hidden Way across the Threshold; or, The Mystery which hath been Hidden for Ages and from Generations. With Plates. Large 8vo. 15s.

STRETTON, HESBA, David Lloyd's Last Will. With 4 Illustrations. New Edition. Royal 16mo, 2s. 6d.

> **Through a Needle's Eye;** a Story. With Frontispiece. Cr. 8vo. 6s.

SULLY, JAMES, Pessimism : a History and a Criticism. Second Edition. 8vo. 10s. 6d.

> **Illusions :** a Psychological Study. Third Edition. Cr. 8vo. 5s. (*I.S.S.*)

SWINBURNE, ALGERNON CHARLES, A Word for the Navy. (Only 250 copies printed.) Imperial 16mo. paper covers, 5s.

SWINBURNE. Bibliography of A. C. Swinburne, 1857–87. Cr. 8vo. vellum gilt, 6s.

SYMONDS, JOHN ADDINGTON, Vagabunduli Libellus. Cr. 8vo. 6s.

SWIFT, JON., Letters and Journals. Edited by STANLEY LANE-POOLE. Elzevir 8vo. vellum, 7s. 6d. ; parchment or cloth, 6s. (*Parchment Library.*)

> **Prose Writings.** Edited by STANLEY LANE-POOLE. With Portrait. Elzevir 8vo. vellum, 7s. 6d. ; parchment or cloth, 6s. (*Parchment Library.*)

TARRING, C. J., Elementary Turkish Grammar. Cr. 8vo. 6s.

'TASMA,' A Sydney Sovereign, and other Tales. Crown 8vo. cloth, 6s.

> **In her Earliest Youth.** Cheap Edition. Cr. 8vo. 6s.

TAYLOR, Col. MEADOWS, Seeta : a Novel. With Frontispiece. Cr. 8vo. 6s.

> **Tippoo Sultaun :** a Tale of the Mysore War. With Frontispiece. Cr. 8vo. 6s.
>
> **Ralph Darnell.** With Frontispiece. Cr. 8vo. 6s.
>
> **A Noble Queen.** With Frontispiece. Cr. 8vo. 6s.
>
> **The Confessions of a Thug.** With Frontispiece. Cr. 8vo. 6s.
>
> **Tara :** a Mahratta Tale. With Frontispiece. Crown 8vo. 6s.

TAYLOR, Canon ISAAC, The Alphabet : an Account of the Origin and Development of Letters. With numerous Tables and Facsimiles. 2 vols. 8vo. 36s.

> **Leaves from an Egyptian Note-Book.** Cr. 8vo. 5s.

TAYLOR, R. WHATELEY COOKE, The Modern Factory System. 8vo. 14s.

TAYLOR, Sir H., Works. 5 vols. Cr. 8vo. 30s.

> **Philip Van Artevelde.** Fcap. 8vo. 3s. 6d.
>
> **The Virgin Widow, &c.** Fcap. 8vo. 3s. 6d.
>
> **The Statesman.** Fcap. 8vo. 3s. 6d.

Technological Dictionary of the Terms employed in the Arts and Sciences (Architecture, Engineering, Mechanics, Shipbuilding and Navigation, Metallurgy, Mathematics, &c.), with Preface by KARL KAMARSCH. Fourth Revised Edition. 3 vols. imperial 8vo.

> Vol.   I. German-English-French. 12s.
> Vol. II. English-German-French. 12s.
> Vol. III. French-German-English. 15s.

THACKERAY, S. W., The Land and the Community. Crown 8vo. 3s. 6d.

THACKERAY, W. M., Essay on the Genius of George Cruickshank. Reprinted verbatim from the *Westminster Review*. With 40 Illustrations. Royal 8vo. 7s. 6d.

Sultan Stork, and other Stories and Sketches, 1829–44, now first collected; to which is added the Bibliography of Thackeray. Large 8vo. 10s. 6d.

THOM, J. HAMILTON, Laws of Life after the Mind of Christ. Two Series. Fourth Edition. Cr. 8vo. 7s. 6d. each.

THOMAS, E., The Numismata Orientalia. Part I. Ancient Indian Weights. With Plate and Map of the India of MANU. Royal 4to. paper wrapper, 9s. 6d.

THOMPSON, E. MAUNDE, Handbook of Greek and Latin Palæography. With numerous facsimiles. Cr. 8vo. 5s. (*I.S.S.*)

THOMPSON, Sir H., Diet in Relation to Age and Activity. Fcp. 8vo. 1s. 6d.; paper covers, 1s.

Modern Cremation. Second Edition, revised and enlarged. Cr. 8vo. 2s.; paper covers, 1s.

Through North Wales with a Knapsack. By FOUR SCHOOLMISTRESSES. With a Sketch Map. Sm. 8vo. 2s. 6d.

THURSTON, Prof. R. H., History of the Growth of the Steam Engine. With numerous Illustrations. Fourth Edition. Cr. 8vo. 5s. (*I.S.S.*)

Manual of the Steam Engine. For Engineers and Technical Schools. Parts I. and II. Royal 8vo. 31s. 6d. each Part.

TIELE, Prof. C. P., Outlines of the History of Religion to the Spread of the Universal Religions. From the Dutch by J. ESTLIN CARPENTER. Fifth Edition. Post 8vo. 7s. 6d. (*Philosophical Library, and Trübner's Oriental Series.*)

History of the Egyptian and Mesopotamian Religions. Translated by J. BALLINGAL. Post 8vo. 7s. 6d. (*Trübner's Oriental Series.*)

TIRARD, H. M. and N., Sketches from a Nile Steamer, for the use of Travellers in Egypt. With Map and numerous Illustrations. Cr. 8vo. 6s.

TISDALL, W. ST. CLAIR, Simplified Grammar and Reading Book of the Panjābī Language. Cr. 8vo. 7s. 6d.

Simplified Grammar of the Gujarotī Language. Cr. 8vo. 10s. 6d.

TOLSTOI, Count LEO, Christ's Christianity. Translated from the Russian. Large cr. 8vo. 7s. 6d.

TORCEANU, R., Simplified Grammar of the Roumanian Language. Cr. 8vo. 5s.

TORREND, J., Comparative Grammar of the South African Bantu Languages, comprising those of Zanzibar, Mozambique, the Zambezi, Kafirland, Benguela, Angola, The Congo, The Ogowe, The Cameroons, the Lake Region, &c. Super-royal 8vo. 25s.

TRANT, WILLIAM, Trade Unions: their Origin, Objects, and Efficacy. Sm. 8vo. 1s. 6d.; paper covers, 1s.

TRENCH. Letters and Memorials of Archbishop Trench. By the Author of 'Charles Lowder.' With 2 Portraits. 2 vols. 8vo. 21s.

TRENCH, Archbishop, English Past and Present. Fourteenth Edition, revised and improved. Fcp. 8vo. 5s.

On the Study of Words. Twenty-third Edition, revised. Fcp. 8vo. 5s.

Notes on the Parables of Our Lord. Fifteenth Edition. 8vo. 12s; Cheap Edition, 61st thousand, 7s. 6d.

Notes on the Miracles of Our Lord. Twelfth Edition. 8vo. 12s.; Cheap Edition, Fourteenth Edition, 7s. 6d.

TRENCH, Archbishop, Household Book of English Poetry. Fifth Edition, revised. Extra fcp. 8vo. 5s.

Essay on the Life and Genius of Calderon. With Translations from his 'Life's a Dream' and 'Great Theatre of the World.' Second Edition, revised and improved. Extra fcp. 8vo. 5s. 6d.

Gustavus Adolphus in Germany, and other Lectures on the Thirty Years' War. Fourth Edition, enlarged. Fcp. 8vo. 4s.

Plutarch: His Life, His Lives, and His Morals. Second Edition, enlarged. Fcp. 8vo. 3s. 6d.

Remains of the late Mrs. Richard Trench. Being Selections from her Journals, Letters, and other Papers. Edited by her Son, Archbishop TRENCH. New and Cheaper Edition. With Portraits. 8vo. 6s.

Lectures on Mediæval Church History. Being the substance of Lectures delivered at Queen's College, London. 2nd edition, 8vo. 12s.

Poems. Eleventh Edition. Fcp. 8vo. 7s. 6d. Library Edition. 2 vols. sm. 8vo. 10s.

Proverbs and their Lessons. Eighth Edition, enlarged. Fcp. 8vo. 4s.

Sacred Latin Poetry, chiefly Lyrical. Third Edition, corrected and improved. Fcp. 8vo. 7s.

Select Glossary of English Words used formerly in Senses different from their present. Seventh Edition, revised and enlarged. Fcp. 8vo. 5s.

Brief Thoughts and Meditations on some Passages in Holy Scripture. Third Edition. Cr. 8vo. 3s. 6d.

Commentary on the Epistles to the Seven Churches in Asia. Fifth Edition, revised. 8vo. 8s. 6d.

On the Authorised Version of the New Testament. Second Edition. 8vo. 7s.

Sermons New and Old. Cr. 8vo. 6s.

Westminster and other Sermons. Cr. 8vo. 6s.

The Sermon on the Mount: an Exposition drawn from the Writings of St. Augustine. Fourth Edition, enlarged. 8vo. 10s. 6d.

Shipwrecks of Faith: three Sermons preached before the University of Cambridge. Fcap. 8vo. 2s. 6d.

Studies in the Gospels. Fifth Edition, revised. 8vo. 10s. 6d.

Synonyms of the New Testament. Eleventh Edition, enlarged. 8vo. 12s.

TRENCH, Major-General, Cavalry in Modern War. Sm. cr. 8vo. 6s. (*Military Handbooks.*)

TRIMEN, ROLAND, South African Butterflies: a Monograph of the Extra-tropical Species. With 12 Coloured Plates. 3 vols. 8vo. £2. 12s. 6d.

TROUESSART, E. L, Microbes, Ferments, and Moulds. With 107 Illustrations. Second Edition. Cr. 8vo. 5s. (*I.S.S.*)

TROWBRIDGE, J. M., The Cider Maker's Handbook: a Complete Guide for Making and Keeping Pure Cider. Illustrated. Cr. 8vo. 5s.

TRÜBNER'S Bibliographical Guide to American Literature. From 1817 to 1857. 8vo. half-bound, 18s.

Catalogue of Dictionaries and Grammars of the Principal Languages and Dialects of the World. Second Edition. 8vo. 5s.

TRUMBULL, H. CLAY, The Blood-Covenant: a Primitive Rite and its Bearings on Scripture. Post 8vo. 7s. 6d.

TURNER, C. E., Count Tolstoï, as Novelist and Thinker. Lectures delivered at the Royal Institution. Cr. 8vo. 3s. 6d.

Modern Novelists of Russia. Lectures delivered at the Taylor Institution, Oxford. Cr. 8vo. 3s. 6d.

Tyll Owlglass' Marvellous and Rare Conceits. Translated by KENNETH MACKENZIE. Illustrated by ALFRED CROWQUILL. 3s. 6d. (*Lotos Series.*)

D

TYNAN, KATHARINE, Louise de la Vallière, and other Poems. Sm. 8vo. 3*s.* 6*d.*
    Shamrocks. Sm. cr. 8vo. 5*s.*
    Ballads and Lyrics. Sm. cr. 8vo. 5*s.*
    A Nun: her Friends and her Order. Being a Sketch of the Life of Mother Mary Xaveria Fallon. Second Edition. Cr. 8vo. 5*s.*

TYNDALL, J., Forms of Water: in Clouds and Rivers, Ice and Glaciers. With 25 Illustrations. Tenth Edition. Cr. 8vo. 5*s.* (*I.S.S.*)

TYRRELL, WALTER, Nervous Exhaustion: its Causes, Outcomes, and Treatment. Cr. 8vo. 3*s.*

UMLAUFT, Prof. F., The Alps. Translated by LOUISA BROUGH. With 110 Illustrations. 8vo. 25*s.*

Under King Constantine. Cr. 8vo. 6*s.*

VAN EYS, W., Outlines of Basque Grammar. Cr. 8vo. 3*s.* 6*d.*

VAN LAUN, H., Grammar of the French Language. Cr. 8vo. Accidence and Syntax, 4*s.* ; Exercises, 3*s.* 6*d.*

VELASQUEZ, M. de la CADENA, Dictionary of the Spanish and English Languages. For the use of Young Learners and Travellers. Cr. 8vo. 6*s.*
    Pronouncing Dictionary of the Spanish and English Languages. Royal 8vo. £1. 4*s.*
    New Spanish Reader. Passages from the most approved Authors, with Vocabulary. Post 8vo. 6*s.*
    Introduction to Spanish Conversation. 12mo. 2*s.* 6*d.*

VELASQUEZ and SIMONNE, New Method of Learning the Spanish Language. Adapted to Ollendorff's system. Revised and corrected by Señor VIVAR. Post 8vo. 6*s.* ; Key, 4*s.*

VIEYRA'S Pocket Dictionary of the Portuguese and English Languages. 2 vols. Post 8vo. 10*s.*

VIGNOLI, TITO, Myth and Science: an Essay. Third Edition. With Supplementary Note. Cr. 8vo. 5*s.* (*I.S.S.*)

VINCENT, FRANK, Around and About South America. Twenty Months of Quest and Query. With Maps, Plans, and 54 Illustrations. Medium 8vo. 21*s.*

VIRGIL. The Georgics of Virgil. Translated into English Verse by J. RHOADES. Sm. cr. 8vo. Second Edition. 2*s.* 6*d.*

VOGEL, HERMANN, Chemistry of Light and Photography. With 100 Illustrations. Fifth Edition. Cr. 8vo. 5*s.* (*I.S.S.*)

VOLCKXSOM, E. W. von, Catechism of Elementary Modern Chemistry. Sm. cr. 8vo. 3*s.*

WAGNER. Richard Wagner's Prose Works. Translated by W. ASHTON ELLIS. Vol. I.: The Art Work of the Future &c. 8vo. 12*s.* 6*d.*

WAITE, A. E., Lives of Alchemystical Philosophers. 8vo. 10*s.* 6*d.*
    Magical Writings of Thomas Vaughan. Sm. 4to. 10*s.* 6*d.*
    Real History of the Rosicrucians. With Illustrations. Cr. 8vo. 7*s.* 6*d.*
    Mysteries of Magic : a Digest of the Writings of Eliphas Lévi. With Illustrations. 8vo. 10*s.* 6*d.*
    The Occult Sciences. Cr. 8vo. 6*s.*

WAKE, C. S., Serpent-Worship, and other Essays. With a chapter on Totemism. 8vo. 10*s.* 6*d.*
    Development of Marriage and Kinship. 8vo. 18*s.*

WALLACE, ALFRED RUSSELL, Miracles and Modern Spiritualism. Second Edition. Cr. 8vo. 5*s.*

WALLACE, WILFRID, Life of St. Edmund of Canterbury from Original Sources. With Five Illustrations and Map. 8vo. 15*s.*

WALPOLE, C. G., Short History of Ireland. With 5. Maps and Appendices. Third Edition. Cr. 8vo. 6*s.*

WALSHE, W. H., Dramatic Singing Physiologically Estimated. Cr. 8vo. 3*s. 6d.*

WANKLYN, J. A., Milk Analysis: a Practical Treatise on the Examination of Milk and its Derivatives, Cream, Butter, and Cheese. Second Edition. Cr. 8vo. 5*s.*

Tea, Coffee, and Cocoa: a Practical Treatise on the Analysis of Tea, Coffee, Cocoa, Chocolate, and Maté (Paraguay tea). Cr. 8vo. 5*s.*

WANKLYN, J. A., and COOPER, W. J., Bread Analysis: a Practical Treatise on the Examination of Flour and Bread. Cr. 8vo. 5*s.*

Air Analysis: a Practical Treatise. With Appendix on Illuminating Gas. Cr. 8vo. 5*s.*

WANKLYN, J. A., and CHAPMAN, E. T., Water Analysis: a Treatise on the Examination of Potable Water. Eighth Edition. Entirely re-written. Cr. 8vo. 5*s.*

WARD, BERNARD, History of St. Edmund's College, Old Hall (Ware). With Illustrations. 8vo. 10*s. 6d.*

WARD, H. MARSHALL. The Oak: a Popular Introduction to Forest Botany. Cr. 8vo. 2*s. 6d. (Modern Science Series.)*

WARD, W. G., Essays on the Philosophy of Theism. Edited, with an Introduction, by WILFRID WARD. 2 vols. 8vo. 21*s.*

WARNER, Prof. F., Physical Expression: its Modes and Principles. With 50 Illustrations. Second Edition. Cr. 8vo. 5*s. (I.S.S.)*

WARTER, J. W., An old Shropshire Oak. 4 vols. 8vo. 56*s.*

WATERHOUSE, Col. J., Preparation of Drawings for Photographic Reproduction. With Plates. Cr. 8vo. 5*s.*

WATSON, JOHN FORBES, Index to the Native and Scientific Names of Indian and other Eastern Economic Plants and Products. Imp. 8vo. £1. 11*s. 6d.*

WATSON, R. G., Spanish and Portuguese South America during the Colonial Period. 2 vols. Post 8vo. 21*s.*

WEAVER, F. W., Wells Wills. Arranged in Parishes, and Annotated. 8vo. 10*s. 6d.*

WEBER, A., History of Indian Literature. From the German by J. MANN and T. ZACHARIAE. Third Edition. Post 8vo. 10*s. 6d. (Trübner's Oriental Series.)*

WEDDING'S Basic Bessemer Process. Translated from the German by W. B. PHILLIPS and ERNST PROCHASKA. Roy. 8vo. 18*s.*

WEDGWOOD, H., Dictionary of English Etymology. Fourth Edition. Revised and Enlarged. 8vo. £1. 1*s.*

Contested Etymology in the Dictionary of the Rev. W. W. Skeat. Cr. 8vo. 5*s.*

WEDGWOOD, JULIA, The Moral Ideal: an Historic Study. Second Edition. 8vo. 9*s.*

WEISBACH, JULIUS, Theoretical Mechanics: a Manual of the Mechanics of Engineering. Designed as a Text-book for Technical Schools and for the Use of Engineers. From the German by E. B. COXE. With 902 Woodcuts. Second Edition. 8vo. 31*s. 6d.*

WELLER, E., Improved French Dictionary. Roy. 8vo. 7s. 6d.

WESTROPP, HODDER M., Primitive Symbolism as Illustrated in Phallic Worship; or, The Reproductive Principle. With Introduction by Major-Gen. FORLONG. 8vo. 7s. 6d.

WHEELDON, J. P., Angling Resorts near London: the Thames and the Lea. Cr. 8vo. paper covers, 1s. 6d.

WHEELER, J. TALBOYS, History of India from the Earliest Ages. 8vo. (Vol. I. *out of print.*) Vol. II., 21s. Vol. III., 18s. Vol. IV., Part I., 14s. Vol. IV., Part II., 12s.

　**** Vol. III. is also published as an independent work under the title of 'History of India : Hindu, Buddhist, and Brahmanical.'

　Early Records of British India : a History of the English Settlements in India, as told in the Government Records and other Contemporary Documents. Roy. 8vo. 15s.

WHERRY, E. M., Comprehensive Commentary to the Quran. With SALE's Preliminary Discourse, Translation and Additional Notes. Post 8vo. (Vol. I. *out of print.*) Vols. II. and III. 12s. 6d. each. Vol. IV. 10s. 6d. (*Trübner's Oriental Series.*)

WHIBLEY, CHAS., In Cap and Gown : Three Centuries of Cambridge Wit. Second Edition. Cr. 8vo. 7s. 6d.

WHINFIELD, E. H., The Quatrains of Omar Khayyám. The Persian Text, with an English Verse Translation. Post 8vo. 10s. 6d. ; Translation only, 5s. (*Trübner's Oriental Series.*)

　Masnavi I Ma'navi : the Spiritual Couplets of Maulána Jalálu-'d-Din Muhammad I Rúmí. Translated and Abridged. Post 8vo. 7s. 6d. (*Trübner's Oriental Series.*)

WHITAKER, FLORENCE, Christy's Inheritance : a London Story. Illustrated. Roy. 16mo, 1s. 6d.

WHITNEY, Prof. W. D., Life and Growth of Language. Sixth Edition. Cr. 8vo. 5s. (*I.S.S.*)

　Essentials of English Grammar. Second Edition. Cr. 8vo. 3s. 6d.

　Language and the Study of Language. Fourth Edition. Cr. 8vo. 10s. 6d.

　Language and Its Study. With especial Reference to the Indo-European Family of Languages. Edited by R. MORRIS. Second Edition. Cr. 8vo. 5s.

　Sanskrit Grammar. Including both the Classical Language and the older Dialects of Veda and Brahmana. Second Edition. 8vo. 12s.

WHITWORTH, G. C., Anglo-Indian Dictionary : a Glossary of Indian Terms used in English, and of such English or other non-Indian Terms as have obtained Special Meanings in India. 8vo. cloth, 12s.

WICKSON, E. J., California Fruits, and How to Grow Them. 8vo. 18s.

WIECHMANN, FERDINAND G., Sugar Analysis. For Refineries, Sugar-Houses, Experimental Stations, &c. 8vo. 10s. 6d.

WILBERFORCE. Life of Bishop Wilberforce of Oxford and Winchester. By HIS SON. Cr. 8vo. 6s.

WILDE, HENRY, Origin of Elementary Substances. 4to. 4s.

WILDRIDGE, T. TYNDAL, The Dance of Death, in Painting and in Print. With Woodcuts. Sm. 4to. 3s. 6d.

WILLARD, X. A., Practical Dairy Husbandry. Complete Treatise on Dairy Farms and Farming. Illustrated. 8vo. 15s.

　Practical Butter Book. Complete Treatise on Butter Making, &c. 12mo. 5s.

WILLIAMS, S. WELLS, Syllabic Dictionary of the Chinese Language: arranged according to the Wu-Fang Yuen Yin, with the Pronunciation of the Characters as heard in Pekin, Canton, Amoy, and Shanghai. Third Edition. 4to. £3. 15*s.*

WILLIS, R., Life, Correspondence, and Ethics of Benedict de Spinoza. 8vo. 21*s.*

WILSON, H. H., Rig-Veda-Sanhita : a Collection of Ancient Hindu Hymns. From the Sanskrit. Edited by E. B. COWELL and W. F. WEBSTER. 6 vols. 8vo. (Vols. I. V. VI. 21*s.* each ; Vol. IV. 14*s.* ; Vols. II. and III. in sets only.)

The Megha-Duta (Cloud Messenger). Translated from the Sanskrit of KALIDASA. New Edition. 4to. 10*s.* 6*d.*

Essays and Lectures, chiefly on the Religion of the Hindus. Collected and Edited by Dr. REINHOLD ROST. 2 vols. 21*s.*

Essays, Analytical, Critical, and Philological, on Subjects connected with Sanskrit Literature. Collected and Edited by Dr. REINHOLD ROST. 3 vols. 36*s.*

Vishnu Puráná : a System of Hindu Mythology and Tradition. From the Original Sanskrit. Illustrated by Notes derived chiefly from other Puránás. Edited by FITZEDWARD HALL. 6 vols. (including Index), £3. 4*s.* 6*d.*

Select Specimens of the Theatre of the Hindus. From the Original Sanskrit. Third Edition. 2 vols. 21*s.*

WILSON, Mrs. R. F., The Christian Brothers: their Origin and Work. With Sketch of Life of their Founder. Cr. 8vo. 6*s.*

Within Sound of the Sea. With Frontispiece. Cr. 8vo. 6*s.*

WOLTMANN, ALFRED, and **WOERMANN, KARL, History of Painting.** With numerous Illustrations. Med. 8vo. Vol. I. Painting in Antiquity and the Middle Ages, 28*s.* Vol. II. The Painting of the Renascence, 42*s.* The two volumes may be had bound in cloth with bevelled boards and gilt leaves, price 30*s.* and 45*s.* respectively.

Woman's Crusade, A. By a DAME OF THE PRIMROSE LEAGUE. 3 vols. 31*s.* 6*d.*

WOOD, M. W., Dictionary of Volapük : Volapük-English and English-Volapük. Cr. 8vo. 10*s.* 6*d.*

WOODBURY, CHAS. J., Talks with Ralph Waldo Emerson. Cr. 8vo. 5*s.*

WOOLDRIDGE, L. C., On the Chemistry of the Blood, and other Scientific Papers. Arranged by VICTOR HORSLEY and ERNEST STARLING. With Introduction by VICTOR HORSLEY. With Illustrations. 8vo. 16*s.*

WORDSWORTH Birthday Book. Edited by ADELAIDE and VIOLET WORDSWORTH. 32mo. 2*s.* ; cloth limp, 1*s.* 6*d.*

WORDSWORTH, Selections from. By WILLIAM KNIGHT and other Members of the Wordsworth Society. Printed on hand-made paper. Large cr. 8vo. With Portrait. Vellum, 15*s.* ; parchment, 12*s.* Cheap Edition, cr. 8vo. 4*s.* 6*d.*

WORSAAE, CHAMBERLAIN J. J. A., The Pre-history of the North. Based on contemporary Memorials. Translated by H. F. MORLAND SIMPSON. Cr. 8vo. 6*s.*

WORTHAM, B. HALE, Satakas of Bhartrihari. Translated from the Sanskrit. Post 8vo. 5*s.* (*Trübner's Oriental Series.*)

WORTHY, CHARLES, Practical Heraldry : an Epitome of English Armoury. With 124 Illustrations. Cr. 8vo. 7*s.* 6*d.*

WRIGHT, G. FREDERICK, The Ice Age in North America, and its Bearing upon the Antiquity of Man. With Maps and Illustrations. 8vo. 21*s.*

Man and the Glacial Period. With 111 Illustrations and Map. Cr. 8vo. 5*s.* (*I.S.S.*)

WRIGHT, THOMAS, The Celt, the Roman, and the Saxon: a History of the Early Inhabitants of Britain down to the Conversion of the Anglo-Saxons to Christianity. Fifth Edition, corrected and enlarged. With nearly 300 Engravings. Cr. 8vo. 9s.

WRIGHT, W., The Book of Kalilah and Dimnah. Translated from Arabic into Syriac, with Preface and Glossary in English. 8vo. 21s.

WURTZ, Prof., The Atomic Theory. Translated by E. CLEMINSHAW. Fifth Edition. Cr. 8vo. 5s. (*I.S.S.*)

WYLDE, W. The Inspection of Meat: a Guide and Instruction Book to Officers supervising Contract Meat, and to all Sanitary Inspectors. With 32 Coloured Plates. 8vo. 10s. 6d.

YOUNG, Prof. C. A., The Sun. With Illustrations. Third Edition. Cr. 8vo. 5s. (*I.S.S.*)

YOUMANS, ELIZA A., First Book of Botany. Designed to Cultivate the Observing Powers of Children. With 300 Engravings. New and Cheaper Edition. Cr. 8vo. 2s. 6d.

SHAKSPERE'S WORKS.

THE AVON EDITION,

Printed on thin opaque paper, and forming 12 handy volumes, cloth, 18s., or bound in 6 volumes, 15s.

The set of 12 volumes may also be had in a cloth box (*see Illustration*), price 21s., or bound in roan, persian, crushed persian levant, calf, or morocco, and enclosed in an attractive leather box, at prices from 31s. 6d. upwards.

THE PARCHMENT LIBRARY EDITION,

In 12 volumes elzevir 8vo., choicely printed on hand-made paper, and bound in parchment or cloth, price £3. 12s., or in vellum, price £4. 10s.

The set of 12 volumes may also be had in a strong cloth box, price £3. 17s., or with an oak hanging shelf (*see Illustration*), £3. 18s.

LONDON: KEGAN PAUL, TRENCH, TRÜBNER, & CO., LTD.

THE AMERICAN PATENT
REVOLVING BOOKCASE.

The Revolving Bookcase will be found a great convenience by those who wish to have from 80 to 200 volumes accessible while seated at a table or by the fireside. This bookcase occupies no more space than an ordinary whatnot, and can be wheeled from one part of a room to another. It is particularly suitable for Private Libraries, for Studies, and for the Consulting Chambers of Barristers, Physicians, &c.

Size No. 1, 36 inches high.

PRICE FROM 4 GUINEAS.

These Bookcases are made in various sizes, 24 inches square, 36 to 59 inches high, with eight, twelve, or sixteen shelves, in ash, walnut, mahogany, oak, and ebonised, and neatly finished so as to form handsome pieces of furniture. A special form of Revolving Bookcase has been designed to hold the set of 'Encyclopædia Britannica.'

Specimens of the different sizes and woods can be seen in use at

PATERNOSTER HOUSE,
CHARING CROSS ROAD, LONDON.

KEGAN PAUL, TRENCH, TRÜBNER, & CO., Ltd.,

SOLE AUTHORISED AGENTS.

Illustrated Price List on receipt of one Stamp.